Isn't that just like . . .

ELIZABETH
BEVARLY

Just Like a Man

"I'll go," Michael said, "and I'll just call you at school tomorrow."

"No!" Hannah exclaimed, surprising him. "I mean," she hastily backpedaled, "I don't mind you being here. You can stay if you want."

Oh, he wanted. He most definitely, most assuredly wanted.

Hannah looked at Michael Sawyer and told herself she really should have stopped after one glass of Chianti. Because if she had, then maybe he wouldn't look so dreamy and winsome and fine. And maybe it wouldn't feel so good to have him here.

And maybe she wouldn't have nearly kissed him just a minute ago. What had come over her? What must he think of her?

And why was she tempted, even now, to lift her hand to his face this time and trail her fingertips over the smile that so sweetly curled his lips, and then press her mouth to his?

By Elizabeth Bevarly

JUST LIKE A MAN
THE THING ABOUT MEN
THE RING ON HER FINGER
TAKE ME, I'M YOURS
HE COULD BE THE ONE
HOW TO TRAP A TYCOON
HER MAN FRIDAY
MY MAN PENDLETON

ELIZABETH BEVARLY

Just Like a MAN

AVON BOOKS

An Imprint of HarperCollinsPublishers

AVON BOOKS
An Imprint of HarperCollins*Publishers*
10 East 53rd Street
New York, New York 10022-5299

Copyright © 2005 by Elizabeth Bevarly
Excerpts from *Just Like a Man* copyright © 2005 by Elizabeth Bevarly; *The Trouble With Valentine's Day* copyright © 2005 by Rachel Gibson; *Flirting With Danger* copyright © 2005 by Suzanne Enoch; *Lady in Red* copyright © 2005 by Karen Hawkins
ISBN: 0-06-050947-3
www.avonromance.com

First Avon Books paperback printing: January 2005

Avon Trademark Reg. U.S. Pat. Off. and in Other Countries, Marca Registrada, Hecho en U.S.A.
HarperCollins® is a registered trademark of HarperCollins Publishers Inc.

Printed in the U.S.A.

10 9 8 7 6 5 4 3 2 1

Dedicated to the memory of
Chester Allen Vittitow III.
Poet, essayist, novelist, humorist.
Scholar, gentleman, wit.
And a friend who came into my life
when I had precious few of those.

There's a terrible disturbance
in the Force without you, Chet.

PROLOGUE

"You have to do this, Raptor."

"No, I don't."

"Yes, you do. You took an oath."

"That oath stopped applying when I turned in my weapon and left the service."

"That oath *never* stops applying. And by the way, we don't have any record of you turning in your weapon. And *nobody* leaves this service. Not entirely."

In a windowless office in a nondescript building in an uninteresting neighborhood in an unremarkable section of the nation's capital, two men ignored government-issue chairs and stood on each side of a government-issue desk where a government-issue lamp lobbed government-issue light into a room made blue and fragrant with *non-*government-issue cigar smoke. The one called Raptor glared at the One Whose Name Could Not Be Spoken—mostly because Raptor didn't know what his name was—and he tried to remember just what the hell he'd done with the weapon he should have turned over to his superior five years ago.

It was probably still in his footlocker, he thought, the one he'd bolted tight after turning his back on this very office and hadn't opened since, because he hadn't wanted to think about this place. At the moment, that footlocker was—damn—probably stowed in the garage. He'd find it somewhere beneath rakes and power tools and an inflatable pool ducky—still inflated, even though no one had used it for years—and that stupid badminton kit he never had gotten set up in the backyard.

Note to self, he thought, *locate and clear out all surviving remnants of previous life. Both physical* and *psychological.* It was way past time.

"I'll mail my weapon to you," he told the other man now. *Just as soon as I find it,* he added to himself. Maybe it was in the locker in the basement where he'd stowed the three gallons of Moroccan Sunset paint he'd never gotten around to putting on the dining room walls. . . .

"Hang on to it," his superior told him. "You're going to need it for this assignment."

"There is no assignment," Raptor countered. "I quit. Five years ago. Remember?"

"You can't quit," the other man replied. "I just told you. Once you join OPUS, you're in for life."

"That wasn't in the job description."

"There is no description for this job."

Which, Raptor had to concede, was true. His position at OPUS had been seat-of-the-pants; probably because the office itself was seat-of-the-pants. Everything at OPUS was on a need-to-know basis. In fact, few people at OPUS knew who was in the know, or knew who decided who would be in the know. All Raptor had known by the end of his time there was that he'd wanted a life. A *real* life. One that contained real pleasures instead of real dangers.

"I'm not coming back," Raptor told his former boss, wondering if *he* was in the know, or knew who was in the know.

"You have to come back," the other man told him. "We need you. Naturally, we have other people who have been working on this assignment, too—a handful of them for years now. But we need *you* specifically to ensure success. We're close, Raptor. So close. And you could help us bring it home."

"Why?" he asked. "What's so special about this assignment that a hundred other agents couldn't complete it just as well?"

The other man said nothing for a moment, only gazed at Raptor as if he wondered how much the other man should know. Finally, though, he uttered a reply. A single-word reply, but one that told Raptor everything *he* needed to know: "Sorcerer."

It was a name Raptor hadn't heard for years, one he had thought he would never hear again. Mostly because he thought Sorcerer was dead. If not literally, then certainly figuratively. Because the last time he'd seen Sorcerer, Sorcerer had been on the road to perdition, and he'd been heavily packed for the trip.

"What are you talking about?" Raptor asked his superior now.

"We have a situation," the other man said. "And it's right in your backyard. And since you and Sorcerer used to be—"

"I haven't seen Sorcerer for years," Raptor interrupted the other man, not wanting to think about that. "He's nothing to me now."

His former boss eyed him intently. "Well, he's about to become your worst nightmare. Hell, he's about to become the entire world's worst nightmare. He's up to something, Raptor. We don't know what yet, but we know it's big. Bigger, even, than before. He surfaced in Indianapolis a few months ago, not long after the announcement that Indianapolis would be playing host to a presidential debate in the fall. He's posing as a legitimate businessman, working for the city's biggest employer, CompuPax Computer Systems. Right now, that's all we know."

"Well, why the hell haven't you brought him in, if you know where he is?" Raptor asked.

"Because, for one thing, we want to see what he's up to," his superior said. "For another thing, what we have on him now is shaky and years-old. There's no guarantee we could put him away for any length of time. But now that he's surfaced again, we have another chance to really nail him. The only thing that would bring Sorcerer out of the woodwork would have to have a huge payoff. And this time, we won't be blindsided by him. We'll be all over the bastard."

"Well, he does have a degree in computer engineering," Raptor reminded his superior. "Maybe he *is* a legitimate businessman now."

The other man didn't even comment on that. And Raptor had to concede that what he'd said was pretty damned ridiculous. "Look," he continued, "what interest could Sorcerer possibly have in what two candidates have to say during an election year, huh? The guy never cared about anything but himself."

"But the guy is especially good at making threats," his former boss said. "Serious threats. And we've never doubted for a moment that he would carry them out if he didn't get what he wanted."

"Has he made any threats since he resurfaced?" Raptor asked.

"Not yet."

"Then why do you need me?"

"Because it's *Sorcerer,* man. What other reason do you need?"

Raptor shook his head slowly, more than a little reluctant to become a part of whatever imbroglio was brewing between OPUS and Sorcerer. "I can't believe this is why you jerked me out of my life on absolutely no notice and flew me here. You should have known I wouldn't take the job. I don't care who it involves."

His superior gritted his teeth, then stubbed out his cigar so brutally that the government-issue ashtray went skittering over the side of the government-issue desk to land in a smoldering heap of broken government-issue glass on the government-issue linoleum beneath. "No, I flew you here," he said fiercely, "because I knew you *would* take the job. I know you, Raptor. You're a man of your word."

"I'm also a father now," Raptor reminded him. "A single father, at that. And that supersedes everything that came before. Everything. Even OPUS."

"Nothing supersedes OPUS."

"Family does."

He could tell by the other man's expression that his ex-boss didn't believe that for a minute, despite the fact that the other man wore a plain gold band on the ring finger of his left hand. "If you don't complete this assignment," he said, "we could be looking at a time when nobody in the world will have a family anymore. Including you."

Raptor swallowed hard. Somehow, he could believe that. Maybe his superior was being overly dramatic. But he doubted it because whatever the hell was going on, Sorcerer was involved. And Sorcerer had always played by his own rules and had always played for keeps. And his rule book, Raptor knew, wasn't anything like anyone else's. In fact, he was pretty sure Sorcerer's rule book contained only one rule: I want the world, and I want it now. Okay, so maybe that was two rules. And maybe they weren't so much rules as they were a personal philosophy. What mattered was that you didn't want to get in Sorcerer's way.

"I'm finished with OPUS," he said halfheartedly, knowing he meant it, but knowing, too, what he had to do.

"Well, OPUS isn't finished with you," his superior said. "We need you again. You know Sorcerer better than anyone does. You always have. We can't do this without you."

Raptor expelled a long, weary breath. "When do you need me?"

"Yesterday," the other man told him.

He shook his head. "Can't yesterday. Can't this week. I'm booked up. I have math/science night at school on Monday, a Scout meeting on Tuesday, a Parents' Association meeting on Wednesday, and it's my turn to carpool swim practice Thursday. Saturday, I have to coach Little League. Look, a week from Friday is the last day of school. How about I go after Sorcerer then?"

He was only half joking. He was a lot more scared of some of the mothers in the Parents' Association than he was Sorcerer. Those women expected him to volunteer for stuff.

"It doesn't work like that, and you know it," the other man said. "This isn't going to be a one-day assignment, Raptor. This will take months. Becoming a father has obviously made you soft."

Damn right it had. And Raptor wouldn't have it any other way.

"Look," his superior began again, "if it will help matters, you can take your son with you on this assignment. He'll get a helluva book report out of it."

Raptor emitted a single, derisive chuckle. "Yeah, right."

His boss turned serious. Too serious. "No, I mean it, Raptor. Your son will come in handy on this mission."

Raptor eyed the other man warily for a moment, fearful he meant what he said. But that wasn't possible. His son was only nine years old, and his boss knew it. So, "Oh, sure," he said. "And I guess you'll be giving him a weapon, too, huh?"

"No, he won't get a weapon. Good God, man, he's only nine years old. But like I said, he'll come in handy for this assignment."

"Very funny. Get real."

"I am real, Raptor. We need your son for this mission. So you're going to have to bring him in, too."

"I GUESS YOU'RE ALL WONDERING WHY I called you here today."

The minute the words were out of her mouth, Hannah Frost regretted them. She was the overworked, overextended, overdressed, but egregiously underpaid—not that she was bitter or anything—director of a tony private school in Indianapolis, not a fez-wearing, hookah-puffing nightclub owner in a Howard Hawks *film noire*. In place of exotic Moroccan attire, she sported a classic—meaning she'd owned it for more than a decade—dove-gray Ralph Lauren suit and crisp white silk blouse, her only accessory discreet pearl earrings. And a fez would have wreaked havoc on the fawn-colored hair she'd cinched into a flawless French twist that morning.

She *did,* after all, have a position as an overworked, overextended, overdressed, but egregiously underpaid—not that she was bitter or anything—director of a tony private school in Indianapolis to uphold. Not to mention scores of trophy wife/mothers to compete with. And the mothers—Hannah hesitated to call them *moms*—of the Emerson Academy were fashionistas out the wazoo. To put it in less-than-academic terms. To put it in even less academic terms, Sidney Greenstreet and Humphrey Bogart would have had their sartorial butts kicked by those women.

Despite the lack of fez and *film noire,* however, Hannah was surrounded by the usual suspects. At least, that was what she was thinking as she surveyed the trio of characters seated on the other side of her desk. One of those people, in fact, was a *too*-usual suspect: Alex Sawyer, the Emerson Academy's newest pupil, who had arrived in their midst only a month before, at the start of the new school year.

His permanent record—yes, in fact, those did exist, in spite of urban legends to the contrary—indicated that his transfer had come about because he hadn't been a "good fit" at his last school. And any educator worth her salt knew that *not a good fit* was teacher code for *major troublemaker.* Especially since Alex's last school had been one that prided itself on accommodating even the most challenging students.

Interestingly, though, Alex had quickly proven himself to be Emerson's brightest pupil, too, remarkably gifted in both math and language arts. Even though he had just started fourth grade, he was reading at a high school level and doing algebra fairly effortlessly. Unfortunately, in addition to being a remarkably gifted student, Alex Sawyer was also a remarkably gifted pain in the butt.

All of nine years old he was, with a mop of unruly brown curls and hazel eyes that could break the heart of a lesser tony private school director. A faint smattering of freckles across the bridge of his nose completed the picture of what could have been a lovable, precocious movie moppet. But Alex Sawyer wasn't a movie moppet, Hannah knew. No, Alex Sawyer was the prince of darkness.

Oh, his conduct was acceptable enough. In fact, there were times when Hannah thought the boy was a little *too* well behaved. He was never late to class, he always had his homework finished neatly and on time, and he voiced all the requisite niceties like *please* and *thank you* and *Wow, is that a new look for you? It's fabulous!*

But the kid was a liar, no two ways about it—which, now that she thought about it, sort of negated that nicety about the fabulous new look thing—and since coming to Emerson, the boy hadn't made a single remark that could be reasonably believed. If he commented one day that the sky was blue, then, by golly, Hannah wanted to call the National Weather Service to find out what was wrong with the atmospheric conditions overhead.

A handful of Alex's prevarications had gone *too* far, though, something that had led him to Hannah's office on more than one occasion. For example, his mother, he had told his new acquaintances at Emerson the week he arrived, had mysteriously disappeared five years ago after being force-fed an untraceable toxin bioengineered by an arcane band of rogue spies in some Eastern European country that Hannah was fairly certain didn't exist. In any event, *she'd* never heard of Badguyistan. Not to mention that, according to Alex's records, his mother and father had divorced five years ago on the very mundane grounds of irreconcilable differences, with his father being awarded full custody. So that was a definite clue that maybe, just maybe, Alex was making up that stuff about the rogue spies.

The father, it went without saying, was currently number two on the list of usual suspects seated across from Hannah, even though the man was anything but usual. This was his first visit to her office, even though she'd tried to see him several times before now. But Michael Sawyer seemed to go out of town a lot for his job, something that—just a shot in the dark—might be contributing to his son's incessant need to invent outlandish tales. Alex obviously craved a more stable family environment. Because he had also told his classmates that he used to have twin sisters, who had, alas, been kidnapped and sold into bondage by an arcane band of rogue slave traders in yet another country that Hannah was pretty confident didn't exist—Outer Villainopolis. According to Alex's records, however, he was—and had always been—an only child. Besides, there was also no mention in those records of him having lived anywhere other than Indiana for the past five years, and before that, he'd been a resident of Maryland, where he was born. And the last time Hannah had checked, indentured servitude hadn't been a major source of income for Indiana *or* Maryland.

And then there was the latest Alex fiction that had begun making the rounds of the Emerson Academy earlier in the week, that his father could hack into the computers of the Pentagon, the Kremlin, the United Nations, the International Monetary Fund, *and* Toys "R" Us, and had done so on a number of occasions. But Hannah knew that Michael Sawyer was a CPA who couldn't hack his way out of a paper bag. She knew the CPA part from Alex's school registration, and about the paper bag hacking because Michael Sawyer had told her about it within moments of his arrival in her office, when presented with the news that his son had been reporting otherwise.

In spite of his reassurances to the contrary, however, there was something about Alex's father that did sort of smack of forbidden entry. Certainly he didn't look like a CPA—or, at least, not like the stereotype of CPA. Maybe he was sort of an über-accountant, Hannah thought. That might explain the aura of . . . of . . . überness . . . about him.

Tall, dark, and handsome really wasn't a fitting description for him, maybe because that was a stereotype, too. But the man was most definitely tall, easily topping six feet. Hannah, at five-ten, wasn't accustomed to having to tilt her head back to make eye contact with anyone, but from the moment Michael Sawyer had walked into her office, she'd felt downright petite. And also strangely uneasy, because there was something about him, something smoldering and urgent and fierce, that made her think he might spontaneously combust at any moment. Or maybe she felt like that because whenever she looked at him, she felt smoldering and urgent and fierce, as if *she* might spontaneously combust at any moment.

In any event, one of them was going to spontaneously combust if she wasn't careful. And then she'd have to completely redecorate her office. And she, for one, rather liked the British Empire feel of the place. It made her feel . . . imperial. And she had precious little of that in her life, despite her position as the One in Charge at the Emerson Academy. Because when one was in charge of children, one was reluctant to act like an empress. Mostly because it went right over the little tykes' heads, since so few of them had read up on their Queen Victoria.

Michael Sawyer was dark, too—and not just outwardly, either. There was something of the cryptic and confidential, the mystique and mysterious about him. He was just dark all over, from his clearly expensive, extremely well tailored, charcoal suit—which, at the moment, was in a flagrant state of rumple, no doubt due to his position as Father of the Liar—to his bittersweet chocolate hair, to his espresso eyes that his black-rimmed glasses did nothing to diminish.

And handsome? Oh, yes. He was that, too. With his dusky complexion and features that appeared to have been hewn by the hands of the gods, there was more than a drop or two of the Mediterranean in his bloodline, Hannah was certain. A name like Michael Sawyer really seemed too generic a moniker for him. Actually, *he* would have fit perfectly into a Howard Hawks *film noire,* cast as the enigmatic antihero who felled the femme fatale with one brutal, burning kiss.

CPA, sure, Hannah mused as she studied Michael Sawyer

again, nudging her thoughts back on track. She could believe he was one of those. Provided, of course, *CPA* stood for *Can't Prove Authentic*.

The last of the usual suspects was Alex Sawyer's language arts teacher, Selby Hudson, who was dressed today in her usual—and quite suspect, really—way, a way that Hannah had cautioned her about before. Selby was fresh out of college, embarking on her very first teaching assignment at Emerson, but she had somehow been tugged back in time, fashion-wise, to the 1960s. Today she had the bulk of her chin-length black bob pushed back from her face with a vinyl, hot pink headband, though her bangs still hung down nearly into her eyes. And she wore the grooviest—and briefest—miniskirt Hannah had seen since . . . well, she had never seen one that groovy or brief, having missed the sixties herself by being born as they were winding down.

Even so, Selby's parents must have only been children during the sixties, and Selby hadn't even been around for the seventies, so who knew why she was so attracted to the skin-tight, crazy-daisy-patterned, long-sleeved T-shirt and hot pink mini? Hannah was going to have to be a bit more stern in explaining to the young teacher that the Emerson Academy dress code concerning skirt lengths extended to the staff, as well as the students. Selby could almost pass for one of their high school seniors. Except that none of their high school seniors would have dared come to school dressed that way, because they knew they'd be sent home to change.

Honestly, an overworked, overextended, overdressed, but egregiously underpaid—not that she was bitter or anything—director of a tony private school's work was never done.

"Now, then, Alex," she began. "Can you tell me why you're here today? *Again?*" she elaborated, just to make clear to the boy that she'd kept track of his numerous visits to her office in his short time at the school. After all, it was only the first week of October. At this rate, Alex was going to end the year being voted Most Likely to Be Living in a Box in the Director's Office for the Rest of His Natural Life.

"No, Ms. Frost," Alex said. "I don't know why I'm here."

She glanced at Selby, who had turned to gape at Alex in disbelief. "Oh, yes, you do, too, know why you're here," Selby told her student in a firm but gentle voice, declining to actually vocalize the *buster* with which Hannah felt certain she wanted to punctuate the remark.

Selby knew, after all, that firm-but-gentle was the one requirement Hannah demanded from all of her teachers. Because firm-but-gentle went a long way with the kind of children who attended Emerson—the kind who were terribly spoiled and even more terribly neglected by self-centered, conspicuously consuming parents who were too busy climbing the social ladder to remember that they had children who needed nurturing and love.

And considering Alex's monstrous fabrications and his father's apparently incessant traveling, Hannah was reasonably confident the boy suffered from the same sort of home life.

Really, sometimes she just wanted to round up all the Emerson parents in the gymnasium, line them up single file, and then go down the line, one by one, smacking each of them upside the head and yelling, "What the hell is the matter with you?"

But she digressed.

She turned her attention back to Alex. "Miss Hudson seems to think you should know why she requested this meeting between her and you and your father and me. Did she not explain the problem to you?"

"Problem?" Alex asked innocently.

"About this latest . . . ah, news . . . regarding your father that you've been telling your friends."

"Oh, that. Miss Hudson thinks I made that up," Alex replied in a voice of complete unconcern. "She thinks I'm not telling the truth."

"That's the problem, all right," Selby confirmed, turning back to look at Hannah, her expression indicating that what she was really thinking was something along the lines of *Do you believe this kid?*, which of course, Hannah didn't, and that was why there were all here.

"But I didn't make anything up," the boy insisted. "I didn't make up any of the stories you've talked to me about. I never make up stories, Ms. Frost. I always tell the truth."

Oh, and there were four more whopping black marks against him in *God's Big Book of Lies,* Hannah thought. Tsk. Tsk. Tsk. Tsk.

"Ms. Frost," Michael Sawyer interjected, peering at her over the tops of his glasses in a way that might have been benign in a less überish man, "if I might have a word with Alex in private?"

Hannah arched her brows at the request, and not just because his voice was as dark and enigmatic as the rest of him. "I can't imagine why you would need to speak to Alex alone," she said coolly. Though how she managed to keep her voice cool with that spontaneous combustion thing happening again was a mystery. "Is there something you want to say to Alex that Miss Hudson and I wouldn't find helpful in some way?"

Michael Sawyer pushed his glasses higher on the bridge of his nose, opened his mouth to say something, evidently decided against whatever it was, and closed his mouth again. Then, "Never mind," he muttered, obviously chastened.

And Hannah tried not to feel too smug that all the time she'd put in on her overworked, overextended, overdressed, but egregiously underpaid—not that she was bitter or anything—director of a tony private school voice hadn't been wasted.

Michael Sawyer turned to his son. "Alex," he said, "we've

talked about this before. About how you shouldn't say the kinds of things that you've been saying. This happened at your other school, too, and you know what happened there."

"But the things I say are true," Alex insisted.

"Alex," his father repeated in a stern voice.

As his father had done only a moment before, the boy opened his mouth to object to the warning, seemed to think better of it, and closed his mouth again. Hannah mentally applauded the elder Sawyer. She'd heard it was possible for parents to master a brook-no-argument voice and posture, but she'd never seen it in action before—certainly the vast majority of Emerson parents hadn't achieved it. Probably because most of them paid other people to raise their children. But never enough so that those other people actually cared about their children.

Not that she was bitter or anything.

Michael Sawyer's voice gentled as he continued. "Look, Alex, I know this is a new school, and I know you think saying stuff like this is a good way to make the other kids notice you and want to be your friend. But that's not the way you make friends. We've talked about this, too. You make friends by *being* a friend first."

"Mr. Sawyer," Hannah said, "it isn't just the frequency of Alex's, oh, shall we say, *inventions,* that concerns us. Though certainly he does seem to, oh, shall we say, *invent,* more often than the average child his age. But it's also the . . . what's the word I'm looking for?" she asked the room at large and no one in particular. *"Enormity,"* she finally settled on when neither the room, nor anyone in it, replied, "of the things he makes up that have us most concerned. I mean, telling his friends that his father has hacked into the computers of the International Monetary Fund? Even putting aside momentarily the fact that most children his age don't even know that the International Monetary Fund exists, let alone what it is—"

"It's an international organization of a hundred and eighty-four countries," Alex offered in as matter-of-fact a voice as Hannah had ever heard. "It was created to help everybody work like a team exchanging money and stuff. And to make business grow and make lots of jobs. And to give help to countries who owe lots of money to other countries."

Both Hannah and Selby stared at Alex openmouthed in amazement. But Michael Sawyer seemed not to be astonished at all, because he only nodded in dispassionate agreement at his son's explanation. There was no beaming pride, no atta-boy to make Hannah think Alex's father had coached him in any way. No, if Alex Sawyer knew that much about the IMF, then she was confident he'd come by the knowledge through natural curiosity and his own research. It wasn't the first time she'd been amazed by his knowledge. But she'd had no idea he could comprehend political and global subject matter that eluded many adults.

"I see," was all Hannah could say in response. And she tried not to think about how she was lying when she said it. Because the truth was, she didn't see at all how such a big brain could fit into such a little boy. "I didn't realize you had such a good grasp of politics, Alex."

Although Alex opened his mouth to reply, it was his father who spoke—so quickly, in fact, that Hannah got the impression he was trying to cut his son off. "Alex and I are both what you might call news junkies and political fanatics. It's kind of a hobby around our house. We watch CNN more than any other channel."

"Well, then, you both must be very excited about the presidential debate Indianapolis will be hosting at the end of the month."

Michael Sawyer smiled. "Already have our tickets."

Hannah smiled back. "I'm planning to attend, too," she said. "All the members of the board of directors of Emerson will be attending, as a matter of fact. Adrian Windsor arranged it for us, since he's a board member. I thought it was very nice of him."

"Especially since he doesn't even have any kids attending the school," Michael Sawyer pointed out.

Hannah was surprised at his knowledge of the school's board of directors. Not that the doings of the board of directors was any secret—on the contrary, she did her best to make parents aware of what was going on with every aspect of the school. But most of the parents just didn't bother to familiarize themselves with such things because most of the parents just didn't care.

Which was why, in addition to ensuring diversity, Hannah had sought board members from outside the school community. CompuPax, Adrian's employer, was the city's largest business, so it had made sense to try and recruit someone in a higher-up position there to sit on the school's board. Adrian Windsor had come highly recommended by none other than T. Paxton Brown himself, the reclusive billionaire who was the founder and CEO of the company.

Adrian's addition to the board had been extremely beneficial, and attracting him had been a substantial coup for Hannah. And if part of Adrian's attraction to the school had resulted from an attraction he had to Hannah herself, well . . .

What was the harm? It was only a little crush, one Hannah had no intention of encouraging, even if she might, from time to time, take advantage of it. She could be shameless when it came to promoting the welfare of her students and her school, but there was no way she would become personally involved with *anyone* connected to the school, including Adrian. And she would never do or say anything that might lead anyone, including Adrian, to think otherwise. But if he wanted to believe he had some small chance of winning her, so be it. Hannah could take care of herself. She always had.

"Adrian's also invited me to attend a reception CompuPax is hosting for the candidates the night before the debate, but I'm not sure yet whether I'll be able to make it."

And why on earth was she telling Michael Sawyer *that*? Hannah wondered. It was none of his business, and she was stepping around the truth with that last remark. She was actually quite sure she wouldn't be able to make the reception, since she already had plans that night. Granted, her "plans" consisted mostly of avoiding Adrian Windsor, since she didn't want him to think he had too much of a chance with her. Even if he *was* a thoroughly respectable local businessman, and even if he *did* have buckets of money, and even if he *had* been voted one of the the city's most eligible bachelors by *Indianapolis* magazine, and even if he *was* handsome and charming and intelligent. He still sat on the board of directors of the Emerson Academy.

And why was Michael Sawyer looking at her as if she'd just told him his eyebrows had turned into caterpillars and were crawling off his face?

Oh, dear, she thought. Michael Sawyer was concluding exactly what she *didn't* want any of the parents to conclude—that she and Adrian Windsor were an item.

"But getting back to the matter at hand," she quickly circumvented before Michael Sawyer could pursue his suspicions, "what's important, Alex, is that you never, ever, make such outrageous allegations again. Do you understand?"

"I've never made allegations, Ms. Frost," the boy said. "Everything I've said is true."

"Alex," she cautioned. Unfortunately, her tony private school director voice carried nowhere near the impact of his father's. Probably because she wasn't a parent. And parents, she knew, still held more weight than school directors. More was the pity sometimes.

"Alex," his father echoed, "just promise you'll stop saying the kinds of things you've been saying, okay?"

Alex nodded, though whether in concession or simply to acknowledge that he'd heard his father, Hannah couldn't have said. What she also couldn't say was why she wasn't quite content with how the meeting had gone. In spite of Alex's cooperation, she felt no sense of problem resolution, couldn't quite convince herself that the boy's lying would now stop. She didn't know why, but she just wasn't satisfied with the outcome.

Then she made the mistake of looking at Michael Sawyer again, and the word *satisfied* took on a whole 'nother meaning altogether. Except that she still didn't feel it. On the contrary, looking at Michael Sawyer generated a potent mix of frustration and yearning that pricked every nerve she possessed and rubbed it raw.

She couldn't imagine any woman having irreconcilable differences with a man like him. The way he was looking at her now, and the fact that he'd been looking at her that way every time she'd glanced in his direction, made her wish she was the center of his attention every day. He was supposed to be focused on his son, but every time she'd looked at him, she'd caught him studying her. Oh, certainly he turned his attention to Alex when he spoke to him, but when he wasn't talking to Alex, he'd been homed in entirely on Hannah.

She told herself it was only because the two of them were in adversarial positions, so naturally he would be watchful, even intense. Yet there was nothing adversarial in his watchfulness. It was, however, intense. In fact, he had watched her in much the same way that a cheetah watches an aging wildebeest—though maybe that wasn't the best description for her to use for herself—as if he wanted to chase her, seize her, fell her, then consume her, methodically and thoroughly, enjoying every moment of the hunt and the pursuit, and savoring every last mouthful once he caught her.

And my, but it seemed warm in her office today. Hannah was going to have to talk to the custodian about her thermo-

stat. The school one, she meant. Her personal thermostat
was something to discuss with her doctor at her earliest con-
venience. Almost thirty-six was way too young for a woman
to be experiencing hot flashes. Even if the woman in question had just had a man like Michael Sawyer enter her orifice.

Office, she quickly corrected herself. Enter her *office.* She
squeezed her eyes shut tight in an effort to banish the very
idea of any of her orifices being entered by him. But the idea
held a lot more appeal than she would have liked to admit,
and she could tell right away that it wasn't going anywhere
soon.

Wishful thinking, she thought wistfully, training her gaze
on one of the ornate bookcases on the other side of the
room, instead of on Michael Sawyer. The last thing she
needed to be pondering with longing these days was any of
her orifices. Unfortunately, having gone without anything
even remotely resembling a romantic relationship since
moving to Indianapolis from Chicago two years ago, Hannah found herself wishing for a lot of things these days, not
the least of which was the nearness of another human being
now and then. Preferably a male human being. Preferably a
warm male human being. Preferably a warm male human
being with washboard abs. And bulging biceps. And an
intrepid jaw, and chiseled features. And strong, potent thighs
and a full, throbbing—

Well. Suffice it to say that, these days, her orifices were
just languishing on the vine. To mix metaphors. Badly.

"Ms. Frost," Michael Sawyer said in his dark, enigmatic
voice, tugging her back to the present.

Hannah made herself look at him again, but had to glance
up to meet his gaze, because he was standing. And then she
had to glance up some more. And then more. And then more.
Boy, he was tall. So she stood up, too, hoping to minimize

the impact of his height, but she still had to tilt her head back to connect with him eye-to-eye.

"Yes, Mr. Sawyer?" she said.

But he didn't say anything else at first, only continued to gaze down at her in a way that made her mouth go dry and other body parts go . . . Um, never mind. Then he smiled, a slow, cryptic, cheetahlike smile, and extended his paw—or, rather, his hand—to her. "Thank you for your time," he finally said, dropping his voice to a low, beguiling growl that made Hannah think of saxophones and red high heels and sultry summer nights.

It couldn't possibly be a good idea to touch him, she told herself as she eyed the proffered hand. Not when the summer night got more sultry and the red high heels started to tango and the saxophones began murmuring "I Got You Under My Skin," which sounded way too much like "I Got You In My Orifice."

Not wanting to be rude, though, Hannah accepted his hand, only to have it completely swallow hers at the first brush of her fingertips against his. Michael Sawyer's hand was nearly twice the size of her own, warm and rough and strangely familiar. Then she realized it wasn't his hand in particular that was familiar. It was simply the fact that it was so masculine, and somewhere way back in the darkest recesses of her memory, she recalled how nice it was to have big, manly hands skimming over her body. Michael Sawyer, she felt certain, would know exactly how—and where—to touch a woman.

Hastily, she withdrew her hand from his, telling herself she only imagined the way he tried to hold on to it for a fraction longer than was necessary. Or acceptable, under the circumstances.

"Hopefully, it won't be necessary for us to meet again," she said.

"Not under these circumstances," he qualified. And once again, she noted his fierceness. And his urgency. And his smoldering.

"Or any others," she made herself say. Then, to avoid sounding impolite, she clarified, "Save a few school-related functions. I'm certain Alex will be the picture of honesty from now on."

Unfortunately, she wasn't certain of that at all. But it wasn't until her office door clicked shut that she finally realized the reason for her uncertainty. Yes, they'd addressed the existence of Alex's inappropriate word-weaving. And yes, his father had told Alex that the things he had said were unacceptable. And yes, he'd made Alex promise to stop saying them.

But not once had Michael Sawyer conceded that Alex didn't tell the truth.

Out in the parking lot, Michael Sawyer paused by his Volvo sedan and ran a frustrated hand through his dark hair for about the billionth time since Alex's new school year had started. He eyed his son with much agitation. Alex had promised he wouldn't pull a stunt like this again. He'd *promised*. Granted, the kid was only nine years old, so maybe he didn't appreciate the magnitude of a promise the way Michael did. It was still no excuse. Nine years old or not, Alex had to understand how unacceptable his behavior was. Because if it didn't stop, Ms. Hannah Frost was going to . . . to . . . to . . .

Ah, hell. He couldn't make his brain go any further than *Ms. Hannah Frost*. Because the minute the woman's name entered his head, his brain shut down and other body parts took over. Body parts that had no business being in control, either, since they'd gotten him into trouble before.

He hadn't expected the director of the Emerson Academy to be so beautiful. So young. Not that he was competing with

Old Man Time himself—his fortieth birthday was still two months away, dammit—but she couldn't be far into her thirties. Whenever he'd spoken with her on the phone, she'd always sounded clipped and inhibited and no-nonsense. So Michael had formed a mental picture of a pewter-haired, crew-cutted, persimmon-lipped, evil-eyed matron of extended years, whose disposition was harsh and joyless.

But even all buttoned up and battened down the way Hannah Frost had been, he'd been able to sense a barely restrained . . . something . . . simmering just beneath her surface. He hesitated to ponder exactly what that *something* might be, though, mostly because it made something equally *something* simmer inside himself. Instead of a gray crew cut, her hair had shone like pure honey in sunlight, the elegantly twisted style making him think it must be long and silky when allowed to flow free. And instead of evil eyes, she had the eyes of an angel, as blue and as big as the heavens above. And as for persimmon lips . . .

Oh, baby. Nothing could have been further from the truth. Hannah Frost's mouth had been as soft as the rest of her promised to be, full and lush and ripe. It had been way too long since Michael had kissed a mouth like that. And there were other things he could imagine that mouth doing, too. Things to him, in fact. Things *on* him, in fact. Things he *really* shouldn't be thinking about when his son was anywhere in the same ZIP code.

So instead of mentally undressing Hannah Frost, he made himself think about the way she *had* been dressed, an austere study in gray. The suit hadn't suited her at all, yet she'd seemed perfectly at ease wearing it. It was yet another puzzle he would doubtless spend hours ruminating about.

Because ruminating about Hannah Frost was as far as Michael would let things go with her. And that was more than he should be doing. She was one cool customer, to be sure. Too bad she didn't have the same cooling effect on him. She made his blood run hot and wild, even after one brief, passionless exchange.

Damn. This was an unexpected development he certainly couldn't afford.

And what the hell did she think she was doing going anywhere near Adrian Windsor? Okay, so the guy sat on the board of directors of the Emerson Academy. After all, that was the reason Michael had been instructed to enroll Alex at Emerson. And okay, so to the casual observer, Adrian Windsor was a forthright, upright, do-right, citizen. Michael knew things about the guy no one else at Emerson knew. For example, he knew that his name wasn't really Adrian Windsor. It was Adrian Padgett. And he knew that Adrian was trouble with a capital *T*. And that rhymed with *D*. And that stood for *Dammit*.

If Hannah Frost was involved with the guy, that was really going to cause some problems. And not just for Michael, either.

Later, he instructed himself resolutely. He could think about that later. Because he *would* think about Hannah later. Over and over again. Mostly, he'd think about what she was wearing—or not wearing—under that starched-and-pressed suit.

Later, he repeated to himself more adamantly. Right now he had more immediate problems to see to.

"Alex," he said firmly to his son, "why do you do this? Why do you say these things that you know aren't true? Why did you tell your friends all that stuff about me hacking into the computers of the Pentagon, the Kremlin, the United Nations, the World Monetary Fund and Toys 'R' Us? You know that's not true." He did his best to glare at his son. "I have *never* hacked into the computers of Toys 'R' Us. That was *you* who did that."

"But you did those other ones," Alex complained.

"The United Nations was a complete accident, and you know it."

"But the others—"

"The others," Michael interrupted his son, "are none of your business. And you wouldn't even know about them if you hadn't hacked into *my* files."

"But—"

"But nothing. I don't want to hear, ever again, that you're telling stories like these to your friends." He frowned. "I mean, c'mon. Twin sisters sold into bondage? Where did *that* come from?"

Alex had the decency to look contrite. He dropped his gaze down to the ground and halfheartedly kicked a chunk of asphalt with the toe of his sneaker. Obviously the Emerson Academy hadn't vacuumed their parking lot as well as they should have this morning, Michael thought wryly. He wished Alex could attend a school that wasn't so . . . so . . . so prissy and overpriced, the kind of school that normal kids attended. But even without his current assignment, he needed for Alex to be someplace like this. Michael was a security freak—for good reason, too—who needed to know his son was safe at all times. And Emerson, like Alex's last school, had a security system that put Fort Knox to shame.

It also had Adrian Padgett.

"I'm sorry," Alex said now. "But I never told anyone Susie and Lily were my sisters. I only mentioned them by name. And they *were* twins. A couple of the guys just assumed they were my sisters, and I guess I let them go on thinking it."

He glanced up at his father, and when Michael saw the earnestness in Alex's expression, he knew his son was telling the truth. Just as he always did.

"And I didn't say they were sold into bondage, either," Alex added fervently. "Just that they were taken against their will. I don't know how that part got messed up." He blew out a melancholy breath. "But I sure do miss Susie and Lily."

"They're guinea pigs, Alex," his father said, striving for patience. "And they weren't taken against their will. They moved to Pensacola with the rest of the Faradays next door."

"They wanted to stay with me," Alex said.

"They belonged to Timmy Faraday," his father reminded him. "Really, I think you should put the past behind you, kiddo."

"Oh, like you have?" Alex challenged him, his head snapping up again to meet his father's gaze.

Boy, Michael hated it when Alex did that. Not just because it put him on the spot, and not just because Alex reminded Michael of his ex-wife when he did that. But because it also emphasized how big his son was getting, and how quickly time was going by. Even though Alex had Tatiana's fairer coloring, he took after Michael in his features and his size. The kid was already nearly five feet tall. He'd be in double digits on his next birthday. Man, where had the past nine years gone?

"My past is none of your business," Michael told his son decisively. "And you wouldn't even know about it if you hadn't decided to do a little snooping in my files. I'm not kidding, Alex," he stated emphatically. "You have to forget everything you saw there. We have a good life here in Indianapolis, and there's much to like here. Let's not screw it up."

Immediately, an image of Hannah Frost materialized in Michael's brain, and, just as quickly, he did his best to vanquish it. He should just leave thoughts of her here in the parking lot, because the last thing he needed was to get involved with someone at Alex's school. Hell, the last thing he needed was to get involved with *anyone* on a more than superficial level. Superficial had worked really well for him since his divorce from Tatiana five years ago. If he had kept things superficial with Tatiana, too, that whole sordid chapter of his life might never have happened. Of course, then he wouldn't have Alex, but that was one of those cosmic *thangs* best not thought too much about.

"Look, just watch what you say at school, all right?" he told his son as he unlocked the back door of the Volvo and opened it. "The last thing we need to do is to bring attention to ourselves."

"I didn't lie," Alex said as he tucked himself into the car and slung the seat belt over himself. "Everything I said was true."

Michael nodded morosely as he closed the door behind his son and circled the car to the driver's side. Yeah, he knew his son had been telling the truth about everything.

That, of course, was the problem.

TWO

ALTHOUGH HANNAH HAD NEVER HAD what one might call a normal upbringing— hoo-boy, was that an understatement—she had watched enough television as a girl to know that even the most upper-crustiest private schools had secret societies and ancient taboo traditions that harked back to a time when politically incorrect thinking had led to despicable behaviors. They were cruel, shadowy customs that put mascot-stealing to shame, practices that no right-thinking person would, in this day and age, tolerate or condone, yet somehow they had survived and even flourished.

The Emerson Academy was no exception.

It, too, had a dirty little secret tradition that Hannah had learned about immediately after beginning her stint as director, an archaic, loathsome annual ritual she detested and in no way endorsed. But it was a custom, a school *tradition,* one staunchly defended by both the students and parents of Emerson. Generations of school directors before her had been forced to tolerate it, and as much as she would have loved to squash the heinous practice, the very mention of abolishing it had been met with boos and hisses and how-dare-you's. A good number of the Emerson parents—and even grandparents—were Emerson alumni, after all. And tradition was everything at Emerson.

So as heinous, archaic, and loathsome as Hannah found the custom, she had no choice but to tolerate the ugliness again this year. Worse than tolerate it. She would have to, as she had before, *participate* in the hideous affair. All the Emerson directors had been forced to participate. So she had no choice but to suffer through yet another . . .

Potluck dinner.

Oh, just the thought of the abuse that lay ahead made her flesh crawl.

And it wasn't just one potluck dinner, as if that would have been odious enough. No, there were *thirteen* of them she was required to attend, for kindergarten through twelfth grade, two to four per month throughout the first half of the school year. Thankfully, she wouldn't be expected to take part in the most abominable rite of the custom—bringing a covered dish—but just having to be present was repugnant enough. One could only make so much chitchat, after all. And one could only handle so many minutes—nay, so many *seconds*—in the presence of several of the Emerson parents.

It was something of a paradox—among other things, but those things were identified with words best not used by someone who worked with children, so *paradox* was what Hannah decided to go with. Although she would have loved to see more parent participation at the school, there were a number of Emerson parents—quite a large number, in fact—with whom she would rather not participate person-ally. And several of them would be attending the evening's horror—ah, dinner—though not so much because they were school-minded, but rather because there would be a decent wine selection. Nevertheless, Hannah would be expected to chitchat with *all* of the parents who attended tonight's func-tion. And she would have to *like* it.

Nothing like coming home from work after staying late on a Friday, she thought as she entered her house after coming home from work late on a Friday, *and having to go back to work.*

Because even though tonight's potluck—for the fourth-grade parents, if she remembered correctly—would be held at the radiant and rambling estate of Bitsy and Cornelius Wainwright, Hannah would still be going to *work.* Being anywhere in Bitsy Wainwright's sphere of existence was work. She just didn't get paid any overtime for it. Or worker's comp. Or hazardous duty pay, for that matter.

She did go home to her tidy brick bungalow in Broad Ripple long enough to sort through her mail, of which there were only bills and credit card offers, and check her phone messages, of which there was only one: Bitsy Wainwright reminding her of the cruel, shadowy, secret, heinous, archaic, loathsome potluck. And also long enough to shed her beige suit for a more evening-friendly black suit. As she fastened a strand of pearls around her neck, she pretended, as she always did when she donned them, that they had been a gift from her doting Great-Aunt Esmeralda on the evening of her high school graduation ceremony.

Even though Hannah had actually purchased them for herself earlier this year from a mall jeweler's on a twelve-months/no interest plan. And even though she didn't have a Great-Aunt Esmeralda, doting or otherwise. And even though she hadn't made it to her high school graduation ceremony because she and her father had been too busy that night slinking out of a crummy tenement because they'd stiffed their landlord for three months' rent.

In spite of being a reasonably sane grown woman of almost thirty-six, Hannah still found herself pretending things from time to time, because she hadn't quite been able to abandon the rich fantasy life in which she had often lost herself as a child. A rich fantasy life, after all, was what had permitted her to *become* a reasonably sane grown woman of almost thirty-six.

Her mother had abandoned her and her father when Hannah was barely walking, and although her father had done his best to eke out a living to support them both, the living he had eked out had been, alas, conning people out of their hardearned money. Which, in addition to being morally reprehensible, not to mention illegal, meant that he and Hannah had been forced to move around a lot in the hope that the police *du jour*—and landlord *du jour*—wouldn't catch up with them.

Regardless of where they had lived, however, there had always been one constant in Hannah's life—television reruns. Particularly reruns of shows like *Leave It to Beaver, Make Room for Daddy,* and *The Donna Reed Show,* where family life had been depicted in a way that had made Hannah yearn to live family life herself—normally. Or, at least, a young girl's idea of normal. Hey, even on *My Three Sons,* which had featured a motherless family, the Douglases still managed to have a nice, stable, secure life, well rooted in the heartland of America.

Nobody wandered from town to town under cover of darkness in an old Dodge Dart station wagon. Nobody lived in dingy hotels and stinking apartments—and, sometimes, an old Dodge Dart station wagon. Nobody ate the majority of their meals at places that served more insects than humans—or in the back of an old Dodge Dart station wagon.

Hannah had known, even as a little girl, that there were people out there who lived life the way it was supposed to be lived. Normally. Uneventfully. Securely. And she had spent most of her days pretending that she was one of them. She had spent the rest of her days planning how, someday, some way, she was *really* going to be one of them.

Her tidy brick bungalow in Broad Ripple was exactly the

kind of home she'd yearned for as a child, right down to the white wicker swing swaying at one end of the broad porch, and the terra-cotta pots of chrysanthemums—geraniums in the summer—that lined the front walk.

She had stopped short of furnishing the house in the tradition of the Eisenhower and Kennedy eras—like her favorite TV families—and had instead opted for more of a thatched Irish cottage look, complete with lace curtains and hooked rugs and hardwood floors, flowered chintz chairs in the living room, a claw-foot tub in the bathroom, a white iron bed in the bedroom, and Blue Willow china in the kitchen. Finally, Hannah had indeed achieved the lifestyle she'd always wanted, one that was the very picture of normalcy, uneventfulness, and security.

Oh, all right, so her job as the overworked, overextended, overdressed, but egregiously underpaid—not that she was bitter or anything, and not that she'd planned *that* part— director of a tony private school in Indianapolis wasn't entirely uneventful. It *was* secure and it was fairly normal. The events that did take place were episodes that didn't directly affect *her* life and its normalcy, uneventfulness, and security. So that was a big plus.

Unfortunately, she did have to attend potluck dinners, but no job was perfect. At least she wouldn't be sitting in the back of an old Dodge Dart station wagon eating cold Beef-a-roni from a can, wondering if the police car behind them was about to pull them over.

The radiant and rambling estate of Bitsy and Cornelius Wainwright was made even more radiant by the stretches of gilded light that spilled over it from a sun dipping low in the sky. As she pulled her Honda sedan to a halt in the wide circular driveway among an eclectic mix of Jaguars, Mercedes, and BMWs, it occurred to Hannah that the exuberant

Tudor mansion seemed almost to glow, as if it were an enchanted fairy-tale castle. The image was only reinforced when Bitsy Wainwright, a fey, tiny creature with golden hair and emerald eyes, opened the front door to greet her, the decor of the house behind her resplendent in its richness and excess.

"Oh, Hannah, *so* glad you could come," Bitsy gushed as she ushered Hannah inside. "*So* looking forward to having you." It was then that Hannah recalled how Bitsy Wainwright seemed to have never quite mastered pronouns. Nor had she seemed to ever quite master moving her jaw when she spoke, because all her words seemed to come through her gritted—though perfectly straight and blindingly white—teeth. "Oh, don't step off the carpet," she hastily added when Hannah's foot skirted the fringe of the narrow Aubusson. Hannah's expression must have registered her confusion, because Bitsy quickly clarified, "Sicilian marble. Doesn't take scuff marks well. Bonita would have a fit."

"Bonita?" Hannah asked, recalling that the Wainwright children were named Devon, Somerset, and Durham. She had often wondered why the Wainwrights had named their children after counties in England. Maybe because, had they opted for counties in Wales, their children would be named Dyfed, Powys, and Clwyd, all of which would look a bit clunky on corporate letterhead someday.

"The cleaning girl," Bitsy explained. "Came from Guatemala. Practices that Santeria. Mustn't cross."

Okay, Hannah thought, so maybe the Wainwright home was less an enchanted fairy-tale castle than it was a giant step backward for the civil rights movement. Lots of people got those confused.

Bitsy led Hannah through the massive foyer and what seemed like hundreds of rooms—never once straying from the carpets—until they arrived in a kitchen that was larger than Hannah's living and dining rooms combined. A kitchen that was also as empty of guests as the rest of the house seemed to be. The reason for that, however, was because the big backyard—or perhaps a more appropriate term in this case would be *the acres and acres of skillfully sculpted grounds behind the radiant and rambling Wainwright estate*—was crawling with people.

It was downright Gatsby-esque, Hannah couldn't help thinking as she gazed through the windows at the scene, the scores of people standing outside in their finery, sipping wine beneath a purpling sky and trees illuminated with tiny white lights. She could almost convince herself there wasn't another world beyond this one, a real world, one populated by real people who had real problems and could use real pronouns. Only the Wainwrights, she thought, could turn a potluck dinner into an elegant, F. Scott Fitzgerald affair.

"Such a nice evening," Bitsy said when she saw where Hannah had directed her gaze, "decided to move the party outside. So much more fun. Drink?"

"Club soda, please," Hannah replied automatically. Then she realized that amid all the Forgotten Generation imagery, she had forgotten her pronouns, too. Horrified by the idea of being Bitsified, she hastily amended, "I mean, *I'll* have a club soda, please. *It* would be great. Thank *you*."

"Lovely," Bitsy said. "Go on out. Appetizers by the roses. Drinks by the pool. Dinner at eight. Feel free to mingle until then."

Mingling, Hannah echoed to herself. Another revolting ritual practiced by the Emerson families at these heinous ceremonies. Bracing herself to shoulder the onerous task she was about to undertake, she headed out into the fray. And as she scanned the faces of the people dotting the patio and nearer reaches of the broad lawn, she told herself she wasn't looking for one face in particular.

She was *not* looking for Michael Sawyer.

* * *

Michael saw Hannah the moment she stepped outside, despite her conservative black outfit. Still, she was the director of the ultra-conservative Emerson Academy, so he could see how she'd want to reflect that. Or make herself invisible to the naked eye so she wouldn't be spotted by some of the other parents and drawn into conversation, since Michael was fast coming to realize that most of the Emerson parents tended to converse about really boring things like golf and Republican politics and 401(k)s.

And, man, he really wished the word *naked* hadn't worked itself into that observation.

He had been thinking—besides the naked stuff—that he himself would be way overdressed for the fourth-grade parent potluck, having come to the Wainwrights' house straight from work. But he'd figured he'd shed his claret-colored tie and dark pinstriped suit jacket—all right, so Hannah wasn't the only one who exuded conservativeness—once he arrived, and do his best to fit in with what he'd been sure would be an ocean of polos, khakis, and chinos on the male partygoers. He'd also assumed there would be loud eighties tunes blaring from a portable boom box, a couple of grills sizzling with burgers and brats, picnic and card tables loaded down with casseroles and brownies and pies, and an off-kilter volleyball net set up for a good no-rules, last-man-standing tournament. He'd been prepared for someone to toss him a brewski and yell, "Hey, Sawyer, go long!" before hurling a football at him from across the yard.

Never mind that he hadn't had time yet to cultivate friendships with any of the parents at his son's new school. Never mind that he didn't *want* to cultivate friendships with any of the parents at his son's new school. That was just the way potlucks were. At least, that was how potlucks had been done when Michael was growing up. Then again, he hadn't attended an overpriced private school like Emerson when he was growing up. He'd been a middling student in a mid-sized public school in middle-of-the-road, middle-class America.

But there was nothing middle-anything about the guests at the Wainwrights'. Michael had wandered into the backyard to find it peopled by individuals dressed in suits and cocktail ensembles, murmuring low in small groups, twisting wine and martini glasses in their fingers as muted jazz music flowed from what might very well have been heaven above, since he sure hadn't spotted any speakers anywhere. Nobody was playing volleyball or football. And the only thing in the pool was a bunch of floating candles—nobody was playing Marco Polo or having chicken fights. And in place of the picnic and card tables, a seemingly endless buffet—wearing a skirt, no less—circumnavigated the patio, filled with the kind of food that only came from a really nice restaurant. Evidently, to the Emerson Academy crowd, the term *covered dish* on the invitation really meant *elegant comestibles from the caterers'*.

Great. Now he was going to have to go out and buy one of those Zillionaire/English dictionaries.

So much for the deviled eggs he'd picked up on his way over. He didn't even see them put out. Bitsy Wainwright must have deemed them unpotluckable, even though the woman behind the deli case at the supermarket had assured Michael they were just the thing. Though Bitsy probably would have had a better word than *unpotluckable*. But it would be one Michael wouldn't recognize, since it doubtless only appeared in the Zillionaire/English dictionary that he didn't own. And it wouldn't be a pronoun, either, since Bitsy seemed to have been absent from school the day they covered those.

Still, there was no reason for him to feel so uncomfortable, Michael told himself. This shindig was no different from a million other such gatherings he had attended in the past. The distant past, granted, but it never seemed distant enough. In fact, this alleged potluck was way too much like those dazzling, dizzying diplomatic dinners he'd been forced to endure with Tatiana as a young man. He'd always hated those damned things.

But then, they'd never had someone like Hannah Frost in attendance.

Friday night, he mused, and she was still at work. Not that he was surprised or one to talk. But he knew his reasons for his lifestyle, and they were good ones, by God. He couldn't imagine why someone like Hannah, someone beautiful and intelligent and successful—and okay, a bit anal-retentive, too, which maybe explained part of it—wouldn't be relaxing and enjoying her life on a Friday night. A life that surely included a man who appreciated beautiful, intelligent, successful—if a bit anal-retentive—women, because no way would Michael believe she was uninvolved.

Then he remembered she wasn't uninvolved. Though Hannah was certainly showing a profound lack of good judgment by seeing Adrian Padgett socially. And probably romantically, too, if Michael knew anything about Adrian. And, of course, he knew everything about Adrian. Even more, he'd wager, than Adrian realized he knew.

Without paying attention to what he was doing, Michael began to gravitate toward Hannah, but the nearer he drew to her, the farther away she seemed to be, almost as if she were avoiding him on purpose. Then he noticed she was moving from one group of people to another, obviously just doing her job, chatting with all the parents present. Except him. Then again, she might be reluctant to chat with him, what with him stalking her the way he was . . .

Stifling a growl of frustration that he could be so enchanted by a woman who should have been in no way enchanting, Michael made himself stop following her around like a lovesick puppy. Maybe she'd find him instead and engage him in a little one-on-one.

And, man, he really wished the phrase *one-on-one* hadn't worked itself into that observation.

What the hell was the matter with him? he wondered. How could he possibly be having libidinous thoughts about a woman dressed in a black getup that was all straight lines, her silky hair fashioned into the sort of 'do usually reserved for Mother Goose? She in no way invited libidiny—was that even a word?—the way she was outfitted.

As if she'd sensed him thinking about her—oh, sure, *now* she sensed him, when he was comparing her to Mother Goose—Hannah's gaze finally lit on Michael, her eyes widening in what he could only liken to panic. Oh, so it wasn't the Mother Goose thought she'd picked up; it was the libidiny one. Damn. Still, at least he'd gotten a reaction out of her. He'd take whatever looks he could get from her at this point, even a deer-in-the-headlights one. Before she had a chance to glance away and pretend she hadn't seen him— like he'd let her get away with *that*—he lifted a hand in silent salutation and began to make his way toward her. And she was polite enough to pretend she was happy about it.

"Mr. Sawyer," she said when he drew within speaking distance. It wasn't a greeting so much as an acknowledgment, but Michael decided not to take it personally. At least she hadn't bolted to hide behind the nearest shrubbery. "How good to see you here, taking an interest in your son's school," she added.

She was so formal, so serious. There wasn't even a hint of casualness or whimsy in her. Had something—or someone— in her past caused her to be that way? It just wasn't natural to be that starched and pressed.

"So how's Alex done at school this week?" he asked without preamble. Or greeting, for that matter. Hey, she started it. "Have there been any more problems since our meeting on Monday?"

"No," she said, "Alex has been fabrication-free this week."

"Good," Michael said. "Hopefully, that will be the end of it, then."

She hesitated for a moment, clearly giving much thought to something, then began, "Actually, Mr. Sawyer—"

"Call me Michael, please," he interjected, trying to alleviate her oppressive air of correctness because it was threatening to wrap around him, too. He really didn't want to get formal with this woman. He hadn't been formal for years, and he'd been very happy.

But Hannah only continued where she left off. "I'm not sure the problem has been solved." And then, with extra coolness, she added, "Mr. Sawyer." Just so Michael would know where he stood with her. Which was ironic, since he actually felt like he was flat on his back. If anything, she was the one letting him know where she stood with him. Specifically, with the heel of her shoe over his esophagus.

Gee, this conversation really wasn't going as well as he'd initially hoped. He'd been thinking he'd walk over and strike up a harmless conversation with Hannah about Alex, then gradually move the subject matter into her work at the school, then ask what had gotten her interested in education in the first place, then follow that with a polite query into her background, and then segue logically into an invitation to meet him at a cheesy hotel later for hours and hours of unbridled sex. But, gosh, that unbridled sex was starting to look kind of unlikely. Where could he have gone wrong?

And what was the question again?

Oh, right. Alex hadn't been lying. What was up with that?

"But if he hasn't said anything inappropriate . . ." Michael continued, stepping forward, dipping his head toward hers because he wanted to lower his voice for the rest of this conversation. But Hannah immediately stepped back, a gesture he couldn't help noting. Jeez, it wasn't like he was stalking her. He hadn't done that for a good five, ten minutes, at least. So he decided to say nothing further, and hope maybe she'd conclude the conversation right there and move on to some other unsuspecting parent. Then, after she'd cooled off a bit, he could approach her again about that unbridled sex.

No such potluck.

"After you and Alex left Monday, Mr. Sawyer," she said, "it occurred to me that you never really did acknowledge the fact that your son lies." Her voice was lower, too, now, but not as low as his. Maybe she'd backed away, Michael thought, but she wasn't going to back down.

"Michael," he automatically corrected her again. Not that he knew why he bothered. She obviously didn't want to call him that, and there was no reason for him to encourage a familiarity in their relationship that wasn't there. For some reason, though, it bothered him to be called Mr. Sawyer by her. Probably because it bothered him so much to call her Ms. Frost.

"And I couldn't help wondering why you didn't," she added when he offered nothing in response. "Especially since Alex obviously does tell lies. You can't possibly argue with me on that score."

"I'd rather not argue with you on any score, Ms. Frost," Michael told her, telling himself he was *not* arguing with her by saying that. Especially since what he really wanted to do with her was get her alone in a cheesy hotel room for hours and hours of—

"Excuse me."

The interruption came not from Hannah, but from a third person who had intruded upon their argument . . . ah, conversation. Not that Michael minded, quite frankly. On the contrary, he was grateful for the reprieve, since at this point he neither wanted to argue with Hannah nor converse with her. Hell, he was even beginning to reconsider the hours and hours of unbridled sex. Well, a little. But then he turned his attention to the owner of the voice, and all he could do was stare dumbfounded at the tawny-haired, green-eyed man who seemed to have sprung up from nowhere. Well, stare dumbfounded and also battle the urge to tell the man to go to hell. Because hell was the only place that could have spawned Adrian Padgett.

"Excuse me, Hannah," he said again, adding her name to the interjection this time, his deep, rumbling voice edged with more than a little intimacy when he spoke it the way he did.

And Michael somehow refrained from grinding his teeth into powder when Hannah did nothing to correct Adrian's use of her first name. Nor did she curdle at his obvious affection for her. No, in fact, she spun around to smile at him with a warmth and regard that was unmistakable. The prick.

Then Adrian turned to look at Michael, presumably to introduce himself and invite him into the conversation. But Adrian didn't need an introduction, something he obviously realized, since he already knew—

"Michael," Adrian said, his tone of voice now revealing absolutely nothing of what he might be feeling. Not that Michael couldn't have guessed. "Michael Sawyer," he further elaborated. Not that it was necessary, since there was little chance Adrian wouldn't have recognized him. Still, although Adrian might recognize him—although Adrian might know him—he had no idea who Michael really was these days.

"Adrian," Michael replied, amazed at his ability to sound courteous, even amiable, in return.

"You two know each other?" Hannah said, sounding surprised. Looking surprised.

And Michael decided to take that surprise at face value and not interpret it to mean she couldn't believe he would be capable of moving in the same social circles as Adrian. Which was pretty humorous, because there had been a time when he and Adrian both had moved in circles that were anything *but* social.

Still, yes, he did, by God, know Adrian. The SOB. So Michael forced himself to smile blandly, and although he looked at Adrian when he spoke, the words he said were intended for Hannah. "Yes, we know each other. But it's been a while. We have some catching up to do."

And once I've caught you up, Adrian, Michael added to himself, *then I'm going to take you down.*

Hannah watched the byplay between Adrian and Michael with interest. Not once in the six months she had known him had she seen Adrian caught off guard. He was normally the most unflappable person she knew—well, besides herself, of course—unaffected by everything from a smudge on his five-hundred-dollar shoes to a stock market that put many people out on a building ledge.

But he had visibly stiffened the second he'd looked over and seen Michael, and he had yet to relax his stance. Oh, he was smiling pleasantly enough, and probably to a casual observer he seemed fine. But Hannah detected the merest bit of agitation in Adrian's posture. And she found it very curious indeed that it had resulted from the simple presence at a fourth-grade potluck of Michael Sawyer.

"Then I don't suppose I need to introduce you?" she asked anyway.

"No," the two men chorused as one.

"That won't be necessary," Adrian added. He smiled again, and this time he seemed more himself.

Himself being a man who was supremely confident— many had called him arrogant, but Hannah wasn't sure she'd go so far as that—a man who was thoroughly at ease in any situation, and who could be at varying times charming and generous, exacting and cautious. He had the capacity to be ruthless, too, Hannah knew, a quality that had surely aided him in his quick climb up the success ladder. And for that reason, she wouldn't have gotten involved with him even if he wasn't on the board of the Emerson Academy. Ruthlessness was a quality in a man she could just as soon do without. She wondered if Michael was ruthless.

And then she told herself it didn't matter. Because she wouldn't be getting close enough to him—ever—to find out.

"Adrian often attends these potlucks in his capacity as a board member," Hannah explained to Michael. Though why she would explain something he would doubtless infer was a mystery to her. Especially since she suspected Adrian attended these potlucks less as a board member and more because Hannah attended them, too. So she hastily added, "Where do the two of you know each other from?"

For a single, uncomfortable moment, both men remained utterly silent, utterly still, as if neither was sure how to answer so simple and straightforward a question.

Then, "As Michael said, he and I go way back," Adrian told her.

Strangely, she detected something in his voice that was almost antagonistic, but there was something there, too, that was almost affectionate. How very interesting.

"And how do the two of you know each other?" she asked, realizing that although he had responded, Adrian hadn't answered her question. Belatedly, she realized it was actually an inappropriate question to ask. Not only was it none of her business what kind of history the two men shared, but there was a chance that the shared history wasn't exactly good, and now she'd set them both up for an awkward situation.

She began to suspect that that was the case when both men still hesitated to reply, and instead only exchanged a hasty, meaningful glance. At least, Hannah assumed it was meaningful to them. She herself had no idea what it might have signified. Other than that she'd just *faux pas*-ed herself into a really big pile of *merde*.

"We, ah . . . we went to school together," Adrian finally said.

"Really," Hannah said. And then, even though she told herself not to, she continued with her same line of questioning. "Was Mr. Sawyer studying computers, or were you studying accounting?"

Adrian chuckled. "Accounting?" he echoed, turning his attention back to Michael. "You're an *accountant* now? Is that the career path you actually pursued? Are you serious?"

"I am an accountant," Michael replied a bit testily. "As for serious, well . . . you should know better than to ask, Adrian."

Adrian nodded. "I remember you were more serious about some things than others," he said.

"As were you," Michael rejoined. And there was a definite edge to his voice when he spoke.

It quickly became evident that the edge was elsewhere, too, because as a wine-laden waiter passed by them, Michael snagged a glass of red from the tray and downed half of it in a single, rapacious swallow. Not once did he take his eyes off of Adrian as he did so. And not once did Hannah take her eyes off of Michael. Something about the way he was looking at Adrian gave her pause. As did the way his strong throat worked over the swallow, and how, after completing it, he pressed the back of his hand to his mouth, still cradling the wine glass with complete ease. His grasp was the only thing about him that was easy, however. Because he looked tense and angry, and Hannah realized to her surprise that she wanted very much to do or say something to Michael that would counter his tension and anger.

And when, she wondered, had she started to think of him as *Michael,* instead of *Michael Sawyer*?

"Mr. Sawyer's son attends Emerson," she said, turning to Adrian. "This is his first year."

"Alex," Adrian said. "He must be in, what . . . fourth grade now?"

"Yes," Hannah replied, surprised, too, that Adrian knew that about Michael. Sawyer. Michael Sawyer.

"Yet this is his first year at Emerson, you say," Adrian added. "How interesting. The timing, I mean."

"Not really," Michael said. "I wasn't all that crazy about his last school. Emerson has a better program for him."

In response to Michael's comments, Adrian looked very thoughtful. "And how is the little tyke? Not so little anymore, I'd wager." He smiled cryptically as he added, "For that matter, how is his mother doing?"

Something cold and vicious sliced through Michael's expression as Adrian posed the questions, something Hannah hoped to never see in his face again. Because it made Michael look less like an accountant and more like, oh . . . she didn't know. An assassin, say.

"Alex is fine," he said evenly. "But his mother and I rarely speak. We divorced five years ago."

Hannah tried to discern some reaction from Adrian to that news, but he showed no emotion whatsoever. "And what, she doesn't ask about, ah . . . your boy?"

"Not often, no," Michael said, the words chilly and sharp.

And Hannah found herself hanging on every one of them. Michael had told her the first time he'd visited the school, in preparation for Alex's registration, that his ex-wife lived in Europe, and for that reason, Alex seldom saw her. But he'd offered no other information to further enlighten her about the circumstances surrounding the divorce, and he hadn't said a word about Alex's relationship with his mother.

Hannah had wanted very badly to know why Michael had been the one awarded custody when, in normal situations, Alex would have gone to live with his mother. Courts overwhelmingly favored mothers in such cases, unless they were chemically dependent, cruel, or unable—or unwilling—to take care of their child. Which had it been for Alex's mother? she wondered. And why did the woman not even call?

She waited to see if Michael would say anything more, but he didn't. So she waited to see if Adrian would press, but he didn't. And then she told herself to stop acting like she was watching a soap opera on television. This was real life. These were real people. And their situations were none of her business. Unless they affected Alex, in which case, Hannah figured she had a right to pry. She cared about the boy, too.

"Where in Europe does Alex's mother live?" she heard herself ask. "I mean," she backpedaled when she saw the expression on Michael's face—the assassin one was back— "I've always wanted to visit Europe. It must be so interesting to live there."

Michael narrowed his eyes at her, a gesture she somehow suspected she should interpret as a warning. Nevertheless, he answered, "Last I heard, she was in Prague."

"Oh, the Czech Republic," Hannah said. Then, when she realized she knew very little about the country, she added inanely, "They make lovely crystal there."

Adrian stepped up beside Hannah then and curved his arm around her waist, a gesture that could be interpreted as nothing but proprietary. It was also unexpected, and inappropriate. And unwanted, too. Okay, so it could be a lot of things other than proprietary. They were all things Hannah didn't like. So she started to step away, only to have Adrian pull her closer still, and she was so surprised by *that* gesture that she honestly wasn't sure what to do.

Especially when he looked down at her and said, "You'd love Europe, Hannah. I have a meeting in London next week. Come with me. We can stay overnight at the Dorchester. We'll have a wonderful time."

Before she even had a chance to reply—not that she had

any idea what to say, so stunned was she by his invitation—
Adrian turned back to Michael. "So where are you living
now? Here in Indianapolis, of course, if Alex is attending
Emerson. When did you get back?"

Get back? Hannah echoed to herself. And then she realized it was a very good suggestion. So she got back. Spinning as gracefully as she could out of Adrian's arm, she took
a few steps away, ostensibly to place her empty tumbler on
the tray of another passing waiter, who was just out of her
reach. And then she stayed just out of Adrian's reach once
she was finished.

"Get back?" Michael echoed this time, out loud. "I never
left, Adrian. Not really."

And my, but wasn't that a cryptic statement? Hannah
thought. Even more cryptic, however, was Adrian's reply.

"No, I don't suppose you did," he said. "Nor will you
ever. There will always be something of the Indiana boy in
you, won't there?"

Hannah was about to open her mouth to ask something
else—though, honestly, at that point she had no idea what
would come out of her mouth next—when Bitsy Wainwright
stepped onto the patio and rang a delicate crystal dinner bell,
the soft *ting-a-ling-a-ling* carrying surprisingly well across
the quiet murmurs of the crowd. And until that moment, Hannah had genuinely forgotten where she was, and what she
was doing, and in what capacity she was expected to behave.

But Bitsy reminded her then, calling out in a voice as clear
and delicate as the dinner bell had been, "Attention, please!
Attention! Welcome to the Emerson Academy fourth grade
potluck! So fortunate to have director Hannah Frost tonight.
So delighted." And then she turned to Hannah and extended
her hand, palm up, in what Hannah supposed was meant to
be an invitation. "Hannah?" she prodded. "A few words?"

And then Hannah had no choice but to separate herself
from Adrian and Michael and make her way through the

crowd toward the steps where Bitsy stood. It couldn't have taken her more than fifteen seconds to make the trip. But after climbing the creekstone steps, when she turned around again, directing her gaze at the spot where she had just stood, it was to find that Adrian and Michael had retreated to opposite corners of the patio.

Like two boxers in the ring, she couldn't help thinking. Because although they had parted, they continued to gaze intently at each other from their respective places, as if they were sizing each other up to . . . *something.* Hannah had no idea what. But there was no sense of camaraderie in their positions, no suggestion of friendliness at all. On the contrary, she couldn't help thinking that the next time Bitsy rang her bell, the two men would come out swinging.

Very odd indeed, she thought. Odder still was her rampant curiosity about the two men's relationship. But the oddest thing of all was that instead of being more curious about Adrian, whom Hannah knew fairly well and should have cared more about, she found herself more focused on Michael. Michael Sawyer, CPA.

Michael Sawyer, *Can't Prove Authentic.*

Michael wasn't surprised, when he left the potluck early, to find Adrian waiting for him by his car. Nor was he surprised that Adrian knew which of the scores of cars parked outside was his. Nor was he surprised that Adrian had slipped away from the party without being noticed or missed. Adrian had always been good at all of those things. Better, alas, even than Michael had been. And, of course, where Michael had left all the subterfuge and stratagem and sneakiness behind, Adrian had continued honing and refining his skills for future endeavors.

Like, for instance, this one. Whatever the hell it was. For all the agents assigned to Adrian over the past six months, OPUS still couldn't pinpoint what the guy was up to. He truly did seem to be an average Joe, marketing software for CompuPax during the day, pursuing women—like Hannah Frost, damn him—at night. He kept regular hours, held a membership at a country club where he played tennis on the weekends, subscribed to the opera, held a position on the board of directors of the Emerson Academy. He hadn't had so much as a parking violation since surfacing in Indianapolis. His whereabouts prior to his reappearance remained a complete mystery, as did his identity prior to that. Oh, he'd forged some excellent credentials for himself, credentials that had enabled him to be hired by CompuPax in the first place, but as Adrian Windsor, the man appeared to be living a perfectly normal life.

And now he stood, as he had so many times before, in the shadows, a tall yet indistinct figure leaning against Michael's car. And it occurred to Michael with uncharacteristic whimsy as he observed him that this was the first time he'd actually ever *seen* Adrian at work. Because Adrian was most assuredly working, there was no question about that. Adrian never stopped working. There had been times when Michael had wondered if he even knew how.

"Raptor," Adrian said by way of a greeting when he drew within earshot.

"Sorcerer," Michael greeted him just as succinctly.

He came to a halt just shy of swinging distance, though whether that was because he feared Adrian might punch him, or he might pop Adrian, he wasn't entirely sure. He only knew he didn't want to get too close. Not now. Not ever again.

"You can't touch me, you know," Adrian said without preamble. "You, OPUS, none of you. Because I haven't done anything wrong."

"We won't touch you," Michael agreed. But he qualified, "Because we can't *prove* you did anything wrong. Big difference, Adrian. But that's about to change."

"I sincerely doubt it. I am, after all, a law-abiding citizen now, a working stiff just trying to make my way in the world."

Michael smiled sarcastically and echoed, "I sincerely doubt it."

"And now you're an accountant," Adrian added, intoning the final word as if he were voicing the name of God Himself. "Among other things," he added with a grin.

Michael let that go. "Yeah, so I know what it really is to be a law-abiding citizen and a working stiff. If you think I'll buy that crap coming from you, you're out of your mind."

Adrian's smile grew broader, but he said nothing more about that. "I suppose I should have realized you'd show up sooner or later," he continued. "I must be losing my touch to have been surprised by your presence here tonight. Really, the only thing that should be surprising is that it took you this long."

Michael feigned shock. "What? Doubting yourself? That's not like you, Adrian."

Adrian smiled. "Not doubting myself," he said. "Just reminding myself that I shouldn't get too complacent."

"Oh, go ahead," Michael told him. "Get complacent."

Now Adrian's smile grew feral. "What, and make your job easier? Not bloody likely."

"My job?" Michael echoed blandly. "What does the fact that I'm an accountant have to do with anything?"

Adrian chuckled in response, and there was something rabid in the sound. "Oh, right. Like I'm supposed to believe you've really become an accountant? You? Crunching numbers for a living?"

Michael shoved his hands carelessly into his pockets and shrugged. "Well, I did major in accounting, after all. And it isn't so different from what I did before."

Adrian leveled a dubious gaze on him. "It's entirely different from what you did before."

Michael shook his head. "No, it's different from what *you*

did before. But then, you were always different, weren't you, Adrian? You always wanted something the rest of us didn't. And you could never understand why we didn't want it, too."

"Not anymore," Adrian replied cryptically.

Michael eyed him narrowly. "What?" he said. "You understand now? Or you don't want it anymore?" He grinned cynically. "Or am I supposed to believe you're not different anymore? That you're just like the rest of the world now?"

"I am like the rest of the world," Adrian stated with all confidence. "I've always been like the rest of the world. You, Michael, you're the one who was always different. You're the one who actually believed good would always triumph over evil. That the average human being was inherently decent. Do you still? After everything that happened, do you still believe that?"

Michael ground his teeth together hard. "Yeah, Adrian. I do still believe that. In spite of everything. Because I still think you're the aberration."

"Well, Tatiana rather liked me, didn't she?"

Michael waited for the white-hot rage that should have come with the other man's remark, and was surprised to find it was only a little bubble of irritation now. Wow. Time really did rub away the rough edges. Because what else could have explained why he no longer cared that much about what had happened between Adrian and his wife? "Yeah, well, I guess there's no accounting for taste, is there?" he said.

"Mm," Adrian replied. "But then, if you'll recall, Tatiana tasted—"

"Button it," Michael said before he could finish. "You won't get a rise out of me. Not this time. Not anymore. What's done is done, and frankly, all things considered, I'm glad it worked out the way it did." He could tell by Adrian's expression that he didn't believe him. But hell, Michael didn't care. "Alex and I have a good life here," he continued. "And everything that's in the past? That's where I left it."

"Until now," Adrian said.

Michael remained silent.

"And now OPUS has you dancing to their tune again, don't they?"

It was useless to deny it. Adrian knew how OPUS worked. He knew the rules. He knew the ropes. He knew the ties that bind. Nevertheless, Michael still said nothing.

"You're wasting your time," Adrian told him. "You, OPUS, all of you. I know you're watching me, but there's no reason to. I'm a law-abiding citizen now. A scion of the local business community. A hometown boy made good."

Somehow Michael refrained from rolling his eyes. "You're a pain in the ass, Adrian, that's what you are. It's what you've always been. Nothing more."

"Then why are you here?"

"Because of a number of developments that add up to trouble," Michael said. "You in Indianapolis. A presidential debate in Indianapolis. Not a good combination, I'm thinking."

Adrian smiled again, that vaguely predatory smile. "What on earth would I have to do with a presidential debate?" he asked.

"That's what I'd like to know," Michael told him. "Just a shot in the dark here, but it probably has something to do with the fact that you've always wanted to rule the world."

Adrian laughed out loud at that, a full, uninhibited laugh that probably carried all the way to Bitsy and Cornelius's back forty. "Oh, I love how you say that. 'Rule the world.' It makes me sound like a comic book villain."

"Well, you were always pretty cartoonish," Michael said. "In any event, it didn't take long for OPUS to put two and two together."

"No, it didn't," Adrian agreed. "I'm just not sure you got the right answer when you did."

"What's that supposed to mean?"

"Just that, as always, OPUS can't see the trees for the forest."

"And what's *that* supposed to mean?"

Adrian continued to smile. "Figuring out what it all means was *your* job, Michael. Assimilate, evaluate, articulate. Remember?"

Of course Michael remembered. He remembered his three-word job classification too well.

"And after you do all those things," Adrian added, "you can penetrate it where the sun don't shine."

"Ah, go fornicate yourself, Adrian," Michael retorted blandly.

"I don't want to take away *all* your fun by telling you everything right off the bat," Adrian said, ignoring his comment. "But you're a smart boy, Michael. You always were. You'll figure it out. Eventually. One can only hope it won't be too late when you finally do."

And before Michael had a chance to say another word, Adrian had turned away to fade into the darkness.

The very place that had spawned him to begin with.

THREE

THERE WAS NOTHING WORSE, IN MICHAEL'S opinion, than Monday mornings. Unless maybe it was cold, rainy Monday mornings. Cold, rainy Monday mornings when he overslept, then had to rely on lousy drive-thru coffee, because he was in a big hurry. Cold, rainy Monday mornings when he overslept, and then had to rely on lousy drive-thru coffee because he was in a big hurry to commit a felony.

Yeah, it was gonna be one of those days.

As he sipped his lousy drive-thru coffee, it occurred to Michael that this was the kind of day that reminded him why he had left his previous job behind. Yet here he was, back in the saddle again. Or, to be more specific, in the driver's seat of a generic white utility van, dressed in generic navy blue coveralls. Of course, there was no *back* or *again* in this situation, since he'd rarely worked in the field before. Still, what he was about to do came as naturally to him as anything else he'd ever done. Only this time, he didn't feel natural doing it. Because where before he'd never had much of a personal stake in the job he was performing, this time it was most definitely personal.

But it wasn't Adrian he was thinking about then. It was the woman who owned the house a half block up from where

Michael had parked the van, the woman who should have already left said house for work, the woman who evidently had also overslept that morning and would have to make do with lousy drive-thru coffee, just as Michael had. The big difference in their situations was that he was reasonably certain Hannah Frost was *not* on her way to commit a felony. No, Hannah would just be doing her job.

But then, that was what Michael was doing, too, wasn't it? The fact that it was work he'd sworn he'd never return to again was immaterial. He'd known the job was dangerous when he took it, and in spite of what he'd told his superior that late spring day in Washington, he'd known, too, that nobody ever left it completely behind. Which was why he shouldn't be surprised to find himself in this position.

Gee. Hindsight really was twenty-twenty.

He was lifting the cardboard cup to his mouth again when, through the streaks of rain glazing his windshield, he noticed movement at Hannah's house. He hit the wiper handle once, to clear the windshield only long enough for a clear view, and saw the garage door slowly rolling upward. Another quick flick of the wiper handle, and he saw Hannah's blue sedan rolling backward from that garage and into the street. Her taillights flashed red as she halted and threw the car into gear, and then she drove off in the direction opposite from where Michael had parked.

He continued to sip his coffee for another ten minutes, just to make sure she didn't return for anything she may have forgotten, and when he was confident she was gone for the day, he hiked up the collar of his coveralls, grabbed what looked to the casual observer like a garden-variety toolbox, and exited the van.

A trench coat would have been nice about now, he thought as he climbed out, even if it would have been *such* a cliché. Though how that cliché had come about, Michael still didn't know. In all the years he'd worked for OPUS, not once had he seen an agent in a trench coat. Not even when it was raining.

It was still early enough in the morning to be semi-dark, something which, added to the rain, made his job infinitely easier. Though that wasn't saying much, seeing as how it had been years since he'd performed a job like this. Still, he supposed, there were some things people learned that never left them, no matter how long they went without practicing. Riding a bicycle, for instance. Swimming. Driving a car. Shooting pool. Playing chess.

Breaking and entering.

His head tucked low—because it looked like he was trying to avoid rain in his face when in fact he just didn't want his face to be seen—Michael ducked into a conveniently placed hedge growing between two houses up the block from Hannah's. He'd driven by twice over the course of the weekend to make a mental map of the area and plan his approach. Fortunately for him, the neighborhood was an old one, filled with overgrown trees and shrubs, and populated by neighbors who eschewed fences, most likely because the neighborhood association frowned upon them. In any event, what made for an aesthetically pleasing environment also made for good cover. So Michael had no trouble making his way to Hannah's back door without being seen. Once there, he withdrew from his pocket a small device and with a few hasty adjustments slipped it easily into the lock of her back door. A soft click told him he hadn't lost his touch, and he easily pushed the door open and stepped inside, making a mental note to wipe up his wet footprints before he left.

Then, with a swiftness and expertise that time hadn't diminished, he moved through the house, placing tiny listening devices where they would be least likely to be discovered. Of course, Hannah couldn't possibly have any idea that she would be under surveillance, so Michael could probably drop a few bugs right in the open, and she'd have no idea what they were. Nor would she guess that two tiny, undetectable cameras could record her daily life.

Gadgetry really wasn't his milieu, but he'd always found the technology created by OPUS to be nothing short of amazing. He himself had been in statistics and examination, one of the people who took the information the field agents gathered and who analyzed and scrutinized, calculated and estimated, and then put everything together. Assimilate, evaluate, articulate, just as Adrian had said. Those had been the code words of his job classification. And that part of the job he did miss.

Not that Michael—or anyone else at OPUS—was interested in Hannah's statistics, or her daily life. Well, except for those parts of her statistics and daily life that included Adrian Padgett. Other agents were watching Adrian in other capacities, but Michael had been assigned to keep tabs on his activities that revolved around the Emerson Academy. And, by extension, on his activities that revolved around the Emerson Academy's director. Because judging by the way Adrian himself had revolved around the Emerson Academy's director at the potluck three nights ago, he was certainly no stranger to Hannah. Therefore one might conclude that he was also no stranger to Hannah's house. And wherever Adrian Padgett went, OPUS needed to be as well. Even if it was Hannah Frost's house. Even if it was Hannah Frost's living room.

Even if it was Hannah Frost's bedroom.

Michael really, really hoped he wouldn't need to activate the bedroom cam over the next few weeks. Hell, he hoped he wouldn't need to activate the living room cam, either. Bad enough he'd be listening in on her. But for the first few days, at least, he'd sit in his van parked a block or two from Hannah's house, and he'd listen to Hannah's life. If he found no reason to think Adrian was sharing that life, Michael would bow out of the surveillance and feel relieved and remove all the surveillance equipment from her home. And he'd hope like hell that Hannah never found out about any of it. If there was any indication, however, that he might uncover more about Adrian by watching Hannah, then, by God, he'd keep watching Hannah.

And he'd hope like hell that she never found out about it.

Once he had everything in place that needed to be in place, Michael moved through the house a final time, giving it a once-more-over to make sure nothing was obvious to the casual observer. Or to the intent observer, either, since Adrian would certainly know what to look for, should he decide to look. But even after a close scrutiny, Michael was confident his work was well hidden. So he began to make his way back to the kitchen . . .

. . . and then realized he might never have an opportunity like this again. He might never have another chance to get a look at Hannah's life up close and personal.

Not that it was any of his business what her life was like even far away and impersonal. But he couldn't resist stealing a few more moments to see the place not from the point of view of someone working, but from the point of view of someone who might have been invited as a guest. And what he saw as a guest—however uninvited—made Michael puzzle even more over Hannah.

Her house was very nice, he'd grant her that. But it looked like a photo spread from a decorating magazine. The furnishings and appointments evoked the feel of a cottage in the English countryside—or, at least, of a photograph of a cottage in the English countryside. But it was just a little *too* quaint, a little *too* tidy, a little *too* charming, a little *too* perfect. Almost as if it were a set for a TV show or movie instead of someone's actual living quarters.

From one room to the next, Michael received the same impression. There was nothing in the place that evoked a sense of who Hannah Frost really was. There were no photographs of family members, no collections, no memorabilia. Nothing that might offer any insight into where she had come from, what she liked to do, or who she might be under the starched, pressed suits.

It was one thing, Michael thought, to keep yourself hidden from the outside world. But it was something else entirely to hide yourself in your own home.

He returned to her bedroom, the one room he would have expected to find *some*thing that offered at least a clue as to who she might really be. But her dresser contained only a mirror and a brush, a bouquet of fresh flowers, a small porcelain tray onto which she had placed a couple of stray earrings, and a bottle of perfume. A writing desk tucked into the corner of the room held only a calendar, a clock, a cup of pencils and pens, a scratch pad, and a small, orderly stack of as-yet-to-be-paid bills. All things functional. No things personal. Even the bottle of perfume didn't appear to have been used, because it was full. And although Hannah, he had noticed, smelled very, very nice, he was reasonably sure the scent didn't come from a perfume bottle.

Before he realized what he meant to do, Michael moved to the dresser and lifted a hand to one of the drawer pulls. He stopped himself before opening the drawer, reminding himself that his job did not include snooping into Hannah's private things. But he couldn't quite force himself to drop his hand. His heart, he was amazed to discover, was thundering in his chest. Never, not even once, had he become edgy while on assignment. Even in matters of life and death, he had always been able to remain cool. So it wasn't the fear of getting caught that made his heart race the way it did. It was the simple prospect of learning something about Hannah that he had no right—or permission—to learn.

In for a penny, he told himself, *in for a pound.* And he tugged gently on the metal drawer pull.

Before the drawer was even open, he was assailed by a

soft, sweet scent, and he immediately identified it as the one he associated with Hannah. He discovered the reason for that soon enough, because the drawer he had opened, as luck would have it—or maybe it was just a sixth sense he had about these things . . . or, at least, about Hannah—was her lingerie drawer. And sitting atop the collection of garments was a silky, tasseled sachet in the shape of a tiny boudoir pillow, the color and, he presumed, fragrance of lavender.

Finally, he was learning something more about Hannah, something deeply personal and very interesting: She liked beautiful underthings. Because beneath that sachet lay an assortment of filmy, delicate confectionery—bras and slips and panties fashioned of the merest lace and the softest silk, in the gentlest palette of colors Michael had ever seen, each decorated with tiny pearls or miniature bows or little satin roses. It was quite a contrast to the severe suits in which he'd seen her attired so far. And, somehow, knowing that this was the sort of thing she wore underneath them made Michael itch to learn more.

Impulsively—because, honestly, he had no idea what possessed him to do it—he filched a pair of peach-colored panties from the silky mélange and tucked them into the pocket of his coveralls. Then he replaced the lavender sachet exactly as he had found it and eased the drawer closed again.

And then he had to lean against the dresser for a minute, holding on to its edge as if it were his only link to reality, because his heart was pounding so hard it was dizzying him and making him see spots.

Good God, what was wrong with him? he wondered. He'd never gotten sick on an assignment before. And hell, he'd done things infinitely more dangerous than bugging the home of a school director. Hell, he'd even done things more dangerous than stealing a woman's underwear. This was nuts.

Although he had been quick in completing the job he had

come to do, it was long past time for Michael to be leaving. So he hurried back to the kitchen, eliminating any sign that he had been there as he went, and slipped back out the way he had come in. The rain had lessened to a fine mist, and the sun was up, if obscured by thick slate clouds. But by now the majority of the neighborhood's residents would be at work, and the few who remained at home, if they saw him, would see only a man in utility coveralls returning to a utility van with a phony license plate. Michael was in no danger whatsoever.

Unless Hannah Frost came home from work tonight, looking for a pair of lavender-scented, peach-colored underwear.

Hannah came home from work toting two overflowing bags of groceries and feeling more exhausted than she had felt in a very long time. Probably that was because she hadn't slept well the last few nights. And probably *that* was because she had lain awake in her bed for hours, pondering two conundrums that defied solution.

The first conundrum was Adrian Windsor. She couldn't imagine what had gotten into the man, but since the fourth-grade potluck three nights ago, Adrian had called her four times—twice at home, and twice at school.

The first time had been early Saturday morning, to reiterate his invitation to accompany him to London. When Hannah had pointed out that she couldn't possibly take time off from work—and that it would be inappropriate for her to socialize with a member of the board—Adrian had backed off.

But then he had called her that afternoon to ask her if she wanted to see *Rigoletto* the following weekend, since he suspected she was the sort of person who loved opera. When Hannah had pointed out that she wasn't much of an opera fan—and that it would be inappropriate for her to socialize with a member of the board—Adrian had backed off.

But then he'd called her "just to talk." Twice. At school. And Hannah hadn't known how to tell him without insulting him that she didn't like "just talking"—whether she was at work *or* at home. So she had "just talked" for five minutes and then excused herself with some fabricated reason why she had to hang up.

It didn't take a genius to figure out that Adrian had moved from being attracted to Hannah to wanting to become her hunka hunka burnin' love. And Hannah just wasn't sure what to do about that. Other than be absolutely certain she had no intention of becoming Adrian's hunka hunka anything, burnin' or otherwise. Not just because it would be inappropriate for her to become romantically involved with a member of the board that way, but because Adrian just didn't . . . float her boat. Rev her engine. Toast her melbas. Burn her hunka. That sort of thing.

And it also didn't take a genius to realize that Adrian's sudden acceleration of attention had come about, oh . . . a nanosecond after he'd recognized Michael Sawyer at the potluck. And Hannah still couldn't stop thinking about—or puzzling over—the way Adrian had looped his arm around her waist and tried to pull her close, as if she were his own personal love muffin. Never, ever, had he done something so boorish and ill-mannered before. And it simply wasn't in the man's nature to do anything boorish or ill-mannered, least of all manhandle a woman in Hannah's position. He could have done it only as a reaction to Michael's presence. Or, perhaps, to see what kind of reaction he might get from Michael.

The question Hannah wanted an answer to was: *Why?*

Short of asking Adrian—or Michael, whom she also intended to avoid—she supposed she wasn't going to receive an answer. But that didn't make the question stop circling around in her brain. Nor did it keep thoughts of Michael—and, to a lesser degree, Adrian—from circling around in her brain. The worst part, though, was how thoughts of Michael continued to intrude into her brain after she fell asleep at night. And those thoughts were the ones over which she had no control.

So if, say, he wanted to appear in a dream, she couldn't stop him. And if, say, he wanted to appear in that dream holding a banana, she couldn't stop him from doing that, either. And if, in that dream, he offered his banana to her, she couldn't help that. Nor could she help it if she also appeared in that dream, holding a doughnut, through which she slid Michael's banana after he offered it to her. And she also couldn't help it if they were both naked in the dream. She couldn't help that any more than she could help waking up all hot and sweaty and agitated afterward, with her tangled sheets bunched between her legs.

Still, she was confident that the dream wasn't symbolic of anything. Unless maybe it signified that she needed to go to the grocery store because she was running low on phallic symbols . . . ah, food, she meant. Surely that would have been the way Freud would have interpreted it. So here she was, home from work with two bags of groceries. Bags of groceries that did *not* contain bananas or doughnuts, since Hannah suspected maybe an excess of carbohydrates might just be to blame for her sleep problems in the first place. So she'd bought lots of protein and vegetables—hot dogs and sausages and pickles and cucumbers and zucchini and . . . and . . . and . . .

Hmm. Maybe it was an excess of something else she should be worrying about.

Shaking the thought off almost literally, Hannah kicked closed the back door and settled her burdens on the kitchen counter. Then she shrugged out of her trench coat and hung it on a peg on the basement door to dry. It had rained all day, a development that rather suited her mood, and she looked forward to a cozy evening at home. Alone. Just her and her phallic symbols. And also a private celebration to which she had been looking forward. Because among the groceries she unpacked was a birthday cake, chocolate with white frosting, her favorite. It wasn't a big cake, but it was beautifully decorated with pink and yellow roses and pale blue trim. Across the top of the cake, plastic pastel prima ballerinas posed in perfect pirouettes, and fancy pink script across the middle read, *Happy Birthday, Hannah.* And Hannah smiled, because it was exactly the kind of birthday cake she had always wanted as a little girl, the kind of cake she'd never once had.

She sighed with much contentment and made her way to the bedroom, shedding her workday clothes as she went, anxious, as always, to be free of them. After making herself comfortable in a loose-fitting, long-sleeved white T-shirt and even looser-fitting pale blue lounging pajama bottoms decorated with clouds, she plucked the pins from her hair and gave it a thorough brushing, looping the elbow-length tresses through each other to form a loose knot at her nape. Then she returned to the kitchen to prepare for her celebration, calling the number of Pizzarama to order a large garbage pizza and cheese sticks. Then she opened a bottle of Chianti and poured herself a generous glass. And then she went to the hall closet to retrieve her presents.

Naturally, they were presents Hannah had bought for herself, since no one she knew had an inkling that today was her birthday. But because she'd never been able to celebrate her birthday as a child, when birthdays meant so much—mostly because her father always forgot when her birthday was—she made sure she celebrated them as an adult. Because even as an adult, birthdays meant so much to Hannah. Each one marked another year in which her life had been stable, secure, and uneventful, and in which she had been reasonably happy.

The Pizzarama guy came and went, and by the time Hannah finished dinner, she was halfway through the Chianti and was feeling pretty festive and eager to open her gifts. She'd save the one from her imaginary Great-Aunt Esmeralda for last, since Auntie always gave her the nicest gifts. But she always got things from her pretend parents, too, not to mention her mythical Nana Frost, and her fictitious Cousin Chloe. And of course Patsy, her fabricated best friend from first grade, always sent some kind of joke gift that made Hannah smile. Oh, boy, she couldn't wait to tear into the brightly colored paper and stick the bows on her shoulders like epaulets, the way she would have done had she ever had a birthday party as a child.

But first things first. First, the *pièce de résistance*. First, she had to have some ballerina cake. And some music. Couldn't forget to sing herself the birthday song. It was, after all, a tradition. So Hannah carefully inserted ten candles onto the cake, then lit them and carried the cake out to the dining room, where she had stacked her presents into a dappled pyramid. And then, as she placed the cake on the table, she began to sing.

Out in his nondescript van, still wearing his navy blue coveralls, Michael Sawyer wondered just what the hell was going on inside Hannah Frost's house.

Oh, the evening had been uneventful enough for the most part. In fact, it had been so uneventful, he'd dozed off a couple of times. At this rate, he'd be home in time to put Alex to bed himself and send the sitter home early. All he'd heard coming from Hannah's house had been a call to Pizzarama—and man, his mouth had started to water when he heard her order the garbage pizza, with anchovies, since all he had to eat himself was a bag of Fritos—and soft, muffled sounds of movement, and what he was pretty sure had been a cork coming out of a bottle of wine. His mouth had watered at the sound of that, too, since all he had to enjoy with his Fritos was a Chateau Café Froid, vintage two hours ago, which although full-bodied and robust—oh, man, was it full-bodied and robust—just wasn't as smooth as he might have liked. And behind all those sounds had been the faint strains of classical piano—Debussy, if Michael wasn't mistaken—which, now that he thought about it, could account for why he'd dozed off a couple of times.

But then the weirdest thing had happened. A different kind of music had suddenly started up. But it wasn't Debussy, not by a long shot. In fact, it had sounded sort of like the birthday song, except that it was being sung in the key of . . . well, it seemed to be an extremely minor key that Michael was fairly certain must be undetectable to anyone but feral, frothing-at-the-mouth mongrels who could appreciate sounds like that. Though maybe *appreciate* wasn't quite the right word to use. . . . On the upside, having heard it, he probably wouldn't have any trouble staying awake for the rest of the evening. On the downside, he might never sleep again.

Just what the hell was going on in there? Hannah was home alone. Wasn't she? But why would she be singing the birthday song—in any key—if she was there all by herself? He thought for a moment that the singing might have come from the television or radio. But then he decided there had to be some kind of FCC regulation forbidding broadcasting that might potentially turn the population into rabid dogs. No, it was definitely Hannah singing—or something. But who was she singing—or something—to?

Immediately Michael thought of a way he might find out the answer to that question. Unfortunately, it involved committing another felony. But being a Peeping Tom couldn't be more than a class D felony, could it? Then he recalled the purloined panties which were still in the pocket of his coveralls, and he realized he might be convicted of a few other crimes, as well. Unable to help himself, he retrieved the panties, holding them up to his nose to inhale their sweet lavender scent again, growing dizzy just remembering the madness that had overtaken him that morning, when he'd snatched them from Hannah's lingerie drawer.

Great. He was OD-ing on underwear. This was just what he needed—a lingerie addiction. He was becoming a panty junkie. He was going to wind up one of those vacant-eyed, slobbering guys who stood outside Victoria's Secret, gazing through the display windows at the scantily clad dress forms that didn't even have a head or limbs, mainlining thongs and garter belts. *He used to be such a nice, normal guy,* they'd all say, *but now he's got a V-string on his back.*

Tucking the lacy garment back into his pocket, Michael unzipped and shed his coveralls, revealing blue jeans and a lightweight, oatmeal-colored sweater beneath. Then he checked all his equipment to be sure it was still taping, and, deciding not to question his actions, he left the safety of his hideout and headed for Hannah's house. Yes, he could have just activated the living room cam to see what she was doing, but something in him revolted at the thought, because it was so, well, revolting. That seemed like such an extreme—and unnecessary—invasion of her privacy, and he didn't want to be guilty of that.

No, he'd much rather invade her privacy in person.

The rain had finally stopped falling, but the air was cumbrous and chill with the lingering damp. The sun had set, smudging the sky a murky soot, but a street lamp on the corner spilled bilious light over much of Hannah's front yard. Michael cleared the four porch steps in two quick strides, then, before second thoughts prevented him, he pushed his thumb against the doorbell. Instead of a melodic *ding-dong,* a shrill, quick buzz shot through the house on the other side of the door. The jerky sound was at odds with his quiet surroundings, and the juxtaposition made him even edgier. After a moment of silence, he heard the creak of hardwood flooring as someone approached. Another moment passed in silence as Hannah, he was certain, viewed him through the peephole and tried to figure out where the hell he had come from and what the hell he was doing here. Then, finally, the door opened, a scant few inches, and her face appeared on the other side.

Only then did Michael realize what a stupid thing he was doing. How on earth was he supposed to explain his arrival at her front door at this hour of the night? Not that it was that late—it couldn't be much past eight—but it *was* night, and normally, parents didn't visit the director of their child's school at night. Nor did they visit the director of their child's school at home. Nor did they show up without calling first. Nor did they show up without a vehicle of some kind. What the hell had he been thinking?

Oh, right. He hadn't been thinking. He'd been sniffing Hannah's panties. So that explained that. And there were thick shrubs obscuring the driveway, so maybe she wouldn't notice the absence of a car. How to explain the rest of it, though . . .

"Uh, hi," he began eloquently. And for the life of him, he could think of not one single additional thing to say. So he stood there foolishly, hoping maybe this was all just a hallucination brought about by a lingerie high.

Hannah eyed him warily for a moment before replying, and when she finally did, her words were tinged with suspicion. "Hello. Mr. Sawyer. What brings you out?"

So it wasn't a hallucination. Her voice was too clear, too pure, too reserved for it to be anything other than the real thing. He strove for a lighthearted, faintly comedic tone when he said, "Would you believe I was just in the neighborhood?"

"No."

He waited for her to elaborate . . . but she didn't. So much for lighthearted and faintly comedic. "Well, then," he tried again, "would you believe I needed to talk to you about Alex and it couldn't wait?"

Oh, fine, he told himself derisively. *Just use your son to further your own treacherous agenda, why don't you? Some father you are.* But then he realized maybe he *did* want to talk to Hannah about Alex. Maybe.

"I might believe that," she said, interrupting his self-contempt. Not that he wasn't grateful. "But I don't know why you'd drive all the way to my house when you could have picked up the phone," she added. "For that matter, I don't know why you wouldn't call me at work. During the work *day,*" she added meaningfully.

"I usually get pretty busy at work, during the work *day,*" he said. "And I get so focused, I tend to forget about things that aren't work-related," he added, proud of himself for at least telling the truth about that. "By the time I remember I need to call you, you're gone for the day."

"You could call me at home," she said. "My number is in the school directory, and I'm always available to talk to parents about any concerns they might have. Though," she added in that meaningful voice again, "usually the parents try talking to their child's teacher first."

"I, ah, I've never much been one for chain of command," Michael said. "I'd just as soon go straight to the top. Besides," he added, hoping he sounded meaningful, too, "Alex's teacher said in her first note home to the parents that she'd be unavailable on Monday and Thursday evenings."

Hannah nodded. "That's right. She teaches adult returning education classes those nights."

Funny, Michael thought, but Hannah sounded kind of ticked off that he'd been right about that. And she hadn't opened the door any farther, and she was still looking at him suspiciously. Gosh, he couldn't imagine why.

"And I really was in the neighborhood," he added, congratulating himself for the truthfulness—sort of—of that statement. "I was hoping you wouldn't mind if I dropped by. So can I come in?" he asked, knowing he was pushing his luck and preparing himself for her rebuff.

But she didn't rebuff him. Not yet. "Is it terribly important?" she asked, cracking the door open a little more.

Her tone was one of reluctant capitulation, so Michael, being the sort of man he was, back on the sort of job he had performed for so long, did what he normally would have done. He took advantage of it.

"It is," he told her. "I wanted to see how he's been faring since we spoke that day in your office. I wanted to talk to you about it at the potluck Friday, but I didn't get the chance. Adrian really monopolized you that night."

Oh, bravo, Michael applauded himself. *Play the guilt card.* Hannah Frost, School Director, hadn't been doing her job on Friday, because she'd been too busy making time with a member of the school's board of directors. She'd *have* to talk to him now.

"You just wanted to check up on him and see how he's faring?" she echoed dubiously. "That doesn't seem terribly important to me."

In contrast to her objection, however, she opened the door even wider, enough for Michael to see she was in her pajamas—kind of. It struck him as odd that she'd be ready for bed so early in the evening. And then he wondered if maybe she wasn't alone after all, if he'd somehow missed someone coming over to see her. And he wondered, too, if that someone was Adrian Padgett, and he really, really, really hoped it wasn't.

Strangely, though, his hope that she wasn't seeing Adrian in her pajamas sprang not from Michael's unwillingness to keep spying on her, but from something else entirely, something he didn't want to name or even think about, because it just didn't seem possible. Or smart.

"It's important when you're a father," he told her. And again, he spoke the truth. Because there was a part of him that would always worry about Alex, no matter how old his son got, no matter how far his son traveled, no matter how responsible, independent, and self-supporting his son became. Michael really did want to know that Alex was faring well at school. The fact that he was going about it in ways that were a bit unorthodox just went along with everything else in his life these days. Because whenever Adrian Padgett was around, things always got unorthodox. To put it politely.

"All right," she said, the words punctuated with a weary sigh. "You can come in."

She took a step backward and pulled open the door, and before she had a chance to change her mind, Michael stepped over the threshold and into her house—into her life—for the second time that day. This time, though, he *had* been invited. Even if it was under false pretenses. Really, he told himself, his presence here now was no more acceptable than it had been earlier that day. At least, it wouldn't be if Hannah knew what was actually going on.

He realized once he got inside that what she was wearing might not, technically, qualify for pajamas, at least not on a less astringent woman. On Hannah, though, the outfit was downright whimsical, a soft white shirt that flowed over her curves instead of hiding them the way the suit jackets did, and pants with . . . nah, couldn't be. Those could not be clouds on her pants. She must have spilled something on herself that landed in the shapes of clouds. But the color made her blue eyes seem even bluer somehow, even larger, and her hair . . . Wow. Her hair. It really was long, spilling out of a knot at her nape—literally, a knot, her hair having been looped through itself—down between her shoulder blades, as thick and glossy as honey.

She'd accessorized her outfit with a glass of red wine,

something which again made Michael reassess his view of her. Of course she would relax with a glass of wine in the evening, he told himself. Why should he be surprised that she would enjoy such a leisurely activity? She was an adult woman with a high-pressure job. Naturally, she'd need to unwind a bit at night. The fact that her expression was kind of dreamy, and her cheeks were kind of flushed, and her eyes were kind of brighter than usual—as if maybe she'd enjoyed more than one glass—was beside the point. As was the fact that, at the moment, she also looked incredibly approachable and agreeable and desirable and kissable and—

And what was the point again?

Oh, yeah. He'd come here to find out if she was alone. And if she *was* alone, then maybe he could . . .

Nothing, he told himself firmly. He could—*would*—do nothing. If she was alone, then he'd chat with her for a bit about Alex, and then he'd turn around and go back out the way he'd come in. Through the front door. Down the front steps. Feeling really frustrated and wondering what the hell was going on. Only this time he wouldn't be wondering about what the hell was going on with Hannah. No, this time, he'd be wondering what the hell was going on with himself. Because never in his life had he been so thoroughly fascinated by a woman so soon after meeting her.

He was trying to think of some mundane question to ask about Alex that would get the conversation going, but something to his right caught his attention and held it, a faint, flickering light that drifted through open glass French doors dividing the living room from what he assumed was the dining room. But watching that weird light, Michael got the distinct impression that there truly was a birthday cake in that other room. A birthday cake with candles lit. A birthday cake over which the birthday song had just been sung.

And before he could stop himself, he heard himself ask, "Is today your birthday?"

Her eyes widened in obvious alarm at the question. "Why do you ask?" she said, her tone of voice contributing to the aura of alarm.

Michael pointed toward the light. "Because if it isn't your birthday today, then your house is on fire."

At that, Hannah spun around in panic, though somehow he got the impression that her panic stemmed less from the threat of her house being on fire than it did from him intuiting that today was her birthday. When she turned around again, she was blushing, though this time it had nothing to do with the wine. And damn, she was even more beautiful when caught unawares.

"The house isn't on fire," she said.

Michael couldn't quite help smiling. "So then it *is* your birthday."

She nodded quickly, once.

"Happy birthday," he told her.

"Thank you," she replied. But her voice was so soft and so quiet, and she was so disconcerted when she said it, that had he not been looking right at her, he might not have even registered the acknowledgment.

"I'm sorry to interrupt the party," he said further. "Had I known . . ."

"There's no party, just me," she said, verifying what he had suspected all along. And still she spoke softly. Still she spoke quietly. Still she was so disconcerted. "I just, um, I like cake," she finally finished, as if that should explain everything.

Michael had no idea what it was inside him that responded to her just then, but something, some unknown thing he'd never felt before, something he probably couldn't have explained in a million, billion years, went all soft and gooey as he watched her. In the gauzy golden light of her living room, surrounded by her too-tidy, too-perfect, too-quaint furnishings, wearing her soft, curvy clothes, Hannah

Frost just looked . . . well, she looked lost, truth be told. Which was bizarre, because whenever he'd seen her before, she'd always seemed to be completely in control of herself and her surroundings. Now, though . . .

Man, he must be losing it. Because at the moment, Hannah Frost, uptight school director, looked very much like a woman who just wanted to be held. *Unguarded,* that was the word that came to him just then. That was how she seemed to be. Unguarded. And more than anything else in the world, at that moment Michael wanted very much to guard her. To keep her safe. To reassure her that everything was fine.

And he wanted even more to kiss her.

So much so, in fact, that he actually took a step forward and, before he even realized what he was doing, found himself lifting a hand toward her face. But he didn't seem to be the one controlling the gesture. Not consciously, anyway. Something else inside him was acting just then, was responding just then, and Michael, even consciously, had no wish to stop whatever it was. Higher and higher his hand rose, but he was too busy drowning in Hannah's blue, blue eyes to really notice it. She didn't seem to notice, either, at least not the movement of his hand, because she was too busy gazing back at him.

And then he did see his hand, hovering near her jaw, his index finger slightly extended past the others, all of them curling slightly toward his palm. Closer and closer his hand drew to her face, to the softly flushed flesh he wanted so desperately to touch. And then his hand was turning outward, forming itself into a cradle as it nestled under her jaw, and then he *was* touching her, just barely, the warmth of her skin seeping into the palm of his hand, and just that slight touch set his heart to racing, ignited tiny explosions in his midsection. Hannah's eyes fluttered closed at the soft contact, her lips parting ever so slightly, as if she knew he wanted to kiss her, as if she wanted that, too.

And then Michael's head was following the path of his hand, dipping toward her face, toward her jaw, toward her mouth. It was almost as if time had stopped, as if reality had simply ebbed away, and he'd been transported over the last few minutes to another place, another body, another life. Hannah tilted her head a little to the right, and he tilted his a little to the left, and as the narrowing space between their bodies grew narrower still, he could almost feel the heat of her mingling with the heat of him, and the wanting of her mingling with the wanting of him, and the need in her mingling with the need in him.

He could feel her breath against his mouth, and he thought he heard her utter a soft sough of surrender, when suddenly whatever it was inside him responding to her was finally overridden by his conscious mind. Because that was when Michael's conscious mind stepped in and reminded him that Hannah did need guarding at the moment, and she did need to be kept safe—from him. If he kissed her now, regardless of how genuinely he felt about her—not that he could quite identify what it was he felt for her, only that it was indeed genuine—he would do so as the man who was spying on her. Who was misleading her. And although Michael had done some pretty questionable things in his time, kissing a woman while lying to her wasn't one of them. On the contrary, he'd been kissed himself while being lied to, and he hadn't liked it much. The last thing he wanted to be was someone like Tatiana.

So he stopped himself from doing what he wanted to do, forced himself to rescind his hand from Hannah's face and take a step backward, then shoved his hands deep into the pockets of his blue jeans so they wouldn't break free again. Hannah sensed his withdrawal, because she straightened and opened her eyes, blinking a few times in rapid succession as if just awakening from a trance. Michael sympathized. He felt a little fuzzy around the edges of his brain, too.

"Yeah, I, uh, I guess there comes a time in our lives when we don't want birthday parties anymore," he said, trying to pick up the threads of their conversation where they'd dropped it, amazed that he even remembered where they had been. "A time when birthdays don't seem so much like something to celebrate." He expelled a rough sound that he hoped didn't sound like dejection, but feared very much did. "Must happen around the same time we stop referring to ourselves by fractions. I mean, me, I'd be thirty-nine and three-quarters now. Somehow, though, I just don't feel compelled to tell people that."

Hannah smiled back, albeit a little shakily. Her smile seemed to result more from gratitude, though, than from any kind of amusement his comment may have inspired. But whether she was grateful for his deflecting the potential embarrassment of her situation away from her, or for the fact that he'd stopped himself from kissing her, he couldn't have said. He hoped it was the latter. Because he still wanted to kiss her. Still intended to kiss her. Once he was in a position to do so. He just hoped he *would* be in such a position. Soon.

"Thanks," she said, cementing his suspicion that she was more grateful than anything else. And then, more forcefully, "But I actually do enjoy celebrating birthdays," she told him. "I just keep my observances to myself, that's all. Well, usually," she amended, and he told himself she was too polite to be making a dig at his intrusion.

In spite of that, "I'll go," he said, "and I'll just call you at school tomorrow."

"No!" she exclaimed, surprising him.

Surprising herself, too, judging by her expression. But then, it had been a night for surprises, hadn't it? Surely she had found their near-embrace just now as unexpected as he had.

"I mean," she hastily backpedaled, "I don't mind you being here." She lifted one shoulder and let it drop in what he supposed was meant to be a shrug. "You can stay if you want."

Oh, he wanted. He most definitely, most assuredly wanted. So maybe he'd do like the song said and stay-ay-ay, just a little bit longer.

Hannah looked at Michael Sawyer and told herself she really should have stopped after one glass of Chianti. Because if she had, then maybe he wouldn't look so dreamy and winsome and fine. And maybe it wouldn't feel so good to have him here.

And maybe she wouldn't have nearly kissed him just a minute ago. Good heavens, what had happened with that? One minute, she'd been wondering where he had come from and why his presence in her home had been even nicer than the presents in her home, and the next minute, he'd been *this* close to kissing her, and she'd been *this* close to letting him. Letting him? she echoed to herself. Hah. She'd been *encouraging* him. She'd closed her eyes and tilted her head, just like a dewy starlet in a fabulous forties film. Could she have *been* any more obvious? What had come over her? What must he think of her?

And why was she tempted, even now, to lift her hand to his face this time and trail her fingertips over the smile that so sweetly curled his lips, and then press her mouth to his?

Chianti, she thought. The libation of love. Except that love had nothing to do with it. No, it was another *L*-word, she was certain, that was ruling her just then. Surprisingly, though, it wasn't lust, either. It was simple loneliness, that was all. Because ever since Michael Sawyer had walked into her office, her condition had been especially acute.

And speaking of cute, Michael was certainly that tonight. She had thought him handsome in a suit and tie, but dressed in more normal clothes like jeans and a sweater, the man was quite . . . She sighed in spite of herself. Breathtaking. That was what he was. Because he seemed so . . . normal. So accessible. So available. And even though she tried to tell herself otherwise, she was pretty sure that that, at least, had nothing to do with the wine.

"Please," she said, stirring herself almost physically from the strange reverie that wanted to encompass her, "stay. You can even have some cake, if you want."

And that, she decided, *had* to be the wine talking. Because never had Hannah wanted to share her birthday—especially her birthday cake—with anyone. Something about having Michael here, though, in her home, on a special occasion like this, just felt . . . good. Normal. Right. And she couldn't remember anyone ever feeling that way.

Chianti, she told herself again. That had to be it. It was just one of the many reasons Italians were such gregarious people.

In silent invitation, she turned and made her way back to the dining room, smiling over her shoulder when she saw that Michael was following. Too late, she remembered the stack of gifts sitting on the table beside the cake, and she hoped he wouldn't comment on them. It would be too unsettling—not to mention flat-out humiliating—to have to share her imaginary family and friends with someone else.

"You even have gifts to open," he said, dashing her hope before it was even fully formed. He hesitated in the doorway. "Honestly, I can go. I really don't want to intrude."

"You're not intruding," she said to be polite. Then she realized it wasn't courtesy at all that made her say it. He really wasn't intruding. She actually liked having him here. "I can open my gifts later."

"Looks like you have a generous family," he said, dipping his head toward the stack. He smiled, a sympathetic sort of smile that made Hannah melt a little more inside. "So who are your gifts from?" he asked.

She really wished she could have headed off that question. Ah, well. She could fib a bit. He'd never know the truth. And there was certainly no harm that could come as a result of what she would be fibbing about. It wasn't like she was going to tell him she could hack into the computers of the International Monetary Fund. "The big one on the bottom is from my Great-Aunt Esmeralda. The others are from my parents, my Nana Frost, my Cousin Chloe, and my best friend from first grade, Patsy."

Hannah started to change the subject after that, but Michael continued before she had a chance.

"I don't have much family myself," he said. "Me and Alex. That's about it."

"Your parents are gone?" she asked.

This time he was the one to nod. "I lost them both within a few years of each other not long after I graduated from college."

"I'm sorry," she said.

"Thanks. They were quite a bit older than me. I was kind of a late-life surprise to them. They'd tried for years to have kids without being successful, and just when they gave up, I came along."

"I bet they doted on you," Hannah said softly.

He nodded. "Oh, yeah. Spoiled me rotten, only child that I was. Like Alex. Not that he's spoiled, I mean. Well, not too bad. Is your family close by?" he asked quickly, and somehow she sensed that he was the one trying to change the subject this time.

"Ah, no," she said. "No. My parents, both of them—they're still married," she lied effortlessly, because lying about her parents had always been effortless to her on account of the truth would have been so much harder to tell. "They live in Kansas. Where I grew up."

She said that because Kansas had always been her idea of the perfect place to live, centered as it was at the heart of the nation. Nothing terrible ever happened in Kansas. It was where amber grain waved. It was home to Dorothy, the place she had always insisted there was no place like. Hannah would have loved to have grown up in Kansas and be able to tell people that was where she was from. So that was the lie she'd always chosen to tell other people, too. And now Michael. Because she really didn't see any harm in telling lies like those. Who would be hurt by them? What harm could they do?

"Is that where your great-aunt and cousin are?"

"Uh, Chloe is there, yeah," she said. Because that was the history she had chosen for herself and her favorite cousin. After all, in order to be that close, they would have had to grow up together. "But Auntie lives in Minnesota. I used to spend my summers with her." Which was what Hannah had always pretended when she was a child. And that was what she'd told the kids at school on the last day. That the reason she wouldn't be able to see any of them over the summer was because she'd be visiting her great-aunt in Minnesota. That sounded a lot better than telling them it was because her father would be fleecing their families and then leaving town.

"And Patsy?"

"Oh, Patsy," she said, warming now to the subject, thanks to the tongue-loosening—and truth-loosening—Chianti. And also thanks to the fact that Michael seemed to be falling for her story hook, line, and sinker. And she tried not to think about how that was probably because, in some ways, as hard as she'd tried to escape her legacy, maybe she really was her father's daughter, after all. "Patsy lives in New Mexico now. But she moves around a lot. She's married to a pilot," Hannah said, having invented a dashing aviator husband for Patsy. She figured it was the least she could do for the imaginary best friend who had stood by her for so many years. "They have four kids," she added. "All blond, like Patsy. They all look exactly like her. It's amazing."

"What's amazing is that you're still friends with someone from that long ago."

"Mm," Hannah said, telling herself the response did *not* come out sounding strained, even strangled. "You don't have any friends you've kept since childhood?" she asked, finding it strange that he would be amazed by such a thing. After all, from what she had gathered about him and Alex, they seemed to have had reasonably normal, secure, uneventful lives, both of them.

His mouth, which only moments ago had been curved into such an amiable smile, flattened into a grim line. "No," he said.

"Oh." She wondered why he didn't make some up, then. Oh, well. Different strokes and all that.

"So you don't have any brothers or sisters?" Michael asked.

She shook her head. "No. My mother always told me that she and my dad were just so enamored of me after I was born that they couldn't imagine creating a second one as good."

After that, Michael suddenly seemed to grow agitated. "Look," he said, the word coming out clipped and cool, "I really don't want to intrude. We can talk about Alex some other time. I'll call you at school. Tomorrow. During the day."

"O-okay," Hannah stammered, unprepared for his sudden, but very real this time, withdrawal.

She was even less prepared for the way he abruptly spun on his heel and made his way back to the front door. Almost as an afterthought, he tossed a quick, indifferent " 'Bye" over his shoulder, and then he was gone.

Almost as if he'd never been there at all.

Hannah looked at the glass of wine in her hand—her third, granted, but the glass was small, and she'd barely touched it—and set it gingerly on the table. Chianti had never made her hallucinate before, but she had been working harder than usual the past month or so, thanks to it being the beginning of the school year. Yes, of course, that's what Michael Sawyer must have been—a hallucination. Because he'd been so handsome, and so nice, and he'd felt so comfortable here in her home. She must have just conjured him up from thin air. That could be the only explanation.

It had to be. Because as Hannah listened for the sound of a car engine, it never materialized. And how could he have assumed it was her birthday, just because he'd seen a little candlelight flickering in the dining room, a not at all unusual place to find candlelight flickering? If Michael Sawyer had indeed been in her home, he must have traveled there by magic carpet. Yes, that must be it. Magic.

Because magic was the way he'd made her feel.

Out in the van, Michael fired up his laptop and pulled up the files he'd been sent on Hannah Frost. He'd learned a lot in her house that he hadn't known before, in spite of the fact that he had only been making chitchat because he'd wanted to be polite—and, yes, lull her into a false sense of security. Or, rather, just a sense of security. There had been nothing false about it.

What *had* been false were some of the relatives she claimed had sent her gifts. As had been the entire personal history she'd cited for herself.

Because Michael knew, thanks to the handiwork of OPUS, that Hannah's only living relatives were her parents—and they had divorced when she was a small child—and that she'd lived just about everywhere *but* Kansas. Hell, if he'd paid closer attention, he would have realized in advance that today was her birthday, too. She was thirty-six. So who the hell was she talking about when she mentioned married parents, a great-aunt, a cousin, and a grandmother? Gee, he'd even make the leap and wager she wasn't still friends with Patsy from first grade, either. So if Hannah Frost didn't have any of those people in her life, how could they have sent her gifts?

Unless maybe, just maybe, she wasn't Hannah Frost at all.

FOUR

AT FIVE MINUTES TO SIX ON MONDAY EVEning, Selby Hudson strode into the classroom she had been assigned for her adult returning education class, balancing a teetering blend of anticipation and trepidation. But after just one quick, camouflaged study of her students, trepidation won the battle hands down.

It was going to be a long six months.

A rapid count told her exactly one dozen pupils were present, ranging in age, she guessed, from early twenties to early sixties. And, gee, there were some celebrities among them, she was surprised to note. Because there, front and center before Selby's desk, sat a woman who *had* to be Dame Edna, right down to the pink hair and rhinestone cat's-eye glasses. Not far from Edna sat Norman Bates, complete with narrow, faultlessly ironed Levi's and a worn cardigan sweater just baggy enough to hide a butcher knife. Behind Norman and to the left a bit was Baby Jane—Selby had always wondered whatever happened to her—and beside Jane sat Jojo the dog-faced boy. Near him was . . . Wow. Gandhi. What an honor. And there, in the very back corner of the room, Selby wasn't positive, but she was pretty sure she had just discovered the missing link. Rounding out the group appeared to be Sammy Davis, Jr., the guy from the

Bounty paper towel wrapper, Granny Clampett, Winston Churchill, Whoopi Goldberg, and a nondescript guy in his fifties who looked to be harmless.

Teaching returning ed, Selby decided then, was going to be more than just a job. It was going to be an adventure. She just hoped she could be all that she could be, the few, the proud, an army of one. Because she suddenly felt besieged by geeks.

Immediately, she mentally reprimanded herself. She shouldn't make fun of her students. At least they were people who were striving to better themselves and their situations by returning to their studies in order to earn their diplomas. Selby understood about striving to better oneself. More to the point, she understood being made fun of. And she understood about being a geek, too, since she'd spent the better part of her life being one. Besides, Gandhi, Churchill, Sammy, Whoopi, and the Bounty guy weren't really all that geeky. Each had made the world a better place in some way.

So Selby smiled at the motley group and made her way across the scarred wooden floor to the scarred wooden desk at the front of the scarred wooden room, shrugging out of her black pearl-buttoned sweater to drape it over the scarred wooden chair. Almost primly, she straightened the Peter Pan collar of her white shirt and tucked her plaid pleated skirt beneath her fanny before seating herself. Hannah Frost's admonition the week before about Selby's wardrobe choices were still fresh in Selby's mind, and she'd swung to the other extreme, pulling pieces out of her closet that would in no way offend the school director. And if she currently looked like, oh . . . a geek . . . she'd just have to do her best to remember that she really wasn't one. Not anymore.

She removed her books and papers and curriculum from her battered leather satchel and arranged them all on her desk just so. Then she crossed her hands efficiently on the short stack of books, smiled encouragingly at her students,

and opened her mouth to introduce herself. But she was
halted before uttering a sound when the door to her classroom was thrust open again, hard enough to send it banging
against the wall.

Her entire body jerked at the crash of the door, so nervous
was she already about the evening ahead. Automatically, she
glanced over at the reason for the disturbance, but seeing the
newcomer only left her feeling even more disturbed. The
good news was that, with one glimpse of him, her nervous-
ness fled. The bad news was that the reason for that was
because she needed to make room for the feeling of unmiti-
gated terror that took its place.

Number thirteen, she couldn't help thinking as the man
strode through the door. Not just because he was her thir-
teenth student, but because something about him made
Selby think her luck had changed, and *not* for the better. Not
that her luck had ever been all that great to begin with.
Which made this downturn even more troubling.

Oh, this *really* wasn't good, she thought. Not good at all.
So much for her job being an adventure. This guy was going
to turn it into an out-and-out feat of derring-do.

Because the man who entered was every bad boy Selby
Hudson had ever gone to school with. And that was saying
something, since she'd gone to school with a *lot* of bad boys.
And a lot of bad girls. And a lot of missing links, now that
she thought about it. Having grown up on the wrong side of
the wrong side of the tracks, she had more than a nodding
acquaintance with badness. And the man who had just
walked into her classroom reeked of it.

Clad in faded, ripped blue jeans and a disreputable black
leather motorcycle jacket, his heavy black boots clinking
with chains and his inky hair badly in need of a cut, he could
have easily passed for an extra on the set of *The Wild One*.
Except that, even without having said a word, he radiated an
utter and unapologetic command that would have zapped

him right to the center of the action, eclipsing even Marlon Brando as Johnny. Although it was October, his complexion was sun-darkened, as if he worked outside. Dark, too, were his eyes, the color of rich espresso coffee, and a few days' growth of beard shaded the lower half of his face. Beneath the battered jacket, he wore a ragged black T-shirt, as if he were composed entirely of shadows.

But there were threads of silver woven through his black hair, and faint lines of paler skin fanned out from his eyes and bracketed his mouth, alleviating a little of the darkness. Instead of detracting from his looks, however, the signs of age only made him seem that much more experienced, that much more potent. Even though the man wasn't young—he probably had almost two decades on Selby—he didn't seem middle-aged, either. Nevertheless, he carried himself as someone who had seen a lot of the world. But he didn't appear to have liked much of what he'd seen, since he scowled at her by way of a greeting.

And then he demanded, in a rough, coarse—and, she couldn't help thinking again, *dark*—voice, "Am I late?"

He was, but Selby sure wasn't going to be the one who told him that. In fact, she shook her head hard enough to send her chin-length black tresses skirting along her jawline. "No, not yet," she told him. "Please. Come in. Sit down."

And with any luck at all, she might even be able to come up with a few words that contained more than one syllable. That would be oh-so-helpful for the language arts segment of her show.

But he didn't move to take a seat, only remained standing in place for a moment, all his weight shifted to his left foot, his hip thrust impudently to the side. He gazed at Selby for a moment in silence, driving his gaze from the top of her head to the toe of her shoe, feeling, evidently, not one iota of self-consciousness at making so thorough a survey of her person. And he did make a survey of her person. Although she was seated, she hadn't pulled herself up to the desk much, and suddenly, for some reason, her plaid skirt and white shirt felt ridiculously indecent. Which was crazy, because what man in his right mind would be turned on by an outfit like hers, complete with black cable tights and updated Mary Janes?

Okay, so maybe a lot of men would be turned on by that, she thought, recalling some of the questionable reading material—as if anyone *read* that kind of magazine—she used to find wedged beneath the mattresses and box springs of her brothers' beds when she'd had to change the sheets. Men who suffered from arrested development. Men who still had to curb a giggle whenever they heard the word *nipple*. Which, in her opinion, pretty much included anyone with a Y chromosome, regardless of his age.

But this man didn't seem to suffer from arrested anything, and something told her he'd know *exactly* what to do with any nipple he might have the privilege of encountering, and it *didn't* involve laughing.

She felt herself blush at such uncharacteristic thoughts and glanced away. Or maybe she was blushing—not to mention glancing away—because of his frank appraisal of her. At this point, both her thoughts and her nerves were so frazzled, Selby could scarcely remember her own name. She had to be frazzled, she thought. Otherwise, why would she find herself worried that she had come up lacking in his evaluation of her?

"Please take a seat," she told the man, hoping he didn't hear the quaver in her voice that she felt.

"Yes, ma'am," he said readily.

But there was something mocking in his tone, something that sounded vaguely like amusement. And if there was one thing Selby hated, it was being an amusement to someone. So she clamped her jaw tight and waited for the man to cross the room and find an unoccupied desk, of which there were plenty left. And once he was seated, with his black leather jacket slung over the desk beside him, and his long, long, denim-clad legs stretched out before him, and his sinewy arms folded over his broad chest—not that Selby noticed, mind you—she went to work.

"Hello," she started off, congratulating herself for being able to voice the greeting with nary a quaver to be heard. "I'm Ms. Hudson. Welcome to adult returning education. I'll be your teacher every Monday and Thursday evening, from six until nine, for the next six months. During that time, we'll cover language arts, mathematics, science, and everything else you studied in high school but were never able to finish. By the end of the program, if you all work hard and take your studies seriously, you'll earn your high school diplomas. But we have a lot to cover before then, so let's get started now by calling roll."

Strangely, as Selby called roll, she realized that all of the people in her class were traveling incognito. Dame Edna was posing as someone named Doreen, Baby Jane was trying to pass herself off as a woman named Robin, and Winston Churchill was claiming his name was Bruno. As if. And on down the line it went, until she reached the end. But of all the dubious names she called, Number Thirteen's was the most suspect of all. Because Marlon Brando's booted sidekick claimed the unlikely moniker of Thomas Brown. Right. As if any man who looked like he did could possibly have a name that normal and unremarkable. Obviously, he had pirated someone else's identity. Obviously, he was hiding from the authorities. Obviously, she should keep an eye on him. Obviously, she should install a metal detector at her classroom door. Between him and Norman Bates, who insisted *his* name was John Smith—oh, *sure*—it could prove a wise move.

Still, once Selby went into teacher mode, everything moved smoothly. Even though she had just received her M.Ed. the previous spring, she was comfortable as a teacher.

It was what she had always wanted to be, what she had worked so hard to become, and she was suited to it. As long as she was teaching, she felt good about herself. She felt smart. Talented. Capable. Valuable. All the things she had always been told she wasn't.

Class was winding down when Harmless Guy, who hadn't spoken a word since roll call, raised his hand. Selby settled her chalk—which had grown stubby from use over the past few hours—into the tray beneath a blackboard covered with everything from sentence diagramming to algebraic rules to the molecular structure of table salt, since she had decided to use her first class as an introduction to everything they'd be studying in the coming weeks. Then she lifted a hand toward Harmless Guy and said, "Yes? Do you have a question?"

"Will we be covering history, too? Because I'm kind of a World War Two buff, and I really think society has been misled about Hitler. He did some really wonderful things for the twentieth century."

Selby bit the inside of her jaw as she digested that. Hookay, so Harmless Guy was actually Hermann Goering. At least she'd had his initials right.

"I'm sorry, and your name again?" Selby asked, approaching her desk to scan her list of names when she realized she didn't remember his.

"Herman," Harmless Guy said in what she now realized was a vaguely foreign accent.

Selby narrowed her eyes at him. "Herman?"

"O'Malley," he finished.

Oh, sure, Selby thought. Aloud, however, she said, "Yes, we'll be covering history, as well, Mr. *O'Malley.* For this first part of the session, though, we'll focus on the big three—language arts, math, and science. Okay, people," she added with a weary sigh. "That's it for tonight's lesson. For homework, let's see . . ."

Selby flipped through her notes and assigned the necessary lessons, then dismissed her class and began to gather up her things. She took a few moments to jot down some notes to herself regarding Thursday's class, murmuring distracted good-byes to her students as they passed, then closed her books and began shoveling them into her satchel. When she looked up again, her thoughts were jumbled and the room was empty.

Oh.

Except for Number Thirteen, who still slouched in the desk he had occupied all evening, and who still gazed at her in the vaguely hungry way he had since his arrival.

And it occurred to Selby, too late, that maybe, just maybe, it wasn't a good idea for her to leave *after* her students.

"Was there something else you wanted?" she asked Thomas Brown—*his* name she remembered. Too well. And—again too late—she realized that maybe, just maybe, she should have phrased the question a little differently. Because Thomas Brown definitely looked like a man who wanted something else, but it was something Selby had no intention of giving him.

His response was a loose, and very predatory, smile. "As a matter of fact . . ." he began.

But he said nothing more than that, only smiled in a way that was even more predacious, a development that reinforced Selby's certainty that he wanted that thing she was saving for someone else, someone she hadn't met yet, granted, but someone else all the same, someone to whom it would mean something, someone who would take care of it, and cherish it, and never mistreat it at all. Someone who was the complete antithesis of Thomas Brown.

And, oh, but it would be so helpful if whoever that someone was rode in right then on a bright and brilliant steed, to sweep her up into his arms and carry her to his castle far, far away, safe from the fiery breath of this wicked, unholy dragon.

Unfortunately, it wasn't a knight in shining armor who rose to the occasion. No, it was dark and denim-clad Thomas Brown. Because he stood then. And he stretched, a long, languid stretch that seemed to harden and toughen every powerful muscle he possessed. And then he gathered his jacket and his notebook and tucked both under his arm. Then he strode forward, one ... leisurely ... step ... after ... another, the soles of his boots scraping across the floor as he approached, sounding like distant thunder predicating an awesome storm.

And all the while, he eyed Selby as if she were the tastiest morsel he'd ever seen. And all the while, Selby felt helpless to do anything but cower in her seat, as if she were a tasty morsel waiting to be devoured.

"Hey, teach," he said as he halted in front of her desk. "That was an awful lot of homework you gave us tonight. And I was kinda planning on hanging out at the soda shop for a while before going home." His words were flirtatious, harmless. His expression was anything but.

"I'm sorry if you find the workload overwhelming, Mr. Brown," Selby said. "I'm just following the curriculum."

"What happens if I don't finish it by Thursday?" he asked.

Selby forced herself to smile and hoped the gesture came out lighter than it felt. "Well, I won't send you to the principal's office, if that's what you're worried about."

"Actually, I was wondering if you'd spank me. But I wasn't worried about it. In fact, I was kind of looking forward to—"

"That's enough, Mr. Brown," Selby said coolly, wanting to make clear both her zero tolerance for come-ons and the fact that she was completely unaffected by him. Not that she really *was* unaffected by him, since something manic and hot splashed through her midsection at the mention of spanking him. But there was no reason he had to know that. "I don't appreciate comments like yours from my students. And I can have you thrown out of the program for making them." Actually, she wasn't entirely sure about that last part. But she'd do her best to make it happen if he kept it up.

He seemed stymied by her reaction, as if he hadn't expected her to be so unruffled and straightforward. As if he'd wanted her to be shocked and humiliated, and squeal her disgust like a schoolgirl.

Finally, though, "Then how about having a drink with me?" he asked. "And then I'll be more than a student, and you might receive comments like that differently."

Selby could scarcely believe the audacity of the man. "Not likely," she told him. And she managed to remain calm and direct as she added, "I repeat: I can have you removed from the program for something like this. And I will." And she was proud of herself for standing her ground, when what she really wanted to do was turn tail and run. She even stood up then, as if to punctuate the statement physically, and flattened her palms on her desktop to lean forward. She was crazy, she told herself. The man was a good foot taller than she, probably weighed nearly twice as much as she did, and she was completely alone with him. Yes, there were other classes that met in the school, on this floor. But they were, by now, almost certainly gone.

Selby's heart hammered hard in her chest when Thomas Brown made no motion to leave, and a hot flush rushed through her entire body. For one long moment, neither of them moved, neither of them spoke, neither of them glanced away. And even though a part of her had never been more frightened in her life, she somehow knew that if she so much as flinched or glanced away, Thomas Brown would run roughshod over her.

And she didn't even want to think about what a man like him could do to a woman like her.

"Class dismissed," she finally said, amazed at the steeliness and calmness in her tone.

Strangely, Thomas Brown smiled at the words. "Yes, ma'am," he said. And then he winked at her, a gesture so quaint, and so old-fashioned, Selby almost smiled back.

He dipped his head forward in silent acknowledgment, then continued on his way to the door and through it, never looking back once. For a full minute, Selby stood at her desk, her palms damp with nervous perspiration, wondering what the hell had just happened. Gradually, she managed to steady her breathing and will her pulse rate to slow. Then she finished collecting her things, put on her sweater, slung her satchel over her shoulder, and headed out, trying not to think about how she was retracing every step Thomas Brown had just taken.

Outside, the night was dark and the wind was crisp, and the street was utterly deserted. Somehow, Selby made herself not look over her shoulder every step of the way as she walked to the bus stop a block from the high school. She wasn't fearful, walking the streets at night alone. She'd grown up walking alone. But she was afraid of Thomas Brown. Afraid he might return. Afraid of what would happen on Thursday, when her class met again. Afraid tonight's episode was simply the first of many. Afraid she wouldn't be able to remain unruffled and unaffected the next time.

Because that was what scared Selby more than anything else—her reaction to Thomas Brown. There was something about him that made her feel hot and wild and restless, something that made her want things she had no business wanting. Not from a man like him.

Never from a man like him.

* * *

Thomas Brown, who was known elsewhere in Indianapolis—and elsewhere in the world—as T. Paxton Brown, rolled his Harley to a stop in one of the five parking spaces reserved for the CEO of CompuPax Computers, barely noticing the solid gold nameplate affixed to the wall. He had other things on his mind at the moment, things that were infinitely more appealing than gold. Miss Selby Hudson, for example. And Miss Selby Hudson's little plaid skirt, for another. And what it would be like to push Miss Selby Hudson's little plaid skirt up, and pull Miss Selby Hudson's panties down, and set Miss Selby Hudson bare-assed back on her desk so that he could do to her all the things he'd spent the evening fantasizing about.

Hell, if he'd had more teachers like her in high school, he never would have dropped out.

Christ, man, she's young enough to be your daughter, he chastised himself. *But only if I got her mother pregnant in high school,* he quickly replied. Because Pax knew from the material he'd received from the adult returning education program that all the teachers who worked in the program had master's degrees or higher. So Selby Hudson had to be around twenty-three years old. Which only made her nineteen years Pax's junior.

And hey, nineteen wasn't so much. Especially for a man who was planning to live forever.

Unsnapping the black helmet, Pax pulled it forward, off of his head, and ran his gloved hands briskly through his hair. He'd been thinking he needed to get it cut, but now he thought he might grow it long. Or, at least, longer. No need to spook the board of directors again by letting it get too out of hand. They were still steamed over the tattoo he'd had inked on his back two summers ago. He couldn't imagine why. The dragon that completely obscured his left shoulder blade and half of his lower back was a goddamned work of art.

Pax nudged down the kickstand with the heel of his boot,

then looped his leg gracefully over the vehicle's seat, not bothering to lock it up or take any security precautions. The CompuPax Pavilion, where Pax both lived and worked, was a fortress, plain and simple. No one came in without his say-so. And no one left without it, either. Nothing happened on any of the twenty-one floors that he didn't know about himself. And there was scarcely an inch of the place that wasn't in view of a security camera, many of which fed right into the media room of the penthouse he claimed as his home. He covered the half dozen steps to his private express elevator and shoved his key into the lock, and with a soft, immediate *swoosh,* the copper-covered doors unfolded. In a matter of seconds, they were opening again, this time onto a suite of rooms so elegantly and artistically appointed, they had been featured in *Architectural Digest.* Twice.

Harry Rutherford, Pax's personal assistant, was waiting by the elevator when the doors opened, standing at ramrod attention the way a good gentleman's gentleman should. Although it was nearly ten o'clock at night, Harry was still dressed for his workday, in an impeccable black suit with a conservative burgundy necktie knotted in a perfect Windsor at his throat.

He should have been standing in the foyer of a stately manor home on the English moors, Pax thought. Instead, his backdrop was a sleekly furnished urban penthouse. No stuffy antiques or mahogany paneling or chintz chairs or Persian rugs for Pax, no way. T. Paxton Brown was a technological wonder, and his decor reflected that, all neutral, smooth-lined leather furniture and brushed-copper accent pieces and abstract art in muted earth tones. He could never remember the name of the artist who had rendered them, but his decorator had assured Pax they'd be worth a fortune in no time, and she'd been right.

Whatever.

"Hello, Harry," Pax said as he entered his home and felt, as he always did upon entering, out of place.

Until a few years ago, Pax had always hired women to be his personal assistants. Mostly because he had fully expected things to become more personal once he hired a personal assistant, and, invariably, he was right. But women had an unfortunate tendency to stop being professional when things got personal, so, invariably, Pax had always eventually had to let his personal assistants go. The one before Harry had been especially difficult to dispose of, however, and it had cost Pax a bundle to settle a laughable sexual harassment charge—if anyone had been sexually harassed in the relationship, it had been Pax—so he'd decided to stick with his own gender when he hired her replacement.

So far, Harry had worked out great. Well, except for needing to drop everything at four o'clock on the dot every day for tea. Still, Harry's staunch Englishmanness was an idiosyncrasy Pax could overlook, since there was little chance it would lead to charges against him.

"Good evening, sir," Harry replied as Pax stepped back into his normal life.

Oh, yeah. And Harry's formality was another idiosyncrasy Pax had been forced to endure, since no amount of insisting that the other man call him Pax, as everyone else at CompuPax did, had swayed Harry. Automatically, Pax went through the rest of the evening ritual, listening to Harry's rundown of the mail, phone calls, e-mail, faxes, and every other manner of communication that came through on any given day. As always, though, Harry had already handled almost all of it.

"How was your class?" Harry asked.

Only two people in the world besides Pax knew that T. Paxton Brown, billionaire, had gone back to school to receive the high school diploma he had considered so unnecessary twenty-five years before. Harry was one, and only because Pax trusted him implicitly. And also because he'd had to give the man a damned good reason why he needed to keep Mondays and Thursdays open for the next six months. The other person was Pax's Great-Aunt Ina.

He still bristled at how easily he had let the cagey old dame talk him into this.

But there had been a time, long ago, in a galaxy far away, when Pax was neither Thomas Brown, adult returning education student, nor T. Paxton Brown, billionaire. No, when he'd quit high school in his junior year, he'd just been Tommy Brown, rebel without a clue. Not to mention a dateless computer geek who'd had no friends whatsoever. But Tommy Brown had been brilliant, and he'd been surprisingly ambitious and driven. Ultimately, even without a high school diploma, he'd built a technological empire in the form of a computer company called CompuPax. These days, the entire world ran on user-friendly CompuPax computers. And if Pax had his way, the world always would.

In spite of his monster success, however, it had always bugged the hell out of Pax that, even though he earned his GED and went to college and ended up with not one but three degrees, he never officially graduated from high school. It had also bugged the hell out of Great-Aunt Ina, who, at eighty-nine years of age, had been recently diagnosed with kidney problems.

A former high school teacher, she'd been making it clear since her diagnosis that she'd go to the great beyond feeling much more content if her favorite nephew got that diploma she'd always considered so sacred. And even though Pax knew she wasn't going off to the great beyond for a great long time, he'd ultimately conceded to what she still insisted was her "dying wish" and had enrolled in night classes at a local high school that, once completed, would win him a real, honest-to-God high school diploma. But he'd felt like he needed to do it as Thomas Brown, incognito, because the last thing T. Paxton Brown needed was for the press to get wind of it. Although Pax had never made a secret of his diplomaless condition, he'd just as soon not advertise it, thankyouverymuch. And he sure as hell was never going to go anywhere as Tommy Brown again.

It helped that T. Paxton Brown had always been something of a recluse who didn't court public scrutiny. Yeah, Pax was sometimes a womanizing party animal, but he only womanized the most discreet members of the opposite sex—well, save one unfortunate ex-personal assistant—and he attended only the most exclusive parties. As a result, there weren't many photographs of him that had circulated in the tabloids, or anywhere else—at least not good, clear ones—so it wasn't going to be all that hard for him to pass himself off two nights a week for six months as Thomas Brown, high school dropout.

Still, he hadn't anticipated that his teacher, Miss Selby Hudson, would be such a nice fringe benefit, one that brought out the womanizing party animal in him even more than usual. But the minute he'd walked into the classroom and seen her sitting there, Pax had been completely enthralled by her. Because she was young and beautiful and spirited and fine . . . just like all those girls who had spurned and laughed at Tommy Brown in high school.

"Class went great," Pax told Harry now. "Better than great, in fact." He thought again about Miss Selby Hudson. And Miss Hudson's skirt. And her panties. And her bare ass. And he decided he wanted to get to know all of them better.

"Refresh my memory, Harry," he said. "How old am I?"

Harry, to his credit, didn't seem to be at all surprised by the question. "Forty-two, sir," he replied.

Pax nodded slowly. "That would put me right around the age when a lot of men start having a midlife crisis, wouldn't it?"

"In this country?" Harry asked, though Pax knew no reply from him was necessary, as Harry always answered his own questions. "Yes, I believe most American males do begin to behave like children when they reach the age of forty or so."

"Do you recall," Pax continued, "if I myself have had a midlife crisis yet?"

"Well, there was that small matter of the tattoo," Harry said, his voice reeking his disapproval of the decoration.

Somehow, Pax refrained from rolling his eyes. "That wasn't a midlife crisis," he said. "That was something I'd been wanting to do since I was a teenager."

"Well, there was also the purchase of that . . . that . . . that vehicle."

The Harley, Pax translated. "That wasn't a midlife crisis, either," he insisted. "That was an investment. That bike's already appreciated by thousands of dollars."

He wasn't sure, but he thought Harry sniffed his disapproval this time. Pax, however, let it go. "What I mean, Harry," he tried again, "is a *midlife crisis*. You know. A full-blown episode of stupid, irresponsible, embarrassing behavior. Like, say . . . dating a woman half my age."

"*Dating* a woman half your age?" Harry asked dubiously.

"All right, all right. Having a woman half my age," Pax amended.

"If you mean sexually—"

"That's exactly what I mean," Pax said through gritted teeth.

"No," Harry replied. "You're not one of those middle-aged men who chase after young, nubile women because those men are clearly terrified people will think they can no longer . . ." He cleared his throat indelicately. "Cut the mustard. At least, you haven't been one of them yet. You've always seemed to appreciate more experienced women."

"You got that right," Pax agreed enthusiastically, ignoring everything else Harry had said, because Harry was never able to go more than a few minutes without offering some kind of social commentary. "So then I haven't had a midlife crisis yet," he said instead.

Harry pretended to give the remark much thought. "Well, *I* certainly never scheduled one for you."

"I didn't think so," Pax replied. "I would have remembered."

"Well, I don't know about *that*," Harry said, not even trying to hide his disapproval now. "There's been more than one morning when you woke up not remembering what happened the night before. And I recall more than one woman *I* had to send home, because *you* couldn't even remember her na—"

"I think, Harry," Pax said, interrupting his assistant, because sometimes Harry just needed interrupting, "you should put me down for a midlife crisis as soon as I have an opening."

Without hesitation, Harry tucked a hand into the inside breast pocket of his jacket and withdrew a slim, leather-bound notebook, then flipped easily through the pages for a moment. "You're completely booked up tomorrow," he said. He flipped the page and scanned the next day's entries. "And Wednesday, as well." After another page flip, he added, "But I can probably rearrange Thursday so that you have both the afternoon and evening free. Shall I schedule you for a midlife crisis then? It won't interfere with your studies?"

Pax thought again about Selby Hudson and her little plaid skirt and her schoolgirl shirt and her prim, button-up sweater. He recalled her expression when he'd asked her to spank him, a mixture of shock and surprise and being generally pissed off. He'd rattled her, but she'd stood her ground. Not that it would do her much good in the long run. Still, he had to hand it to her. Instead of squealing like a girl, Selby Hudson had done her best to nail him to the wall. He couldn't help wanting to return the favor. Only when he nailed her to the wall, he'd really nail her.

Because he also remembered the way she had looked, standing in a puddle of pale blue lamplight on the street corner as she waited for her bus—he had been parked in the shadows nearby, waiting for her to come out, because he'd wanted to see what kind of car she drove, just in case, you know, he wanted to look for it whenever he was out driving around. He'd been surprised to see her go to the bus stop instead.

And as he'd watched her standing there, he'd been reminded of other girls standing on corners, waiting for buses, in their plaid skirts and white shirts and prim, button-up sweaters. And he remembered, too, the way they'd always laughed at him behind their hands whenever he walked by, and called him names before he was safely out of earshot. The taunts in elementary school had never even made any sense, but they'd cut to the bone anyway. *Tommy, Tommy, run to Mommy. She'll make you some hot pastrami. Tommy Brown is such a clown, he wears his undies upside down.* And in high school, it had only gotten worse.

Geek.

Dork.

Pizza Face.

Freak.

"No," he told Harry, "this midlife crisis won't interfere with my studies at all."

FIVE

"READY FOR YOUR SPELLING TEST?"

"Yes."

"Ready for your math test?"

"Yes."

"Got your book report?"

"Yes."

"How about—"

"Yes, my science reading is done. And I have my lunch, too. I have everything I need, Dad. Everything."

Even though Michael knew that wasn't quite true, he smiled at his son over his shoulder, from his position in the driver's seat. "All right," he said, relenting. "I'm sorry. I just wanted to be sure. I know I've been working a lot lately, and I haven't been around as much as I should, and I just want to be sure . . ."

Of what? he asked himself. That Alex was okay? That life was everything it was supposed to be? That the universe was operating exactly as nature dictated it should? That good always won out over bad, no matter what? Would he ever be sure of any of those things? Could anyone be?

He sighed inwardly and reached across the back of the seat to give Alex's shoulder a squeeze as his son freed his seat belt and turned to open the back door. "I love you, kid," he said. Then, because he couldn't think of any other way to say the million, billion things ricocheting through his head where his son and his son's welfare were concerned, he added, "Have a good day."

Alex smiled back at him. "I will, Dad. I love you, too."

And then he was out of the car, out of Michael's sphere of influence and protection, on his way toward the front door of his school. Michael supposed he would never quite get used to that—turning his son over to the care of others, having faith that no harm would come to him while they were apart during the course of the day. One thing Michael had learned immediately after becoming a parent was that he would know fear for the rest of his life. It was something that had never been a problem for him before Alex's birth. Even with Tatiana, he hadn't feared for her. He'd always known she could take care of herself, that she was smart and capable enough not to get into trouble. Well, not too much trouble. Nothing she couldn't handle. But Alex ... He'd been so small, so fragile, so totally helpless. And even though he wasn't helpless anymore—or even fragile or small— Michael would always be frightened for him. Always.

He watched as his son strode to the front door of the school, not once looking back at Michael. He envied his son that ability. Nine was such a weird age. There were days when Alex seemed not to even know he had a father, so self-aware was he, so self-reliant in everything from making his own breakfast, to doing his homework without having to be told, to brushing his teeth and putting himself to bed with a good book. But there were other days when Michael had to nag him about everything, or nothing would have gotten done. And there were still nights, too, when Alex woke up with nightmares, when he'd run into Michael's room and crawl into bed with him, and ask his father to tell him a story, the way he had when Alex was a preschooler.

When the parent behind him in the carpool line honked to

get him moving, Michael finally had to throw the car into gear. He glanced irritably into his rearview mirror as he shifted into first. It was Roberta Harrigan—Bertie Harrigan, to her friends—whose son was in Alex's class. After she'd cornered him at the fourth-grade potluck and he'd had to listen to her ramble on for nearly an hour about her new house in Naples—Italy, not Florida—he'd come to think of her as *Wordy* Harrigan instead.

As he pulled out of Emerson's parking lot and into the flow of traffic headed toward downtown, he thought again about Alex, about how he seemed to be breaking away from and clinging hard to Michael at the same time. Michael supposed he understood. He'd done the same thing himself a time or two in life. When he left home to go to college. When he left college to join OPUS. When he left OPUS to start life anew.

When he met Hannah Frost.

Ever since that first day in her office, he'd been drawn to her. Big time. He didn't understand the whys or wherefores of that, only that there was something in her that tugged at something in him, as if she had a string wrapped around her finger that she began winding tight whenever he came near her. Yet he had to keep his distance from her. Of course, he hadn't kept his distance Monday night, had he? Idiot. Then again, allowing himself to get close, even for that short time, had been enormously helpful. Helpful, and also confusing. Because now he was really wondering who she was.

The Hannah Frost in the OPUS files had no known family beyond her parents, from whom she was estranged. Her mother and father had split when she wasn't even two, and she'd been raised by her father alone. There was no Nana Frost, her father's mother having died before Hannah was even born. And there was no Great-Aunt Esmeralda, either. And since she'd switched schools with the frequency most kids traded bubble gum cards back then, he found it hard to believe she'd maintained contact with anyone named Patsy, either. Just to be sure, he'd had OPUS run a check on the roster of the school she had attended as a first-grader. And there hadn't been a single Patsy listed there.

Because that was the thing about OPUS. They knew everything about everybody. So Michael had been able to learn more about Hannah with a few clicks of the mouse than she would ever volunteer on her own. Hell, he probably knew more about her than she would *want* him to know. For instance, he knew that she had been born in Florida, and that her father had dragged her all through the South while doing his part to cheat good, decent citizens out of their hard-earned cash through a variety of cons and swindles. Billy Frost had been arrested twice, but had been released both times long enough to disappear before his cases came to trial. Mostly he had slithered from town to town with a few ill-gotten gains before anyone knew what had hit them.

Michael supposed Hannah, even as a girl, must have known what was going on. She was a smart woman. She would have been a smart kid. He wondered how she'd felt about her father's way of life, whether she'd been forced to help in the cons or if she'd tried to steer as clear of them as she could. Not for a moment did Michael fault her for any of her father's behavior. On the contrary, when he pictured someone putting Alex through that, he wanted to hit something. Hard. She had evidently taken care of herself, though, because as an adult, she had made a good life, in spite of her beginnings. She'd probably be horrified to learn that Michael knew as much about her past as he did. If she'd made up a family and friends and a fictitious history for herself, she obviously wanted to keep all that hidden—not that he blamed her for that, either. She might even be as horrified to find out Michael knew the truth about her past as she would be if she found out he was spying on her present.

Really spying on her. Because Hannah might not know

where her mother was living now, but Michael did. Audrey Simmons Frost had remarried a few years after divorcing Hannah's father—and then remarried again after divorcing husband number two, and then again after divorcing husband number three, and then again after number four, making her Audrey Simmons Frost Hemple Donnelly Madigan Durant—and she was now divorced again and working as a cocktail waitress at Fort Benning in Arkansas.

Michael knew, too, where Hannah had gone to school growing up—all ten of them—where she'd gone to college, that she'd worked three jobs to pay her tuition, that she'd graduated with two degrees in education, and that she'd lived in Chicago before coming to Indianapolis, in a small apartment a few blocks from Michigan Avenue, over a Greek restaurant. She'd done her laundry at the Spin Dry Launderette across the street, had kept both a checking and savings account at Citibank, and had often gotten carry-out curry at Vijay's.

He knew how much she had made at every job she'd ever had, how much she earned at this one—not nearly enough, as far as he was concerned—how much she had saved, how much she had invested, how much she spent in any given month, and what she bought when she spent it. She was financially responsible to a fault, really. There were few frivolous expenses, and those had been modest, even by Michael's frugal standards. He wondered what she was saving up for, since she had no children's futures to see to, and a more than decent retirement package from Emerson. He knew where she shopped—but she didn't shop much—and how she spent her free time—mostly at home. He knew what she bought at the grocery store—right down to the birthday cake Monday afternoon—and he knew what she rented at Blockbuster—old and new romantic comedies and classic melodramas. Oh, yeah. OPUS was really good at knowing what people did. So thanks to OPUS, Michael knew everything there was to know about Hannah Frost.

Except for why she had made up all those friends and relatives she didn't really have. And except for who had bought her those presents, if not those people she had claimed.

He could hazard a guess. But he'd rather not. Mostly, he supposed, because he didn't want to think about her being a lonely woman who had to make up people to keep her company and buy herself presents to ease the melancholy of not receiving them otherwise. And that was probably because thinking about that was hitting a little too close to home.

Not that Michael made up people to keep him company. He had Alex, after all. But he was lonely sometimes, even with Alex. Lonely for things he couldn't even identify. He only knew there was something missing from his life. He would have sworn it *wasn't* the presence of a woman. He'd had women since his divorce from Tatiana, sometimes even women he cared about. But none had filled that empty place inside him. Hell, truth be told, Tatiana hadn't filled that, either. No one had. So maybe, in that sense, at least, he could understand Hannah's desire to have someone close. He only hoped her imaginary loved ones filled the bill for her. Because he'd never found anything to fill the bill—or the emptiness—for him.

By the time Michael pulled into the self-storage lot where he kept the van, he had shoved all his troubling thoughts about Hannah aside and was operating efficiently on automatic pilot. It was an old defense mechanism he'd developed to keep himself sane while working on cases that had run the gamut of boring-as-hell busts to man-we-barely-escaped-with-our-skivvies matters of national security. One thing about working for OPUS—you never knew what the job would bring.

But he was reasonably sure he was wasting his time with

this job, at least when it came to keeping Hannah under surveillance at her home. For the past three nights, she'd been home alone, and the most exciting thing Michael had heard was the bathtub spigot kicking on. She liked long baths by candlelight—if the flickering illumination behind her frosted bathroom window was any indication—and with classical music, because that was all he'd heard between intermittent splashes of water and the occasional sigh of contentment.

And always, always, he'd sat in the van, picturing Hannah in that bathtub, surrounded by candles and the faint strains of a piano concerto, her skin slick and shiny with water as the light danced across her flesh, her body as warm and fragrant as the steam rising from the water, her hair piled high atop her head, a few errant tresses falling damply over her shoulders, clinging to her wet nape, her wet breasts. And then he'd been able to picture himself in that scene, half naked himself, leaning over the tub as he sluiced soapy water over her back, the candlelight gilding every poetic ripple of her skin. And then, in that vision, he'd move his hand forward, over her damp shoulder, across her chest, and lower still, curving under one heavy breast, lifting it, caressing it, and—

And then he'd started reciting every baseball statistic he knew, starting with the roster for the 1976 World Series and ending with the Marlins-Cubs lineup the night before.

So, since he was obviously spinning his wheels when it came to watching Hannah's house—not to mention feeling things he'd just as soon not be feeling, at least not when he was sitting all alone in a van, eavesdropping on someone in the bathtub—last night he had broken into the school to place wiretaps and a camera in Hannah's office, and, it went without saying, bug her phone.

As far as he could tell, Adrian hadn't contacted Hannah at home since the potluck a week ago. But then, he hadn't surveilled her over the weekend, and Adrian could be contacting her at school, the way guys like Adrian—guys who weren't out surveilling in a van and then stupidly approaching the surveillee's front door after hearing the birthday song sung—would do. With any luck at all, Michael would find that out today.

And with even more luck, he wouldn't be picturing Hannah naked when he did.

Hannah looked forward to Fridays with the same enthusiasm she had as a child. Every Friday, every single Friday, as she drove home from work, she thought happily to herself, *There's no school tomorrow!*

Alas, on this particular Friday, that precious declaration was still hours away. Because the morning had barely started, and already she was fielding a half dozen problems. Mrs. Terry, the sixth-grade social studies teacher, was missing—again. One of the second-graders had been found locked in a seventh-grader's locker. A toilet was backed up in the teacher's lounge. And there had been a small fire in the Senior Foods class when Heather Kimmelman tried to light her spinach soufflé, thinking *soufflé* was French not for "puffed" but for "ignited." So now she would be receiving a C in both Senior Foods *and* French, and she was none too pleased about that. Mr. and Mrs. Kimmelman were even less pleased. And the Carmel, Indiana, fire department was most displeased of all.

And then there was Adrian, whom Hannah had done her best to put off, but who was not going to be put off any longer. Not over the phone, at any rate, because he continued to call her at school. And now he'd done the meanest thing she could imagine him doing, a heinous, hateful thing that had been completely uncalled for. He'd invited her to a dazzling gala affair, a black-tie fund-raiser at an elegant five-star hotel downtown that would feature fine dining, classical music, and every celebrity Indianapolis boasted.

The fiend.

There was no way Hannah could turn down his invitation. Not when she would have the opportunity to solicit so many moneyed bastions of the community for financial sponsorship of her school. In spite of its exorbitant tuition, the Emerson Academy never had enough money to operate as well as it *should*. As well as it *could*. So even with the tuition, there was always some kind of fund-raising going on, and Hannah was always looking for people who might be interested in sponsoring or underwriting one aspect of the school or another. Obviously Adrian knew that. And he knew her well enough to be confident she wouldn't turn down such a chance to rub elbows—and pry open the pockets—of so many of the city's wealthy elite. He was confident she wouldn't turn *him* down.

She twisted the phone cord in her hand as she spoke to him, but her mind was miles away. Would that the Kimmelmans were miles away, too, instead of sitting in her outer office waiting to talk to her. "No, really, Adrian, I'm sure it will be wonderful," she said.

"You sound about as enthusiastic as you would had I asked you to accompany me to an autopsy," he replied wryly.

Well, if he had, at least she'd have a reason for the sick feeling in the pit of her stomach, she thought. "No, it isn't that. You just caught me at a bad time, that's all. It's been one of those days. Again." *Translation,* Hannah thought, *stop calling me at work.* "I'm sorry."

"I know it's last-minute," he said, "barely twenty-four hours' notice. But I wasn't sure myself if I'd be going until just now. I'm glad you're free." *Translation,* Hannah thought, *I know you don't have a life.*

"It sounds fabulous," she said. And it did. Or, rather, it

would, had someone else been the one asking her to attend. Someone like, oh, say . . . Michael Sawyer.

Because she hadn't been able to stop thinking about Michael since she'd hallucinated him at her home Monday night. Though she still couldn't quite bring herself to believe he'd been a hallucination. He'd certainly seemed real. Looked real. Sounded real. Smelled real. She just couldn't quite bring herself to believe he'd *been* real. Because if she conceded to the fact that he had been real, then she'd have to concede, too, to the fact that he'd very nearly kissed her. And she'd also have to concede to the fact that she'd very much wanted him to.

Chianti, she told herself again. Lethal, lethal stuff. Made a person far too fanciful, far too romantic. And now Adrian was talking again, and she realized she had no idea what he was saying, because she'd been thinking about Michael. Again.

"I'm sorry, Adrian, what did you say?"

"I said I'll pick you up at your house at six tomorrow night. How will that be?"

Wonderful, she thought sarcastically. "Wonderful," she said brightly.

And as she hung up the phone, she wondered what one wore to a black-tie gala event, and if her black suit would be all right.

The black suit wasn't all right. Hannah discovered this after going to the Emerson library and discreetly thumbing through the etiquette books, none of which appeared to have been consulted by any of the students since . . . ever. All of the books had stated quite adamantly that for a black-tie event, one needed a gown. This was a problem, since in spite of being a formal person, Hannah didn't own a single formal.

So now she stood beside Adrian in the hotel's crystal ballroom, dressed in a brand-new purchase, one she would doubtless never wear again after tonight, making it a ridiculously unnecessary—well, just plain ridiculous, as far as she was concerned—expense. She told herself the flowing, black strapless velvet number was an investment, one that would more than pay for itself in other ways, in the form of financial remuneration to Emerson. And she reassured herself that at least she hadn't had to buy any jewelry to go with it, since the pearl necklace and earrings from Great-Aunt Esmeralda were the perfect complement. And she decided that the ridiculous expense she'd had to go to was the reason she felt so irritable at such a sparkling gala event accompanied by a dazzling, handsome escort like Adrian Windsor.

It was *not* because she saw Michael Sawyer on the other side of the ballroom looking more handsome than ever in a faultless tuxedo, and that he'd accessorized it with an even more faultless blonde.

Honestly, she thought, talk about robbing the cradle. The woman—hah, *girl* was more like it—couldn't even be out of college yet. And could her dress be cut any lower? And could her hair be any bigger? And could her smile be any shallower? And could her breasts be any perkier? Boy. Some people.

"I told you you'd have a good time," Adrian said as he pressed a glass of champagne into her hand. "Have you ever seen such an impressive display of pretension and ostentation in your life?"

"Never," she replied absently.

And then she realized that Adrian had said *prominence and distinction* not *pretension and ostentation,* and that her own prejudices might possibly be slipping in. Nevertheless, her reply would have been the same, because she really *hadn't* ever seen such a display in her life. She just wasn't talking about the one laid out for the guests, that was all. The way Michael Sawyer and his date were pawing all over each other—now, *that* was a display.

Jeez, people! Get a room!

Honestly. Boy. Some people.

Adrian seemed to notice where her attention lay, because when she turned to look at him—and she was turning to look *at* him, she told herself, and not turning to look *away* from Michael and Perky Breasts Barbie—she saw that he had trailed his gaze in the same direction. And just as he had at the potluck that night, Adrian went rigid beside her.

"Well, well, well," he said. "Look who's here."

Hannah feigned confusion and looked in Michael's direction again, but pretended she didn't see him. Pawing all over the blonde. Who was young enough to be here selling band candy. Except that the band director would surely frown on the microscopic size of her screaming red dress. Then again, it probably wasn't any more revealing than the majorette outfit she normally wore.

"Who?" Hannah said. "I don't see anyone I know."

When she turned toward Adrian again, she could tell by his expression that he thought she was full of hooey. "Your friend Michael Sawyer."

Hannah looked that way again and this time pretended to be surprised. "Why, so it is. I didn't realize he had a daughter in addition to Alex."

She could hear the laughter in Adrian's voice when he replied, "He doesn't have a daughter. But Michael's always liked them young."

Why that should surprise Hannah, she didn't know. She'd seen for herself how many of the mothers at Emerson were second, much younger wives to men who had found themselves denying their own middle—and even later—age. But it did surprise her that Michael Sawyer would be one of them. He really didn't seem like the type of man who would be intimidated by women of his own age and experience. He struck her as the sort of man who would welcome a companion of equal measure. Just went to show how much Hannah knew about men. Which, of course, was very little. She did know herself.

"Well, we can say our hellos to him later," she said, threading her arm through Adrian's, because . . . well, just because, that was all. "If our paths cross later, I mean." And then she tried to steer him away toward anything that wasn't in Michael's direction.

But Adrian stood firm. "Looks like our paths will be crossing now," he said.

And sure enough, when Hannah glanced over again, it was to see Michael and his majorette marching toward her and Adrian. Strangely, though, instead of being focused on his escort—and, my, but wasn't she a *tiny* thing, too? Hannah couldn't help noticing—Michael seemed to be focused on the way Hannah had linked her arm with Adrian's. Not sure why she did it, Hannah snaked her other arm across her waist and settled it, too, in the crook of Adrian's arm. And she noticed that Michael noticed. Because he frowned when she did it, and narrowed his eyes.

"Fancy meeting you here," Adrian said as Michael and the majorette came to a halt.

Michael shrugged off the greeting almost literally. And he didn't return it, Hannah noted. "My firm always sends a couple of representatives to big fund-raisers like this. Someone they can trust to make sure the check arrives. This year, it fell to me and Tiffany."

"Tiffany?" Hannah asked, biting back a smile. Somehow, the moniker was just so appropriate.

The blonde nodded. "Uh-huh. With two *f*'s, two *n*'s, and two *e*'s." For a physical illustration, she held up her index and middle fingers as if to say, *That's this many.*

Ooohhh, Tiffannee, Hannah thought. That was even more appropriate.

"And do you know Adrian Windsor, Tiffannee?" she

asked. "You two have something in common, kind of. He has two *a*'s in his name."

"Oh, how interesting!" Tiffannee said in wide-eyed delight. "What a coincidence!"

"Hannah, too," Michael said.

She looked at him strangely. "What?" she asked.

"Lots of pairs of letters in Hannah," he pointed out. "In fact, your name is made up entirely of pairs of letters. Two *h*'s, two *a*'s, two *n*'s."

Yeah, so what's your point? she thought. It wasn't like she was named Tiffannee. "So it is," she said, feeling suddenly defensive for no reason she could name.

He smiled. "And it's also a palindrome."

"Michael!" Tiffannee said in a chiding voice, swatting him playfully on the arm. "There's no reason to be mean. Just because Hannah's name is old and kind of stiff—"

Old? Hannah echoed to herself indignantly. *Stiff?*

"—doesn't mean you have to insult her by calling it a pal . . . a palin . . . a palind . . ." She screwed up her widdle features into an impatient widdle face and stomped her widdle foot on the floor. "Oh, whatever it was you just called it. That wasn't very nice."

Michael opened his mouth to explain, then evidently thought better of the task and closed it again. But Adrian seemed not to be put off at all, and it was he who saved them from more trouble by asking Tiffannee if she wanted to dance. They were, after all, he pointed out, striking up the chords of a fox-trot, which had two *o*'s and two *t*'s, thus making it the ideal dance for Tiffannee, even if the letters weren't quite paired together.

"And there's also an *f* in it," Tiffannee said, "which is sort of an upside down *t* when it's in little letters. So that makes it kind of like having triplets. Which, omigosh, also starts with *t*. Hey, this is fun!"

Then she tittered. Actually tittered. Hannah was reasonably sure she'd never heard anyone titter before, but now she could say with all honesty that she had. And she was certain she spoke for everyone present when she said, "Amazing." She also found herself wondering if Tiffannee would boost the amazement quotient even higher later by lighting her batons on fire.

Then Adrian and Tiffannee were off—with two *f*'s—to the dance floor—with two *o*'s—and she and Michael were left to stare uncomfortably at each other.

"So what's your problem tonight?" he asked without preamble.

She gaped softly in surprise. "My problem?" she echoed. "I don't know what you're talking about. I don't have any problem."

"You seem to be in a blue funk this evening," he said.

"Actually, it's a black Dior," she quipped.

She could tell he was trying not to smile at that, but he didn't quite succeed. "And you look ravishing, too," he told her. He punctuated the observation by driving his gaze hungrily up and down her body, and suddenly Hannah felt as if she weren't wearing anything at all. Even stranger than that, she found herself *wishing* she wasn't wearing anything at all. And she wished she was with Michael when she wasn't wearing it. And hopefully, he wouldn't be wearing anything, either.

Um, what had they been talking about?

"Hm," he said, "now you seem to be in a brown study."

Oh, right. They were color-coding each other's moods. "Well, I suppose it's better than being in a purple haze."

"Actually, now I'm beginning to see red."

She narrowed her eyes at him. "So now that we've covered the spectrum," she said, "have you delivered the check you came to deliver?"

"Actually, Tiffannee's the one who brought the check," he said. "She just asked me along for the ride."

And Hannah really, really, really didn't want to think about what—or whom—he would be riding. "Someone actually entrusted her with a large sum of money?" she asked.

"Don't underestimate Tiffannee," he said. "Those who have have regretted it."

Probably, Hannah thought, that was because they'd had to go so low to underestimate Tiffannee that they'd drowned at the bottom of the Marianas Trench.

She trailed her gaze back to the dance floor, and was surprised to see that Tiffannee was currently engaged in scientific experimentation and was trying to absorb Adrian through osmosis. Hmm . . . Hannah had never seen the foxtrot danced like *that* before.

"Looks like you might be hitchhiking home tonight," she told Michael. "Your ride seems to have just veered off onto Adrian Street."

Michael followed her gaze and sighed. But all he said was, "Ah, youth."

"And just how young is she, by the way?" Hannah asked. "Shouldn't you be getting her home to study for her spelling test? I mean, I know it's not a school night, but . . ."

Michael didn't respond right away, and when she looked at him again, he was grinning quite openly, and quite wickedly. "Well, my goodness, aren't we waspish tonight?"

Hannah lifted her nose into the air. "That was not waspishness. It was concern for Tiffannee's school performance. Education is very important to me, you know."

"Yeah, right." But he was still grinning. "What do you care how young she is?"

"I don't," Hannah said coolly. "I just wondered how she got hired at your firm when she's obviously still in high school. And speaking of your firm," she added before Michael had a chance to further embarrass her—not that she wasn't doing a fine job of that all by herself—"it occurs to me that I have no idea which accounting firm it is you work for. I don't recall seeing it on Alex's application."

Not that she looked that closely at every student's application, mind you. But since meeting Michael that first day, she had looked over Alex Sawyer's application a time or two—or ten. But only because she wanted to make sure everything was in order, and not because she wanted to find out where the Sawyers lived so she could drive by their house on the way home from school occasionally, as if she were a twelve-year-old girl on a pink Stingray checking out the new boy in the neighborhood. She'd just accidentally gotten lost that time she'd accidentally driven by their house, that was all. It had been accidental. And she had perfectly good reasons for all those other accidental times, too. She did. After all, how could she have known that the Sawyers lived less than a mile away from a tire store she'd been dying to check out for months?

He eyed her narrowly. "That's because I don't think Alex's application asked for my place of employment," he replied.

"Yes, it did," Hannah told him pointedly. "And you left it blank."

"Did I? Must have been an oversight." And then, before she could say more, he added, "Would you like to dance?"

And then, before she could say no—or even yes, for that matter—he was taking her into his arms and leading her out onto the floor, which presented several problems. First, he had to pull her close. Second, he was placing one of his hands in hers, and splaying the other open against the small of her back, an action that sent a thrill of something flaming and furious fox-trotting right down her spine—which, it went without saying, became problem number three. Fourth, it was incredibly nice to be held by him that way. Fifth, there was the problem of how good he smelled, and how warm his palm was against hers, and how his dark eyes seemed to grow even darker as he fixed his gaze on hers. Okay, so maybe that was three things, making them fifth, sixth, and seventh. Eighth, there was the problem of how, when Michael held her the way he did, she realized that she never, ever wanted him to let go. And last, but certainly not least, there was the problem of Hannah having no idea how to dance.

"Ouch," Michael said as soon as he realized that.

"I'm sorry," she hastily apologized, trying to untangle herself from him. But he straightened and continued to hold her, obviously thinking she'd stumbled a bit, or perhaps missed a step. "I've never been much of a dancer," she added.

"Ouch," he said when he realized that, too.

He did halt then, his eyes still focused on hers, but his expression was one of resignation. He inhaled deeply and released the breath on a slow sigh of surrender. He obviously recognized that it would be wise for him to quit while he was ahead—and still had two functioning feet—than to try and teach Hannah the fox-trot. She steeled herself for his withdrawal, braced herself for no longer having the opportunity to enjoy the feel of his warm hand cupped in hers while the other opened so tenderly over her back, and did her best not to become suicidal about it. But the strangest thing happened.

He didn't withdraw.

On the contrary, he opened his hand wider at the small of her back and urged her closer, until her entire body was flush against his. And then the something flaming and furious inside Hannah became explosive and extreme. And although he did release her hand, it was only so that he could move his to her back to join the other, only higher this time, between her shoulder blades. She remembered being in high school, standing in the shadows of the gymnasium, watching the other kids dance, draping themselves over each other in that swaying sort of movement that couples did instead of dancing, as if they were trying to couple with their clothes on. The position should have been indecorous, she thought. Instead, it felt . . .

Well. It felt very nice. Very nice indeed.

Now she knew why the other kids had danced this way. And she wished she'd known some of them—or even one of them—well enough to do it then. Because if she had danced this way then, she might not feel so out of her element now. Then she made herself admit that it wasn't the dance that caused heat to shudder through her. It wasn't even the way Michael was holding her. It was Michael himself doing that. Because had she been standing this way with Adrian or any other man in the room at that moment, no way would she have wanted to pull him close enough to crawl inside him.

But she wanted very much to pull Michael that close.

Tentatively, she looped one arm around his neck and cupped her other hand over the center of his chest. His heartbeat buffeted her fingertips, racing like her own, and when she tilted her head back to look at him, she realized he was no more calm or collected about what was happening than she was. And she took some comfort in that . . .

. . . until she remembered just how hazardous—not to mention pointless—an attraction between the two of them would be. What really troubled her, though, was that this seemed to have gone way beyond an attraction. And she didn't even want to think about where it might ultimately lead.

Just what was happening? she wondered. When had they crossed the line? She told herself it must have been when Michael showed up at her house on her birthday. That night, something between them had shifted, had knocked itself off kilter and brought the two of them closer together—both emotionally and physically. But they had crossed a line tonight, too, just now, when Michael pulled her close. And something told her it wouldn't be easy to go back to the other side of that line now. Not just because of their actions. But because of the way she felt.

She gave herself a moment to get accustomed to the feel of his body so close to hers, to the imperious height of him and the potent strength of him and the sheer magnitude of his presence. Then she decided it wouldn't hurt to give herself another moment to do that. And then another. And another. And another. And then she realized he felt so good, she wanted to give herself a million more moments to simply get accustomed to the feel of him, as many moments as were left in the evening. In the year. In the century. He was so different from her—hard in the places she was soft, angular in the places she was curved, solid in the places she was slight.

The heat of his hands seeped through the velvet of her dress, mingling with her own heat at the base of her spine and between her shoulder blades. Where his chest made contact with hers was more heat, a turbulent heat that seemed to spread to her every extremity. And he smelled good, too, but not of some bottled fragrance or the great outdoors. He smelled scrubbed and vibrant and very, very male.

Michael Sawyer, CPA, she thought again. Michael Sawyer, *Can't Prove Authentic*.

"Just who are you, Michael Sawyer?" she asked softly. The question was out of her mouth before she even realized she wanted to ask it. But she had no desire to retrieve it, wanted very much to hear how he would reply.

He didn't reply, though, not at first. He only continued to gaze down at her face as if he considered it something worth gazing at, and swayed their bodies slowly to the music—much more slowly, in fact, than the music itself. Finally, very softly, he said, "I'm Alex Sawyer's father."

"Oh, you're more than that," she said with much certainty.

Leisurely, he began to turn their bodies, and danced them in a new direction. But Hannah scarcely noticed, because she was too captivated by the way his hand moved on her back, a bit higher, nearing the tantalizing place where her dress ended and her skin began.

"Am I?" he asked, his voice quiet, fluid, pouring over her in a ripe, rimy rill.

She nodded. "And I want to know what else."

Again, he hesitated before replying, but she wasn't sure why, since all he said when he finally spoke was, "I'm an accountant."

"And what else are you?" she asked with a grin, warming now to the exchange.

He grinned back. "I'm a Sagittarius," he told her.

"And what else?"

He thought for a minute, but kept dancing. Then, "A hand-ball player," he said.

"And what else?"

"A Louis Armstrong fan."

"And what else?"

"Type O positive."

She smiled again. "And what else?"

"An art lover."

"And what else?"

This time, before he answered her, he pulled her even closer, something she would have sworn was impossible, something that very nearly stopped her breath. In a very low, very rough voice, he told her, "I'm a man who'd like to take you home tonight."

The playfulness Hannah had been feeling fled, to be replaced by a reaction unlike anything she had ever felt before. A hunger mixed with deprivation, a need mixed with desire. Heat shot through her belly, fire swept through her body. Just the thought of going home with Michael, and what would happen if she did . . .

"You can't take me home," she said softly. "I came with Adrian."

Not that she felt any obligation or commitment to Adrian. On the contrary, she wanted very, very much to go home with Michael. Which was precisely why she answered him the way she did. Feeling as she did just then, all anxious and edgy and hot, she couldn't be responsible for what would happen once they got home.

"Are you going home with him?" Michael asked, his voice belying nothing of what he might be thinking or feeling.

She should tell him yes, she thought, even though she would be lying when she did. She should make him think there was something going on between her and Adrian, even though there was no chance of anything like that ever happening. It would make things easier if Michael thought she was involved with someone else. Easier for her, at any rate. Because maybe if he stopped taking an interest in her, she would stand a better chance of fighting her own interest in him.

In spite of her little chat with herself, though, "No," she said. "I won't be going home with him. Not tonight."

Michael eyed her with much deliberation, as if he were silently willing her to elaborate.

"Not ever," she obliged. "There's nothing between Adrian and me." She waited for him to say there was nothing between him and the majorette, either, but nothing was forthcoming. So, narrowing her eyes at him, she said, "How about you, Michael? Who will you be going home with tonight?"

He smiled at that, a shrewd, confident sort of smile that told her if he couldn't go home with her, then he'd go home with whatever warm body—or, perhaps, bod*ee*—made itself available.

And then he surprised her by saying, "I'm going home with you."

She started to shake her head in denial, but he spun her around so quickly that she began to grow a little light-headed. Or maybe it was Michael himself who made her feel that way. But she didn't have time to think any more about it, because just as she began to regain her equilibrium, she realized there had been a method to his dancing, and that he had managed to sway her into a secluded little alcove hidden by overgrown potted palms and darkened by its distance from the rest of the dance floor.

And then, without warning, he kissed her. Kissed her with a passion and a longing unlike anything Hannah had ever felt before. There was nothing tentative in the kiss, nothing apologetic, nothing uncertain. Michael kissed her as if he'd spent his entire life rehearsing it. His mouth descended over hers, captured it, clung to it, and something inside Hannah sprang to life the moment his lips touched hers. When she gasped in surprise, he took advantage of her reaction to taste her more deeply, his tongue inciting her mouth to commit mayhem. She responded in kind, tangling her tongue with his, each of them warring for possession of the kiss, neither yielding, simply because the battle was too enjoyable. The hand that had crept to the top of her dress in back moved higher, curving over her bare nape, his fingertips dipping into the hair she had so painstakingly arranged.

She didn't care. On the contrary, she wanted him to free the mass and drive his fingers into it, the way she wanted to twine her fingers in his hair. And when Michael went no further, only pressed his hand more possessively against her neck, she surrendered to her own desire and threaded her fingers through his silky locks. He groaned in response to her foray, and deepened the kiss even more, until Hannah grew breathless and unsteady. She tore her mouth from his long enough to inhale a gulp of air, then he was upon her again, as if he were trying to consume her. The hand at her neck dipped lower again, skimmed over her bare back and shoulders before joining its mate at her waist again. But his other hand went exploring, creeping downward at first, over the fine curve of her derriere, making her gasp once more.

And again he claimed her mouth before she could say a word, kissing her greedily, needfully, the way she was kissing him. His fingers pressed into the tender flesh of her bottom, tracing the lower curve before moving to her hip, then up along her rib cage and in between their bodies. And then she felt his hand beneath her breast, cradling it in the wide L of his thumb and forefinger, pushing at it until her flesh erupted from the top of her gown. His mouth left hers to drag a line of openmouthed kisses along the column of her throat, into the divot at its base, and then lower still, to taste the ivory skin above her dress. Her fingers tightened in his hair as he nipped her lightly, and when she cried out softly in response, he darted his tongue over the tender spot to soothe it. And all the while he cupped her breast confidently in his hand, palming her delicate flesh beneath the black velvet, the fabric creating a delicious friction with every subtle movement he made.

"Michael," she managed to gasp as he stole another taste of her flesh. "Michael, we . . . we have to . . . to stop," she stammered. "Please," she added. "We're in a . . . a public place." But the reminder didn't faze him. "Please," she tried again. "If we get caught . . . if *I* get caught . . ." But her voice halted, and she gasped again, when he flicked his thumb adroitly over her taut nipple.

Her words did seem to finally register, though, because Michael paused, his head still bent, his breathing ragged and rapid. After a moment, he straightened, then dropped both hands to her waist, holding her that way while he collected himself. Hannah moved her own hands to his chest, curling her fingers lightly against the fabric of his jacket, not sure what to say or do. When his eyes finally met hers, they were dark and tempestuous. As if he felt as rash and unsatisfied as she.

"I'm sorry," he said softly. "I didn't intend for that to happen. Not here. Not yet."

Meaning he *had* intended for it to happen under other circumstances, Hannah realized. But she couldn't think about the significance of that right now. "You're not the only one at fault," she said. "I didn't exactly discourage you."

She had hoped he would smile at that, but he didn't, only fixed his gaze even more intently on her face. "Come home with me tonight," he said roughly.

She shook her head and uttered one word of explanation: "Alex."

"He'll be in bed by the time we get there," Michael said.

But again, Hannah shook her head. "I can't, Michael."

"Then I'll go home with you. I'll call the sitter. Have her stay late."

Hannah replied with another one-word answer: "No."

He clenched his jaw tight. "Why not?"

"I'm the director of your son's school. It would be inappropriate."

He nodded, but she didn't think it was because he was agreeing with her.

For one long moment, they only stood there in silence, their gazes bound, their hands settled on each other's bodies, their thoughts tangled. Hannah was the first to move away, but she did so reluctantly.

"I should find Adrian," she said. "And Tiffannee will be looking for you." And then, because she honestly didn't know what else to say—and because the look on Michael's face was just too much for her to bear—Hannah turned and fled.

It was nearly two A.M. when the phone rang, but Hannah was still lying wide awake in the darkness when it did. She switched on her bedside lamp and glanced at the caller ID.

The number was blocked, something that would have normally caused her to let the machine pick up. But she answered this time, because somehow she knew who she would hear on the other end of the line.

And before she even said hello, he confirmed it by saying, "I told you I'd be going home with you tonight."

She had to smile at that. In spite of what she had told him earlier, he had indeed come home with her. He had ridden in the car with her and Adrian, and he had been there on the front porch as she turned her cheek when Adrian went to kiss her good night. He had come into her house with her, had undressed with her, had showered with her, had even eased into bed with her. And hearing his voice now, so silky and sexy and sweet, she almost felt as if he'd just reached over and traced a finger along the curve of her shoulder and down between her breasts. Because her heart rate quickened, her blood began to race, and her body grew hot all over. Just from hearing him utter one short sentence. She could only imagine what would be going on if he had *really* come home with her tonight.

Oh, wait. She already had imagined that. It was why she was still lying in bed awake at two in the morning.

"You came home with me, too," he said. "I can't stop thinking about you, Hannah. About what happened tonight."

"Michael, we can't do this," she said. "It's completely inappropriate, and there's no future in it."

"How do you think it's inappropriate?" he asked. "Why do you say there's no future in it?"

She noticed he didn't disagree with her, only questioned why she felt that way. So she told him what she had told him earlier. "I'm the director of your son's school. I can't get involved with one of the fathers."

"Not one of the married ones, no," he agreed. "That, I'll grant you, could lead to trouble. But I'm not one of the married ones, Hannah. I haven't been married for a long time."

Something about the way he said the word *long* made her think it had been a long time for other things, as well. She tried not to think about that, tried not to think about how long it had been for her, too. But remembering the way they'd responded to each other, with such fire and such an utter lack of restraint, how he'd touched her so intimately, in ways that should have offended her, but had instead inflamed her . . .

"But you are the father of one of my students," she reminded him. "And I just don't think it would be wise for us to continue with this . . . this . . ." She expelled a soft sigh of exasperation.

"Yeah, I know," he said when he heard it. "I'm having trouble figuring out what it is, too."

She waited for him to say something more and, when he didn't, told herself to say good-bye. Instead, she heard herself saying, "What happened tonight, Michael, should never have happened. And it won't happen again." And in a way, she thought, that was saying good-bye. So why didn't it feel quite right?

She heard what sounded like a sigh of resolution from the other end of the line. "So then it probably wouldn't be a good idea for me to tell you what I'm thinking about right now, would it?"

"If you're thinking what I think you're thinking, then, no, it probably wouldn't be a good idea."

"Why?" he asked. "Because you're thinking the same thing?"

Deny it, she told herself. *Say good-bye. Hang up.* But she hesitated before doing any of those things.

"What happened tonight, Hannah," Michael said, "was inescapable. And I guarantee you, it *will* happen again."

That, of course, was precisely what Hannah was afraid of. And that, if nothing else, was what finally made her tell him good night.

SIX

IF THERE WAS ONE THING ADRIAN PADGETT hated, it was discovering an unforeseen wrinkle in his schemes. Because his schemes normally played out as smooth as silk. And wrinkles in silk were a bitch to get out without doing irreparable damage to the fabric. And his fabric—that which made him what he was, he meant—was already damaged enough, thank you very much.

Why had he not anticipated Michael's arrival in Indianapolis? he asked himself as he sipped a very fine cognac on the terrace of his high-rise condo in downtown Indianapolis. The city was quiet in the wee hours of the morning, but it sprawled prostrate before Adrian like a dutiful vassal, just waiting to be plundered and robbed. Its taller buildings—he hesitated to call them skyscrapers since this was, after all, Indiana—sparkled like diamond-encrusted towers, and its outlying suburbs slept beneath a streetlight-studded blanket of night. The wind nudged open his white tuxedo shirt, but he scarcely noticed the cold breeze dancing over his bare flesh. He was too busy making plans.

His hometown, he thought as he sipped his cognac again, such as it was. Ironic that he should return to his past to engender his future. But sometimes that was the best thing to do. Start over anew. Except that he was actually much better than new these days. Because new, Adrian Padgett had been poor, plagued, hated, and unhappy. These days, he was rich, carefree, hated and unhappy. All in all, a much better way to live.

Or at least he'd been carefree until a couple of weeks ago. But now that Michael was here . . .

Why had he not seen Michael coming? he asked himself again. He, who knew Michael better than anyone else—or at least who *had* known Michael better than anyone else, once upon a time—should have realized he would come running back to OPUS the minute they crooked their little finger. And Adrian had known for months that OPUS was watching him. He supposed he had just assumed that Michael meant it when he said he was finished with OPUS. Michael, after all, was a man of his word. But no one, Adrian knew, ever left the organization. Not really. Even he himself still used the knowledge he had gained while working for them to his advantage. With Michael thrown into the mix, though, Adrian was going to have to rethink a few ideas, rearrange a few strategies, rework a few details. And he loathed redoing anything. Especially when his original plan had been so perfect.

He remembered how Michael had laughingly referred to his wanting to rule the world. As if ruling the world would be some great gig. As if this world were worth ruling. Adrian didn't want to rule the world. He wanted to be master of time, space, and dimension. And if everything worked out the way it was supposed to, that was what he would be. Because what Adrian would soon control—once he ironed out the wrinkle that was Michael Sawyer—would have him back on track to getting what he wanted.

Everything.

Oh, he did so love being an evildoer.

Michael thought Adrian was in Indianapolis right now

because of the upcoming presidential debates. He probably thought Adrian was planning to assassinate someone. How quaint. How old-fashioned. How technologically backward. That was the problem with OPUS. They kept thinking in terms of traditional mayhem, and couldn't be forward-thinking at all. For all their technology, they still didn't grasp just how much damage one person could do sitting in one room pushing one button. Or if they did think about such a thing, it was in terms of conventional warfare. A nuclear warhead carrying enough explosive power to leave a hole in the earth where once stood Liechtenstein. How quaint. How old-fashioned. How technologically backward.

But Michael, if given enough time, could figure out what Adrian intended to do. Right now he was still working under whatever guidelines and information OPUS had given him, which would be in no way helpful with regard to what Adrian was planning. But Michael, being Michael—and also being a pro when it came to assimilating, evaluating, and articulating—if he amassed enough intelligence, would know what was what. He could be a problem. He could be a major problem. And Adrian couldn't have that. So he was going to have to distract Michael somehow, make sure he didn't get the information he needed to assimilate, evaluate, and articulate. Or if he did get the information, he needed to be so frazzled he could make neither heads nor tails of it. And luckily for Adrian, he knew exactly what kind of distraction to levy. He knew what would frazzle Michael the most.

Hannah Frost.

It didn't take a genius to see that Michael had a thing for the lovely school director. Adrian had a thing for her, too, but his thing was considerably less noble and considerably more ribald than Michael's thing. Because Michael's thing for women was always noble. The moron. But beautiful women had always been Adrian's weakness, too—his only weakness. He'd been ruled by his libido since he was thirteen, and it had only been the realization that he could potentially become master of time, space, and dimension that had turned his head even a little bit. But beautiful women were everywhere, and they were frightfully easy to possess. Mastery of time, space, and dimension, however, that was a bit trickier. And therefore a bit more interesting.

And also a bit more worth having.

So Adrian could sacrifice Hannah Frost to Michael. He could sacrifice her to more than that, if that was what it took to make sure Michael stayed off his back. And if Hannah Frost proved to be uncooperative in that regard, well . . . Adrian had other avenues he could travel. He just hoped he wouldn't have to resort to those. Not just because they were inconvenient and made more wrinkles, but because there was just something about screwing Michael over with a woman again that appealed to him. But then, Adrian had always enjoyed screwing Michael's women. It was what friends like him did.

Adrian enjoyed another mouthful of savory brandy and let the soft strains of mellow jazz flow over him. He remembered a time, years ago, when he and Michael hadn't been rivals, when they'd been friends. And he smiled. Not because the memories were so warm, and not because he felt any sort of fondness for them. He was, after all, emotionally damaged. He didn't feel things like warmth or fondness. Had Michael, and others, realized that a long time ago, things might have been easier for all of them. But he and Michael had had some good times when they were kids. And they'd had even better times when they were young men.

It was just too bad Michael had insisted on being one of the good guys. They could have had even more fun if he'd followed the path Adrian had taken himself.

"Adrian?" a feminine voice called from the bedroom behind him.

The summons was punctuated by the scrape of the glass doors he'd left open a crack, so that he would know when his companion was stirring. It was a signal that he was no longer alone with his thoughts, so he pushed his thoughts to the back of his brain, where they belonged for now and could stew nicely in their own juices.

"Is everything all right?" the soft voice came again.

He inhaled deeply of the silky Indiana evening and glanced over his shoulder to see a tiny blond creature emerging from his bedroom, wrapped in the top half of his silk pajamas. He did so hope she hadn't bothered with the bottom half. Because Michael wasn't the only one Adrian had plans for. He had plans for Tiffannee, too. Especially Tiffannee's bottom half.

"Everything's fine, sweetheart," he told her. He smiled when she reached up to push a length of pale blond hair out of her eyes, the gesture making his pajama shirt gape open to reveal a soft curve of her breast that made him hard all over again. He reached for her as he said, "In fact, now that you're here, everything is perfect."

When the ringing phone woke Michael the morning after the fund-raiser, he thought for some reason that it must be Hannah. He had no reason to infer this, since she'd told him only hours ago that there was no future in anything the two of them might pursue. But even in his sleep-fogged state, he knew the call would have something to do with her. In hindsight, he supposed it was hope that made him feel certain it was her. Unfortunately, as he'd learned on too many occasions, hoping something was true didn't make it so. It was a lesson he really wished he would learn.

"Raptor," a harsh male voice on the other end of the line ground out without greeting.

Even without hearing his code name, Michael recognized at once the voice of the One Whose Name Could Not Be

Spoken. Which really wasn't a problem this morning, since Michael could think of more than a few names he'd like to call the guy.

"What?" he snarled in response.

There was a brief moment of silence, then, "Oh, did I wake you? I am *so* sorry."

The hell he was. Still, Michael could think of more than a few ways to make him sorry.

Although months had passed since he'd been activated for this assignment, he was still pissed off about having been pulled out of his life the way he had been, with no choice, no preparation, and no recourse. It had taken him five years—*five years*—to reach a point where he was reasonably comfortable that his past wouldn't catch up with him, and reasonably confident he'd be able to raise his son in a normal, safe, stable environment. Five years to erase his history and delete his former self so that he could move ahead with his future. Michael had finally stopped worrying that his time with OPUS would sully any possibility he might have at winning happiness. For himself and for his son.

And then just like that—poof—it was gone. All of it. His having been reactivated had opened up the door to all the mischief and malice that had once filled his life, and had invited it right inside. And with its arrival, every last ounce of security and sanctuary he'd won over the years had packed its bags and moved out. Now he would have to start again from scratch. Perpetually worrying, constantly second-guessing, always looking over his shoulder. All because of his connection—long ago severed—to Adrian Padgett.

"What is it?" he asked his superior, not bothering to mask his distaste for everything that had anything to do with this whole endeavor.

"It's been a while since you checked in," his boss told him. "Do you have anything to report?"

"If I had anything to report, I would have checked in."

Silence met his remark.

He sighed fitfully. "What?" he demanded.

"The Frost woman," the other man said. "I think you have something to report with her."

Heat erupted in Michael's belly at the mention of Hannah's name. "What about her?"

"You can use her," his boss said.

"I'm already using her," Michael replied, barely able to restrain his anger. Because he knew what he said was true, and he didn't like using Hannah the way he had been. "I'm watching her at home and at work both. But there's nothing to report there," he insisted.

"She has a relationship with Sorcerer. He likes her."

"Yeah?" Michael muttered. "So do more than a thousand kids at the school. You want me to put them under surveillance, too?"

"Don't be coy, Raptor."

Yeah, I got your coy right here, pal, Michael thought uncharitably. But all he said was, "Coy? *Moi?*"

"Use her," his boss instructed him again. "She has an in with Sorcerer that we don't have. You can work it to our advantage."

Maybe it was his sleep-muddled brain, or maybe Michael just didn't want to go there, but he couldn't for the life of him figure out what his superior was telling him to do. "I'm not sure I follow you," he said. "What can I do that I'm not already doing?"

"According to one of our operatives working Sorcerer from another angle, you're in a position to . . . provoke a situation. Between him and Hannah Frost."

Michael narrowed his eyes. "Provoke a situation?" he echoed warily.

"Sorcerer can be made to become . . . distracted by her," the other man told him. "If you put the wheels into motion."

"Come again?" Michael asked. Because he really didn't want to think that his boss was telling him to do what he was beginning to think his boss was telling him to do.

"Oh, come on, Raptor. Do I have to spell it out for you?"

"Yes."

There was an exasperated sound from the other end of the line, then his superior told him, "You and Sorcerer always got into more trouble over women than you ever did matters of national security."

"That wasn't my fault," Michael said.

"This time it will be."

"How do you figure?"

There was another one of those moments of weighty silence, then, "Go after the Frost woman," his superior said. "Pursue her romantically. It will piss off Sorcerer and make him compete with you. It could sidetrack him enough to buy us some time. It might even distract him enough that he'll botch whatever it is he's planning to do. The presidential debate is less than two weeks away, Raptor. And we still don't know what he's planning."

"Which means we still have almost two weeks to find out," Michael said. "Since when does OPUS bring ordinary citizens into its operations and put them at risk?"

This time, soft, less-than-happy laughter was Michael's reply. "Oh, come on, Raptor. Since when does OPUS give a damn about the individual—ordinary citizen or not—in the big picture? National security is everything. You know that. And if that means risking one person to save millions, that's what we have to do."

Of course, Michael thought. How could he have forgotten that about OPUS? It was, after all, something he'd learned personally. And it was yet another thing that had cemented his decision to leave.

"I categorically refuse to bring Hannah Frost into this," he stated unequivocally. "Especially the way you want me to."

"Yeah, and you categorically refused to come back for this assignment, too," his boss reminded him.

"I won't put her at risk," Michael insisted. "And I won't mislead her—or use her—any more than I already have."

"We don't have much choice, Raptor."

"You mean I don't have much choice."

More silence from the other end of the line.

"I won't do it," Michael said again.

"You will do it," his superior informed him. "You have to. You know it. You always do the right thing, Raptor."

Before Michael could object again, he heard a soft click and the buzz of an empty phone line. And he knew that what his boss had just said was true. He did always do the right thing. And this time would be no different.

On Monday, for the first time since assuming her position as director of the Emerson Academy, Hannah decided to duck out early and go home before the day was done. At first she told herself it was because she couldn't concentrate on anything and wasn't doing any good at work anyway. Then she told herself it was because she was exhausted, having spent the last two nights tossing and turning and not sleeping at all. Then she told herself it was because she wasn't feeling well, and had a migraine that just wouldn't quit. Finally, though, she made herself be honest, and admitted that she just wanted to be alone. Her nerves were still too frazzled after what had happened Saturday night, and her emotions were still too raw for her to associate with people.

She hadn't felt like herself since Michael had kissed her, and she hadn't been able to think about much else. Two days wasn't enough to recover from something like that. Of course, two centuries probably wasn't enough to recover from a kiss like Michael's. But one more day, she figured, wouldn't hurt anyone. Mondays were fairly uneventful around Emerson. It was only as the week wore on that the children became fractious—and the faculty and staff even more so. So when Hannah sat down at her desk to eat her lunch, and realized she had no appetite, she decided it was time for her to go home.

Dorothy, her secretary, looked concerned when Hannah announced her intention to leave early, but assured her they'd be able to handle things in her absence. Hannah had no doubt of that, which was another reason she didn't berate herself for falling down on the job this once. Still, she drove home absently, stopping and starting and turning corners on automatic pilot. It was a picture-perfect autumn afternoon, the sky thick and slate over trees awash in red and gold and orange, a brisk, bracing wind rippling the leaves like the pages of a book. It was cold enough for a fire, so when she stopped for gas, she bought a ricket of firewood, too. Because by then, all she wanted to do was go home, change into something comfortable, and tuck herself into the sofa with a cup of tea and a good book and try to lose herself for the rest of the afternoon.

But fate had something different in mind.

Because no sooner had Hannah freed her long hair and finished buttoning an oversized plaid flannel shirt over a thermal undershirt and blue jeans than someone knocked at her front door. She padded in thick socks to answer it, and wasn't nearly as surprised to see Michael standing on the other side as she figured she probably should be.

"Hi," she said through the screen door when she saw him.

"Hi," he greeted her in return.

And then neither of them said a word for several moments, each only gazing at the other as if unable to believe they really existed in the world. Michael had apparently had as much trouble focusing at work as she had, because he was dressed not in a suit, but in blue jeans and a thick heather-gray sweater, hiking boots on his feet where loafers would have been before. Framed by the pure golden backdrop of the impeccable autumn afternoon, and with the breeze sifting fondly through his hair, he looked almost like a fantasy standing out there.

She could scarcely believe she had kissed this man. He was so handsome, so big, so overwhelming, so very different from any man she had ever been attracted to before. And in that moment, she knew—she *knew*—she could no more resist him than she could stop the sun from rising the next morning.

"I guess I should ask you what you're doing here," she said. "But I think I already know."

And she told herself she was ready. Ready for whatever was supposed to happen between the two of them. Ready for whatever fate, or chance, or destiny, or whatever had in store. The pull she felt toward him was just too strong to ignore. Making love to Michael, she suddenly realized, was inescapable. She just hoped she could handle whatever came afterward, too.

And as she pushed the screen door open to invite him in, she couldn't help wondering if maybe this had all been predetermined somehow, by forces neither of them could comprehend or disobey. That they would both take off from work the same day, and that he would show up at her house within minutes of her own arrival . . . that defied explanation. Maybe this, she thought, was the reason she'd needed to leave work, and she hadn't even realized it. She'd needed to come home to welcome Michael. Into her house. Into her life. Into her heart. Maybe it really was as simple as that.

But his expression had changed some as she spoke, and as she opened the door to invite him in, he looked anything but inviting himself. Nevertheless, he entered, his body brushing hers as he passed her in the narrow doorway. He smelled of woodsmoke and windy afternoon, and his body pressing against hers as he pushed past her generated a delicious sort of friction that crackled through her entire body.

"So what made *you* decide to take the day off?" she asked

as she pushed the front door closed behind herself. Not sure why she did it, she leaned back against it, her hands tucked behind her back, as if she were afraid he might try to bolt, and she wanted to block his path.

He didn't answer her right away, only stood at the center of her living room, hands shoved into the pockets of his blue jeans. "Actually," he finally said, "I'm working right now. And you're a part of that work."

She eyed him curiously. "What are you talking about?"

He opened his mouth to explain, but couldn't seem to find the words to do it. So, abandoning the attempt, he strode over to the fireplace and lifted one of the brass candlesticks at the end. As Hannah watched, confused now, he scraped something off the base with his thumbnail. Then he replaced the candlestick in its original position and returned to where she still stood leaning against the front door. On the pad of his thumb was a tiny metallic circle, so minute, it couldn't have even passed for a freckle.

"Do you know what this is?" he asked her.

She shook her head.

"It's a microphone."

She dropped her gaze to the speck again. "It's what? A microphone?"

He nodded.

She shook her head, not understanding. "What's a microphone doing on the bottom of my candlestick?"

"The same thing as the other ones," he said. "Recording every sound that occurs in this house."

Hannah, too troubled and befuddled to dwell on the last part of his statement, fixed on the first part instead. "What other ones?"

"The ones that are stuck inside your telephone, to the back of your china cabinet, under one of the basement stairs, inside the pencil holder on your desk, on the side of your medicine cabinet, and under the kitchen table."

She shook her head again, more slowly this time, unable—or maybe just unwilling—to process what he was telling her. "I don't understand. Someone's been listening to me? Without my knowledge?"

"Yeah," he told her, his expression harsh. "Not just here, but at school, too. There are a couple of these in your office."

"But—"

"And that's not all," he interrupted before she could say more. "Because there's something else you should know about, too," he added, moving this time toward the sofa.

He reached toward the picture hanging above it, a large oil-on-canvas reproduction of a bouquet of flowers, and plucked out something that had been affixed to the dark center of the sunflower in the middle. It had been positioned in such a way that it had looked like part of the painting, a shadow at the base of a petal. But even after Michael brought it to Hannah and showed it to her, she had no idea what it was.

Her face must have illustrated her confusion, because Michael told her, "It's a camera."

She glanced back up at him, wide-eyed, a sick feeling roiling through the pit of her stomach. "A *camera*?" she gasped. "Someone's been *watching* me?"

"No," he said, swiftly and firmly enough that she almost believed him. Almost. "The camera was never activated," he assured her. "I swear to you, Hannah. No one ever watched you like that." He opened his mouth to say more, but hesitated, as if he were considering something very carefully. Then, having evidently made up his mind, he said, "There's one in your bedroom, too."

"Oh, my God," she whispered, the sick feeling now swirling into her chest. And then, almost too afraid to ask, but knowing she had to, she said, "How did you know about all those?"

He met her gaze levelly, grimly. "I'm the one who put them there."

She felt as if the floor suddenly tipped forward at a ninety-degree angle, and she fell forward with it, staggering over to collapse onto the sofa before her knees buckled completely beneath her. "When?" she asked, amazed she could even find her voice.

"While you were at work one day," he told her.

She looked up at him, but his expression now was hard, impenetrable. He looked nothing like the man who had kissed her Saturday. God, had that only been two nights ago? "You broke into my house while I was gone?"

He didn't flinch once. "Yeah. I did."

"You were here when I wasn't?"

"Look, I'm sorry, Hannah," he said. But she could detect nothing apologetic in his tone. What he sounded was angry. As if he were the one who had a right to feel that way. With a casually tossed-off shrug, he added, "That's not the worst of it."

"Oh, goody, there's more," she managed. She wrapped her arms around her midsection and pulled her knees up before herself, effectively curling herself into a ball.

He blew out an exasperated breath. "I'm the one who's been listening to you, too," he told her, his voice gentling some. "It's how I knew you'd be home right now. I heard you tell your secretary you were leaving. But even if I hadn't, I was sitting in a van parked a block away from the school, eavesdropping. I saw you leave. I followed you here. You never even noticed me."

And did he actually sound as if his feelings had been hurt by that? she wondered. Golly. She hated to think she'd *hurt his feelings*. Especially after all the nice things he'd done for her.

So much for thinking his arrival at the house just after hers had been preordained by kismet. So much for inviting him into her home and her life and her heart. So much for being ready. So much for not being able to resist him. So much for making love with him.

Oh, God . . .

"I don't believe this," she said. "I don't believe this is happening. People don't get their houses bugged. That only happens in spy books and spy movies. Next you'll be telling me that's what you are. A spy."

When he said nothing in reply to what she had intended as a joke—albeit a not especially amusing one—Hannah glanced up at him again. And again, he was wearing that strange expression, the one that made him look dangerous and sinister and coarse.

And then he said, "Well, actually, if you must know . . ."

She couldn't quite stop the bubble of nervous laughter that erupted inside her then, and she clapped a hand over her mouth when she heard it, fearing it might just be the beginning of complete hysteria. But she removed it long enough to ask, "You're a *spy?*"

He nodded. "I work . . ." He halted for a moment, then shrugged, as if to say, *What the hell?* "I work for OPUS."

She narrowed her eyes at him and dropped her hand into her lap. "OPUS?" she echoed. "What's OPUS? I've never heard of it."

"You're not supposed to have heard of it," he said. "Very few people have. And of those who have, ninety-nine percent of them only know about it because they work for OPUS, too."

"What is it?"

He smiled, a clearly forced and very uncomfortable smile. "If I told you, I'd have to kill you."

She didn't smile back. "If this plays out the way I think it's going to play out, you're already killing me."

Michael's smile—what there was of it—fell. "I'm sorry, Hannah. I can't tell you any more than I already have. As it is, I've violated a direct order by coming here and showing you that you've been under surveillance. And violating a direct order is something you just don't do in OPUS."

"Oh, no, you don't," she said, feeling some righteous indignation moving in on the bruising sorrow. "You're not going to come in here and show me this stuff and then say it's none of my business. Whatever's going on, I'm in it, too. And it's not like I volunteered," she reminded him. "I think I have a right to know, Michael, *what the hell is going on.*"

For a moment, she didn't think he was going to tell her anything more. He only stood in front of her, towering over her, glaring down at her as if all of this were somehow *her* fault. His dark eyes were furious, his jaw was set ruthlessly, and his arms were crossed impatiently over his broad chest. Finally, though, he relented, relaxing his stance, and he dropped down onto the sofa to sit beside her. Without even thinking about what she was doing, Hannah pushed herself back up again, then moved to a Queen Anne chair on the opposite side of the room. He duly noted her movement and seemed resigned to it.

"I guess you do have a right to know," he said, sounding exhausted now. "Hell, who am I kidding?" he added. "I don't pledge any more allegiance to OPUS these days than I pledge to the Mickey Mouse Club." He sighed wearily. "All right, I'll tell you. But, Hannah, what I'm about to say to you goes no further than this room. If they find out you've said *any*thing to *any*one, they can make you disappear."

Gee, that sounded ominous. "Disappear?" she repeated.

He met her gaze unflaggingly. "Like you never even existed before."

She swallowed hard, but nodded. "I won't say a word."

Her vow was evidently good enough for him, because he told her, "OPUS stands for Office of Political Unity and Security. We're an intelligence branch of the OSS."

"Like the CIA?" she asked.

He shook his head. "Not exactly."

"Like the FBI?"

He shook his head again. "Not quite. But we've worked in concert with both of those organizations."

"Well, gosh, Mr. Secret Agent Man, that just makes it all crystal clear," she said sarcastically.

He sighed again, sounding very, very tired. "I wish I could tie it up in a simple package for you. But the fact is, even people who work for OPUS don't always know what we are. What *they* are," he quickly corrected himself. "I'm actually working for them now as sort of a consultant."

"Now?" she said, confused again. "So you're not really employed by them full-time?"

"Not anymore. But OPUS used to be my career. My calling," he told her. "There was a time when that was all I was. An operative for OPUS. I started off analyzing numbers and bank accounts and such, looking for anything that might suggest terrorist stockpiling of money or what have you. Then I worked very briefly in the field. After that, and for the biggest chunk of my employment, I worked for the part of the organization that analyzes the information gathered by other operatives. Operatives in OPUS work in partnerships. Two people to a team. One is a field agent, and the other mans the equipment. The computers, the files, the radios, the Internet, whatever's available. My partner would go wherever there was a threat, and he'd gather whatever information he could and feed it back to me. I'd take what he found and make the connections, find the patterns, fill in the blanks. I'd put the puzzle pieces together until they made a picture. Then I'd send that picture to the guys upstairs, and they'd decide what action to take, if any, and who would take it."

"And who were those guys?" Hannah asked, trying to digest everything he was telling her, but making sense of only bits of it.

"I can't tell you," Michael said. And before she could ask why not, he told her, "Because I don't know who they are. Nobody at my level did." Then he tilted his head to the side, a gesture of concession. "Okay, actually, that's not entirely true. One person at my level did find out who the big boys were. And then he blackmailed every last one of them for a boatload of money, said he'd reveal their identities and the identities of other operatives to the world unless he was paid outrageously well. So they paid him. And then he disappeared. For years. He resurfaced this past spring, and we've been watching him since then. He's done his best to look like a normal citizen, going to work every day, collecting a paycheck, buying a home, doing all the things regular people do. But this guy, Hannah, he's not regular. He's not normal. He's up to something."

"What's he up to?" she asked. "Can you at least tell me that?"

He shook his head. "Not because you're not entitled to know. Because *we* don't know. Not yet. That's why I'm here. They pulled me out of retirement because I know this guy better than anyone. We're reasonably certain that whatever he's up to, it has something to do with the presidential debates later this month. But we can't quite pin down what that something is."

"But what does this guy have to do with *me*?" she asked. "Why has my house been bugged?"

"Because you know him," Michael said. "And we needed to find out if you knew him in a way that was anything other than casual."

Okay, now she was *really* confused. "But how do I know him? I don't know anyone outside the Emerson Aca—" She halted right there, panic seizing her. "It's someone at school, isn't it?" she said, terrified to think that Emerson might be caught in the middle of something dangerous, something menacing. That her children and her coworkers might be at risk. That even Alex—

Oh, God, Alex, she remembered then. "That's why you enrolled Alex at Emerson, isn't it?" she asked. "It wasn't because he was a bad fit at his last school. It was because you . . . because this OPUS thing . . . needed some way to get into the school environment."

Two bright spots of red stained his cheeks at her supposition, and Hannah knew she was right.

"My God, Michael, you brought your own son into this? Put him at risk? He's only nine years old. You really are a ruthless sonofa—"

"Alex has *never* been at risk," he interrupted her angrily. "I would *never* do anything to put my son in danger."

Oh, sure, Hannah thought. Lots of fathers enrolled their kids in schools where they knew there was criminal activity. Specifically *because* there was criminal activity. And if Michael had used his own son to get at whoever this guy was, he sure as hell wouldn't have any qualms about using Hannah, too. Obviously he *wasn't* the kind of man she'd assumed him to be. He really was a ruthless sonofabitch.

And then another thought struck her. All those things Alex had said about his family, about his father being able to hack into all those computers, and his mother's disappearance . . . considering what Michael had just revealed, could Alex have actually been telling the *truth*?

She looked at Michael. "So if you used to be a spy," she backtracked for a minute, "then does that mean Alex's mother really *did* mysteriously disappear five years ago after being force-fed an untraceable toxin bioengineered by an arcane band of rogue spies in some Eastern European country that I was fairly certain didn't exist? Was she a spy, too? Is that why it happened?"

"Ah, actually," Michael said, "that was just a case of food

poisoning brought on by some bad pâté at the Russian embassy in Paris. But yeah, Tatiana did disappear into a Parisian hospital for a few days. She came back totally fine," he hastened to reassure her. "And, yes, she was a spy, too. Originally for her own country, but then she came to work for us at OPUS."

"Tatiana?" Hannah repeated. "That was really her name?"

Michael didn't seem to think it particularly significant. "Yeah. She was born in Russia."

Of course, Hannah thought. Where else would a glamorous spy wife be born? She developed a quick mental picture of flowing platinum hair that swept over one eye, wet red lipstick, and a long cigarette holder from which curls of wispy white smoke rose. Tatiana had probably dressed in black leather and been able to toss back enough vodka to send lesser men under the table. She'd probably always had a stiletto tucked into her spike-heeled boots. *Dahlink,* she'd probably called Michael. *My little babushka,* she'd probably murmured from the other side of the bed after they'd spent hours and hours steaming up the sheets upon their return from a dangerous assignment. Had to get rid of all that extra adrenaline somehow, right?

And why in God's name was she thinking about stuff like this?

Avoidance, she told herself. Anything to *not* think about what was really happening.

"So then you really *can* hack into the computers of the Pentagon, the Kremlin, the United Nations, the International Monetary Fund, and Toys 'R' Us?" she said.

"Well, Toys 'R' Us is still eluding me, but Alex managed to crack their code. He now knows when all the new Xbox and GameCube games will be hitting the stores long before anyone else does. It's made him something of a legend in Internet gaming rooms."

"So then, you're not an accountant," Hannah guessed astutely. Which, of course, came as no surprise at all.

"Actually, I am an accountant," Michael told her.

She narrowed her gaze at him. "You are not."

"I am, too," he said, sounding defensive. "I have my own firm. Why is that so hard for everyone to believe?"

"Have you looked in a mirror lately?" she asked.

"What's that got to do with anything?"

She would have laughed had this whole scene not been so bizarre. As it was, she only told him, "Never mind. So Saturday night, when you said, 'My firm always sends someone to this fund-raiser with a big check,' you were talking about . . ."

"*My* firm, yes," he said.

So then he'd been the one who hired Band Candy Barbie, Hannah thought. How nice.

"And how have you been running *your* firm while working this gig, too?"

"Not very well, lemme tell ya," he said. "Fortunately, I have a very capable team of accountants working for me. And fortunately, I had some vacation days coming. And fortunately— very fortunately—this isn't tax season. But if I don't have this thing wrapped up by the end of the year . . ."

Hannah still couldn't believe everything he'd told her. This was nuts. This sort of thing didn't happen in real life. It certainly didn't happen to people like her, people who strove to live a normal, stable, uneventful life. How could she have become a part of something like this? Was her luck really that bad?

"So, what, is there a secret handshake or something that you have to learn to join this OPUS organization?" she asked sarcastically.

"No, of course not," he replied impatiently.

"Do you have, like, a decoder ring?"

He leveled an intolerant look on her. "No."

"Invisible ink?"

He set his jaw hard for a moment, then, "Actually, a little lemon juice on onion skin works better," he said.

She nodded. "How about a code name? Have one of those?"

The spots of red appeared on his cheeks again, and she gaped at him. "No," she said. "You don't really. I was being sarcastic. You don't honestly have code names."

He dropped his gaze to his lap then, worrying a loose thread in his blue jeans. "Uh, yeah, actually. We do."

"And you are?"

He blew out another one of those exasperated sounds, but still didn't look at her. "Raptor," he said.

Hannah, in turn, felt another one of those hysterical giggles bubble up inside her again. "Like . . . a bird of prey?"

He nodded quickly. And continued to not look at her. "Yeah. Like that."

"It fits you," she said.

He snapped his head up at that, gazing at her full-on. "You think so? I've never much liked it."

"Oh, yeah. Trust me."

"Look, Hannah," he said, his tone returning to the no-nonsense, ruthless sonofabitch one he'd had such good command of earlier, "the reason I've told you all this is because now that you know about it, it taints you."

And, oh, wasn't *that* something a woman wanted to hear from a man with whom she had, only a couple of nights before, engaged in a very compelling oral examination?

"*Taints* me?" she echoed.

He nodded, more eagerly than he had since they'd started talking. "Once the guys at OPUS know I've told you what's going on, they can't make me 'use' you."

And, oh, wasn't *that* something a woman wanted to hear from a man with whom she had just been anticipating a thorough body cavity search? "Oh, I think it's a little late for that," she said. " 'Cause believe me, Michael, I feel plenty used."

He closed his eyes tight and actually flinched, as if she'd just slapped him across the face. "I'm sorry about that, Hannah," he apologized again. And this time, he sounded sincere. He opened his eyes and met her gaze levelly again. "Really, I am sorry. If I'd known what was going to happen between us . . ."

"Yeah, about that," she said, regaining her hold on her righteous indignation.

He looked at her expectantly, almost hopefully. "What about it?"

"It won't happen again," she told him decisively.

Now he looked resigned. Unhappy, but resigned. He nodded again, disconsolately this time. "I understand."

"Oh, I sincerely doubt that," she said. And then, because she really didn't want to dwell on it, she added, "You still haven't told me who the guy is that you're after. And I have a right to know that, too. Especially if my school is at risk."

"I don't think the school is at risk," he said.

"You don't *think* so." It was a statement, not a question.

"I'm reasonably confident that the school isn't in any sort of danger," he qualified. Sort of.

She waited until his gaze met hers again before saying, "And I was reasonably confident that you cared about me."

"Hannah . . ."

"Who is it, Michael?" she asked point-blank. "I deserve to know."

For a minute, she didn't think he would tell her. Then, dipping his head forward in concession, he said, "Adrian Windsor."

She couldn't have been more surprised if he'd told her it was her secretary Dorothy. "Adrian? But he's so . . . he's so . . ."

"He's so dangerous, Hannah," Michael finished for her. "And his name isn't really Windsor. It's Padgett. Adrian Padgett. You should stay away from him. Especially since we still have no idea what he's up to. Or even what he's capable of. All we know is that where Adrian goes, trouble follows. And it just keeps getting worse."

"And you think he's going to do something at the presidential debates," she said. "What? Like an assassination attempt or something?"

"That's one possibility, yeah."

"Do you really think he'd try something like that? That he's capable of it?"

"At this point, Hannah, I honestly don't know what Adrian is capable of doing."

She thought for a minute about everything Michael had just told her, mulling it, dissecting it, analyzing it. Much, she supposed, in the same way he had once performed his job. But she thought, too, about things Michael didn't know. Things about Adrian. Things about Emerson. Things about herself. And then she made a decision.

"No, I'm in," she said.

This time it was his turn to look confused. "What do you mean?"

"I mean I'm in," she repeated, even more forcefully than before. "You guys brought me into it, and now I'm staying in it."

He shook his head, his eyes wide. "Oh, no, you're not."

"Oh, yes, I am," she told him. "My school, my kids, may be at risk, Michael. Adrian sits on the board of directors. And I won't tolerate my school being at risk. If there's any way I can prevent something terrible from happening, I'll do it."

"Hannah, there's no evidence to suggest something terrible is going to happen to Emerson."

"Is there evidence to suggest something terrible *isn't* going to happen to Emerson?"

He didn't answer her on that one. Which was really all the answer she needed.

Knowing that he wasn't going to allow her to be part of what was happening, regardless of her role at Emerson, she played her trump card. "You have no choice but to let me be part of this, Michael."

"Oh, don't I?"

"No. You don't."

"Why not, pray tell?"

"Because I can get closer to Adrian than any of you can."

"How?"

"He's invited me to be his guest at a reception the night before the presidential debates that his employer is hosting. He's told me he'll even get to meet the candidates. He might even get to sit at one of their tables. I told him I'd have to check my calendar, and I've been putting him off, because I really didn't want to do it. But suddenly I remember that I'm totally available that night, and I can tell him I'd be delighted to come."

"Hannah . . ." Michael said warningly.

"Bet none of you OPUS guys has an official invitation to the reception," she said.

"Hannah . . ."

"Bet none of you gets to sit at the candidates' tables."

"Hannah . . ."

"So now, Michael, you'll have to let me play your little spy game. Won't you?"

SEVEN

LON CHANEY, IT HAD BEEN SAID FOR YEARS, was the Man of a Thousand Faces. Selby Hudson, on the other hand, had been, for years, the Woman of a Thousand Jobs. Because if there was a demeaning, dead-end, poorly paying position out there, Selby had held it at one time or another—often several of them at once—beginning at the age of fourteen, when she'd started running the dishwasher at her mother's diner after school.

Not that her mother had owned the diner, mind you. No, Sheila Hudson had only worked there as a waitress. But she'd finagled a job for Selby even before it was legal for Selby to work, because she'd told the owner her daughter was sixteen and needed a job. Though really it wasn't Selby so much who had needed the job. It was the entire Hudson family who had needed it. They had needed all the jobs—all the income—they could get, thanks to Frank Hudson's pre-occupation with Pernod and the ponies, two things that frequently left him without jobs himself.

Selby's three older brothers had all worked, too, in jobs no better paying—or personally fulfilling—than hers had been. But the boys had received one perk Selby hadn't. They had escaped the nonpaying position of housekeeper, which she had been required to perform alongside her mother as soon as she was old enough to wield a mop and broom. She was, after all, a girl. And that was pretty much all girls were good for. Never mind that they brought home an outside pay-check, too. Girls weren't nearly as important as boys were. All they were good for was taking care of the house and the men. And someday, if they were good at it, bringing more men into the world.

At least, that was what Selby's father would have had her believe, and that was what he taught her brothers to believe, too. Even her mother had bought into it, probably because Sheila had had a father just like her husband. But Selby had always been smarter than the average Hudson. And she'd known, deep down, that someday she'd do more than clean and cook and breed. Someday, some way, she was going to do something no one else in her family had ever even aspired to do.

Someday, Selby Hudson was going to travel all the way around the world. If she had to lie, beg, borrow, or steal to do it.

So far, though, she hadn't had to resort to any of those means. Because she'd resorted to hard work instead. It was, after all, what she knew. Even when she'd been working at the diner, she'd always siphoned off a little bit of her weekly pay before handing it over to her father, and had stashed a buck or two in a rusty coffee can that she kept wedged beneath a rotting tree root in the woods near the double-wide trailer the Hudsons had called home.

Since then, Selby had first paid her own way through col-lege and graduate school—God forbid Frank Hudson should waste what little money he had on the education of a female—and she'd supported herself since then by living as frugally as she could. She walked or rode the bus wherever she went, bought her clothes in thrift stores, even grew some of her own food in the backyard of the modest apartment building where she lived.

And she worked. Oh, boy, did Selby work. Her job teaching fourth grade at the Emerson Academy constituted the bulk of her income. But she also waited tables on Friday and Saturday nights at Trino's, an upscale restaurant in downtown Indianapolis. And she worked as a salesclerk on Saturday and Sunday afternoons at Mathilda's, a chic boutique two blocks from the restaurant that sold romantic—and sometimes exotic—gifts for women that cost way more than anything Selby would ever be able to afford for herself. And she picked up whatever odd, temporary jobs came her way, too, things she usually heard about from coworkers at the restaurant or shop. Catered parties. Deliveries. Proofreading. Secretarial. Anything that would earn her a few more dollars to sock away in her "Around the World" fund. Because on her thirtieth birthday, Selby intended to embark on a years-long journey of circumnavigation. She would see and do all the things she'd read about as a girl, whenever she could sneak away to the Indianapolis Free Public Library and hide in the reference section, stretched out alongside the *Encyclopedia Britannica*.

The job teaching returning ed had been a nice windfall, one she hadn't expected. For six hours a week—plus some late nights planning classes and grading homework—she was stashing a tidy sum into her traveling account. Of course, had she known she was going to wind up with a student like Thomas Brown . . .

Dammit. Why did thoughts of the man always seem to intrude, no matter what she happened to be thinking about? Only two weeks had passed since their first encounter, but it felt like two years of her life had gone by. She couldn't believe she still had five and a half more months of seeing him regularly. He'd behaved himself a little better after their first encounter, but he still pushed his luck—and Selby's buttons—every night they had class.

Always, he hung back and waited for everyone else in the class to leave, so that the two of them ended up alone. Always, he managed to corner Selby before she had a chance to escape. No matter how hard she tried to get away before everyone else was gone, she was never quite able to make it. Because Thomas Brown always had some question or comment or observation about whatever material they'd gone over that night, and he always needed for Selby to address it before the next class began. She'd try to encourage him to walk and talk at the same time, so that they could exit with the other students. But Thomas would forget something, or he'd drop his notebook and spill his notes everywhere, or he'd find some other way to detain them, or distract her, and suddenly, even though she'd promised herself it wouldn't happen again, Selby would be alone with him.

And once she was alone with him, she lost every scrap of sense she possessed. Because Thomas would look at her in ways that made her blood run hot. And he would say things to her. . . .

Since that first night, he hadn't been as bold or as brazen as he had been with the spanking comment. But he still managed to say . . . *things,* and say them in . . . *ways* that made Selby want to go home and stand under a cold shower. And then there was the way he looked at her, as if he wanted to remove every article of clothing she was wearing, piece by piece, then stretch her out on the desk and—

Ahem. There was just something about the way he looked at her, that was all.

She wasn't sure how he did it. There was just something about him that went way beyond Selby's personal sphere of experience. Not that her sphere of experience was especially large, but still. The man just oozed sex appeal simply by being in a room.

So Selby was understandably hesitant about entering her classroom for her fifth session with her returning ed students only two weeks after starting as their teacher. Even though she was ten minutes late, thanks to missing her usual bus and having to wait for the next one, she slowed her steps as she approached her classroom. She heard the voices of her students coming from inside, a jumble of overlapping murmurs, none of which she should have been able to identify individually. But she did identify one. Too clearly. Thomas Brown's rich, deep baritone seemed to rise above all the other voices, in much the same way that he himself seemed to rise above all the other members of the class.

It was odd, that. Selby was very good at reading people, thanks to having worked with so much of the public over the years. And she could recognize traits in each of her students that she was certain had contributed to their to dropping out of high school way back when. Insecurity, perhaps, or a feeling of unworthiness—heaven knew Selby identified with both of those herself. Some members of her class were shy, others sullen, and still others were sort of vague. But Thomas Brown was none of those things. On the contrary, he was utterly full of himself, supremely confident, and appeared to be completely in command of his destiny. He didn't seem like the kind of person who had ever had the sort of social or emotional or life problems that would lead him to drop out of high school.

So why was he in her class? What was his story?

Certainly she wondered about the stories of everyone else in the class, too. In addition to being able to read people well, Selby was intensely curious about them, probably also because she had worked with so much of the public over the years. It was yet another reason why she wanted to see the rest of the world and all its denizens. But she was more curious about Thomas Brown than she'd ever been about anyone. But she *couldn't* read him. No matter how hard she tried.

And it bothered her to realize just how much time she'd spent on that particular endeavor over the last couple of weeks, too. Not just because she was beginning to think she'd never figure him out, but because Selby wasn't normally one to waste time. And time spent thinking about Thomas Brown was definitely time wasted. Because no woman in her right mind would go courting trouble like him. Bad enough she had to try and teach trouble like him.

Hitching a final breath, Selby made herself enter her classroom, speaking loudly as she went so that her own voice would drown out the others and, hopefully, quiet them all.

"I'm sorry to be late," she said as she moved directly to her desk and settled her battered satchel atop it. "I missed my bus and had to catch a later one."

Hastily, she unbuttoned and shrugged out of her oversized, faded denim jacket, then pushed up the sleeves of her cognac-colored sweater, swept her long, denim skirt under her fanny, and took her seat. Although it was mid-October, the weather hadn't yet turned cold. Still, Selby had donned brown cable-knit tights and hiking boots to round out her ensemble. And she told herself she hadn't been trying to minimize her physical appearance when she'd done so. Which was strange, because for the past few years, she'd been really proud of her physical appearance. Mostly because, until a few years ago, she'd been so unhappy about it.

"I'll do my best to keep us on track," she told the class. "We should still get out of here on time."

And they did. Thanks to shortened breaks and Selby's good command of the class, she managed to cover all the necessary material by nine. What she didn't manage to do—again—was avoid being alone with Thomas Brown.

"Hey, Teach," he called from behind her as she bolted for the door, hoping that *this* time she'd make it through before he noticed she had fled. Ah, *left*. Before he noticed she had left.

With a resigned sigh, she halted and turned around. "Yes, Mr. Brown? Was there a question?"

Although Selby may have deliberately dressed to tone down her appearance, she decided Thomas Brown would never even try. Because, as always, his jeans were more rip than denim, and his white V-neck T-shirt bore a faint stain of oil—or maybe blood. She couldn't be sure. Along with the leather jacket and boots, not to mention the five o'clock Mack truck shadow, he looked . . .

She sighed. Dammit, he looked too yummy for words.

He smiled at her question. "Mr. Brown," he echoed. "It sounds funny when you call me that. Nobody calls me Mr. Brown."

"I can't imagine why not," Selby said, even though she could imagine why not perfectly. He may have been a lot of things, but a *Mr. Brown* wasn't one of them.

His smile kicked up a little at her comment. "Yeah, well, probably because I've never been in the position to be called Mr. Brown," he told her. "Including this one," he added pointedly. "Call me Thomas, please. That whole Mr. Brown thing is just too weird."

Selby neither acquiesced to nor rejected his request. She simply made a mental note to herself not to address Thomas Brown as anything at all.

He must have interpreted her silence as encouragement, however—then again, the man was so brazen, he'd probably interpret a sharp stick in the eye as encouragement— because he grinned that arrogant grin again and added, "I mean, there can't be *that* much difference in our ages. Just enough to make it, you know . . . interesting."

Selby told herself not to rise to the bait. So instead she repeated, "Was there a question?"

He nodded, but seemed disappointed that she hadn't played along with . . . whatever it was he was playing. "Can I call you Selby?" he asked.

"That's your question?"

"One of them."

"What's the other one?" she asked, again replying in neither the affirmative nor the negative. Telling him he could call her Selby might make him think she was interested in getting to know him better. But telling him *not* to call her Selby might make him think she was interested in getting to know him better. Which, of course, she was *not*. But he did seem like the kind of man who would buy in to that whole "women say one thing and mean another" propaganda. So it was probably best, when dealing with a man like him, to say as little as possible.

Naturally, though, that didn't work, either. "So can I?" he asked. "Call you Selby?"

Selby was about to tell him no, he couldn't call her that, and Ms. Hudson would be preferable, but he hurried on before she had a chance to say anything. Probably because he'd been able to tell she was about to say no, he couldn't call her that, and Ms. Hudson would be preferable.

"It's an interesting name, Selby," he said. "It's like the kind of name rich people would give to their daughter. Must have been your mother's family name or something."

Somehow Selby refrained from bursting into laughter over his speculation about the vast Hudson fortune. "Actually," she said, "it happened because of a screwup on my birth certificate. My mom meant to name me Shelby, but she accidentally misspelled it. Still groggy from the painkillers, I guess," she added by way of an explanation, even though it was just as likely because her mother honestly hadn't known how to spell Shelby. "But when she realized her mistake," Selby continued, "she decided she liked Selby better, so she kept it the way it had originally been recorded."

Actually, what had happened was that it would have cost her parents money to change the birth certificate, since the mistake had been her mother's, so her father had decided his daughter's name would stay the way it had originally been recorded. But there was no reason Thomas had to know that. Besides, Selby had always liked her name, and had enjoyed being the only girl she knew who had it. Even if it had been the object of ridicule on more than one occasion while she was growing up. Mostly because she was the only girl who had it.

The look Thomas gave her then was mildly speculative, though she couldn't imagine what he might be speculating about. And, really, she was probably better off not knowing.

In an effort to hasten her departure, she made a big deal of checking her watch and said, "Oh, gosh, I have to get going if I'm going to make my bus. It's the last number 6 bus of the day. If I miss it, I'll have to walk six blocks to catch the number 20 instead. And having missed one bus today already, I'm not in the mood to have it happen again."

And why on earth had she told him that? she wondered even as she concluded the announcement. She sounded like she was fishing for a ride home, which she most certainly was not. Not just because she was doing her best to avoid him, but also because she'd seen the vehicle he rode to class, and there was no way she would climb on the back of a motorcycle, especially when the driver was a rebel without any visible means of support. She was adventurous, not suicidal. Plus, by telling him she could take the 6 or 20 bus and still make it home, she had given him a clue as to where she lived. Granted, not a good one, but if he was halfway intelligent—and even after two weeks, she knew he was way above average in that regard, something else that only made her wonder why he'd dropped out of school—he could put 6 and 20 together and find out what neighborhoods they shared in common. Namely, hers.

"I have to go," she said quickly, before he could figure all that out.

"But I need to ask you something about tonight's lesson," he objected. "It'll just take a minute, I promise."

Selby glanced at her watch again. "I can spare five minutes," she told him. "But no more than that, or I'm screwed."

And somehow, she made herself not blush or close her eyes in embarrassment at the double entendre she'd inadvertently made.

Thomas, however, made no pretext of pretending he didn't notice it. "Well, gee, Teach, if you want me to take you home and have my way with you, just say so."

"Don't," she warned him, what little benevolence she'd begun to feel toward him evaporating completely. "Do not start this again. I told you I can have you removed from the program. And I am *not* interested, Mr. Brown."

He held up a hand, palm out, and even had the decency to say, "I'm sorry. Really, I apologize." And he honestly sounded like he meant it. "I have a bad habit of speaking before I think, especially when I'm talking to a beautiful woman. I didn't mean anything by it."

The hell he didn't, Selby thought. But she didn't belabor the point. And she did appreciate his apology. She even appreciated his compliment, due to the fact that she'd received precious few of those in her life. What she didn't appreciate was the steamy way he looked at her when he offered it. Mostly because it had the desired effect of making her feel steamy, too. Good heavens, what made the man so potent?

In an effort to hurry them along—and also in an effort to cool herself down—she said, "What did you need to ask me?"

"It's about the math," he said. "I'm still having trouble with the algebra."

"More than five minutes' worth of trouble?" Selby asked halfheartedly.

"Just problem number seven, that's it. Can you just show me again how you got the answer you did?"

Had it been any other student, Selby would have taken the extra time to offer a quick explanation. It would be rude—not to mention unfair—not to help Thomas if she could. Just because he made her heart flutter wildly by looking at her, and just because there was a dark, mysterious part of her that, even then, was wondering what it would be like to go home with Thomas Brown and let him have his way with her . . . well, that was no reason not to help him with his math. She just wished she could believe it was his math that he really wanted help with.

"Okay, quickly," she said, relenting.

But it ended up not being quick at all. Thomas simply could not seem to grasp what should have been a fairly easy principle for him. And if he couldn't get this, then he was going to struggle for the rest of the session. So, resigned to walking the six blocks necessary to catch the number 20 bus, Selby pulled out a clean sheet of paper and went over the work with him one more time. Then two more times. Then three. Then four. By the time he finally understood the problem—and smacked himself in the forehead good and hard for not having seen it before, *Man, that was so easy, am I an idiot or what?*—it was too late for Selby to catch the number 20 bus, too.

"Thank you so much for taking the extra time to explain all that," he said. "I really appreciate you staying late to—" He halted midsentence and gazed at her, obviously chagrined. "Late," he repeated. "Ah, hell. I've made you late, haven't I?" This time he was the one to glance down at his watch. "How long did we take? You didn't miss your bus, did you?"

"Actually, I missed both of my buses," Selby told him.

"But that's okay. I can call a cab. There's a pay phone in the school lobby."

"I'll walk with you, to make sure you get one," he said. "And I'll wait with you till it gets here."

"That's okay, you don't have to do th—"

"It's the least I can do," he interrupted. "I'm the one who made you late. Or better yet, let me give you a ride home."

Oh, no, Selby thought. *No, no, no, no, no.* That wasn't doable *at all.* "That's okay," she said. "A cab is fine."

Even if it was a complete waste of money. Her apartment was way too far for her to walk, especially after dark, since it wasn't in the greatest neighborhood to begin with. Oh, it was pretty much fine during the day, and it was cheap, which suited her needs perfectly. But it wasn't the kind of place to be out alone at night. Not if you were a law-abiding citizen who spent your evenings abiding the law, at any rate.

"Well, at least let me stay with you until I know you've got a ride," he said.

Gee, what a choice, Selby thought. Hang out alone in a deserted high school after dark, or hang out with a potential hoodlum in a deserted high school after dark. She had no idea what to do. So she did what she always did in such situations. She went with her gut.

Probably, she thought, Thomas Brown wasn't the kind of guy who would hurt people. Probably he was just a smart-ass. Probably she'd be safer with him than without him. Probably.

But then she looked at his face again, at the jet hair that tumbled rebelliously over his forehead, at the dark brown eyes that were bottomless, mysterious, perilous, at the full, seductive mouth that hooked into a smile that was at once charming and menacing.

And she realized it wasn't her personal safety she was worried about. What worried her was that, at the moment, looking at Thomas Brown, her personal safety was the last thing on her mind. Because something about him made her feel very impulsive and very irresponsible. And that was the last way she needed to be feeling. Especially around a man like him. Because he was impulsive and irresponsible, too. Worse than that—he was downright reckless. And to a woman like Selby, recklessness was a romantic fantasy. To a man like him, recklessness would be a way of life.

"Okay," she said in spite of her misgivings. Because, truth be told, her misgivings really weren't all that strong. Which was something else she should be worried about, she told herself. But she couldn't quite bring herself to feel that, either. "You can walk me to the phone and make sure I get a cab. Thank you," she added belatedly, trying not to sound ungrateful. "I appreciate it."

And strangely, Selby realized that that was true. She did appreciate having Thomas around for a bit longer. What she didn't appreciate was just how good it made her feel that he would be.

Pax eyed Selby Hudson from the other side of a Formica-topped table in a downtown diner, marveling again at his amazing good luck this evening. Because it certainly hadn't been his usual skill with women that had made this little interlude possible, since Selby Hudson seemed to be remarkably immune to that. Go figure. No, it was an amazing series of plain dumb luck that had won him the most glorious of prizes: a cup of coffee with her. Because she appreciated him having given her a ride home, and the least she could do was buy him a cup of coffee, and no, of course it wasn't because she didn't want him to know which of the four buildings on the corners of the intersection where they had parked was her apartment building, don't be silly. She just wanted to repay him somehow, and he looked like he could use a cup of coffee, and gosh, so could she.

So here Pax sat, in the kind of restaurant he would normally *never* patronize, in a neighborhood he would never have visited under circumstances that didn't involve wanting to get robbed and beaten senseless, curling his fingers around a chipped stoneware mug that the dishwasher hadn't managed to quite rid of lipstick. And he was *happy* about it. What he couldn't figure out was, why?

Oh, yeah. Because he was lucky, that was why.

Lucky that Selby had missed her bus the first time that day. Lucky that she'd told him about it, thereby giving him the idea of making her miss her bus again. Lucky that the phone in the school lobby had been vandalized beyond repair—and he hadn't even had to be the one to do it. Lucky that she hadn't had any coins to make a phone call for a cab company once they had found a phone. Lucky that she'd believed him when he told her he didn't have any change either.

Hell, he was even lucky someone had invented the cell phone in the first place, thereby heralding the demise of the pay telephone so that they'd had to walk four blocks before even finding one—though he couldn't imagine why Selby wouldn't have a cell phone herself. Even teenagers carted around cheap phones these days. And a woman who worked nights and walked the streets alone should definitely have one in case of emergencies. Or in case she met a man who might be looking to compromise her. Still, he knew better than to complain, because he'd used that four-block walk to lull Selby Hudson into a false sense of security and convince her that he was a good guy. And he was *really* lucky she'd bought that.

But then, Pax had always been lucky. Well, since college anyway. And he knew how to use good luck to his advantage. Always.

"You really didn't have to do this," he said as the waitress dropped a handwritten check onto the scarred tabletop and walked away, change jingling in the stained, once-white apron tied around her waist.

"I wanted to," Selby told him. And she sounded like she was telling the truth, too. "I appreciate you giving me a ride."

Pax chuckled at that. Appreciate, hell. She'd looked like she was going to faint dead away when he straddled the big bike and kicked the starter into gear and yelled for her to climb aboard. For a minute, he'd thought she was going to decline and brave the streets alone. So he'd goaded her, dared her, called her chicken, and she'd immediately set her jaw and cocked her chin and swung her leg over the seat. He'd made a mental note that Selby Hudson didn't like being called a coward, knowing he could use that little tidbit of info again later. And then he'd reveled in the feel of her slender arms wrapping tentatively around his torso.

And he recalled with some astonishment the splash of heat that had doused his midsection when she'd touched him. He hadn't been prepared for that at all.

"So how'd you get into teaching night school?" he asked now, pushing the memory away until he could ruminate on it further, later, when he was alone.

She shrugged, rubbing the pad of her thumb over the handle of her own chipped stoneware mug, directing her gaze at her coffee, at his coffee, at a gash on the tabletop, at the clock on the wall to their right, out the window to their left. Anywhere but at Pax. "Same way I got into teaching day school," she told him. "I answered an ad."

"You teach during the day?" he asked, wondering why that surprised him. Of course she'd have a day job, he told himself. And the fact that it involved teaching, too, made complete sense. "Where do you teach?"

"I teach fourth grade," she told him, not answering his question, but enlightening him just the same.

"Fourth grade?" he repeated, unable to mask his surprise.

She did look at him then, but her gaze met his only long enough to let him know she found his bewilderment bewildering. "You sound surprised," she said before glancing away again, as if even that small measure of eye contact had made her uneasy.

"I am surprised. I guess I see you more teaching high school than elementary school."

"I like teaching little kids," she said, smiling, her gaze still fixed on the gash in the table, which she began to trace with the pad of her thumb. And something in her smile tethered a breath in Pax's chest for a minute, long enough to make little dots dance before his eyes, long enough to make his brain feel fuzzy. He had thought her beautiful since the day he'd walked into class, but when she smiled like that, Selby Hudson was downright dazzling.

"Why?" he asked.

She shrugged again, but she continued to smile and worry the scar on the table. "They're just fun, that's all. In fourth grade, they're still pretty naive, but they're so curious about everything, and they want straight answers. You have to be honest with kids that age. They know when you're lying to them."

He eyed her with much consideration, wondering if there was some underlying significance to what she had said. Nah, he decided. She was just stating a fact, that was all. She wasn't overly hung up on honesty. And she sure as hell didn't suspect he was being dishonest with her.

"So why did you become a teacher in the first place?" he asked.

She didn't answer right away, only continued to trace her thumb over the gash in the table, as if in doing so she might somehow be able to heal it. Finally, she said, "I don't know. Because I was curious when I was a kid, too, I guess. I always liked learning new things. So now I like helping other kids learn new things, too."

For some reason, Pax didn't like her answer. It made him feel . . . well, not guilty, he thought. But . . . uncomfortable. Yeah, that was it. So he did what he always did when faced with something that made him uncomfortable—he changed the subject. "Did you grow up in Indianapolis?"

She shook her head. "Southern Indiana. A small town. You've probably never heard of it."

"Try me."

Her gaze flew to his, and there was nothing timid or tentative in her expression now. "I'd rather not," she said coolly. "Thanks, anyway."

Oh, dammit, Pax thought. *Here we go again.* "Selby, I didn't mean it like that," he told her. And he hadn't. "Jesus, I've never seen anyone more skittish than you."

"Oh, please," she countered indignantly. "I think I have a right to be skittish around you, after the way you've been since walking into my classroom that first night. My God, you asked me to *spank* you."

Her voice had risen in direct proportion with her indignation, Pax noticed, and by the time she came to the word *spank,* what few people were sitting in the diner had all looked her way, and a dead silence settled over the place. Selby blushed furiously when she realized what she had done, then she folded her elbows onto the table and dropped her head into her hands, something that made Pax's chuckles evolve into full-fledged laughter. He couldn't help himself. She was just so . . . cute.

"Please don't laugh at me," she said softly.

And immediately, his laughter stopped. Because there was something in her voice when she spoke that just commanded him to. "I'm not laughing at you," he said softly.

"Yes, you are."

"No, I'm not," he assured her.

"Then why are you laughing?" she asked, her voice muffled, since it was coming from behind the hands that still cradled her head.

Pax smiled. And before he could stop himself, he heard himself saying, "Because you make me feel good, that's why." And only after voicing the sentiment did he realize it was true.

For a minute, he was afraid she was going to think he was hitting on her again, when in fact that wasn't what he was doing at all. He was just stating a fact, pure and simple. Selby did make him feel good. And he couldn't remember the last person who had done that.

Gingerly, she moved her hands and lifted her head to look at him, her long bangs hanging down in her eyes and making her seem vulnerable somehow. She looked so young, he thought, not for the first time. She had to be fresh out of college and almost totally ignorant of the world. But there were times, too, when he would swear she was his age or older.

She said nothing, but she dropped her hands to the tabletop and sat up straight, curling her finger around the handle of her mug once again. She seemed to want to pretend the last few minutes hadn't happened, so Pax did, too. And like Selby, he hooked a finger through the handle of his mug and lifted it to his mouth for a sip. But he nearly spat out the mouthful of coffee when Selby asked him what she did next.

"So what do you do for a living?"

Damn. He should have realized their conversation would eventually turn to him. But he hadn't been prepared for that at all. Somehow, he swallowed his coffee, but it was with obvious difficulty, something Selby noted.

"I'm sorry," she apologized. "Did I say something I shouldn't have?"

Pax quickly shook his head. "No, not at all. It's just that I . . . um . . . ah . . . I mean . . ."

Realization seemed to dawn on her then, because she

blushed again, albeit less furiously this time. "Oh, I'm sorry," she said again. "I didn't mean to embarrass you. I mean, if you're unemployed, that's—"

"I'm not *unemployed*," Pax said, stung that she would think such a thing. Jesus, he was considered one of the hardest-working men in America. He headed up a Fortune 100 company. He'd built it up from scratch, practically with his bare hands, and he toiled ninety hours a week sometimes to keep it running. How could she possibly think he was *unemployed*?

Gee, Einstein, maybe because you're in an adult returning education class, and you've deliberately misled her about your true identity, and given her absolutely no reason to think otherwise?

Mmm, could be.

"I mean," he tried to recover, "it's just that . . . um . . . ah . . . I mean . . ." Okay, so maybe his attempt at recovery failed abysmally. At least he'd tried. Not that he usually had to even try, since, normally, he could bluff his way out of anything. With Selby, though, his brain had turned to oatmeal. That was probably significant, but he didn't want to think about why.

"That's okay, Thomas," she said, calling him by the name no one else had ever used until now. "You don't have to be embarrassed. There's no shame in being unemployed in times like this. At least you've gone back to school for your diploma. That will make you a more desirable prospect."

"Will it?" he asked, hoping she meant what she surely did not.

"For employers, I mean," she said.

"Oh."

"I, um, I should go," she said abruptly. "It's late, and I have to work tomorrow."

She stood, obviously intending to call it a night. So Pax stood, too, wishing she'd end it with him, knowing that wasn't likely. Not yet, anyway. Though he was confident he'd be spending the night with her soon. And not just one night, either. But as many nights as he wanted. Until he grew tired of her and moved on to someone else, which was what invariably happened.

For tonight, though, he resigned himself to going home alone. Not that he could take Selby home with him, anyway, because then she'd find out who he really was, and he couldn't have that. He intended to only enjoy her for a short time, after all, and then toss her aside like yesterday's newspaper. He needed for her to know him as Thomas Brown, jobless high school dropout, not T. Paxton Brown, billionaire. Because if she knew he was T. Paxton Brown, billionaire, she could come looking for him after he was finished with her and demand retribution of the financial sort. No way was he going to get bogged down in something like that again.

It had nothing to do with his suspicion that if Selby knew he was T. Paxton Brown, billionaire, she wouldn't like him, the way she might like Thomas Brown, jobless high school dropout. And Pax decided not to wonder why that bothered him so much.

"Here, at least let me get the tip," he said. He reached into his pocket and pulled out four quarters, then tossed them onto the table.

Selby watched the shiny silver coins skitter across the Formica, then she looked up at him, her lips parted in surprise.

"What?" he asked.

She pointed at the quarters. "Earlier, when I needed to make a call at the pay phone, you told me you didn't have any change."

This time it was Pax's turn to blush. What was weird was that he hadn't blushed in nearly twenty years, and this was such a minor infraction, it hardly called for such a thing. "Uh . . ." he said.

But to his surprise, Selby smiled. That same dazzling smile to which she had treated him when talking about how much she enjoyed teaching. She said nothing, though, only turned and made her way to the diner exit. Having the advantage of surprise, she was through it before Pax could even shrug on his jacket and make a move to catch up with her. And by the time he stepped outside, the street was empty, save a couple huddling in a doorway across the street. But whether they were saying good night or conducting business, Pax couldn't have said. It was just that kind of neighborhood. Neither of them was Selby, however, of that he was certain.

He looked at the building directly in front of him across the street, at the one to his left, and at the one catty-corner to where he stood. And he waited. After a minute, in the one to his left, on the sixth floor, a light went on in a window, drawing his gaze. And then a woman moved to that window, silhouetted against the light. A woman in a bulky denim jacket, he saw before she drew the curtains together. A woman with chin-length black hair. Selby Hudson had made it home safely after all.

And now Pax knew exactly where to find her.

EIGHT

THE WEEK THAT FOLLOWED MICHAEL'S self-inflicted outing at Hannah's house was damned near the worst week he'd ever endured. Worse than the one he'd spent holed up in a stinking ghetto while keeping tabs on a potential defector. Worse than hell week at the end of basic training for OPUS. Worse than any given week while Alex had had colic. Worse, even, than the week he had discovered that his wife was having an affair with what had passed for his best friend. Because in the week that followed Michael's self-inflicted outing, he had to watch Hannah cozy up to Adrian more and more every day. And he learned pretty quickly that he cared a lot more for Hannah than he'd begun to suspect.

What the hell was she thinking, to insist on being part of this thing? he asked himself for perhaps the millionth time since that fateful afternoon at her house. He still couldn't believe she had been so determined to wedge herself into the operation. And he really couldn't believe the One Whose Name Could Not Be Spoken had gone for it. Michael had done his best to talk the guy out of it, but noooooo. . . .

Hell, he'd thought he would be called to the mat by his boss for telling Hannah the truth. He'd figured the guys upstairs would want his head on a platter, and that they'd for sure relieve him of his duties. Not that *that* had had anything to do with his decision to tell Hannah the truth about the situation, no way. But No-Name had been even more determined to include Hannah directly in the operation than Hannah had been. He'd pointed out there was no agent who could get closer to Adrian than Hannah. Since she'd be there at Adrian's invitation, there was little chance he'd become suspicious of her presence. No-Name had thought Michael was nuts for taking exception to the plan.

So now here Michael was, sitting in his van again, listening in on Hannah's life again. But this time, she knew he was listening, because she was wearing the microphone he'd planted in a strand of phony pearls. And unlike before, Michael didn't want to hear what was going on. Because she wasn't splashing in the bathtub. And she wasn't singing the birthday song to herself. She was having dinner with Adrian at a five-star restaurant, and the guy couldn't have been more obvious if he'd affixed a lit neon sign to his forehead that blinked off and on with the message, *I want to diddle you.*

So far, Adrian had fed Hannah oysters and caviar by hand, had insisted they share an order of truffles, had ordered—for both of them—the salmon, with artichokes and asparagus, and had opted for the cherry chocolate torte for dessert. According to Michael's admittedly limited knowledge of aphrodisiacs, they ought to be rutting and bleating like mountain goats under the table any minute. And that was something Michael *really* didn't want to listen to.

He hated this. Hated it even more than when Hannah hadn't realized he was listening in on her. Because he didn't know Adrian anymore, and hadn't for years, and he couldn't be sure how far the guy would go. Even when the two of them had been partners, Michael had never completely trusted him.

And before that, when they were kids, he'd always felt

like there was something in Adrian that was just . . . wrong. He'd been such an angry kid, so resentful of everyone else. A lot of that was due to his upbringing, Michael knew. Adrian had never known his father, and his mother hadn't been home much. She'd worked as a salesclerk during the day, and at night . . . well, as an adult man, Michael realized she'd been working then, too. But when they were kids, he and Adrian both had figured she was out on dates. One date after another. With a different man every time. And if Michael had eventually figured out what she was really doing, he was certain Adrian had, too.

Still, a lot of the kids at their school had come from lousy neighborhoods and broken homes, and they hadn't become criminal masterminds. Adrian, though, had always felt as if he deserved so much more than he had. So much more than anyone had. No, he'd felt as if he were *entitled* to it. And maybe he had deserved more, Michael thought. But that didn't mean it was okay for him to go out and take whatever he wanted.

Which was what he had discovered Adrian was doing one day when they were both around twelve. They'd gone into a drugstore to buy comic books. Well, Michael was going to buy them, since Adrian didn't have any money. Adrian never had any money. But that was okay, because Michael, the dutiful son who completed all his chores, always had his allowance. And he was always willing to share whatever he bought with his friend.

That day, though, Adrian hadn't wanted to share. He had wanted comic books, however. And even though he hadn't had any money, he'd helped himself to a few anyway. Michael had watched in astonishment as his friend slipped three of them under his jacket and started to make his way to the front of the store. He'd gotten caught by the owner on the way out, naturally. And Michael had been fingered as an accomplice. That day, they'd gotten off with a warning and a report to their parents, and an admonition to never set foot in the store again. That hadn't kept Adrian from stealing, though. He'd just opted for other venues.

They'd been forced to put their friendship on hiatus when Michael went to Princeton and Adrian stayed in-state, at IU in Bloomington. Truth be told, though, by that point Michael had needed a break from Adrian. Adolescence had brought a wildness to his friend, an almost amorality that had manifested itself in reckless, even dangerous behavior. Adrian had always been in some kind of trouble, whether at school or at home or at the computer store where he had worked. Michael knew for a fact that Adrian had become a regular lawbreaker, everything from stealing cars to burglarizing homes to taking home smuggled stock from the store where he worked. But not once—not once—did he get caught.

Yet Michael hadn't been able to sever his ties to Adrian completely, even knowing he was bad news. He didn't want to abandon his friend the way so many other people in Adrian's life had. And he'd still kind of liked the guy, even with his outlaw tendencies. Adrian was smart and funny, and he liked the same things Michael did. Of course, that last trait would prove less attractive later, when Adrian started liking Michael's wife. But until then, despite Adrian's borderline behavior, Michael remained his friend. So much so that when he'd been recruited for OPUS, he'd immediately thought of Adrian, too, thought it would be a career to which his friend would be well suited. And he'd hoped, too, that maybe going through the training at OPUS would curb some of Adrian's wildness—or, at least, offer a more acceptable outlet for it. He'd hoped Adrian would channel his anger and resentment at society in general into a more specific enemy—the threat to his country. And for years, that was exactly what Adrian did.

But when all was said and done, Michael should have realized that Adrian would never pledge allegiance to any-

one but himself. It shouldn't have surprised him when
Adrian turned on all of them, or that he'd used Tatiana the
way he did—to hurt Michael in a way that he'd never been
hurt before. Michael had been forced to realize then that
Adrian hated everyone, even the people he'd chosen for his
friends. And maybe Michael, by getting closer to Adrian than
anyone else had, became the most hated of all.

Michael had hoped that by leaving OPUS, all of that
would stay in the past. For five years, he'd pretty much convinced himself that it had. His feelings for Adrian now were
only a shadow of what they had once been. Time had
blunted the edges of Michael's fury. And he'd decided that
what Adrian was, at his core, was bitter. Probably even
Adrian didn't know why. But that not knowing why was precisely what made him so dangerous. And it was why he had
to be stopped. Because Adrian would always be bitter. He
would always be angry. And that bitterness and anger would
only grow. Just as it had grown from a childish resentment
into an adolescent rage. As an adult, Adrian might have better control over his feelings, but his feelings were still the
same. He still felt like he was better than anyone else. And
he still felt entitled. And he would still do whatever he had to
do to get whatever he wanted.

Which was why Michael feared for Hannah's safety. If
Adrian decided he wanted her—and after the way he'd pursued her this evening, there could be no doubting that he
wanted her—he wouldn't stop until he had her. Whether she
gave her consent or not. All Michael could do at this point
was hope that tonight wouldn't be the night Adrian decided
to collect. Then again, if it was the night, at least Michael
would be around to stop him.

Oh, hell, he thought then when he heard Adrian's voice
coming through the headphones again. Now he was ordering
anisette to go with the torte. Wasn't that overdoing it? Hannah
had to be on to him by now. She was too smart for this crap.

And that was another weird thing. Adrian never went for smart women, unless they happened to be the wife of a friend. He went for women he could manipulate. Women were nothing more to him than a repository for his over-whelming libido. So why had he taken an interest in Hannah?

"Really, Adrian," Hannah was saying now, and Michael adjusted the volume so that he could hear her better. "No anisette for me. I don't have room. As it is you're going to have to eat the torte all by yourself."

Yeah, that's it, Hannah, Michael thought. *Tell him to eat it.*

"Nonsense," Adrian replied. "There's enough here for both of us."

"If I eat that," Hannah said, "I'll be awake all night."

Silence met her comment, but Michael suspected Adrian well enough to know he'd be throwing her one of those come-hither smiles of his that should have made any right-thinking woman run screaming in horror in the opposite direction, but which had always worked amazingly well for the guy. And Michael was sure that was what Adrian had been doing when he heard him reply, "That's all right. I can think of a few ways to pass the time."

Michael rolled his eyes. Great. The diddle sign was blinking again.

Somehow he managed to listen to the rest of the revolting dinner conversation without losing his own dinner, then he discreetly followed Adrian's car back to Hannah's house. He parked the van a block over, close enough that he was still within listening range, but out of sight. Then he listened to more revolting conversation as Adrian walked her to the front door and did his best to wangle an invitation inside. And then—then—Michael had to listen to the most revolt-ing thing of all.

He had to listen while Adrian kissed her good night.

And it wasn't one of those namby-pamby kisses on the cheek he'd hoped it would be, either. No, to make it look good, to prevent Adrian from becoming suspicious, Hannah kissed him good night the way she would kiss a guy she wanted to make her own. With a soft laugh, and a quiet murmur of acquiescence, and the rustle of fabric that implied the arrival of much touching, though Michael was confident she would keep it all above the waist.

At least, Michael hoped that was why Hannah kissed Adrian that way. Then again, Adrian had charmed an awful lot of women in his time. And Hannah had been seeing him before Michael entered the picture. Oh, sure, she'd sworn there was nothing serious going on between them—and Michael believed her—but she *had* been attracted to Adrian. Otherwise she wouldn't have been seeing him, however superficially. So when Adrian's breathing starting coming in great, hulking gasps the way it did just then, that was no reason for Michael to think Hannah was getting more into the kiss than she should be, right?

Because this was Hannah, he reminded himself. She wasn't the type of woman to be charmed by a man she knew was trouble. Adrian could pull out every amorous weapon in his arsenal, and she'd remain unmoved, right?

Right?

So then why was she moaning the way she was just then? And why was her breathing suddenly as raspy and unbridled as Adrian's? Just what the hell was going on out there?

Knowing he shouldn't, but unable to stop himself, Michael jerked off the headphones and exited the van, leaving the tapes running, but locking up behind himself. Then he stole between the houses that abutted Hannah's backyard and ducked through a shrubbery that landed him behind her detached garage. It was dark by now, but there was enough streetlight available to cause him problems if he wasn't careful. He crept across the backyard and edged the side of the house that lay in shadow, halting when he came to the front corner. Now he could hear Hannah and Adrian without the benefit of the microphone. But it still sounded pretty revolting.

Risking a peek around the corner, he saw them, and his stomach pitched at the sight. Adrian's back was to him, but he had pulled Hannah close—too close . . . too goddamned close—-and Hannah's arms were roped around his waist. Michael clenched his hands into fists, and ground his teeth together hard. Then he forced himself to pull back, pressing himself against the brick, and waited for the torture to end. And he told himself that as hard as this was for him to stomach, it had to be even worse for Hannah.

Finally, though, it did end. The kiss, anyway. Adrian's cajoling, however, had just begun.

"Come on, Hannah," he said. "Let me come in for a little while."

"Adrian, I can't," she said. "I wish I could, but I can't. I have to work tomorrow."

"So do I," he told her. "But that doesn't have to spoil our fun unless we let it."

"I'm sorry, Adrian," Hannah told him. "Maybe next time. On the weekend."

"The reception is coming up," he reminded her.

"Let's plan to spend more time together that night, then," she said.

And that faint promise seemed to appease Adrian. For now. But OPUS damned well better figure out what the hell was going on before then, Michael thought, or else Adrian would collect on that promise, however faint. Michael had until next Friday to keep Hannah safe, he thought. Because Adrian Padgett didn't take well to people who went back on their word. Never mind that he was an expert at that himself.

With one final, parting kiss, Adrian left, fairly skipping down the walkway as he went. The prick. Michael heard Hannah open her front door and go inside, then close it behind herself. And he heard her slide the deadbolt into place. He waited until Adrian's car pulled away from the curb, counted slowly to fifty, then circled to the back of the house. Hannah might think her evening was over. But Michael had one more thing he needed to do before he could call it a night.

Hannah had stripped off the dress she'd worn to dinner with Adrian and tossed it into the garbage—she never wanted to wear it again, since he had pawed all over it—when she heard a soft knock at her back door. It couldn't be Adrian, because he wouldn't go to the back door. Nor would he knock. Had he returned for what he had so reluctantly surrendered tonight, he wouldn't let something so crass as a locked door stop him. She lifted a flowered silk robe off its hook inside the closet door and pulled it on over her slip, then strode barefoot to the back door and pushed aside the curtain to see who was there.

Michael. She should have known. He'd probably come to debrief her. Or maybe he wanted to pick up where Adrian left off and, um, debrief her. If so, then the joke was on him, because she was actually wearing bikini panties. She winced inwardly at the lame attempt at humor. She was getting punchy. Or maybe she was just trying to think of something—anything—that would take her mind off of the evening she'd just spent with Adrian.

Michael, she was sure, had come to do the first kind of debriefing. Because that was what they did to people after completing a mission, right?

She still couldn't believe she was involved in this . . . this . . . this *Mission: Implausible*. All she'd ever wanted was a normal life. A secure life. An uneventful life. She'd spent years trying to win that for herself and had finally accomplished it. She should have just butted out and let Michael and his OPUS pals do their jobs. But she'd gone and offered herself up for the task, too, even though it was a job for which she was completely untrained and in no way prepared. What had she been thinking, to volunteer herself for this?

She'd been thinking about her kids, she recalled. She'd been thinking about the school. She'd thought she could avert any trouble that might befall the Emerson community. If Adrian was as bad as Michael said he was, she wanted to do whatever was within her power to stop him. Before he did something that would, at best, compromise the school, and, at worst, destroy it.

And now that she was involved, no matter how bad things got, she was determined to see it through to the end. Hannah Frost was no quitter. When she decided to do something, she did it until she got it right. She just hoped this something was the right something. Then again, having Michael appear at her back door just then did feel strangely right.

He didn't come in, only stood on her back porch in the darkness, his hands shoved deep into the pockets of a leather bomber jacket that was zipped halfway up over blue jeans and a navy blue sweater. She liked this more casual side of him, thought he was more suited to it than to the suits she'd initially seen him wearing.

And the more she'd seen of him, the more she'd realized how much she liked him, in spite of his having misled her, in spite of her having misjudged him. Yes, he was different from other men she had known, and yes, he was more ruthless than she cared to admit. But that was probably why he had such a potent effect on her. She just didn't know yet if it was so potent she'd never recover from it.

He didn't say hello as he stepped over the threshold, didn't ask about her dinner with Adrian. Instead, he strode to the center of the kitchen and turned around. And he said, very softly, "Are you okay?"

Hannah pushed the back door closed and crossed her arms over her midsection, telling herself it was to ward off the chill of the night air that had scurried in behind him, and not because she suddenly felt so vulnerable. She nodded in response to his question, even though she felt anything but okay. She hadn't thought it would be difficult to insinuate herself into Adrian's life. After all, she'd already been a part of his life, in a way. She hadn't thought it would feel much different. Now, though, she realized she hadn't been thinking at all. She'd been so shell-shocked that afternoon by everything Michael had told her that she hadn't been capable of coherent thought. She'd reacted, that was all. And if she was starting to regret that reaction, well . . . that was just too bad. She was in it. She would finish it. That was all there was to it.

"You sure you're okay?" Michael asked her again.

She nodded once more, but knew it was with less conviction this time. "I'm fine," she said, the words coming out more quietly than she intended. So she tried again, saying more loudly, "I'm fine. Really."

"You don't look fine."

"Well, I am fine."

"Hannah . . ."

"Just drop it, Michael, okay? Please?" But even she thought she sounded pretty pathetic the way she said it.

She thought he would let it go, but he expelled a sound of unmistakable irritation.

"What?" she said, suddenly feeling defensive.

He shrugged, but there was nothing casual in the gesture. "Nothing," he said, his voice clipped.

"No, you want to say something," Hannah said. "What is it?"

He eyed her levelly for a minute, as if he were deciding whether or not he should say what he obviously wanted to say.

"Come on," she cajoled. "What is it?"

He blew out another one of those exasperated breaths, and said, "Okay, fine. It's just that this part of the assignment tonight was nothing, but you look like you've been through a war zone. I'm worried you're not going to be able to hold your own for the rest of the operation."

"Nothing?" she echoed incredulously. "You think what I did tonight was *nothing*?"

"Oh, please," he said. "You had a three-hour dinner at a five-star restaurant, and you didn't even have to pay for it. Oysters, caviar, champagne, salmon." He removed his hands from his pockets to tick off each course on his fingers. "Good God, Hannah, we've had operatives go for weeks in isolated areas with nothing but powdered rations and water to drink. You wouldn't last five minutes in a situation like that."

"No, I wouldn't," she agreed. "But this isn't a job I chose to do."

"The hell it isn't," he countered. "I *told* you to stay out of it, but you wouldn't listen. And hell, you even got a good night kiss out of it."

Oh, now, *that* was going too far, Hannah thought. She gaped at him. "You talk like you think I enjoyed that."

He chuckled derisively. "I was listening in, remember? I heard how you reacted, Hannah. You think I'm going to believe you were repulsed by that kiss?"

"Yes, that's exactly what you're supposed to believe. It *was* repulsive." She couldn't believe he was acting this way. "God, how can you think I *enjoyed* it?"

"You sure the hell sounded like you were enjoying yourself."

"Oh, please," she spat. "The only way I managed to kiss him without becoming physically ill was to pretend he was—"

It was only at the last possible moment that Hannah was able to cut herself off before she revealed something to Michael she absolutely did not want to reveal. But she was too late. He'd heard enough to want to hear more.

"Was to pretend he was what?" he asked.

"Nothing," she snapped. "I didn't pretend anything."

"No, you were going to say something, Hannah. What was it? You only managed not to get sick by pretending Adrian was . . . ?"

In an effort to put as much distance between them as she could—and also to stall, because she *really* didn't want to pursue this line of questioning—she moved to the other side of the kitchen and leaned back against the counter, crossing her arms over herself again. "I pretended he was someone else, all right?" she said curtly, hoping that would satisfy him.

Fat chance.

"Who?" Michael asked. "Who did you pretend he was?"

She fluttered her hand in front of herself dismissively. "Just someone else, that's all."

"Who, dammit?" he insisted. And she knew he wasn't going to stop until he had the answer he wanted. The answer, she had to admit, that was true.

"You," she finally said softly. "I pretended he was you, okay? There. Are you satisfied?"

He looked at her from his place on the other side of the kitchen, bathed in the pale yellow light of the bulb burning over the stove. He shook his head. "No. I'm not satisfied. Not by a long shot."

And then he was across the kitchen and standing in front of her. She started to say something, but he cupped his hands over her shoulders and dipped his head to hers, and before she could even catch her breath, he was kissing her. Softly, at first, his lips brushing tenderly across hers, feathery little touches that lit tiny fires throughout her body. Then he moved his hands to her face, curving his palms over her cheeks, threading his fingers into the hair at her temples. He tilted her head to the side a bit and swooped in again, angling his mouth this time so that he could kiss her more deeply.

Unable to help herself—not wanting to help herself—
Hannah slid her arms around his waist, silently cursing the
barrier of his jacket, but loving the feel of the soft leather
beneath her fingertips. It was almost like touching his skin,
except that his skin would be warm, not cold, and it would
move beneath her fingers where she touched him. He
smelled of sweet tanned hide and strong black coffee, and
she knew she would never be able to inhale those scents
again without thinking of him. He sighed, an echo of her
own, then roped an arm around her waist to pull her closer,
tangling his other hand in the ponytail that fell between her
shoulder blades. Then he was freeing her hair from the ribbon that bound it, and threading his fingers through the long
tresses, bunching a fistful in his hand to bring it to her nape
before letting it cascade back down as he seized another
handful.

Again and again he kissed her, his hands sweeping over
her back, her waist, her hips, until Hannah was unaware of
anything but him. It just felt so good to hold him and be held
by him. She never wanted to let go. She lifted her own hand,
curving her fingers over his nape, but the moment she
touched him, skin on skin, he pulled back.

He didn't, however, let her go.

"There," he said as he lifted his head and gazed into her
eyes. "Take that one to bed with you tonight. Forget about
the one you suffered from Adrian."

For a minute, she honestly wasn't sure what he was talking about. Then she smiled and asked, "Who's Adrian?"

Michael smiled back, then ducked his head to hers again.
This time, though, he kept it brief, taking her mouth once,
twice, three times in succession. And then, with obvious
reluctance, he released her, and turned to make his way out.

So *that* was how they debriefed people after a mission,
Hannah thought vaguely as she watched him go. No wonder
so many people wanted to be spies.

He pulled the back door open and stepped through it, and, for a moment, she feared he would leave without looking back, without saying good-bye. "Michael?" she called out softly before he could close the door behind himself.

She noted when he turned to look at her that his cheeks were flushed, his breathing was ragged, his hair was a mess, and he was in no way steady on his feet. And she smiled to know she had the same effect on him that he had on her.

"Yeah?" he said.

She had been thinking there was something very important she needed to tell him, but she couldn't quite wrap her mind around the appropriate words. So she settled on a quiet but heartfelt, "Thank you."

"You're welcome," he said. Then he added, "Have dinner with me tomorrow night. Me and Alex. At our house."

Her first impulse was to tell him no, that she couldn't, that it wouldn't be appropriate for the director of the Emerson Academy to have dinner with the father of one of its students. Then she remembered how she had originally told Adrian she couldn't have dinner with him, because it wouldn't be appropriate for the director of the Emerson Academy to have dinner with a member of its board of directors. And there was no way she'd show Adrian preferential treatment.

So she said, "That would be nice. Thank you for that, too."

"I'll leave work early, and we'll pick you up after school," he said. "That way we'll have part of the afternoon, too."

"No, that's out of your way," she told him. "And I usually stay for a while after the kids have gone. I'll drive over to your house when I finish up. Around four? Four-thirty? That way Alex will have time to do his homework first."

And that way, she added to herself, no one at school would see them leaving together.

"Then we'll expect you by four-thirty," he said. "Bring an appetite."

Not a problem, she wanted to say. Especially not after that kiss. Then she realized he was talking about an appetite for *dinner*. At least, she was pretty sure he was talking about that. Alex would be home, after all. But then she noticed how he was looking at her, and she found herself reconsidering. Alex had to go to bed sometime, right? But would he be the only one doing so?

Oh, stop, she told herself. She would *not* be going to bed with Michael, regardless of whether his son was home or not. It was dinner, that was all. And it would serve the same purpose as the kiss just had—to give her a better memory to replace the dinner she'd had with Adrian. Michael was being polite, that was all.

And he was also working, she reminded herself.

Don't let him charm you, she told herself. *You thought Adrian was charming, too, at first, and look what he turned out to be.*

Deep down, she thought, Michael really wasn't all that different from Adrian. Two sides of the same coin. There had been a time when the men were virtually two of a kind, working side by side for the same organization. Eventually one went one way, and one went the other. But they'd both started from the same place. And it was safe to assume that they'd both been drawn to that place for similar reasons. Because they were similar men. Michael had spied on her. He'd entered her house when she wasn't home. He'd misled her. He'd deceived her. Yes, he'd ultimately come clean about everything he'd done, had even apologized for doing it. But he'd been able to do all those things in the first place. And any man who had the capacity to act in such ways, regardless of how charming he might seem, wasn't a man Hannah needed to have in her life.

She started to tell him then that she'd just remembered a previous commitment tomorrow evening, and that she wouldn't be able to make dinner after all. But his gaze hooked hers just then, and there was something in his expression . . .

"I'll be there by four-thirty," she promised.

"And bring an appetite," he repeated.

She did her best to smile, but somehow the gesture didn't quite feel right. "I will."

And then Michael was gone, almost as if he hadn't been there at all. But the faint smell of leather and coffee lingered, and Hannah inhaled it as deeply as she could into her lungs. Then she switched off the light over the stove and headed back to her bedroom. And, later, as she fell asleep, the only thought wandering through her head was how soft Michael's hair had been caught between her fingers, and how wonderfully warm and wanton his mouth had been on her own.

And she hoped that, in the morning, she didn't wake up too hungry.

At home, Michael paid Alex's sitter and sent her on her way, then went up to his son's room to check on him. He'd bought the house in Carmel right after coming home to Indianapolis, after leaving OPUS behind. He'd chosen the roomy Victorian because it was exactly the sort of house he wished he'd grown up in himself, the kind of house where Alex could put down roots. Deep enough roots that maybe someday, after Michael was gone, Alex would even move his own family into it. Because roots, Michael had come to realize, were very important.

Not that it had always been that way. On the contrary, he hadn't been able to light out of Indiana fast enough when it came time to go to college. And landing the job with OPUS had exceeded his wildest dreams. He'd majored in accounting because he was good with numbers, and because he'd let his parents sway him into thinking it was better to go with a sure thing than to take chances with a career path that might

ultimately dead-end. The world would always need accountants, they'd assured him. Of course, the fact that they were
both accountants themselves may have had something to do
with that.

But Michael had discovered that people who were good
with numbers could find other kinds of work, too. Enter
OPUS, where his skill at finding patterns and locating hidden funds had ultimately made him one of the best at assimilating, evaluating and articulating. It was Adrian, the
risk-taker, with his borderline morality, who had been the
perfect candidate to send out into the field. Field work was
easy for him, Adrian had once said, because he never felt
fear. Fear, he had told Michael, only existed in people who
had something to lose.

And when Alex came along, Michael had been forced to
really look at what he was doing, and decide if that was what
he wanted to continue to do. He'd talked to Tatiana about it,
of course, had asked her if she didn't think that now that
they had a child, they might try to make their living in a
more conventional fashion. But Tatiana had wanted none of
that. She'd been a risk-taker, too. And Alex hadn't been
planned. Michael was as honest with himself about that as
he was everything else. He and Tatiana hadn't intended to
start a family, ever. But the moment he'd taken his newborn
son into his arms for the first time, Michael had known a
love unlike anything he had ever felt before. And he'd
known that Alex's arrival would be the greatest thing that
ever happened to him, past, present, or future.

Now, as he made his way upstairs to check on his son,
Michael knew a satisfaction that had been a long time in
coming. He had a great kid. A beautiful home. A job he
enjoyed. Well, his usual job, anyway. Not so much the one
he'd been performing for the past several months. But even
his return to OPUS obligations had provided an unexpected,
and very nice, surprise: Hannah Frost. And soon that job

would be over. But Michael intended to do whatever he had to do to ensure that Hannah Frost would still be around afterward.

He had his work cut out for him.

He knew she didn't trust him. And he didn't blame her for that. And he'd seen the way she looked at him tonight before he left, had known she was trying to think of some way to back out of the commitment she'd made in a moment of weakness to come to dinner tomorrow night. He'd deliberately invited her at a time when he knew she was vulnerable, right after kissing her, because he'd known if she had time to think about it, she would have turned him down. But in the end, she hadn't turned him down. In the end, his manipulation of the situation—and of her—had worked out the way he'd planned.

And realizing that made him wonder just how much better a man he was than Adrian Padgett after all.

But then, Michael *was* like Adrian in some ways. He just hoped Hannah eventually realized there were differences between the two of them, too.

Then again, he thought with a smile as he padded down the hallway toward Alex's room, his footsteps muffled by the thick Persian runner spanning the hardwood floor, if her reaction to that kiss tonight was even half what his own had been, he stood a pretty decent chance of her figuring that out. Eventually.

Nevertheless, Michael did have his work cut out for him.

He flipped on the hall light and peeked into his son's room, where Alex was sprawled on his stomach on the top bunk. His moon and stars comforter was still glowing subtly in the dark, just like the luminous stars Michael and his son had stuck all over the ceiling immediately after moving in. There was a space shuttle lamp on the desk, a poster of Neil Armstrong on the wall, and every Lego Mission to Mars model that had been invented, not to mention a half dozen free-style versions Alex had created himself.

Surprisingly, he wanted to be an astronaut when he grew up.

Michael moved to the top bunk and tugged on the comforter that Alex had kicked off, gently pulling it over his son's sleeping form. But Alex stirred when he did, turning his head to the side, smiling sleepily when he saw his father.

"Hey," he said softly.

"Hey," Michael greeted him back.

"You worked late again."

"Yep."

"Been doing that a lot lately."

"Yeah, I know. I'm sorry."

"But it's not tax season."

"I know. But I've kind of been on a special assignment. Only temporary, though, I promise."

"How much longer will it last?"

"Not much longer," Michael promised him. Because one way or another, this assignment would be drawing to a close soon. He just hoped when it did, everything fell into place the way it was supposed to.

"Did you see Ms. Frost tonight?" Alex asked.

And Michael didn't ask how his son knew he'd been seeing Hannah. Alex just had a knack for knowing what was going on. He supposed all nine-year-olds did. They might *look* like they were wrapped up in the latest Super Mario game or *Yu-Gi-Oh!* DVD, but they still had one ear tuned to what was going on in the grown-up world.

"Yeah, I saw Ms. Frost," Michael said. Because he never lied to Alex.

Alex nodded. "Good. I like her."

"I like her, too."

Alex smiled. "I know you do." And then he started in with the "Dad and Ms. Frost sittin' in a tree, K-I-S-S-I-N-G" thing, so Michael pulled the comforter all the way up over his head.

"Yeah, yeah, yeah," he said. But he smiled, too. He

wouldn't mind being up in a tree with Hannah K-I-S-S-I-N-G. Hell, he wouldn't mind doing that under a tree, either. Or on a rock. Or in a stream. Yeah, in a stream would be good. Or maybe in the back seat of his car. Or the front seat of his car. Or, hell, the trunk of his car. Or on the roller coaster at King's Island. Or—

Well, he could think about that later. And he no doubt would.

"Go to sleep, kiddo," Michael told his son. "It's late."

Alex nodded and reached out to his dad, and Michael leaned in for a hug and a kiss. Then Alex lay his head down on the pillow and closed his eyes, and with one final adjustment to the comforter, Michael turned to leave. He was almost out the door when Alex called out to him again.

"Dad?"

He turned around. "Yeah, sport?"

"Promise me again that you won't be working late much longer."

"I promise."

"Good. 'Cause I miss you, you know."

"I know. I miss you, too."

Evidently satisfied that he had said everything he needed to say, Alex wished his father a good night and turned his head on the pillow.

Michael stood in the doorway for a long time, watching Alex sleep. It had been years since he'd done such a thing. But he remembered when he and Tatiana both had stood beside the crib in the middle of the night, watching the soft rise and fall of their infant son's back, just to reassure themselves he was still there, still breathing, still alive.

And he remembered how Tatiana had always been the first to go back to bed, and how Michael would stand by himself watching Alex, being terrified something would happen to him. Night after night, he'd had to reassure himself his fear was groundless. But then he'd go to work the next day, and he'd realize how what he was doing could potentially piss off an awful lot of people, should those people ever find out Michael was the one doing the work. And he'd realize that some of those people, being amoral and vengeful, might opt to exact their revenge not on Michael, but on someone whose life he considered infinitely more important than his own. Eventually, he decided he needed to find a new line of work, if for no other reason than that he didn't want any of those amoral, vengeful people to find out about his son.

Unfortunately, he hadn't been quick enough to give up his old lifestyle. Because there was still one amoral, vengeful person out there who might consider his son a viable target. And if Adrian dared to touch a hair on Alex's head, Michael would kill him. Swiftly and neatly. And never lose a moment's sleep. But Adrian knew that, so there was little chance he'd come after Alex. Still, Michael didn't want to underestimate him. There were other people, after all—or, at least, one other person—whom Adrian knew he cared about. So, one way or another, this thing would be over soon. Michael just hoped, when it was, the people he cared about were still around.

And he hoped they—or, at least, she—still liked him.

NINE

THE SAWYER HOME WAS THE TYPE OF storybook house Hannah wished she could have grown up in herself, a three-story frame Victorian with diamond-paned windows and lots of interesting angles and a winding cobbled walkway that led from the driveway to the front door. In the absence of an English garden, which one might have expected with such a property, there were terra-cotta pots of greenery placed along the walkway and situated along the front porch, Michael's concession, she supposed, to more time-consuming landscaping. The front door was arched and painted dark red, and if she listened very hard to the wind whiffling through the trees, she could almost hear a voice whispering, *Nibble, nibble, little mouse, who's that nibbling on my house?*

That front door opened as she approached it, almost as if by magic, adding to the enchanted feel of the place. And where she had felt grateful to Michael the night before, when he gave her that staggering kiss good night that had completely erased the lingering bitterness of Adrian's mouth on hers—well, okay, and she also felt some other things in addition to grateful, things like careful and fearful and lustful—yeah, there'd been a lotta lustful in there, definitely—and doubtful and hopeful and lustful, and need-

ful and forgetful and lustful—had she mentioned lustful?—
and . . . and . . . and . . .

Where was she? Oh, yeah. Where she'd been grateful—
among other things—to Michael last night for that kiss, finding him waiting for her at the front door with Alex standing
on one side and a golden retriever, tongue lolling out of his
mouth, sitting on the other, made Hannah feel strangely
warm and fuzzy. All over.

And *warm and fuzzy*—never mind that *all over* business—
wasn't what she should be feeling around Michael Sawyer.
The *strangely* part, though, that was no surprise at all, since
her feelings for him were exactly that. But warm and fuzzy?
Nuh-uh. That way lay madness.

And, oh, she really wished the word *lay* hadn't cropped
up in that sentence.

And, oh, she really wished the word *up* hadn't risen in
that sentence.

And, oh, she really wished the word *risen* hadn't come up
in *that* sentence.

And, oh, she really wished the word—

"Hello!" she called out before she even reached the porch.

"Hi, Ms. Frost," Alex greeted her before Michael had a
chance.

The golden retriever, too, barked once in welcome, then
stood with tail wagging, grinning at her. Alex had changed
out of his school uniform and into a pair of blue jeans, the
knees of which were buffed nearly white, and an oversized
football jersey bearing the colors and logo of the Indianapolis Colts. Michael, too, had changed out of his work clothes
and into a pair of baggy khaki trousers and a wine-colored
sweater. Hannah was glad she'd gone casual herself, opting
for a pair of charcoal-colored pants and a dove-gray sweater
set. Well, it was casual for *her.*

"We're really glad you could come to dinner tonight,"

Alex added as she drew nearer. "'Cause Dad cooked lasagna."

"You shouldn't have gone to so much trouble," Hannah said as she stepped up onto the front porch.

Michael pushed open the door and started to say something, but the golden retriever squeezed through first, nudging Hannah's hand.

"That's Foley," Alex told her. "He's glad you could come, too."

"Hello, Foley," Hannah said, grinning when the dog started licking her fingers.

"It was no trouble," Michael assured her. "Lasagna is easy." He gave a little shrug and added, "Alex and I had a lot of fun, didn't we?"

Hannah turned to the little boy. "You helped?"

"With the spinach salad," he said.

Michael smiled. "He put in the chocolate chips."

Hannah smiled back. "Ooohhh. Sounds yummy."

"It was an experiment," Alex told her. "But I think it turned out really good."

In fact, all of dinner turned out "really good," Hannah had to admit after they'd finished it. Including the spinach salad. That hot caramel dressing made all the difference. No more boring spinach salads for her in the future, no way. Alex was definitely on to something. While dining, they talked about Alex's favorite subjects at school and his karate classes and the latest duel on *Yu-Gi-Oh!* And they talked about Michael's recent business trip to Washington, D.C., and his plan to add a sunroom to the back of the house come spring. And they talked about Indianapolis, where Michael grew up and with which Hannah was still familiarizing herself, even having lived here for two years.

In fact, they talked about all the mundane kinds of things that people—families—always talked about at dinner. At least, they were the kinds of things Hannah had always imagined people—families—talked about at dinner. And not once was she bored. Not once was she uncomfortable. Not once did she feel anything other than, as Alex had said, glad to have come. Because dinner with the Sawyers was exactly the type of dinner she had always fantasized about enjoying as a child. A dinner where she would come home from school and tell her parents of her day, and tease her little brother and sneak scraps to the dog under the table. For the first time in her thirty-six years, Hannah had the reality instead of the fantasy. And the reality, she thought, was even better than the fantasy. Because the reality included Michael.

And after Alex went upstairs to finish his homework and get ready for bed, the reality consisted of Hannah and Michael alone. And she knew she didn't want to leave just yet. She didn't want to return to her house. Her reality at home *wasn't* what she had fantasized for herself as a child. It didn't feel like home at her house. It didn't feel like this.

And that, she told herself, was Not Good.

Because instead of returning to the place where she lived her life—the place where she belonged—she wanted to stay here with Michael, in the place where he lived his life and where *he* belonged. She wanted to help him clean up, help him do dishes and keep discussing the day, as if this were the sort of thing the two of them did every evening. She wanted to kick off her shoes once they knew Alex was asleep, and then switch off the lamps and light some candles and snuggle on the sofa before the fire. She wanted to sit quietly at the end of her day with a man she— With a man she cared very much about. And for that reason, if no other, Hannah told herself she needed to go.

Because she didn't care about Michael in the idealized, storybook way. She couldn't care about him like that.

Because he wasn't an idealized, storybook man. As she had told him that night at the fund-raiser, Michael was much more than Alex Sawyer's father. And it was that *much more* that Hannah had to keep reminding herself about. Because although this side of him was soft and warm and fuzzy, his other side—with which she had a more than nodding acquaintance—simply could not be trusted.

So after Alex trundled off, when Michael asked her if she'd be interested in an after-dinner brandy, Hannah told herself to tell him thanks, but no, she really had to be leaving. Instead, she heard herself say that yes, that would be nice, thanks so much.

And *then* she would leave, she told herself. As soon as she was done with her brandy. But since she was driving, she figured she better drink that brandy pretty slowly, so that it didn't impair her in any way. Yeah, that was it. Didn't want to rush things like that. Could be dangerous. So she'd just take her time.

"Why didn't you ever marry?" Michael asked as he splashed a *very* generous serving of cognac into a wide-mouthed snifter and handed it to her. Wow, she was *really* going to have to take her time with that one.

They were still seated at the dining room table, but Michael had cleared away the dirty dishes and stacked them in the kitchen, pshaw-ing when she'd offered to help him clean up. He'd moved to her side of the table, though, and seated himself beside her instead of across from her, close enough that she could see the shadow of his beard darkening his face and the black swirls of hair peeking out of the V-neck of his sweater. And when she found herself wanting to reach out and touch the things that made him so masculine, so much different from her—and therefore so complementary—she focused instead on the floral pattern in the creamy damask tablecloth and tried to picture Michael buying it. She couldn't do it. It must have been a gift. Or something his wife had purchased and left behind when they'd split up.

So much of the house was like the tablecloth—cozy, comfortable, traditional. Everything touted a happy family existence. The way Alex was growing up was so different from what Hannah had known as a child. And Michael, even though he was a single father like her own had been, had nothing in common with Billy Frost. Hannah's father had never mistreated her, and she supposed, in his own way, he had loved her. But he hadn't known how to care for a child, and she'd always suspected he would have rather traveled alone. He'd done his best, all things considered, she supposed. He just hadn't cared all that much. Not the way Michael cared about Alex. And as often as Hannah had pretended to have come from a home just like this, she truly couldn't imagine what it would have been like.

But she wished, just once, she might have known.

"Why do you ask?" she said in response to his question as she watched him pour himself a brandy, too. And she hoped Michael would also take his time drinking his, even though the only place he'd be driving tonight would be Hannah to distraction.

He shrugged, then placed his elbow on the table, cradling his jaw in his hand. "I don't know," he said as he looked at her. "Just curious, I guess. I can't imagine some guy not snapping you up a long time ago."

She smiled at his compliment, warmth spreading through her at the casual way he had offered it. "No guy was ever that interested."

"Were you?"

"Was I what?"

"Ever that interested?" he asked. "Interested enough in a guy to be snapped up by him, I mean."

"Not really," she said.

He studied her thoughtfully. "You answered that pretty quickly."

"I didn't have to think about it," she said.

This time Michael was the one to smile, obviously pleased by her response. Idly, he ran the pad of his middle finger around the rim of his glass, tracing a leisurely circle once . . . twice . . . three times . . . four, and Hannah was entranced by the subtle, rhythmic motion. As she watched, he halted, then slid his palm under the bowl of the glass, the stem positioned between his middle and ring fingers, lifting it to his mouth to enjoy a small sip. He savored the flavor of the brandy for a moment before swallowing, his throat working easily over the spirit, then he placed the glass back on the table.

The gesture should have been an unremarkable one, and should have been in no way arousing. But as she watched Michael, Hannah suddenly felt as if he'd just run those fingers over her naked flesh, and had lifted her to his mouth for a long, unhurried sip.

Her thoughts must have shown on her face, because when he looked at her again, clearly meaning to say something else, he stopped with his lips parted, the words unsaid. Then he unfolded his arm from the table and sat up straighter, and although she looked away too quickly to be sure, she thought he started to extend his hand toward her—which was why she looked away too quickly to be sure.

"I, um, I like your house," she said abruptly, a little breathlessly, uttering the first thought to pop into her head, hoping that would banish the odd spell that seemed to have settled over them.

She stood and moved around the table to the other side, hoping maybe even that symbolic barrier would prevent her from doing what she really wanted to do, which was curl up in Michael's lap and thread her fingers through his hair, and kiss him and kiss him and kiss him.

"Did you have a decorator?" she asked as she began to make her way from the dining room into the living room.

Michael rose, too, and followed her, but he didn't try to reach for her again. Probably, she thought, he realized what a mistake it would be. And not just because Alex was upstairs, either.

"No, I didn't, actually," he said. "Most of what's here belonged to my parents."

She nodded, surveying her surroundings again. So this was the way he had grown up, too, she thought. Lucky him.

"And when Tatiana left," he added, "she only took with her what she'd brought to the marriage."

When Tatiana left, Hannah repeated to herself. So it had been she, and not Michael, who wanted the divorce. She was dying to ask more about his ex-wife, wondered what had led to the breakup. She wondered even more how he had felt when it happened. How he continued to feel now. But there was no way she would ask such invasive questions. The last thing she wanted to do was stir up the past. His or her own. And it didn't matter, anyway, because there was no future for the two of them together.

"Tatiana and I both wanted out of the marriage, Hannah," he said anyway, as if he had read her thoughts.

She spun around and met his gaze. "You don't have to tell me about it," she said, half hoping he wouldn't. But the other half hoped very much that he would. And she decided not to think about why.

"I know I don't have to tell you," he said. "But I want to."

He took a few more steps forward, his shoes scraping over the hardwood floor until they connected with the Persian rug spanning the floor between two sofas. They faced each other on each side of the fireplace where the fire had burned low, until only a few flickering flames licked at what was left of a few charred logs. Michael pulled a poker from the collection of fire tools and jabbed perfunctorily at the few flames, but they only sputtered a bit, puffing a few lazy embers up the chimney, and never leapt any higher.

"Tati and I met through OPUS," he said. "She was one of my instructors when I went through training. Their weapons specialist."

Tati, Hannah repeated to herself. A pet name, obviously. And a weapons specialist. How glamorous she must have seemed to him. How glamorous she must have been.

"Looking back," Michael continued, "I guess I was really more infatuated with her than I was in love with her. She was older than me, and I thought she was just incredibly hot."

"Michael, really," Hannah said. "You don't have to—"

"I want to," he said again.

Well, then she just hoped he'd ease up on the *incredibly hot* business and focus more on the *older* business.

"I guess, what it all came down to," he began again, "was that we never should have gotten married in the first place."

Now, that's more like it, Hannah thought.

"Because in the long run, Tatiana's career meant more to her than anything else did."

Wait a minute. Because *Tatiana* didn't think they should be together? That wasn't what Hannah wanted to hear.

"And really, after all was said and done, I realized I never loved Tati the way a person needs to be in love before deciding he wants to build a life with that person."

Oh. Well. That was okay, then.

And why was she thinking these things? Hannah demanded of herself. What difference did it make why Michael's marriage had ended? What difference did anything that had happened to him in the past make? It wasn't like Hannah was a part of his future. Or even his present. They were only here now because they were two people who needed to eat dinner, that was all. She was *not* going to get involved with him. Not only had he invaded her privacy most egregiously—she didn't care if he *was* only doing his job—but that very job was everything she *didn't* want in her life. It was anything *but* normal, stable, and secure.

Even if that job was only temporary—which he had never said it was—there was no reason to believe he wouldn't return to it again whenever he was needed, since he'd been pulled back this time after swearing he'd left it behind. Yes, he had a young child to think about. But if Alex's presence in his life hadn't prevented him from accepting this assignment this time, then Hannah's presence in his life certainly wouldn't prevent him from accepting future assignments. No way would she involve herself with someone like him. She'd grown up depending on a man who could never be counted on because she'd had no choice. She wasn't about to choose that life as an adult.

"And she's not involved in Alex's life?" Hannah said, still finding that difficult to believe. Alex was a great kid. Even when she'd thought he was a pathological liar, she'd been charmed by him.

"Tati wasn't suited to parenting," Michael said. "And don't get me wrong, I don't mean to disparage her when I say that. She cares about Alex. But she also knows her limitations. She's an excellent spy. And she's a lousy mom. She'd be the first one to tell you that. And she didn't see any reason to make everyone unhappy by trying to be something she wasn't. Even before she and I split up, I was Alex's primary caregiver. I worked at home by then, had all my equipment there. Tati was a field agent who had to travel a lot. And she was happiest when she was on assignment somewhere. It would have been unfair to ask her to be anything else."

Hannah nodded. She understood that, too. And when she thought about it that way, she supposed maybe it was better that her own mother had left, instead of staying and resenting Hannah for simply existing. Even if her father hadn't doted on her, she hadn't ever felt unwanted by him. Not really. Well, not *too* much, anyway.

"Alex is lucky to have you," Hannah said. "He's lucky to have the life you've made for him."

"He's no luckier than any other kid," Michael said, shrugging off the praise quite literally.

"Actually, he is," she said. "He's lucky to have a parent who is so devoted to him and puts his needs first. And he's lucky to be growing up in a house like this. He's lucky to have roots and some semblance of stability and security. He's lucky that when he wakes up in the morning, he knows exactly what's expected of him, and what sort of day it's going to be. He's lucky that at night, he goes to bed with a full stomach and happy memories, knowing his father is right downstairs if he needs him. And he's lucky to be able to know that the next day holds more of the same. He's really, really lucky, Michael. Trust me."

Michael said nothing in response to that at first, only studied her in silence, as if he wanted to say something, but didn't quite know how. Finally, though, he told her, "But his life can't be that much different from most. His childhood can't be that much different from, say . . ." He shrugged again, but there was something about the gesture this time that made it seem less than casual. "From, say, your own."

Hannah remembered then Michael's being at her house on her birthday and seeing the gifts she'd told him were from her friends and relatives. And she remembered telling him all the things she'd told him—all the lies she'd told him—about her happy childhood and her adoring family. This was the perfect opportunity, she thought, for her to come clean with him, the way he'd come clean with her that day at her house. To confess that she'd made up all that stuff because she hadn't wanted to seem so pathetic, buying herself presents on her birthday because there was no one else to do it. And she *would* tell him the truth, she assured herself . . . *If* there was some reason to think that the two of them would ever be more to each other than what they were now—weirdly connected by a strange attraction that had no hope of being anything else. But she still feared looking pathetic. Being thought pathetic. To him. By him.

So, reluctantly, she told him, "No, I don't guess his childhood is much different from what mine was."

"Except that your parents are still married," Michael said in a voice that didn't seem quite like his own.

"Right," she said quietly.

"And that they doted on you," he added. "Both of them, I mean."

She nodded. But all she could manage by way of a reply this time was a halfway strangled, "Mm-hm."

"And where Alex doesn't have much of an extended family," Michael continued, "you have your grandmother and great-aunt and cousin. And probably others you haven't mentioned."

"Of course," Hannah agreed dismally.

They were still standing in the middle of the living room, neither of them having taken a seat as they spoke, but now Michael strode over to one of the sofas and sat down, patting the cushion next to him in silent invitation. Hannah told herself that was her cue to bolt, her unfinished brandy be damned. But there was something about the way he looked at her as he patted that cushion that was just so . . . inviting. It was the way a husband would look when he was patting the cushion for his wife after the kids had gone to bed and he felt like being naughty. And Hannah just couldn't resist. With a soft sound of resignation—and a promise to herself that she really would leave soon—she traced his steps and sat down beside him.

"You heard all about my boring childhood over dinner," he said as she sat down. "Now I want to hear about yours."

That was when Hannah remembered why it had been so important for her to leave. So she wouldn't have to be like Foley over there, lying like a big dog.

"Oh, you don't want to hear about my childhood," she hedged.

He turned on the sofa to face her, bracing his elbow on the back and cradling his head in his hand. "Yeah, I do, actually. I want to hear all about your past. You said you've only been in Indianapolis for a couple of years now. Where were you before that?"

She breathed a silent sigh of relief that they had returned to safer subject matter, and that she could speak truthfully about her experiences. "Chicago," she told him. "After I graduated from college with a bachelor's and a master's in education, I took a job as a teacher for a small private school in Naperville that focused on the creative arts. When a position in administration opened up, I became the lower school liaison. That eventually led to the assistant directorship. And when I read about the opening here, I thought it would be perfect. I'd have my own school, and Indiana just seemed like a nice place to live. Very earthy. Very middle-America."

"And that's important to you," he said. "The middle-America thing, I mean."

"It is," she assured him.

"Because that's how you grew up?"

Oh, dear. They were back to that again. "Not just that," she evaded. "It just seemed like a good place to put down roots, that's all."

"New roots, you mean."

"Right. New roots."

"Because your old roots would be . . . where was it again you said you grew up?"

Why did he keep circling back to her childhood? Hannah wondered. "Kansas," she told him. "I grew up Kansas." That was what she always said when people asked her where she was from. Because Kansas was far enough removed from her actual childhood that she was comfortable with it.

He nodded slowly, as if remembering. "That's right. I remember you told me that at your house that night. What city?"

"Kansas City," she said. That, too, was a stock reply. She'd gone there once for a teacher's convention, and she remembered liking it very much. It had been very stable. Very secure. Very normal. Very different from what she'd known as a child.

"And you spent your *entire* childhood in Kansas City?" he asked.

Why did he sound doubtful? she wondered. "Well, most of it," she told him, suddenly worried that maybe the past she'd fabricated for herself really was too good to be true. There *were* people in the world who grew up in one city alone, after all. Weren't there? There had to be. Just in case, though, she said, "We moved there when I was seven. Before that, we lived in . . . um . . ." And just like that, her normally fertile imagination deserted her, and Hannah drew a complete blank. Panicking, she snatched something from her real past to fill it. "The South," she finished. "I was actually born in the South and spent the first several years of my life there."

Michael looked very interested in that. "Oh, I love the South. What part are you from?"

"Um, Georgia," she said. Because she'd probably spent as much time there as anywhere else. She'd need a calculator to know for sure.

He eyed her thoughtfully. "Georgia's wonderful. But you don't have a trace of the accent they have down there."

"It was a, um, a long time ago," she said. And she hoped

she didn't sound rattled when she said it. "Besides, we, ah . . . we mostly stuck to . . . to urban areas."

Now he looked surprised. " 'Stuck to urban areas'?" he echoed. "That's kind of a funny way to put it. What did your parents do for a living?"

Hannah set her brandy on the coffee table, since it was obviously playing havoc with her concentration. Otherwise, she never would have said something like *we mostly stuck to urban areas,* since, as Michael pointed out, that was a funny way to put it. *Unless your father was a man who made a living out of conning people,* she meant. Then she glanced up at him again, at his dark eyes fixed relentlessly on her face, and his full mouth quirked in just a hint of a smile. And she realized it wasn't the brandy playing havoc with her.

"My father was self-employed," she said. "And he traveled a lot for his work. That's what I meant by stuck to urban areas. Sometimes my mother and I went with him."

"Because you were such a close family," Michael guessed.

"Right."

"So did you get to see much of your Nana Frost and Aunt Esmeralda and Cousin Chloe, with them living in other places?"

Wow. He really did remember that conversation at her house, she thought. She was going to have to either continue to mislead him about all that, or admit that she'd been lying to him. Because she was as deep in it as she was—and also since there was no harm that could come of telling him this, since they had no future together anyway—she decided to just go with it for now. "Well, as I said, I spent my summers with Auntie in Minnesota."

"And whereabouts in Minnesota is Auntie?" he asked, pronouncing it "*Ahn*-tie," the way Hannah did.

"In Minneapolis," she replied.

"And what did you do during those summers?" he asked.

"All kinds of things," she told him. "Auntie took me to

movies and the zoo and to plays and concerts. Sometimes we'd go to lunch together. That was always fun. She had a bridge club that met every Friday, and I'd help serve tea and refreshments." She shrugged as she concluded, feeling guilty for the first time she ever had when telling someone about her imaginary visits with her pretend great-aunt.

"Sounds like you guys had a close relationship," Michael said.

Very, very softly, Hannah told him, "We still do."

She waited for him to ask her about her Nana Frost or her Cousin Chloe, or even Patsy, started rehearsing again all their stories and histories in her head to prepare herself. But he didn't ask about any of them. He asked about all of them.

"Do you miss not seeing them?"

And Hannah told him, quite truthfully this time, "Always."

"So how do you spend your summers now?" he asked. "Do you still go up to visit Auntie in Minneapolis?"

Hannah dropped her head to stare at her lap, unable to meet Michael's gaze any longer. "Not like I used to," she said quietly. "I'm so busy these days."

"Well, at least you have some wonderful memories to keep you company," she heard him say.

"Yeah," she agreed, her voice even quieter now. "At least I have those." And because she couldn't stand talking about those falsified memories and those fabricated people with Michael any longer, Hannah stood and told him, "I really need to go."

He stood, too, but looked surprised. "Why? It's still early."

"No, it's actually very late," she said.

Truer words had never been spoken. Because it was indeed very late. Too late, really. Too late for Hannah to undo so many things she had done. Too late for her to unsay so many things she had said. So instead of doing even more damage, it would be better if she just left. Left Michael's beautiful house. Left Michael's delightful family. Left Michael's wonderful life. Left Michael, period.

Because if there was one thing she had learned this evening, it was that what Michael had created for himself was exactly what she had always hoped to find for herself, but which had eluded her in spite of her efforts. Unfortunately, thanks to his job—and her own fears—he wasn't the man who could give it to her now. So with a hasty good-bye and one last look, Hannah left it all behind.

And she told herself that if she was smart, she would never, ever, look back again.

TEN

 AS SELBY SAT AGAIN IN THE DINER ACROSS the street from her apartment, watching Thomas Brown sip his coffee, a part of her hoped this wasn't going to become a habit. But another part of her—a bigger part, she had to admit—was more than a little happy to think maybe it would. Because that part of her was beginning to suspect that Thomas Brown, motorcycle thug, was only a façade, one that camouflaged a much more complex, much more interesting man.

And like most façades, it was pretty flimsy. Because even having known him a short time, she sensed that the come-ons and the put-ons she'd thought made him a smartass were in fact weapons he used to keep people at a safe distance. Why he'd want to keep people at a distance, she couldn't begin to guess. Mostly because she could think of too many reasons herself why someone would want to do that. At this point, she was intrigued by him enough to want to spend a little more time with him, to maybe try and figure him out. Not just because of her intense curiosity about people in general, but because she was starting to like Thomas Brown in particular.

She hadn't missed her bus tonight, the way she had before. No, this time, as the rest of the class was filing out,

Thomas hadn't dropped his books, or had questions or comments, or voiced any trouble with any of the lessons. He had flat-out offered her a ride home, and after only a moment's hesitation, Selby had told him yes. That would be great. Thanks. She wished she could convince herself it was because she was saving more money, even if it was only bus fare. But really, she knew money had nothing to do with it. She'd just wanted to be with Thomas.

Her head had been filled with thoughts of him since the other night—memories of the way he had smiled at her, at the way he had watched her when she talked, even the way he had raked his thumb over the handle of his coffee cup, as if he hadn't realized he was doing it, but just needed to be touching something. She'd recalled the feel of his hard torso under her palms as she'd ridden on the motorcycle behind him. She'd remembered the feel of his broad, solid back vibrating against her softer front as she'd pressed her body close to his in an effort to quell her fears at riding out in the open like that, so dangerously.

And she'd replayed the look of embarrassment on his face when she'd caught him in his lie, when he'd thrown the coins on the table for the tip. He'd looked like a little boy just then, one who felt guilty for having not done his homework when he knew he should have, because he'd wanted to partake of some frivolous, more enjoyable pursuit instead. There had just been something in that expression, something utterly at odds with Thomas's usual aplomb. Something that had revealed a small chink in the impertinent armor he wore. That was when Selby had realized that, deep down, he might not be the sort of man he pretended to be. Deep down, he might not be confident or arrogant or impudent. Deep down, he might be just like her. Full of doubt and self-consciousness and hesitation. Full of dreams and hopes and wishes that things could be different.

And that was why she had said yes to his offer of a ride tonight. Because she wanted to see if she had only imagined that something in his expression, or if he really was, deep down, like her.

Tonight, he wore his standard rebel outfit of black leather jacket, T-shirt, and jeans, but the T-shirt in question wasn't quite as ratty as usual, nor were the jeans as torn. She tugged on her bulky turtleneck sweater, a thick, oatmeal-colored one she'd pulled on over a brown corduroy skirt that morning, and reached for the metal creamer the waitress had dropped off on her last trip by the table.

"So you grew up in southern Indiana," he was saying now, referring to their earlier conversation. "A place you think I've never heard of."

"It was very small," she assured him.

"Suburb of Louisville?"

She shook her head. "Out in the middle of nowhere."

"Farm?"

"No, we weren't farmers. We just lived in a small town. My family was more suited to that, I think," she hedged, not wanting to tell him how they couldn't have afforded to live anywhere else.

He nodded, seeming to mull that over, and she wondered what, exactly, there was in the statement to mull. "Southern Indiana is pretty," he said. "I bet your hometown is a picturesque little place. Am I right?"

Dorsey, Indiana, was pleasant enough, Selby supposed. The town, anyway. It was the area where the Hudson trailer had been situated—near the landfill, though thankfully upwind of it—that had been a tad lacking in the picturesque department.

"It was kind of charming, I guess, now that I think about it," she said, injecting a brightness into her voice she didn't really feel. As charming as the town was, she didn't carry many fond memories of it. Her life there hadn't exactly been enjoyable.

"And you were probably the town darling, weren't you?"

he asked further. "Probably left a string of broken hearts behind when you left."

Selby told herself the faint tinge of bitterness she thought she heard in his voice was only there because it had filtered through her own bitterness. "Not really," she said uncomfortably.

"You're being modest," he said. And again, she thought there was just a hint of something sour in his voice.

But when she looked up at him and found him smiling at her, with nary a trace of distastefulness in his expression, she decided she only imagined it, that the source of it was her, and not him. "No," she told him. "I'm not."

"Your family is still living there?"

She nodded. Oh, yeah. Hudsons never strayed far. Not just because they couldn't afford to, but because they were an indifferent, apathetic lot, for the most part. They didn't want to learn about or experience anything unless it had an effect over whether or not there would be supper on the table come evening. "They're still there," she said. "I don't imagine they'll ever be going anywhere."

"Town founders, huh?" Thomas guessed. "Firm roots and lots of traditions, right?"

Selby did smile at that. He made her family sound like they were the bastions of the community instead of the basement-dwellers. But all she said was, "Yeah. Right. Town founders." Hey, the Hudsons had lived in Dorsey for generations. And belittling the Hudsons had been a town tradition for generations, too. Because before the Hudsons were basement-dwellers they'd been cellar-dwellers. So she wasn't really lying when she agreed.

"You have brothers? Sisters?" he asked.

"Three older brothers," she told him.

"So you're the baby of the family."

"Yep."

"Bet they really watched out for you, didn't they?"

"Oh, yeah," she said mildly. Her brothers had always been watching for her to come home at night. They'd been hungry, after all. They'd wanted their supper. And they'd needed their clothes washed for school or work the next day. God forbid they should take care of any of that themselves. Why should they, when that was Selby's job?

"And I bet your folks doted on you, too, didn't they?"

"Mm-hm," she said. Doted on her paychecks was more like it.

"And you were probably involved in all kinds of activities at school."

"Oh, sure," she said, biting back her derision. "Cheerleading, gymnastics, Spanish Club, yearbook staff. I was involved in all those hip extracurriculars in one way or another."

Because she *had* been involved with those school activities. In one way or another. After all, she'd been teased by the cheerleaders on a regular basis, since being the fat girl who lived in a trailer made Selby their prime target. And she'd been laughed at in PE by all the gymnasts because she couldn't even pull herself up onto the uneven parallel bars. She'd really enjoyed that activity. That had been followed a couple of times by the activity of being thrown fully dressed into the showers and having to go to Spanish class soaking wet, where the activity of being laughed at even more had come into play. And, of course, there had been her favorite activity, having her photo appear in the yearbook under the heading, "Most Likely to Appear Floating in the Sky over the Super Bowl."

Yep, she'd been involved in *lots* of activities in high school.

"But, gosh, enough about me," she said. "What about you?"

When Selby met Thomas's gaze again, she saw that he still seemed to be doing some serious mulling. And she couldn't have him doing that. Because if he mulled long enough, he'd realize how sarcastic she was being. And eventually he would correctly deduce that, when she was in high school, she had been a complete loser. Selby hadn't felt like a loser for a long time. Gee, not since high school, come to think of it. And she hadn't *been* a loser for a long time—not since high school. She wasn't about to let Thomas Brown take her back there again, whether inadvertently or not.

"What about me?" he asked.

She didn't want to bring up his job again, since she pretty much knew he was unemployed, even if he did deny it. She didn't want to embarrass him. So she asked, "Did you grow up in Indianapolis?"

Pax looked at Selby and battled the edginess that was burrowing deeper into him every time she answered one of his questions. He'd been right about her, he realized. She really was like all the girls he'd gone to high school with, pampered, coddled, popular. Always given every opportunity without so much as having to ask for it, always taking whatever else she wanted.

Then he remembered she'd asked him a question and he nodded. "Yeah, born and bred."

"Where did you go to school?"

"Madison High School," he told her. "It doesn't exist anymore. They tore it down to build . . . something else."

What he didn't tell Selby was that he'd been responsible for his school's quite literal downfall. He'd bought his old high school and the land surrounding it from the city for an outrageous amount of money, enough to enable the board of education to build three more schools, and then he'd razed the sonofabitch to the ground. On top of it, he'd built his empire, the CompuPax Pavilion. He worked there, slept there, ate there, entertained there, copulated there. And not a day went by that he didn't rejoice in the knowledge that he'd toppled the building that had once brought him nothing but misery, and had built in its place an edifice of mammoth proportions that was a monument to his colossal success.

"So what made you drop out?" Selby asked, jerking him out of a place he frankly didn't want to revisit anyway.

Pax didn't mind the question. It was a normal one for her to ask, under the circumstances. And he replied truthfully when he said, "I didn't like school. I thought it was boring, and I didn't feel like I was learning anything. So I left."

She nodded, but he could see that she didn't understand. He supposed he didn't blame her. She was a woman who valued education so much she'd become a teacher. And she'd had a good experience in high school. She'd been one of the popular ones. One of the girls who stood on the corner and laughed at boys like Tommy Brown when they walked past.

Geek.

Dork.

Pizza Face.

Freak.

He tried to picture Selby Hudson among the other girls he'd known back then, hurling epithets at him for no other reason than that they were shallow and mean. But the image came out nebulous and not quite right somehow. Selby's face just wouldn't materialize in that group. Still, she had been one of those girls at her own school, he reminded himself. She'd just admitted she'd been a member of all the chic societies, a constituent of all the exclusive cliques. She'd doubtless lobbed more than a few slurs in her time, had doled out her fair share of teasing and humiliation.

Not that Pax would let something like that keep him from wanting her. And having her. Because now that he was the kind of man he was, she was the kind of woman he always sought out. The kind of woman he always wanted. The kind of woman he always had. The women who had been part of the in crowd as girls. The cheerleaders, the homecoming queens, the star athletes. The perky ones. The cute ones. The popular ones. He always dated the women who'd been Someone in high school. He courted them. Wooed them. Charmed them. Bedded them.

Then he discarded them without a second thought.

Selby Hudson, he told himself, was no different. Yeah, maybe she wasn't living the popular life now. Maybe she took the bus and lived in a crummy neighborhood and worked two jobs to make ends meet. That was what often happened to the popular kids, Pax had discovered, both the girls and the boys. Once they got out of high school, out into the real world, once they realized that no one gave a damn whether they'd played sports or been a calendar girl or valedictorian or what have you, they started having to struggle like the rest of the poor saps. And a lot of them had lost the struggle. A lot of them lived the way Selby did. None of *them* had done as well as Pax had. None of *them* was a billionaire, that was for goddamned sure.

"And now you've come back to do the work that will earn you your diploma," Selby said, once again drawing him out of that place he hated to revisit, so why did he keep slipping back there?

"Yeah, I've come back," he said. Because God knew getting that diploma would make him a hell of a lot more employable.

"I'm glad," Selby said. "Education is so important. Without it, people just flounder."

"Mm," Pax muttered. Because he honestly didn't know what else to say.

"I never want to stop learning," she continued, smiling. "I never want to reach a point where I feel like there's nothing left for me to discover, you know? I mean, people talk about how sad it would be to die before they've done everything they want to do or seen everything they want to see. But I think it would be worse to live life and have there be nothing left that you want to do or see. To be so experienced and jaded that nothing seems interesting anymore. That there's nothing left to enjoy. That, to me, would be sad."

Pax didn't know what to say to that, either. Probably because it hit way too close to home. In the past two decades, he'd done more and seen more than most people twice his age. He'd traveled the world over, had met hundreds of Very Important People, had seen every notable landmark, every geographic wonder, every scientific marvel there was to see. He'd mingled with heads of state, partied with movie stars, vacationed with industrial and technological giants. He really had been there and done that, regardless of what it was. Anytime he'd wanted to do something, see something, hear something, taste something, he'd just whipped out his platinum card and done, saw, heard, or tasted it. Usually in its natural habitat. There was nothing left that astounded or amazed him. Nothing he found particularly interesting. Nothing that dazzled. Nothing to marvel at. The world was his oyster, and he'd sucked it down with hot sauce and licked the shell clean a long time ago. And now here was Selby Hudson telling him to expand his horizons. It was almost too funny for words.

Somehow, though, Pax didn't feel like laughing. On the contrary, he felt like he wanted to . . .

"Pie. We gotta have pie with our coffee," he said. And before Selby could object, he hailed their waitress and ordered a slice for each of them. With ice cream. Because you couldn't have pie without ice cream. It wouldn't be right.

By the time they finished their coffee and their pie and their conversation—not that that was finished, mind you, but it was definitely winding down—it was nearing midnight. Selby actually gasped when she finally realized the time.

"I can't believe it's almost midnight. I have to go," she said, gathering up her satchel and shrugging into her big denim jacket. "I have to be at school early tomorrow. The entire fourth grade is taking a field trip."

"Where to?" Pax asked as he reached into his back pocket for his wallet. No way was he letting her buy this time.

But he nearly dropped it on the floor when Selby replied, "The CompuPax Pavilion. They've been studying the Industrial Revolution in social studies, and Mrs. Gaddie, the social studies teacher, thought it would be a good idea for the students to see how the contemporary technological revolution is sort of paralleling that. Completely changing society and the way people do things."

Pax told himself not to panic, that school field trips came through CompuPax all the time. They never made it to his office. And he rarely ever left his office. There was no reason to think Selby would run into him. Still, he was glad to know in advance. He'd be sure not to wander far from his home base.

When they stepped outside the diner, the street was deserted, save a lone male figure standing on the corner, leaning against a street lamp whose light had been broken out—probably by the very guy standing beneath it. Pax looked at Selby, thinking she'd probably planned on telling him good night right here and watching as he pulled away, so that she could go home again without him finding out where she lived. Which, of course, would have done her no good, since he already knew precisely where she lived. Her attention was on the man by the street lamp, but then she turned to look at Pax. She hesitated.

Then, "Would you mind walking me home?" she asked.

He grinned, thinking he should probably tip the streetlight reprobate on his way back. "Sure," he said. Then, smiling to himself, he asked innocently, "Which way?"

Instead of replying, Selby turned toward the building he'd seen her in Thursday night, then positioned herself so that Pax was between her and the guy on the corner. She was good at the whole self-preservation thing, he thought. And he wasn't sure why that bothered him.

They hustled across the dark, deserted street, and when they came to the front door of her building, he reached for the handle to pull it open, frowning when he realized there was no lock on it, and any streetlight reprobate could get in.

"That's okay," she told him. "I can take it from here. Thanks."

"The hell you can," he said, opening the door. "I'll see you up."

But again, she hesitated. "You don't have to, really."

"Yes, I do."

She relented with unmistakable reluctance, and preceded him through the door, making her way to the steps.

"No elevator?" he said.

"It doesn't work," she told him. "It hasn't since I moved in."

"Which would have been?"

"July. I moved to Indianapolis from Bloomington for my job."

"You went to IU?" he asked as they began to climb the stairs.

She nodded. "Cheaper than going out of state. And it's a really good school."

Pax was about to agree and tell her he knew because he'd gone there himself. Then he remembered he wasn't T. Paxton Brown, but a jobless loser named Thomas Brown who was in returning ed. Selby might wonder, if she knew he'd earned two degrees in computer science. And he didn't want her wondering right now. He wanted her comfortable. He wanted her trusting. He wanted her reassured.

Hell, he just plain wanted her.

Which was why, when they finally reached the sixth floor and made their way to her front door, and when Selby turned to tell him good night, he lifted a hand to her face. Her eyes widened in surprise when he touched her, and her lips parted, as if she were about to speak. So before she had a chance to do something crass like ask him what the hell he thought he was doing, Pax dipped his head to hers and kissed her.

He had intended for the kiss to overwhelm her, to be a long, fierce, thorough penetration of her mouth that would throw her off her guard and enable him to take advantage. He had wanted to do to her standing up what he would later be doing to her lying down. He'd wanted her to come undone, to invite him inside, to insist he stay the night. But his first taste of her was so dizzyingly exquisite, so mind-bogglingly intense, so unexpectedly delicious, that his entire body shuddered in response.

It was Pax who ended up being overwhelmed.

He wasn't used to losing control of a kiss, but the sensation of Selby's mouth beneath his made him forget about everything except her. He lost himself in the potent, coffee taste of her, in the sweet, powdery scent of her, in the hushed, gentle murmur of her, in the soft, lithesome feel of her. His hands connected with her then, roving hungrily over her round curves, into the dip of her waist, over the flair of her hips, then higher, to hesitate under the swell of her breast. And as he touched her and deepened the kiss, all he could think about was how badly he wanted to bury himself inside her, surging as deeply as he could, thrusting as hard as he could, lunging as quickly as he could, over and over again, until neither of them could tell where one body ended and the other began.

As thoughts of doing just that to her flashed strobe-light fast through his brain, Pax crowded her back against her front door and pushed his body into hers, his forearms bracing on each side of her head now, his hips pressing into hers, his pelvis rocking forward. Only the need for breath made him tear his mouth from hers, and when he did, Selby gasped and cried out, a sound so fraught with fear, Pax had no choice but to halt what he was doing.

When he looked at her face, he saw her eyes hadn't widened in surprise, but in alarm. And though her hands were splayed wide across his chest, it wasn't because she was overcome with passion, but because she was trying to push him away. She was indeed frightened. And Pax could scarcely believe he was the reason for it. He'd never frightened a woman in his life.

But then, why should he be surprised? he asked himself. Hell, he'd just terrified himself, too.

As he studied Selby's expression more closely, though, he thought he detected something else mingling with her fear, a raw desire he only recognized because it so completely mirrored his own. She was scared, yes. But she was aroused, too. Probably not because she wanted to be, but there it was all the same.

In spite of that, Pax reined in his passion as quickly as he'd loosed it on her, and he pushed his body away from hers.

"I'm sorry," said, taking a giant step backward so that he wasn't crowding her. "I didn't mean for that . . . I mean, I wasn't trying to . . . I just wasn't thinking . . ."

And that was when Pax knew he was in serious trouble. Because not only had he just retreated from a woman—something he'd never done before—but he realized he really *hadn't* meant for that to . . . And he *hadn't* been trying to . . . And he *hadn't* been thinking . . . He'd wanted Selby the same way he'd wanted scores of other women, but he hadn't taken her the way he had scores of other women. Rewinding to the moment he'd dipped his head to hers, he realized he hadn't been plotting and calculating the way he normally did when he kissed a woman. He'd simply been acting on impulse. And Pax was *never* impulsive when it came to women.

Then he realized something even more significant. He realized that the way he wanted Selby *wasn't* the same way he'd wanted scores of other women. Something about her made him want her even more. He wasn't sure what it was or where it had come from or why she should be any different. He only knew he wanted Selby Hudson with an insatiability he'd never felt before.

Which, he couldn't help thinking, would just make it all the sweeter when he had her.

Because he would have Selby Hudson, he promised himself. And he would have her on his terms. He was just going to have to rework his strategy, that was all. Because she made him feel things other women hadn't, and she made him want things he'd sworn he would never want again.

That shouldn't cause too many problems, though, he thought. Because when all was said and done, she was a woman. And these days, at least, Pax knew exactly what to do with them.

"I'm sorry," he said again, feeling strangely sincere when he did.

For a moment, Selby only stood frozen in place, staring at him, her eyes dark with something Pax was too afraid to think about, her mouth pink and swollen from the harshness of his kiss. God, he wished he could read her mind just then. But he could no more guess what was going through her head than he could understand his reaction to her. Finally, though, she nodded, slowly, uncertainly. But she still looked a little dazed by what had just happened.

And then, very softly, very cryptically, she said, "No harm done. I just need to be careful not to let it happen again."

She spoke like she thought he was dangerous, Pax thought. And where before, with other women, he might have kind of liked that response, now he felt oddly uneasy. He didn't want Selby to think him dangerous. Probably because, unlike other women who found an element of danger to their liking, Selby wouldn't consider it a selling point.

So he'd have to go about seducing her in other ways. Fortunately for Pax, he knew all about seduction. Especially when it came to women like her.

"I'll, um, I'll see you in class," she said quietly, her gaze flitting over everything in the hallway except Pax. Then she jingled her keys in her hand in obvious dismissal. "Thanks for the coffee," she added.

"Don't mention it," he replied. Which was an unnecessary remark. Because he was pretty sure Selby didn't want to mention it again.

But that was okay, he thought as he watched her squirrel herself quickly into her apartment and close the door, then listened to the thrust of the deadbolt being jacked into place. He still intended to pick up right where they left off next time they were together. And he'd make sure Selby was so preoccupied then, she wouldn't want to talk anyway.

The night after scaring Selby by kissing her, Pax had the bejeezus scared out of himself by her.

He was minding his own business, sitting at the bar in Trino's with a colleague, waiting for a table to open up amid the Friday night crush of people, when he looked out across the restaurant and saw Selby waiting on one of the tables. At first he told himself it couldn't be her, that it was just some woman with the same haircut and build. The restaurant was dimly lit, after all, and she was a good thirty or forty feet away from him. But then she smiled at the couple she was waiting on, and the breath left his lungs in a long, emptying *whoosh*, and he knew without question it was her.

What the hell was she doing here, waiting tables? he wondered. She already had two jobs as it was. And how was he going to explain his presence here if she saw him? No way could Thomas Brown afford to eat here. And no way would Thomas Brown be wearing what was clearly a very expensive suit.

Damn. How was he going to work this? he wondered further as he turned his entire body on the barstool to face away from where Selby was scurrying around down on the restaurant floor. Fortunately, this left him looking at his colleague instead of away from his colleague. His colleague, Ellen. Ellen Howington. Of Howington Electronics. A knockout redhead who was nothing if not staggeringly gorgeous. So even if he managed to conjure from thin air some lame excuse as to why Thomas Brown would be sitting in an overpriced restaurant wearing an overpriced suit, he'd have to come up with yet another lame reason for why Thomas Brown was here with what, to the casual observer, looked to be an overpriced woman. Because Selby would never believe the truth, that this was a working dinner with an out-of-town associate who would be returning to her home—and her husband and kids—in Chicago next week, after concluding her business in town.

Oh, man. He couldn't risk Selby seeing him here like this. Or, worse, wind up himself at one of her tables. But he and Ellen had just ordered drinks to help pass the time of the thirty-minute wait for a table. And he always brought Ellen to Trino's when she was in town, because she loved the place so much. What was Pax supposed to do? Grab her by the wrist, tell her to forget their drinks—not to mention dinner—and drag her off to the nearby Bob Evans instead? And just hope that Selby didn't see them as they made their escape?

"Ellen," he said as she concluded the call she'd taken as they sat down and folded her cell phone closed, "do me a favor, will you?"

"Sure, Pax, anything."

"Look over my shoulder," he instructed her, "down at the restaurant floor. Do you see a waitress down there, early twenties, black hair about chin length, really cute?"

Ellen grinned, but did as he asked. "Yeah, I see her. Who is she?"

"That's not important," Pax told her. "Just tell me if she comes this way, all right?"

Now Ellen arched her auburn eyebrows in surprise. "You're hiding from her?" she asked incredulously. "Oh, I think who she is is *very* important. Tell me."

He shook his head.

"Tell me, or I'll wave a hand and draw her attention and tell her to come over here."

"You wouldn't dare. I introduced you to your husband."

"And I paid you back by naming our son after you. I don't owe you anything anymore. Tell me who she is. A recent conquest you're trying to avoid?" Her grin turned wicked. "Or did you just find out about a daughter you never knew you had?"

"It's a long story," Pax told her.

"And it's going to be a thirty-minute wait for a table."

"Another time, Ellen," he said. "I promise. I just can't go into it right—"

"She's coming this way," Ellen interrupted him, turning to face him fully. "Just keep your back turned and talk to me, and she'll never be able to tell it's you." And then she launched into what was obviously a fabricated recount: "So I told him, 'You can't talk to me that way,' and he said, 'Oh, no?' and then I said . . ."

Everything Ellen said after that was completely lost on Pax, because Selby sidled up to the bar between him and the woman seated on his other side, her shoulder softly brushing his.

"Oh, I'm sorry," she said as she nudged him. But she was clearly distracted, because she didn't even wait for a reply, and instead beckoned to the bartender. "Bernie, can you change a twenty for me? I'm out of ones."

"For you, Selby Hudson, I'll do anything," Bernie said with a flirtatious chuckle, something that made Pax want to leap over the bar and strangle the guy with his bare hands.

Before he had a chance, though, Bernie took the bill from Selby, and Pax watched from the corner of his eye as he threaded his way through the other bartenders to the cash register in the middle of the bar. Pax held his breath and pretended to be interested in whatever long-winded tale Ellen was recounting, but his body fairly hummed with the frustration of knowing Selby was so close and he couldn't reach out to touch her. It was through no small effort that he forced himself to sit still and not turn around to look at her. But when he heard the outburst from the woman seated next to him, the one on the other side of Selby, he couldn't help but twitch and turn his head just the tiniest bit.

"Selby? Selby Hudson? Omigod, is it you?" the woman said in the shrill, stupefied voice of the overly inebriated.

Even over the din in the bar, Pax heard Selby's responding sigh, a sound that was a mixture of irritation, resignation, and dread. "Yes, Deedee," she replied, obviously having recognized the woman even before being recognized herself. "It's me. Hello."

The woman identified as Deedee expelled a sound of obvious astonishment. "I hardly recognized you! You're not fat anymore!"

Fat? Pax echoed to himself, puzzled. What the hell was she talking about? Selby was just right, round and soft in all the places a woman should be round and soft.

But Selby confirmed the other woman's comment—sort of—when she replied, "Yeah, I've dropped a few pounds since high school."

"A *few*?" Deedee the Shrill repeated. "You were as big as a house in high school." The woman laughed, a sound not unlike what one might have expected to hear from a dying horse. She was evidently speaking to her companion—whoever the unfortunate soul was—when she added, "Selby and I went to high school together in Dorsey. In the senior class superlatives, she was voted 'Most Likely to Hover over the

Super Bowl with the word Goodyear Emblazoned on Her Butt.' Or something like that. Omigod, it was *so* funny."

"Actually, Deedee," Selby said, her voice the very picture of dignity, "it was 'Most Likely to Appear Floating in the Sky over the Super Bowl.' If memory serves, you were the one who nominated me."

Deedee laughed again, and Pax cringed. Though his reaction wasn't just because the sound put his teeth on edge. It was also because he remembered that sort of laughter coming from someone else. Several someone elses, in fact. A gaggle of girls standing on a street corner, right before they started hurling names at him.

"That's right! It *was* me!" Deedee exclaimed, sounding quite proud of herself. "But it was really Steve Saunderson's idea. He put me up to it. I wanted to nominate you 'Most Likely to Cause Damage to an Ice Cream Truck on Two-for-One Day.' But the blimp one was better. Omigod, it was so funny."

"Mm," Selby said.

"Boy, those were fun times, weren't they?" Deedee asked.

"Mm," Selby repeated.

"Don't you wish we could go back?"

"Mm," Selby said again. Then she hurried on, "Excuse me, Deedee, I have to get back to work. Great seeing you again." And amazingly—at least, it was amazing to Pax—she managed not to choke on the words as she said them.

Braving a small glance over his shoulder, Pax watched Selby hustle off, and when she was completely out of eyeshot, he turned around on his stool to face the front of the bar. Ellen had halted her monologue to answer another call on her cell phone, so Pax stole a surreptitious glance at Shrill Deedee, and saw that she was a lovely-looking creature the same age as Selby, blond-haired, blue-eyed, beautifully formed, dressed in a creamy white sweater set that was almost certainly cashmere. A former cheerleader, Pax surmised. Because he knew the look of them well. She was seated with another cheerleader-type, which wasn't surprising, since the breed usually traveled in numbers. Pack mentality, after all, made it much more fun to disparage others. Deedee watched Selby's departure, too, then began speaking to her companion again, and Pax, being Pax, eavesdropped quite shamelessly.

"We used to have so much fun with her in high school," Deedee told her friend. "There was this one day when we threw her in the showers after gym class. She was dressed by then and she was kicking and screaming like a banshee, and, omigod, it was *so* funny. Then she had to go to Spanish class all soaking wet, and the look on her face was just priceless. We laughed so hard. Omigod, it was *so* funny."

Funny, Pax echoed to himself. Gee, he'd be willing to bet from Selby's point of view it had been something else entirely.

Deedee's friend laughed obligingly, but Deedee was obviously just warming up, because she continued, "And once, a bunch of us told her that Buck Reeser, on the wrestling team, had this huge crush on her. She didn't believe us at first, but we really worked on her and finally convinced her it was true. Told her he admired her intelligence, and she bought it. Can you believe that?" She enjoyed a moment of chuckling, then went on, "We told her Buck wanted to meet her after school at the arcade, but was just too shy to ask her. So she showed up, and Buck was there, but he was totally clueless. We never told him what we'd done, and he was so embarrassed. Told her he'd never go out with a fatty like her. Omigod, it was *so* funny."

Oh, yeah. Pax would just bet it was.

"She was *such* a geek," Deedee continued, sipping her cosmopolitan. "*Such* a dork. Just a real freak, you know?"

By now Pax had turned on his stool again, until he was completely facing the odious Deedee. She was so out of it, though—or, more probably, so self-absorbed—that she didn't notice his scrutiny. Nor did her friend, who seemed to be equally intoxicated. And equally narcissistic.

"Yeah," Deedee went on after enjoying another sip of her cosmopolitan, "I figured she'd be living in that double-wide trailer with her loser family for the rest of her life. What guy would want her, you know? And hell, someone had to take care of her father, the boozer. He couldn't keep a job for more than two weeks at a time." She smirked. "I never imagined she'd climb all the way up to the high-falutin' waitress life. Woo-wee. But that's what her mom was, too. At some cheesy diner. I guess serving people just runs in the Hudson blood."

Pax put aside, for now, his discovery that everything he'd assumed to be true about Selby was, in fact, completely false. He'd think about that later. And he told himself that any mature, well-adjusted adult who'd just overheard what he had just overheard would pretend he'd heard nothing and move on with his life accordingly. A slightly less mature, slightly less well-adjusted adult would politely tap the woman on the shoulder and courteously point out to her that other people had feelings, too, and maybe, in the future, she might think about that.

But Pax wasn't well-adjusted. And he sure as hell wasn't mature. So he caught the bartender's attention, and when the young man leaned over the bar, he asked, "Bernie, what's the nastiest, stickiest, most stain-inducing drink you know how to make?"

To his credit, Bernie didn't bat an eye. "That would be my own invention," he said. "I call it a Dark Cloud over Chernobyl. I created it at a frat party I worked a while back. Political science majors. Dark rum, blackberry vodka, Chambord, dark crème de cacao, pineapple juice, splash of grenadine, Cherry Coke for the fizz, a little—"

Pax smiled. "Make one for me, will you?" he asked before

Bernie even finished the recipe. He already knew it was *exactly* what he was in the mood for.

The bartender shrugged. "Sure."

"And Bernie?"

"Yes, sir?"

"Could you set it on fire?"

Bernie shook his head ruefully. "Not this one, Mr. Brown."

Pax's disappointment was acute. "Then make it a double."

"Yes, sir."

He watched as Bernie mixed up the concoction and poured it into the blender with crushed ice—oh, good, it would be nice and cold, too—then poured it into a really *big* glass. It was indeed a nasty, sticky-looking prospect, the consistency of slush and the color of something the cat hacked up. As Bernie placed it on the bar, Pax asked him for the bill, then signed it with a flourish, adding a five hundred percent tip.

Then he looked at Ellen. "Would you object to going somewhere else for dinner? I promise next time you're in town, we'll come back to Trino's."

"That's fine, Pax," she said. "As long as you tell me what's going on."

He nodded. "Any of sign of the waitress?" he asked her.

She looked past him, surveying the restaurant. "None."

"Good. Let's go, then."

And as he turned, he—accidentally, honest—smacked the freshly prepared, and still teeming full, Dark Cloud over Chernobyl right off the bar, and onto the unsuspecting Deedee, who kicked and screamed like a banshee as it splashed onto her face and neck and all the way down the front of her creamy white cashmere sweater set.

Omigod, it was *so* funny.

"Holy shit," Pax said when he realized the magnitude— the gigantic, immense, enormous, colossal, stupendous, glorious magnitude—of the damage. Bernie was going to have to change the name of the drink to Dark Cloud over Kashmir. Or maybe Dark Cloud over Deedee. Yeah, that's the ticket. Because she was a sputtering, gasping mess from head to toe. Quite literally, since bits of the slushy drink clung to her eyelashes and dripped from her lovely blond coif and also trickled over what Pax would wager were Manolo Blahnik shoes.

Wow. He'd had no idea he'd do that much damage. He really should be ashamed of himself.

So he leaned down close to her ear, and he said, "If I were you, Deedee, I'd get that up to the cleaner right away. I bet dark rum is a real *bitch* to get out of cashmere."

Then he straightened and crooked his arm for Ellen, who looped her own arm through it and let him guide her away from the bar. He knew she'd ask what that had been about once they were outside, and Pax would explain then. And he knew Ellen would understand completely.

After all, she'd been a geek in high school, too.

ELEVEN

IT HAD BEEN A LONG TIME SINCE MICHAEL had been called to the principal's office for something he had done. And although he was pretty sure Hannah's reason for summoning him now wouldn't leave a dark blot on his permanent record—like those *really* existed—he still felt as edgy and uncertain as he had all those times in school when he'd found himself in a similar situation.

Because she'd joined the OPUS operation, he had left the bugs in her home and office, including the wiretaps on her phones, and he had continued to surveille her. Now, though, it was with her knowledge. She'd also kept him apprised of what was going on with Adrian elsewhere, in case he said anything of significance during his conversations with her. Most of the things Adrian had said to Hannah on the phone had been significant only in that they made Michael want to vomit, on account of Adrian's terms of endearment consisted largely of food metaphors so sickly sweet they'd put a diabetic into a coma. In the meantime, Michael had tried to take care of some of his real work—the legitimate work he normally performed to earn his living—because that was what he would be returning to eventually, and it would be oh-so-helpful if he had at least a few clients left when he did.

So when Hannah called him and told him to come to the principal's office right away, he reacted with reluctance and dread. All she said was that he needed to come right away, because of something very important that was an emergency. His first thought, of course, had been Alex, but before he even had a chance to ask about his son, Hannah was assuring him Alex was fine, this had nothing to do with Alex, but could he still come to Emerson right away for an emergency of utmost importance because she really needed to tell him something important and it was an emergency and could he please hurry because it was an important emergency?

Such an important emergency, evidently, that she was waiting for him in the outer office when he arrived, and the minute he came through the door, she told her secretary to hold all her calls and visitors and, without so much as a hello, she ushered Michael into her office proper.

And then she immediately closed the door behind them and said, "Did I mention this is important?"

He nodded. "I do believe that word came up a time or two"—*or twenty*—"during your call, yes."

"And did I mention it's an emergency?"

He nodded again. "Yeah, I think you did."

"Then what took you so long?" she demanded.

He eyed her warily. She was dressed, as always, in one of her conservative suits, this one the color of tobacco with a cream-colored blouse underneath. It was a nice outfit, but it did nothing to complement the expression of wild-eyed anticipation she wore with it.

"Well, I wasn't able to bend time or transcend dimensions the way I usually do and just beam myself over," he told her, "so I had to drive. From the other side of town," he added meaningfully. "During the beginning of the lunch rush."

She expelled an exasperated breath. "Well, thanks to you, we now have a half hour less to do this," she said.

"Do what?" he asked. "What's the important emergency?"

Her eyes fairly sparkled, and he could almost see electricity spiking there as she told him, "I have a key to Adrian's place. And Adrian isn't home. And he gave me permission to go over there and look around."

Several thoughts bounced through Michael's head at the announcement. Where had Hannah gotten a key to Adrian's place? When had Adrian given it to her? How did she know he wasn't home? What was she supposed to be looking for there? Who did she think she was, calling this an important emergency? And why was Michael here? She was acting like she planned on doing something with this knowledge and the key to Adrian's place, like go over there and have a look around. And that was just plain—

Uh-oh.

"Maybe you better start at the beginning," Michael told her.

Still leaning back against the door, her eyes still gleaming, Hannah said, "Adrian called me this morning and told me he needed me to do him a favor, because he's in Seymour on business, and he forgot something at home, a computer disc he accidentally left in the CD burner that he really needs, and he wondered if I could possibly go over and get it for him and drive it down to Seymour for him, because he's going to be tied up in meetings all day and he needs it by dinnertime."

Michael narrowed his eyes at her. Putting aside, for now, the fact that this was just a bizarre request on Adrian's part, and the fact that her mouth was running at a hundred miles per hour with her excitement about it, he asked, "Why do you have a key to Adrian's place?"

She toggled her head back and forth impatiently. "Well, I don't have it yet. But he told me where he hides a spare key. In the garage of his building, not far from his assigned parking space. And he told me to go into his home,

Michael. We have permission to go to his condo and look around."

"No, *you* have permission," he said. Not that it mattered, because there was no way he was going to let her go over there.

"But I'm inviting you along," she told him.

"Oh, no," he told her. "I'm not going anywhere near Adrian's place under these conditions, and neither are you."

She gaped at him in disbelief. "Are you nuts? This is the perfect opportunity for us to go search his place and see if we can find out what he's up to."

"Are *you* nuts?" Michael countered. "This is a setup."

"A setup?" she echoed.

"Oh, come on, Hannah, even the boys in the mail room at OPUS know better than to fall for something this obvious."

She straightened up and crossed her arms over her chest, a clear indication that she was feeling defensive. "This isn't obvious. It's a legitimate request. Seymour is forty-five minutes away, and he needs something for a meeting this evening, and he doesn't have time to drive back here to get it. So he asked a friend—me—to do him a favor and bring it to him. I don't see anything suspicious about that."

No, of course she didn't, Michael thought. Because she was so damned trusting of people, even a crook like Adrian. "At best," Michael said, "this is an attempt by Adrian to get you to come to Seymour, and then he'll try to convince you it's too late to drive home, so you should stay and spend the night. In the same hotel he's staying in. In the same hotel *room* he's staying in. At worst, he's still here in town, and he's just waiting for you and me to go over to his place, and there will be a booby trap of some kind waiting for us."

"The caller ID on the phone when he called said it was a

call from Seymour, Indiana. You are just too suspicious of people, Michael."

Now it was Michael's turn to gape. "Of *course* I'm suspicious of people, Hannah. It's my job to be suspicious."

"No, it *used* to be your job to be suspicious. You're just suspicious on a consulting basis now, remember?"

Michael bit back a growl of discontent. "Hannah, we are *not* going over to Adrian's condo," he stated in no uncertain terms. "Not for any reason. You're going to call him back and tell him you've gotten tied up at work, and you can't do this favor for him."

She lifted her chin defiantly. "Fine. You don't want to go with me, don't go. I'll go by myself and have a look around."

Michael started shaking his head before she even finished what she was saying. "Oh, no, you won't."

"Oh, yes, I will."

"No, you won't."

"Yes, I will."

"You won't."

"I will."

"Won't."

"Will."

"Hannah—"

"Michael—"

And just like that, they hit an impasse. She settled her hands on her hips in an "I dare you to try and stop me" way that made him want to stop her just about any way he could. And the way that came to mind just then was a way he would have enjoyed very much. Because something about her posture taunted him, tempted him, and he wanted more than anything in that moment to cover the room in the three quick strides it would take him to do it, pull her into his arms, and kiss her until they were both too addlepated to do anything.

Well, anything but fall to the floor and spend the rest of the afternoon making love.

And, oh, dammit, why did every thought of Hannah lately end up with the two of them falling to the floor—or a bed, or a couch, or a chair, or stairs, or into a shower stall, or a bathtub, or onto a kitchen countertop, or a kitchen table, or, hell, the kitchen sink, he didn't care—and spend the rest of the afternoon/morning/evening/night/sunset/sunrise/dawn/twilight/lunch hour/whatever making love?

And why weren't they making love now, the way he wanted to? Oh, yeah. Because Hannah would rather go over to Adrian's place and rifle through that guy's drawers instead of Michael's.

"I won't let you do this," Michael told her.

Her eyes went wide in obvious outrage. "Excuse me?" she said. "You won't *let* me do this? I don't recall asking for your permission. And I don't have to have it."

"Maybe not," he said. "But when you get over there and realize this is a setup, you'll wish like hell I was there."

"Then maybe you better tag along," she said sarcastically. "Don't want the little woman getting into trouble, do we?"

"The little woman won't get in trouble if she stops acting like a child," Michael pointed out.

She ignored that and said, "We might not ever have another chance like this. We need to take advantage of it."

"The only reason we have this chance right now is because Adrian is up to something," he countered.

"Then I'll go without you, Michael."

He shook his head in defeat. "Man. One little taste of intrigue, and you're turning into Mata Hari."

"And you're turning into Mahatma Gandhi," she told him. "What's wrong with this picture?"

Everything, he wanted to say. Because this should be a picture of two people on the verge of discovering each other's most intimate secrets. Instead, it was a picture of two people who were about to make a terrible, terrible mistake. Hannah by falling for Adrian's ruse, and Michael by doing nothing to stop her.

Stop her? he jeered at himself. Hell, he was going to drive her over there.

He blew out a long, impatient breath and said, "Just promise you'll stay close to me when we get there."

Adrian may have been a despicable human being, Hannah thought as she rifled through a desk drawer looking for heaven alone knew what, but he sure did know how to live in style. He'd probably spent more just to furnish his home office than Hannah took home in a year's time.

Not that she was bitter or anything.

But the computer system whose files Michael was currently plundering was completely state-of-the-art—though she supposed, since Adrian was a big muckety-muck for CompuPax, he probably got a decent deal on stuff like that—and the furniture was all quality hardwood—teak, judging by the look and feel of it. Of course, she knew an executive of a company like CompuPax probably drew a pretty good salary. And, naturally, it never hurt to blackmail your former employer for millions of dollars before leaving, did it? Especially if your former employer was some hush-hush spy group like OPEC. Or OPRAH. Or OPERA. Or ODIOUS. Or whatever the hell the name was of the organization Adrian and Michael used to work for. OPUS, that was it. Even if, to Hannah's way of thinking, she and Michael were currently working for OBTUSE. That would be the Opportunity for Boneheaded, Tedious, Useless, Stupid Efforts. Because they'd been searching Adrian's condo for nearly an hour, and they'd discovered absolutely nothing of consequence. Not even a decent security setup they couldn't easily evade.

On the upside, they hadn't walked into a trap the way

Michael had thought they would. And Hannah had done her best—honestly she had—not to sing, *Nyah, nyah, nyah, nyah, nyah . . . I was right and you were wrong.*

On the downside, though, she now knew where Adrian threw his dirty socks and underwear at day's end. And she also knew his preferred brands of toothpaste, toilet paper, dishwasher detergent, deodorant, and foot powder, which would definitely come in handy, oh, say, the next time he asked her to pick up a few things from the grocery store for him while he was out of town. As for today's enterprise . . .

Well. Suffice it to say she'd never really thought about all the things one discovered upon searching a premises that one *didn't* want to find. Like the aforementioned name brands. And the aforementioned dirty laundry. And the skeezy cheeses in the refrigerator. And the sexually ambiguous, ah, equipment, in the nightstand. Not to mention the *enormous* box of condoms that indicated Adrian was either quite the hound dog or quite the optimist. Though combined with the aforementioned, ah, equipment, in the nightstand . . .

Well, suffice it to say Hannah preferred not to think for too long about what Adrian did in his spare time.

She closed one desk drawer and opened another, and reminded herself that *she* had been the one who insisted they search Adrian's condo. Even if, by some wild chance, it *wasn't* a setup, Michael had told her on the drive over Adrian was too smart to leave anything out in the open. But Hannah had been sure he would feel comfortable enough in his own home to have kept things here that might be potentially incriminating.

Okay, okay, okay. So Michael was the real spy here, and this just proved it, and she should have listened to him in the first place. He hadn't *had* to tag along. Just because he'd thought it might be dangerous for her to come here, that didn't mean he had to come, too. Just because he'd thought there was a chance Adrian would come home while they were here. Just because he thought it might even be an ambush Adrian had coordinated. Just because he thought Adrian was going to show up and catch them red-handed. Just because—

Her thoughts stopped right there when she heard the front door open and close in the other room.

Oh. No.

Oh. Damn.

She really hated it when other people were right and she was wrong.

Her gaze flew to Michael, who had halted with his hands hovering over the keyboard, obviously having heard the same thing she had. He lifted a hand to his mouth, holding his finger to his lips in the international sign language for, *Button it*. Oh, like she needed to go through spy training to know that was how you reacted when someone caught you going through his things. She snatched from the top of the desk the CD she'd pulled from the computer's burner—yes, Adrian had indeed left one in there—and made a face at Michael, then turned and left the room. Hey, he was a smart spy. He'd figure something out. She hoped. Real bad.

"Adrian?" she called out as she exited the office. Her heart was pounding so hard, she was afraid he'd be able to hear it, and it made her feel almost dizzy with the way it was rushing her blood through her body. Her legs felt wobbly as she walked, and she hoped like hell she could keep her voice steady. "Is that you?"

"Hannah?" he called back.

She strode down the hallway to the living room, and he came into view the moment she rounded the corner. "What are you doing here?" she asked. "I was just about to leave." She held up the CD and forced a smile. "Is this what you needed?"

He smiled back. "That's it," he told her. "One of my meetings was a no-show, so I thought I'd have time to run back here and get what I needed and not bother you. I tried to call you at school to intercept you, but they said you'd left." He glanced down at his watch. "That was almost an hour ago."

Meaning he wondered where the hell she'd been and what the hell she'd been doing since then, she realized.

"I went to lunch first," she said. "I was starving, and since you said you didn't need this until dinnertime, I thought you wouldn't mind."

"Of course not," he told her. "But now you won't have to make that long drive yourself. Thank you, though, for agreeing to."

"Don't mention it," she told him. "Anytime."

She covered the rest of the distance between them and handed Adrian the CD, then turned toward the front door, certain he'd want to turn around and leave again, now that he had what he'd come for, so that he could get back in time for whatever he had to get back in time for. So it was with some surprise that she watched him toss his keys onto an end table near the sofa.

"Don't you have to be going?" Hannah asked.

He shook his head. "Oh, I have a few minutes. Since I'm here, there are a few more things in my office I'd like to get."

"The office?" she echoed, much too loudly, and with much too much panic striking her voice. Worse, without thinking, she bolted in that direction, situating her body at the hallway entrance in a way that was clearly meant to keep Adrian from venturing any farther.

Oh, yeah. Mata Hari. That was her, all right. Smooth as extra-crunchy peanut butter. Spread over broken glass. With a pitchfork. In the dark.

Adrian halted in front of her, his expression indicating he thought she was as nutty as extra-crunchy peanut butter. "Yes, the office," he said patiently. Then, to make things even clearer, he added, "*My* office."

"But . . ." Hannah began. And never finished.

"But what?" he asked.

"But, um . . ." she elucidated.

"But, um, what?" Adrian asked.

"But, um, ah . . ." she clarified.

This time Adrian only narrowed his eyes.

"I-i-i-it's just that, I, uh . . . there was a big spider in there when I was in there before," she finally said. "Really big," she elaborated. "Like *this* big," she emphasized, holding the thumb and index finger of her right hand a good two inches apart . . . and then widening them even more when Adrian seemed unimpressed—and unterrified. And then more. And then bringing her other hand into it, ultimately making the spider large enough to cook Adrian's breakfast for him in the morning. And then raise any children he might have later in life. "It's like . . . like . . . like the *king* of spiders," she finally told him, since he still didn't seem to be bothered by its post-atomic-apocalypse size. "I haven't seen one like that since *Damnation Alley*. You should get out now while you still can and call the super to take care of it. That's what I'd do."

Adrian smiled at her benevolently, the way he might smile at an inmate in a mental asylum. "There, there," he told her calmly. "I'll take care of that icky spider for you."

And then, before Hannah could think of a way to stop him, he was pushing past her, making his way down the hall. Hannah spun around to watch him go, feeling helpless and inept and frightened. She watched as Adrian stopped at the office door and settled his hands on his hips, as if he were offended by the sight on the other side. He turned to look at her, his expression one of consternation, then back into the office again. Hannah was on the verge of blurting out an apology and trying to come up with some lame excuse to explain Michael's presence—*My car wouldn't start, Adrian, so I called your archenemy to give me a lift*—when Adrian spoke first.

"There's no spider in here," he said. "Not one as big as you say, anyway. It must have gone out the window."

Well, that certainly brought Hannah up short. Adrian lived on the sixteenth floor of his high-rise. If that spider went out the window, it was nothing but a greasy accountant stain on the street below now.

By the time Hannah made her way to the door, Adrian was inside the office . . . alone. The screen saver danced on the computer monitor the same way it had when she and Michael had arrived, the chair was tucked neatly into the desk, and nothing appeared to have been touched. Hannah remembered leaving some papers scattered on top of the desk and a drawer open when she heard Adrian come in, but Michael had tidied everything and still managed to get out without Adrian's seeing him. But where? she wondered. Where had he gone? Thankfully, the window was closed, so she was confident he hadn't tossed himself through it.

He must still be in the apartment, though, since she and Adrian had both been in full view of the front door. Unless he knew about another entrance that she didn't know about herself. She supposed she and Adrian had been out of view of the office door and hallway when he'd first come in, so *maybe* Michael had had a chance to sneak out. Maybe.

She found some small comfort in knowing he must still be close by, though. If Adrian decided he had more than a few minutes to kill, and decided to kill them by, oh . . . Hannah didn't know . . . by killing *her,* say—or, worse, by having his way with her—Michael would be around to stop him. Unless he'd ducked out for a sandwich or something, she thought further. In which case, if she started screaming for help, he'd be too busy hitting the deli counter to be of much use.

Boy, that would be just like a man. Right when you need him to be a hero, he's going for the Philly cheese steak.

But no, Michael wouldn't leave her alone with Adrian, of that she was certain. She just wished she knew where he was at the moment. If for no other reason than that he was, you know, her ride home.

She watched as Adrian collected the things he needed from his office, and tried not to cringe when he opened and closed the very drawers she had been searching only moments ago. Had she put everything back the way it was? Did he even pay attention to the contents that much? Would he know someone had been going through his things? What would he do if he suspected Hannah of being more than a garden-variety snoop?

And where had Michael gone?

"Well, I think that's everything," Adrian said as he collected a few more CDs from the shelves above his computer. He turned to face Hannah and smiled. "I'm sorry again for bringing you all the way over here like this for nothing."

"Honestly, Adrian, it was no trouble," she said. Well, except for the pesky heart attack she was on the verge of having.

"I'll make it up to you this weekend, after the reception," he told her with a leer.

"And I'm just counting the moments until then," she replied. In fact, she was counting them in much the same way that an inmate on death row counts the moments until they strap him into the chair.

Adrian sighed with something that might have been wistfulness in another man—another man who wasn't, say, a jerk—and said, "It really is too bad I have to get back to Seymour today. I mean, here we are alone at my place, with no one to bother us. And since I'm sure you told them you'd be taking the rest of the afternoon off, you don't have to be back at work until tomorrow."

He strode across the office and lifted a hand toward Hannah, skimming his fingertips along the line of her jaw, and somehow, she managed to make the shudder that wound through her seem like it was one of anticipation instead of revulsion.

"Maybe I'll call and cancel my final meeting in Seymour," he murmured as he drew nearer. "We could spend the rest of the day here enjoying ourselves. . . ."

And then he was dipping his head to hers, and his mouth was hovering over Hannah's, and she was thinking, *Oh, God, no, please, no, not this, not here, not now, not with Adrian,* and he suddenly seemed so big and so powerful and so menacing and so terrible and so everything she had hoped to never come up against in her life, and when had her life stopped being so normal and secure and uneventful and become such a freak show, and where, oh, where was Michael, and—

And then there was a soft, cheery chirp that sounded like a bird on a wire, and Adrian was pulling away with an exasperated sound, and Hannah was breathing again.

His phone, she realized, relaxing some. The telephone on his desk was ringing. She felt almost as if she were having an out-of-body experience as she watched him walk over to answer it.

"Yes?" he said impatiently. "What? I'm sorry, I can barely understand what you're saying." He covered his other ear with the fist that was holding the CDs. "No, I still can't understand you. What's that ungodly noise? What? My car? Oh, for God's sake. Why on earth do I—What? No, don't touch anything. I'll be right down."

Before Hannah could even ask what was going on, he was returning the phone to its cradle and turning around. "It was the garage attendant," he said. "My car alarm is going off."

"Someone tried to steal your car?" Hannah asked, hoping she sounded shocked and outraged instead of relieved and delighted. "Right out of the garage? Who would do such a thing?"

Adrian eyed her warily. "Who indeed?" he asked.

It was in that moment, when Adrian looked at her as if she should have known better than to even ask such a question,

that Hannah became almost certain that Adrian knew everything. Almost. Somehow, she suspected he knew she was
only pretending to be interested in him. Suspected he knew
she had used his need of a favor to search his home. Suspected he knew she was helping Michael. She wasn't positive, but she suspected. And she suspected, too, that Michael
had been right all along, and that Adrian had set up this
entire episode knowing she would enlist Michael's help, and
then Adrian could catch them both red-handed.

Why had he done it, though? She didn't have the answer to
that.

"You better get down there," she said quietly, amazed at
how calm she suddenly felt in light of her discovery. "He
might still be there."

Still looking at her in that way that told her he knew what
was what, he shook his head. "No, I'm sure he's long gone
by now. The alarm—if nothing else—must have frightened
him off." And then he strode forward again, stopping in
front of Hannah when scarcely a breath of air lay between
them. "Come on, Hannah," he said. "I'll walk you to your
car."

"No, that's all right," she told him. "I'm parked on the
street. You go ahead and take care of things down in the
garage."

He didn't move, though, only stood menacingly over her
for another moment, gazing down at her as if he weren't
quite sure what he wanted to do with her. Then he tucked the
CDs he still clutched into his jacket pocket and extended his
hand toward her. She pretended not to understand what he
meant by the gesture.

"My key?" he asked, crooking a tawny eyebrow at her.

She feigned forgetfulness. "Oh, of course," she said,
reaching into her own pocket to retrieve it.

"I'll put it back where it belongs," he said as she handed it
to him.

And she knew that place would be different from the one where he'd put it for her to find today.

He dropped the key into his pocket along with the CDs, then extended his hand toward the hallway this time, toward the front door. Hannah preceded him, even though she figured it probably wasn't a good idea to turn her back on Adrian.

And as she turned to watch Adrian close the door behind them and lock it, she wondered once again where Michael was.

TWELVE

MICHAEL WASN'T SURE HIS HEART WOULD ever be the same again after the episode at Adrian's. He couldn't remember ever being so scared. And he hadn't even given a thought to his own life or well-being. He'd been terrified of something happening to Hannah. At the moment, he wasn't sure what he wanted to do more—kiss her senseless or turn her over his knee and spank her. Although doing both did hold a certain strange—and very erotic—appeal . . .

He would not say, *I told you so,* he thought as they made the drive back to her house in silence. As much as he wanted to say it, he wouldn't. He would think it—a lot. But he wouldn't say it. Or he might hum it to himself. But he wouldn't say it. He might even do some mental Shakespearean rendition of it. But he wouldn't—

Oh, the hell with it.

"I told you so."

In the passenger seat next to him, Hannah growled menacingly.

"I told you," he continued, "that it was a trap. That Adrian was setting you up."

This time Hannah's response was more of a snarl.

"But would you listen to me?" he asked. Then, because he

was pretty sure her ensuing response to that was a word no woman who worked with children should be familiar with, he answered himself, "*Nooooooo*."

"Michael," she said through gritted teeth, "do you think we could do this some other time?"

"There's no time like the present," he pointed out smugly. "Never put off tomorrow what you can do today."

"Gee, and just when I didn't think you could get any more annoying," Hannah said, "you resort to clichés. Is there no end to the marvel that is Michael Sawyer?"

He clamped his jaw shut at that. For all of ten seconds. "He's on to us both now," he said. "You realize that."

"I suspect it," she agreed. "But I don't know for sure."

"There's no way you're going to that reception with him Friday night."

"Of course I'm going to the reception with him," Hannah said. "Why wouldn't I?"

Michael took his eyes off the road long enough to turn and stare at her in openmouthed astonishment. "Why wouldn't you? Why *would* you? It's too dangerous. He knows you've been helping me out. He's not going to misstep or say anything helpful around you now."

"How do you know?"

"Because I know Adrian. He won't make a mistake like that. There's absolutely no reason for you to get within a hundred feet of the guy after what happened today."

"I'll be surrounded by people Friday night," she said. "He won't have the opportunity to do anything to me."

"That's not good enough," Michael said.

"You'll be there, too," Hannah reminded him. "I won't be in any danger. And I think there's still a small chance he might trust me. We should take advantage of that if it's still even a remote possibility."

"Yeah, and you also thought he had a legitimate favor to ask you today, too."

She said nothing for a moment, then, very evenly, she told him, "Don't start that again."

God, why were they so angry at each other? he wondered. Yeah, they'd done a stupid thing, but they'd survived it, and there really had been no harm done. In fact, they were better off, because now Michael could be sure of what he'd been suspecting for a while, that Adrian knew Hannah was helping him. Now he could give his boss a reason for pulling Hannah out of the operation. And now he could go back to concentrating on Adrian without the added distraction of worrying about Hannah's safety. Because that could be the only reason for slipping up as egregiously as he had today. Yeah, it had been five years since he'd done this, but even a greenhorn fresh out of basic training could have handled this assignment better than Michael had. Because a greenhorn fresh out of basic training wouldn't be halfway in love with Hannah.

Ah, dammit. He really hadn't wanted to admit that to himself. But hell, the minute he'd heard Adrian coming home this afternoon, his first thought had been not for himself, but for Hannah. And he'd known then that he was indeed in love with her. What he didn't know was what he was going to do about it.

"How did you get down to the garage anyway?" she asked him now.

He smiled. "Old trade secret. If I told you—"

"You'd have to kill me," she answered for him.

"Maybe for Christmas I'll get you some top-secret clearance," he said. And he was only half joking when he said it. He wouldn't get her top-secret clearance, of course. But he did hope he'd be around to get her something for Christmas.

She blew out another impatient sound and tapped her fingers anxiously on the dashboard. She'd been doing that ever since they left Adrian's place, he realized. Tapping her fingers on the dashboard with one hand, the other fiddling impatiently with the radio. She'd opened his glove compartment and examined the contents—several times—then slammed it shut again. Now she flipped down the visor and inspected his CD collection, pulling the discs out one by one and shoving them back in again, so quickly that he wasn't even sure she could tell what they were.

By the time they pulled up to her house, Michael was feeling nearly as agitated as she was, and he was eager to be on his way. He didn't need to be feeling edgy around Hannah when she felt edgy, too. Not having discovered what he just had about his feelings for her.

"Next time you want to search somebody's house," he said as he threw the car into park, "call someone else, okay?"

She smiled, and there was something in her expression that seemed almost genuinely happy. "Could you come inside for a few minutes?" she asked.

"Why?" he wanted to know.

"Just . . . I think you should come in for a little while," she repeated. "It's kind of important. Do you have to get home right away? School won't be out for another hour."

Michael did some quick calculating. Alex had chess club after school today, then he was going home with a teammate who was a friend of his for dinner. Michael had intended to use the extra time to himself to finish some work at the office. But if Hannah had something she needed to talk to him about . . .

"Okay," he said. "I can stay for a little while."

She nodded, and he noticed the gesture was a little jerky. "Good. That's good."

The moment they were inside, she pushed the front door closed behind them and turned to look at Michael. Judging by the expression on her face, she seemed to want to tell him something very important indeed. So Michael waited, expectantly, to see what it would be. Then he waited some more. And then some more. And then some more. Probably a good two or three minutes passed with just the two of them standing there in the living room, staring at each other in silence. And then, finally, Hannah moved. She took a step forward. Toward Michael.

And she began to unbutton her jacket.

He told himself it was just because she was home now, and wanted to, understandably, shed her jacket in an effort to make herself more comfortable. But when she shrugged the jacket off, she didn't hang it on the coat rack by the front door. Instead, she tossed it aside without even looking at it, oblivious to how it landed in a heap on the floor. Then she took another step forward. Toward Michael.

And she began to unbutton her blouse.

"H-H-Hannah?" he stammered once he understood her intentions. "Wh-wh-what are you doing?"

"I'm taking off my clothes, Michael," she said as she tugged her shirttail free of her skirt and unbuttoned the rest of her buttons. "Then I'm going to take off your clothes," she added. "And then you and I both are going to have sex."

"O-o-oh."

Obviously intending to make good on her promise, Hannah shed her blouse, too, and Michael went hard at the sight of her luscious breasts surging out of the top of a sheer lace brassiere the color of a seashell. It was one of those bras that stopped halfway up, and he could see the very edge of her aureolas peeking out from the tops of the cups. She had a mole on her left breast that he found incredibly sexy, and his mouth opened involuntarily as he envisioned himself tracing it with the tip of his tongue. And then Hannah was reaching behind herself and unhooking her bra, and her breasts spilled completely free.

Oh, gee, had he thought he was hard before? Gosh, he'd had no idea.

By now she was standing in front of him, and she reached

down to take his hands in hers, lifting them to her breasts in invitation. Like Michael really needed one. Eagerly, he filled his hands with her, palming the ripe flesh, kneading, squeezing, thumbing the taut peaks to even greater distinction. She was so soft. So warm. So incredibly beautiful. As he bent over, he lifted one breast to his mouth and pulled her nipple between his lips. He brushed his mouth over her once, twice, three times, four, then drew her inside for a more thorough taste. He darted his tongue against her, then lapped more eagerly, marveling at how sweet she tasted, how fine she felt.

Her hands moved to his hair, her fingers threading and weaving, silently bidding him to continue with his exploration. So he did. Then her hands moved downward, over his shoulders and flat torso, along the waistband of his trousers, over the belt buckle and lower still, her palm flattening, hard, against the part of him that had swollen in response to her little striptease. Then her fingers were closing snugly over him, her palm curving over the long, hard ridge of him. He pulled back, sucking in a harsh breath at the contact, then released one of her breasts to cover her hand with his, holding it firm as he linked their fingers together. Slowly, deliberately, he pushed both their hands downward, over his trousers and his taut flesh, to the very base of his shaft. And then lower still, until their hands were between his legs, and she was cupping him completely in her palm.

He ducked his head into her neck as she caressed him there, panting against her damp skin, his breathing ragged and heavy, his body tight with his need. Still pushing her fingers hard against himself, he drew their hands back up again, growing even harder and thicker against her palm. Again and again, he helped her stroke himself, until their fingers began to grow damp from the friction and perspiration. And then, abruptly, he halted her and drew her hand away, jerking her body against his almost roughly.

"No more of that for a bit," he gasped. "I want to make this last as long as I can."

"But school will be out soon," she said.

"Alex has plans this afternoon," he told her. He reached behind her, locating the back zipper of her skirt. "And so do I."

Hannah had no idea what had come over her, to be behaving so brazenly. She only knew that once they were safely away from Adrian's place, she'd been overcome by a fierce agitation unlike anything she'd ever felt before, as if there were some powerful force bottled up inside her too tightly, an uncontrollable chemical reaction that was about to explode with the strength of an atom bomb if she didn't do something to release it. She had recognized it as a purely sexual response. But to what? She had no idea. She only knew that she had been frightened out of her wits for Michael's safety, but even knowing he was all right, she couldn't let go of the anxiety. It had kept building and building, all through the drive home, until she felt as if she were going to come apart at the seams with it.

She'd known she would stay wound too tight like that unless she could find some kind of release. And the only way to release it, she knew, was to let it out, and let it be what it was. A raw sexual need to be with Michael.

Now she would be with him. Sexually. Rawly. Because never had she needed a man the way she needed him in that moment. And having touched him the way she just had, the way he had made her touch him, she knew he needed her that way, too.

As he drew her zipper downward, he pushed her body close, her pelvis connecting with his, his erection surging against her belly. She moved her hands to the waistband of her skirt, pushing the garment down as he opened the zipper wider, unable to wait for him to finish before she took it off.

She wiggled out of her stockings, too, rolling them down over her legs as gracefully as she could, kicking them aside to join the rest of her discarded clothing. Michael watched her as she undressed, his gaze roving hungrily over her nearly naked body, and there was just something terribly arousing about that. He continued to watch her as she hooked her fingers into the waistband of her panties and pulled them down, too, stepping out of them and casting them away almost frantically, unable to tolerate being dressed a moment longer.

And then she was back in Michael's arms, and his hands seemed to be everywhere at once, first framing her face, then cupping her breasts, then curving around her waist, then stroking her fanny. When had he stripped her naked? she wondered hazily as she reveled in his touches. Then she remembered she had been the one to do that. But why hadn't she stripped him naked, too?

She loosened his tie and reached for the top button of his shirt, but there was something so fundamentally erotic about being pressed naked to his still fully clothed form, and she hesitated, drinking in the sensation. The brush of his cotton shirt over her tender nipples made her gasp her delight aloud, and she rubbed her body more sinuously against his. He groaned at her action, opening his hand wide over her bare bottom, pushing her forward until the damp heart of her was pressed to the hard ridge beneath his trousers. He dipped his head to her neck, kissing her, nibbling her flesh, darting his tongue over the tender wound, then nibbling her again. Finally, though, Hannah wanted to know what he was like beneath his garments, too, and she shoved his jacket over his shoulders, tugged the knot in his tie free, and went to work on the buttons of his shirt. Michael helped by removing his belt and unfastening his trousers, and with both their fumbling efforts, they finally had him naked, too.

They should go to the bedroom now, she told herself. Somehow, though, she knew they'd never make it . . .

As she fell back onto the sofa, Michael knelt before her, parting her legs with one fluid move. Instantly, shamelessly, he pulled her ankles wide apart and pressed his face to her center, laving her, licking her, savoring and devouring her. Hannah cried out loud at the jagged jolts of heat that shot through her every time his tongue moved against her. Never, ever, had she felt such a wild conflux of sensations. His tongue darted over her, inside her, as if he wanted to drink deeply of her essence to quench a long-unassuaged thirst. Her head rolled back against the sofa and her eyes fluttered closed, and she tangled her fingers in his hair as he relished every taste of her. Vaguely, she registered the feel of his hands moving up her legs, over her calves and shins and knees, then higher still, over the outsides of her thighs, then moving inward. His thumbs joined his tongue in parting her, pleasuring her, then she felt him slip a finger inside her, deep inside her, before withdrawing it slowly again. She thought she gasped his name aloud, but she wasn't sure. She wasn't sure of anything then, only that she'd never have enough of this man.

He slid his finger inside her again, moving the other hand above his mouth to find the sensitive little button of her clitoris. He stroked it once, lightly, and she gasped at the wave of pleasure that rolled through her. His finger moved inside her again, a second joining the first, and she nearly came undone.

He pulled back then, with obvious reluctance, but joined her on the wide sofa, pulling her up to her knees, her back to his front. He took a moment to free her hair from the untidy bun it had become, plucking the pins out one by one and tossing them aside, sifting the long strands through his fingers reverently, as if they were spun gold. Then he reached around her with both arms, dipping one hand between her legs to gently plow the flesh he'd made so wet and hot with his mouth. The other hand found her breast, covering it with sure fingers, squeezing and massaging, catching her taut nipple tight between index and middle finger. In response, Hannah pressed herself backward, more intimately against him, the press of his hard member parting her buttocks and rubbing against her sensitive flesh with a delicious sort of friction she hoped would never end.

"Oh, God, Hannah," he said, grinding out the words as if they were painful to say. "I've wanted you this way, so much, for so long."

"I've wanted you, too," she confessed. "I've wondered what it would be like between us when it happened. If it happened," she hastily corrected herself.

He hesitated, then said, "If I tell you I have a condom in my wallet, will you think I've been taking for granted this would happen?"

She smiled a little weakly. "What if you have been?" she asked. "Don't guys always take it for granted they'll get laid?"

The hands he had been skimming over her body stilled. "This isn't getting laid," he told her, his voice steel-edged now.

She nodded. "I know," she said.

He brushed his fingers lightly over her torso, down over her thighs and hips, and back up to her breasts again. "So then you won't be mad that I was prepared for something like this? Not that I was, you know, *prepared* for something like this."

"Michael?" she said.

"What?"

"Are you going to go through your pants to find the condom, or should I?"

She heard him chuckle from behind her. "You already went through my pants once, and look what happened."

"So hurry up, and it can happen again."

He did, and it did. In no time, Michael was kneeling behind Hannah again, one hand covering her breast, the other delving between her legs. And a part of her wished that moment would never end, that they would remain this way forever, naked, passion-filled, needy, and *almost* coupled together.

But then they were coupled together, Michael entering her from behind, deeply, confidently, thoroughly. For one long moment, he stilled, letting her adjust to the feel of him, the size of him, the depth of him, and Hannah marveled at how she had never felt so complete. With one gesture, Michael had filled all the empty places inside her, had made warm all the places that had been cold for too long. His breath hammered her neck in ragged gasps, and his heart buffeted her back, and she knew he felt as overwhelmed by what was happening as she did.

He bent forward, his chest pressed firmly to her back, making Hannah bend forward, too. And as their bodies curved against each other, Michael withdrew himself from inside her, only to plunge in again, more deeply even than before. Bucking his hips against hers, he took her from behind, each thrust deeper and more arrant than the one before. Closer and closer to the edge she teetered, riding the crest of her orgasm. And just as she thought she would go over the edge, he withdrew from her completely, falling to his back on the sofa.

For one heartbreaking moment, Hannah thought he was through with her, was going to stop before either of them reached completion. But when she braved a glance over her shoulder, she saw him smiling at her, a dark, lascivious smile. Then he reached for her.

"Now you ride me," he said as he wove his fingers through hers. "You set the pace. But turn around first. I want to see your face when you come."

She nearly did then, simply hearing him say what he did. Never had sex been like this for her. Never had it been so primal, so potent, so raw. So fierce, so electrifying, so intense. In one swift, fluid move, she was atop him, sheathing him, sliding her body down over his until her legs pressed his torso and she pressed him. Acting purely on instinct, because sensation had long ago replaced cogent thought, Hannah moved atop him, rolling her body forward, then back, rising and falling until she felt the heat generating inside her again. Michael seemed to feel it, too, because he moved his hands from her hips to her breasts and back again, splaying his fingers wide as he caressed each in turn, bunching fistfuls of hair in his hands in between. Gradually, Hannah picked up the pace, moving her body faster, until she felt as if she were on the verge of total and complete eruption.

And then, suddenly, she was erupting, her entire body flaming and fracturing in a white-hot rush of fever. She cried out as the heat flared inside her, and she heard Michael's echoes coming from what seemed like a million miles away. For one long moment, they both seemed to hang suspended in time and space, and then, as one, he reached for her and she fell forward, both of them clinging to each other as if they feared what would happen once they let go.

It was a long time later, after they'd finally made it to Hannah's bed and the sun was dipping low in the sky, casting her bedroom into shadow, that either of them spoke. And only the growing darkness seemed to make that possible. And perhaps because of the growing darkness, too, when Hannah finally did speak, she felt compelled to speak the truth.

"It's never been like that for me," she said softly. "Not even close. Michael, that was . . ." Try as she might, though, she couldn't find a single word that would adequately describe what had happened.

But he seemed to understand, because she felt him nod, his head brushing softly against hers as he pulled her close. "It was never like that for me, either."

"So then I guess it's true what I've read," she said.

"What's that?" he asked.

"That imminent danger heightens the sex drive."

He chuckled at that and pulled her close, tucking her head beneath his chin.

"I didn't mean for it to be funny," she said soberly.

His chuckles stopped. "Then how did you mean it?"

"I meant . . ." She shook her head, not entirely sure what she meant, and gazed up at the ceiling. The truth, she reminded herself. She was going to tell him the truth. Very softly, she said, "I guess what I meant was that this shouldn't have happened. Not the way it did. That it wouldn't have happened if we hadn't gone over to Adrian's this afternoon. We got all worked up and turned on because of a dangerous situation, and sex was just a natural release for that." She swallowed hard and tried not to think about how he hadn't disagreed with anything she'd said so far. "So I guess what I'm saying is that this . . . that what happened here this afternoon . . . the way it happened . . ." She inhaled one final breath and said quickly, "It was a mistake."

For a moment, Michael said nothing, and she figured that was because he agreed with her, and she didn't want to think about why that bothered her—why it scared her—so much.

Then, as quietly as she had spoken, he said, "You think that's why we ended up making love today? Because of some weird sexual response we had to a dangerous situation?"

She nodded, but couldn't bring herself to look at him. "Of course that's why we ended up . . . having sex today," she corrected him. "Why else would we?"

Because what they'd done certainly hadn't been a response to a mature, adult emotion, she thought. If it had been, they would have turned to each other before now. Or later, once they understood their feelings better. They wouldn't have had the explosive physical reaction they had experienced today.

This time Michael's response was a sound of derision. "You know, for being the director of a tony private school, you sure do have a hell of a lot to learn about stuff."

"And what's that supposed to mean?" she asked. She struggled to sit up in bed, wrapping the sheet around herself, because she suddenly felt very exposed. The springs of the antique bed squeaked beneath her, so fierce were her movements as she shoved herself up toward the headboard and turned to face him.

Michael, too, pushed himself up to a sitting position, but he didn't bother with the sheet, letting it pool negligently around his hips. In spite of her antagonism, Hannah had to concede in that moment that she had never seen a more beautiful sight than his naked body bathed in the pale evening light. It was almost enough to make her take back what she'd said. Almost. But she needed to make clear to him that what had happened to them today wouldn't happen again. Not until—not *unless*—both of them could make sense of whatever was going on between the two of them. If they could even ever make sense of that. And not until she could feel confident they had a chance of building a future together.

The next time she and Michael had sex, they would make love, she promised herself. And it wouldn't be because of some chemical reaction in their bodies brought on by the fear and the thrill of being in jeopardy. The next time it would be because the two of them felt a deep emotional bond that transcended a simple physical response. And it would be because they'd both come to terms with everything that was happening. She just hoped that somehow she could come to terms with that.

"It means," he said, "that if you think this happened because danger is an aphrodisiac, then, sweetheart, you don't know jack."

She gaped at that. "Oh, you're so smart, then why do you think it happened?"

"I can't believe you even have to ask me that," he said.

And she couldn't believe he was playing games. "Oh, come on, Michael," she said, "today was totally unreal."

"You can say that again."

"No, I mean it wasn't like anything that ever happens in real life. It was like some old movie. Like we were Ingrid Bergman and Cary Grant, and Adrian was Claude Raines and—"

"Oh, sure," he sneered before she had a chance to finish. "And of course you'd know, since you've rented *Notorious* at Blockbuster more than a dozen times this year. You ought to just buy it, Hannah. It would save you a bundle."

She went absolutely still at his words. "How do you know what I've rented at Blockbuster this year?" she asked softly.

Even in the nebulous light, she could tell he was turning red. He dropped his gaze to his lap and tugged on the sheet until it covered his chest, as if he were trying to hide something from her. Himself, say. Or his thoughts, maybe. Or maybe something even worse.

"Michael?" she asked. But it was pointless to keep asking him, since she was pretty much figuring it out all by herself. She was, after all, an educated woman. Maybe not smart, but educated. "It isn't just Adrian you've been spying on all this time, is it?" she said, her stomach pitching with the realization. "You've been spying on me, too, haven't you?"

He neither confirmed nor denied her charge. But it was that last that made her want to curl up into a ball and disappear.

"Oh, God," she said, drawing her knees up before her. She looped her arms around her shins and hugged herself hard. "Just how much do you know about me?"

"Hannah . . ." he began. But he didn't get any further than her name. Probably, she thought, because he was having some trouble coming up with a reasonable explanation for how he knew about her video rental habits, when in fact there wasn't a reasonable explanation at all.

Except for him having investigated her video rental habits. And if he'd investigated those, then he must know about a whole lot more.

"You've really been doing it," she said. "You've been spying on me. *Really* spying."

"Hannah—" he tried again.

But this time he didn't get any further because she cut him off. "Not just listening in on my life at home and at work," she went on, "but you've done some digging, too, haven't you? Into my personal life. All this time that you've been seeing me," she said, "what you've really been doing is investigating me. Spying on me."

She had never felt sicker in her life than she did in the moment she understood what had been going on. What had been going on for nearly a month. Michael had been spying on her. Really, truly, honestly spying on her. The way spies did. The way they spied on terrorists or assassins or any miserable excuse for humanity. Her entire life had probably been thrown open to him.

"What else do you know about me?" she asked again.

"Hannah . . ." he said for a third time. But he only shook his head, and, again, said nothing more.

"No, I want to know, Michael," she insisted. "If you know what I rent at Blockbuster, you must know all kinds of things about me. So what else do you know?"

He held his jaw clenched tight and didn't reply.

"Do you know where I was born?" Then she chuckled nervously. "What am I saying? Of course, you know where I was born. You probably know where I went to college, where

I've worked, whether I've ever had a traffic ticket, and how much I owe on my taxes."

He continued to remain silent, but she was sure he did indeed know all those things about her.

"Everything's on file somewhere these days, isn't it?" she asked. But really, she wasn't asking anyone in particular. Especially since she already knew the answer. "I mean, I've read where people can even find out what you buy at the grocery store. So have you done that, too, Michael? Checked my supermarket purchases? My favorite brand of coffee and cereal? That I prefer high pulp over no pulp? That I will occasionally binge on Mrs. Field's cookies? How about—"

She halted abruptly when she remembered the night he'd come by on her birthday. She met his gaze levelly. "How about birthday cakes?" she asked, her voice dropping so low, she almost couldn't hear it herself. "Do you know about those, too? That night you came by my house, I never heard a car leave. That's because you weren't in a car, were you? You were somewhere close by, eavesdropping on me. God, why didn't I realize that before? How could I have been so stupid? How could I have been so trusting?"

Her voice broke on that last word. She closed her eyes in mortification, remembering how she'd sung 'Happy Birthday' to herself that night. When she opened them again, Michael's expression was hard, and she knew he had indeed been listening in. Oh, God. How *could* she have been so stupid?

"You must have thought I was pretty pitiful that night, huh?" she said. "Of course, I suppose I *am* pretty pitiful, buying myself a birthday cake. Singing the birthday song to myself. You must have laughed yourself silly over that."

"Hannah, stop," he finally said. "Stop this. It wasn't like that. It hasn't been what you think. It hasn't been like that at all."

She nodded slowly. "You're right," she said. "I haven't been pitiful. I've been victimized."

This time he was the one to close his eyes, but he kept them shut, as if she'd flung a knife into his back and the pain was too much to bear. *Good,* she thought. She wanted him to feel the same way she did.

"Hannah," he said, opening his eyes, "I swear to you, I never meant for it to turn out like this."

She chuckled morosely. "Oh, I'm sure you didn't. I'm sure you never anticipated getting caught."

"No, I mean the way it turned out between us. You and me. I never meant to fall in love with you the way I did."

Oh, my. Had she thought she was in pain before? That was nothing compared to what she felt after hearing that. Forget the knife in the back. This one went straight through her heart.

"You don't love me," she told him. Because if he'd loved her, he would have been honest with her. Of course, he wasn't the only one who hadn't been honest, was he? she taunted herself. But her dishonesty hadn't been nearly as damaging as his had been. And when she'd been dishonest with him, she hadn't realized she loved him. Now, though . . .

Oh, God. *Now.*

"Yes, I do love you," he said.

She shook her head. "No, you don't." And before he could deny it again, she added—again, since he still hadn't answered her—"So what else do you know about me?"

"There's no reason for us to go into this," he said, not answering her again.

"Oh, I think there's every reason." Then she fired point-blank. "Where did I live before moving to Indianapolis? My address, I mean, not just the city of Chicago."

He sighed heavily, a sound of surrender, of resignation.

"Six twenty-four Peabody Street, Naperville, Illinois, 60540."

Heat stabbed Hannah in the belly as he recited perfectly her old address. "And before that?"

He sighed again, but there was weariness mixed in with the sound this time, too. "You had a loft apartment in Evanston, near the Northwestern campus."

"Address?"

"Thirty-two fifteen Organdy Street. A brick Victorian. You lived on the top floor."

Wow. It was even worse than she'd thought. He really had been thorough. "What's my favorite restaurant?" she asked.

"Well, you seem to eat at the Blue Iris Café an awful lot," he told her.

Yes, she did. As a matter of fact. "And what did I do every Saturday afternoon during summer vacation this year?"

"You had a ceramics class. That damned dragonfly vase never did turn out as well as you would have liked."

Oh, God . . .

"Where was I born?" she asked him, even though she knew if he already knew those other things about her, he'd surely know that.

And he did. "Tampa, Florida."

"What were my parents' names?"

"William and Audrey Frost."

The next question she wanted to ask was the one she most dreaded hearing the answer to. Because if Michael got this one right, then it would be clear he knew far more about Hannah than Hannah wanted anyone to know. Least of all the man with whom she had fallen in love. Because she knew then that she did indeed love Michael. That could be the only reason for why this hurt as badly as it did.

"What," she began slowly, "did my father do for a living?"

When he didn't answer her right away, a brief, gasping

flicker of hope sputtered to life in her chest. Maybe he didn't know, she thought. Maybe her father had covered their tracks so well that Michael would think he really was vaguely self-employed, as she'd told him that night at his house. Maybe Michael had no idea that her father had been—

"A con man," he said softly. "Your father was a con man."

And that little flicker of hope in Hannah's chest stuttered right out.

"Con artist," she corrected him automatically. Because if there was one thing her father had insisted he was, it was an artist. He'd told her often that only people of exceedingly gifted qualities could rip folks off with the skill and finesse he had, leaving them so befuddled, it was months before they realized just how badly they'd been soaked.

"So if you know who my parents are, and what my father did for a living, then I guess you know they got divorced shortly after I was born."

"I do know that, yes."

"And you know I haven't seen my mother since."

"Yes."

"So you know she never told me the reason they didn't have another child was because they loved me so much."

He said nothing for a moment, then, very quietly, "Yes."

"And you know I don't have a Great-Aunt Esmeralda," she said.

He nodded slowly. "Yeah. I know about that."

"Or a Cousin Chloe."

"Yes."

"Or a Nana Frost or a best friend Patsy."

"Yes."

"You've known since the beginning."

"Yes."

Hannah nodded, feeling sicker still. "So then you know I

lied about all of that. About the storybook childhood and the picture-perfect family and the Norman Rockwell holidays."

He said nothing in response.

"And being the smart guy that you are," she continued, "I guess you know that the reason I made all that stuff up was because I had such a crummy childhood and I'm ashamed of it."

"Hannah, there's no reason for you to—"

"And here the reason we met," she interrupted him, because she didn't want to hear him make excuses for her, especially not when she didn't even want to do that for herself, "was because I called your son to the office after he told what I thought were enormous lies. Bet you think I'm a real hypocrite, huh?"

More silence met her comment.

"Although, really, now that I think about it, I imagine what you've probably been thinking is . . . well . . . that I'm pretty pathetic."

"Hannah, that isn't true at all," he said quickly.

But she ignored him, since she knew he was lying. "No wonder you thought I'd be such a pushover. You're probably surprised I held out as long as I did."

"Hannah . . ."

"I think you should go, Michael. You're probably late getting Alex anyway."

"Alex will have more time to spend with his friend. He'll be delighted I'm not there on time," he said in that swift, certain voice. "I'm not leaving yet, Hannah. I'm not going anywhere until we hash this out."

"There's nothing to hash out," she said, feeling even more swift and certain than he sounded. "I think it's all perfectly clear. You misled me. You used me to get through to someone else. I foolishly believed something I should have known better than to believe." She looked at him again. "So

I guess we're even, huh? Except that you never foolishly believed me, because you already knew you were being misled. You just let me go on talking because you didn't want me to know you already knew. Because if you'd told me the truth, then you never could have gotten close to Adrian, could you?"

He studied her in silence for another moment, as if he were trying very hard to figure out what he should say. Finally, though, he told her, "Hannah, you are so far off the mark here, I'm not sure I'll ever be able to pull you back onto it."

"Then don't try," she said, giving him the out he needed. "Just go, Michael. And let's just pretend this never—"

She stopped herself when she heard what she was saying. Yeah, pretending had always worked for her before. She'd pretended a whole life and family for herself. This time, though, pretending just didn't seem like it was going to be quite as effective as it used to be. And it certainly wouldn't make her happy, as it had in the past.

"Just go," she repeated. "Go back to OPUS and tell them we failed in our mission." She couldn't help the strangled laugh that punctuated the comment. "With Adrian, I mean," she added. "You don't have to tell them how badly we failed at everything else. Though if everyone else at OPUS is like you, I'm sure they probably knew it before we did."

She felt the bed shift then, and the old springs groaned as Michael rose. He pulled the sheet with him, wrapping it around himself, and uncoiling it from Hannah, so that she had to reach for the quilt at the foot to cover herself again.

"I'll go," he said, turning to look at her, "but only because there's no way we can talk about this civilly tonight. We aren't finished, though, Hannah, not by a long shot."

This time Hannah was the one to remain silent as she watched Michael make his way to her bedroom door, out to where he'd left his discarded clothing heaped in piles with her own. But he halted before walking through, turning around to look at her one more time. One last time, she corrected herself. Because there was no way she was letting him back in again after this. Not into her house. Not into her life. And not into her heart, either.

"I love you, Hannah Frost," he said. "That, if little else, has been true all along."

And then he was gone. And Hannah was alone. The way she had been before she met him. Except that this time, she had the echo of his final words to haunt her. And this time, she had memories of a reality unlike anything she had ever known before. And the reality was far better than any fantasy had ever been.

So good, she knew, that fantasy would never be enough for her again.

THIRTEEN

"HEY, HARRY, YOU KNOW WHAT THE absolute best thing is about being self-employed?" Pax asked his personal assistant early Wednesday evening when Pax was ensconced upon the oxblood leather sofa in his home office with his laptop, and Harry was sitting at Pax's desk pretending to be fascinated by the task of answering Pax's correspondence.

Without looking up, Harry replied, "The reeking piles of filthy lucre?"

"Besides that," Pax said.

"No," Harry replied. "Do tell. I am all atwitter wanting to know. What *is* the best thing about being self-employed? Because having always been at the mercy of the mendacious promises and capricious whims of often despotic employers, I wouldn't have any experience with such a thing myself."

Implicit in that statement, Pax was sure—aside from Harry's calling him a lying, fickle tyrant, he meant—was Harry's not caring one whit what the best thing about being self-employed was. But that was okay. It had been a rhetorical question anyway. Pax was going to answer it whether Harry cared or not.

"It's being able to work at home," he told his assistant.

Harry took a break from feigning an interest in his work and gave that some thought. "Considering the fact that your home is located in the same building as your place of employment, thereby making them one and the same, I'd have to conclude that your choice of the best thing about being self-employed is . . . oh, what's that delightfully American term I'm looking for . . . ?" He pressed his fingers to his forehead and made a series of tsking sounds before looking up again with an *A-ha!* sort of expression. "*Lame.* That's the word."

Pax rolled his eyes. "The fact that my home and office are in the same building is beside the point, Harry."

"Is it?"

"Yes."

"I'm sorry, then. I must have missed the point."

"A not unusual occurrence with you," Pax said.

"Mm," Harry replied.

"The point," Pax told him, "is that if I don't want to put on a monkey suit and go down to my office, I don't have to."

Harry gave that some thought, too. Or, at least, pretended to. With Harry it was always hard to tell. "But considering the fact that you're the owner and CEO of the company you work for, why should you feel compelled to put on a monkey suit—or go down to your office, for that matter—in the first place? And the fact that you're working on a Wednesday when the rest of your employees are at home with their loved ones after hours leads me to also conclude that even the best thing about being self-employed—according to your own definition, I mean—isn't particularly . . . oh, what's that delightfully American term I'm looking for . . . ?" He did the head-tapping, tsking, and *A-ha!* expression thing again. "*Awesome.* That's the word." He grinned before punctuating the statement with, "Dude."

"Harry," Pax said flatly.

"Yes?"

"Did anyone ever tell you you're no fun to verbally spar with?"

Harry gave that some thought, too. "No. I don't believe anyone's ever told me that. And actually, I don't think it would be exaggerated to describe myself as captivating. I wouldn't go so far as to say winsome, although I will admit that a lady smitten with my charms did use that very word. Of course, that was years ago, and in a different country. But in this one, I've always been known as quite the interlocutor amongst my peers."

This time it was Pax's turn to reply, "Mm." He gazed at his assistant through slitted eyes. "Interlocutor," he repeated. Though not without difficulty. "I suppose that could be one word to describe you. Another might be—"

"If you won't be needing me this evening," Harry interjected, "I'd like to have a few hours off."

"What makes you think I won't be needing you?" Pax asked.

"The fact that you've so far needed me today only as a receptacle for your bombast."

"Bombast?" Pax echoed indignantly. "Harry, I haven't been bombasting."

"No?"

"C'mon," he cajoled. "You prepared my agenda today. Do you recall, at any time, writing in the mandate, 'Bombast Harry, but good'?"

"Of course not."

"Well, there you go."

"Bombast is a noun. One cannot, by definition, actively bombast another. I would never write such a thing."

Pax decided it would be best to just move things along and make believe he still had the upper hand. "Yeah, okay, you can have the evening off. There's nothing here that can't be done tomorrow. Have at it."

Harry did have the decency—or, more likely, it was just ingrained courtesy, not that he had much of that, either, mind you—to thank Pax as he left the room. Pax was turning his attention back to the laptop sitting on his denim-clad thighs when the phone on his desk trilled softly. It was the ring he'd assigned to the concierge on the first floor of the building, and the guy was probably calling to tell Pax a courier delivery he'd been expecting early this morning had finally arrived. At least he hoped that was what the guy was calling about. He'd needed those documents yesterday.

He glanced at his watch as he rose from the sofa, the well-worn leather releasing him with a softly sighed *wuuufff,* and headed for the phone. Jesus, it was almost seven o'clock. It damned well better be the courier. Not just because Pax needed the info, but because he didn't want to be bothered by any additional work tonight. The concierge confirmed that, yes, the courier was here with a package, and Pax instructed the man to go ahead and send the guy up, since by now everyone else had gone home. Then he settled his laptop on his desktop, saved the work he'd completed so far, and headed out of his office to wait for the guy at the front door.

His penthouse was large, certainly larger than the average suburban home, and his office was located in the back of the dwelling because the room overlooked a park across the street. Not that Pax had the time—or the inclination, for that matter—to do much staring out the window, but the decorator had considered that part of his home a good location for an office, away from the public rooms, where it would be quieter and therefore easier for him to work. Pax frankly hadn't cared where his office was located, since he wasn't the kind of person to open his home to the public anyway. When he socialized, he generally went out. When he had to throw a party for business associates, he hired someone to rent a place and make the arrangements. His home was *his* home. It was personal space. He didn't often share it with others.

Well, except for Harry. But Harry was different. Harry was . . . Harry. He wasn't personal. At all. Au contraire.

But since Pax's office was at the back of his home, it took him a few minutes to make his way toward the front, a few minutes he spent stewing over how much *more* work he could have finished by now if he'd had that damned delivery early this morning, when he was supposed to have received it. Hell, he could have given himself the evening off, too. Maybe called Selby to see what she was doing. Because seeing her only twice a week was really starting to bug the hell out of him. Which was odd, since normally with women it was seeing them more than once a week that got kind of irritating.

But then, Selby wasn't like normal women, was she? No, she was like Pax.

He still hadn't come to terms with what he'd learned about her at Trino's that night. That she was the kid in school who had been taunted and ridiculed by others, just as he had been. Hell, her experiences had been worse than his own. She'd been physically assaulted when she'd been thrown into the showers. As often as the other kids had jeered at Pax, they'd never laid a hand on him. He'd been a tall kid, and big enough, he supposed, that it made even the bullies think twice about coming after him. Selby, though, as a girl, would have been an easy target. And obviously had been.

But she wasn't angry, he thought. She'd actually been polite to the despicable Deedee. She didn't carry around a chip on her shoulder the size of Gibraltar the way Pax did. She seemed okay as an adult. Unbothered. Happy. As if she'd left the past in the past and was focused on the future. He didn't see how she could do that.

But he wanted to learn.

In fact, over the past several days, he'd come to realize he wanted to learn everything he could about Selby Hudson. Where she really came from, what made her tick. Why she was able to be the kind of person she was—warm, generous, cheerful—having come from the background she had. And he'd realized something else, too, something that had rocked him to his very foundation. He'd realized how much he had come to like her. Even before learning about her experiences in high school, even before discovering the two of them had so much in common, Pax had come to see that he liked Selby. He liked her a lot. And he'd begun to wonder if maybe—

Well, he'd just begun to wonder, that was all. And he didn't usually wonder about women.

He nudged thoughts of Selby away for now, and focused instead on the work that would consume his evening. He tugged on the gray sweater he'd pulled on over jeans that morning, then ran his hands quickly through his ebony hair, fuming again about the lateness of the courier. That was the problem with low-paying menial jobs, he thought as he strode past his bedroom, past the one, two, three guest rooms that were never used, past Harry's room—where he could hear Harry singing "I Gotta Be Me" as he readied himself to go out—past Harry's office, past the media room, the game room, the library, the kitchen, and the dining room. Nobody got paid enough to give a damn about their job performance these days. The courier had probably spent the afternoon riding around on his bike instead of making his deliveries, because it was a beautiful day outside, and hey, who cared if the working stiffs didn't get their stuff on time? Who cared that there were other people in the world who took some pride in their work and wanted to make sure things were done the right way?

Grumble, grumble, grumble.

By the time Pax's doorbell rang, he'd worked up a good head of steam and was ready to give the kid what-for. But it wasn't a guy on the other side of the door, he saw immediately. It was a girl, shorter than he by nearly a foot, her build slight, her head, encased in a red baseball cap, bowed over a clipboard upon which she was writing. He really shouldn't have noticed any more than that about her, and her gender shouldn't have made any difference when it came to his wanting to chew her out. But something about her made Pax hesitate. She was dressed casually, in blue jeans and red high-top sneakers, an oversized red jacket zipped halfway over a white T-shirt. The jacket and hat both were embroidered in black with the logo of the courier service, and she had a fat Tyvek envelope tucked under the arm of the hand that was writing.

"Hi, I have a delivery for CompuPax," she said in a friendly voice as she wrote. "Guy downstairs said I should bring it up here."

The moment she began speaking, the hair on the back of Pax's neck leapt to attention. And when she finally glanced up, a shock wave of heat blasted through his belly. The last person he'd expected to see when he opened his door was Selby Hudson. And judging from the expression on her face, he was the last person she'd expected to see opening it.

"Thomas," she said when she saw him, his name coming out as a soft sigh of surprise. Then she smiled. A curious, confused kind of smile that did something to his insides he wasn't sure he liked.

Selby, it appeared, wouldn't have been available this evening even if Pax had given himself the rest of the night off. Because Selby, it appeared, was working, at yet another job. This made, what . . . four? That he knew about, at any rate. Did she ever take time off? Why did she work so many jobs? And why, if she worked four jobs—that he knew about, at any rate—could she only afford to live in a crummy apartment in an even crummier part of town?

Maybe Pax would eventually learn the answers to those questions, but right now, he had an explanation to fabricate and a delivery for CompuPax to think about. A delivery for which he had been waiting so long. A delivery that was late. A delivery over which he'd been about to chew the courier's butt off. But as often as he'd fantasized about nibbling on Selby Hudson's behind, this hadn't been quite what he'd had in mind.

And as for his fabricated explanation, how the hell was he going to explain Thomas Brown's presence in the penthouse of the CEO of CompuPax? And what was he going to do if Selby knew the name of the CEO of CompuPax was T. Paxton Brown? She was a smart woman. A teacher—among other things. Twice over, at that. It wouldn't be difficult for her to put two and two—or rather T. Paxton and Thomas—together, and calculate the common denominator of Brown.

"Selby," he said. Mainly because that was the only one of billions of thoughts ricocheting around in his brain that he could get a handle on.

Her gaze bounced from his to scan the door and the wall above it for a number or a sign—fruitlessly, since there was nothing to mark the residence—then back at Pax's face again. He wanted to reassure her that yes, she did indeed have the right address. She just had the wrong idea. Not that he for a moment intended to set her straight. No, if Pax had any hope of salvaging anything of their . . . whatever the hell it was they had—and he decided not to think just then about why it was suddenly terrifyingly important that he salvage it—he was going to have to make sure her wrong idea got even wronger.

"I, uh . . . What are you doing here?" she asked flat out. "Do you work for CompuPax?"

He couldn't let her think he had anything to do with CompuPax. One niggling little suspicion that he had anything to do with the company, and she'd eventually put it all together. She'd know he'd been lying to her. And then she'd want nothing to do with him. Not just because he was a liar, either. But because she wouldn't want T. Paxton Brown, billionaire, the way she wanted Thomas Brown, dropout. And he couldn't stand the thought of Selby not wanting him.

"I, ah . . ." he began. "Yeah, um, I—I'm working, but not for CompuPax. Not, you know, technically."

Woo. Good thing he'd gone back to school recently. His vocabulary in particular needed work.

"I was just, um, I mean, I was, ah . . ." he continued as articulately as before, "working on the computer," he finished in a fit of ingeniousness. Not to mention honesty. Hey. Cool how that worked out. Maybe he could bluff his way through this without even having to bluff.

"What, you're the computer repairman?" she asked.

"Yeah," he said, that honesty stuff going right up in smoke. "That's kind of what I do. Repair computers. Part-time, I mean. Weekends and evenings, I mean. When I can find the work, I mean. What little comes my way, I mean," he finished. Because, hey, if he was going to be a liar, he might as well be a big, fat liar, right?

And why did the realization that he was such a big, fat liar with Selby suddenly bother him so much? He'd lied to people. Lots of times. Nobody attained the level of success Pax had without telling a few whoppers along the way. And nobody held on to such colossal success by being sincere or fair. He'd never considered virtue a virtue. And integrity? Please. What the hell was that? He'd lied to and misled all manner of people, from housekeepers to IRS agents to captains of industry. And he'd been misrepresenting himself to Selby for weeks. Why, suddenly, did he feel so damned guilty for telling her something that wasn't true?

"So then you do have a job," Selby said, smiling.

He nodded, hoping the gesture didn't look as jerky and panicky as it felt. "Part-time, like I said."

"Well, good," she said. "Once you get your diploma, with experience like that, you should be very employable."

"Yeah," Pax said. And then, because he couldn't think of anything else to say, he added, "Yeah."

And then he gazed at Selby, a sick feeling in the pit of his stomach, because even dressed as a courier, she looked so damned pretty, he wanted to pull her into his arms and kiss her again, and part of him knew then that somehow, eventually, this was all going to blow up in his face, and he'd never see her again.

"So . . . who do I give this to?" she asked, tugging the envelope out from under her arm. She held up the clipboard, too. "Somebody has to sign for it."

"Right," Pax said. "Hang on. Mr., ah . . . the, uh, the guy who runs CompuPax is home. I'll go get him."

"Okay, thanks."

And before he succumbed to the look of utter bewilderment on her face and told her everything—the *truth,* for God's sake, like *that* was going to help him out—Pax wheeled around and made his way back to Harry's room, where his assistant had finished the final chorus of "I Gotta Be Me" and launched into "I Feel Pretty." *Me, me, me,* Pax thought inanely as he rapped on Harry's door. Everything with Harry always started with both the letter and the word I. And Pax tried not to think about his mother's admonition that whenever he pointed a finger, he had three more pointing back at himself.

"Harry," he whispered harshly as he concluded his rapping. "Open the door."

Harry did so, his expression one of complete annoyance. "You already told me I could take the evening off," he reminded Pax by way of a greeting.

"Yeah, I know. And you can. But you have to do one thing for me before you go."

Harry held up his wrist and tapped his watch. "Sorry. Off the clock. Employer said so."

"This will just take a minute."

Harry tapped his watch again and enunciated more slowly, "Off . . . the . . . clock."

Pax settled his hands on his hips. "You want your Christmas bonus this year or not?"

Harry's mouth flattened into a tight line. "What is it that you need me to do?"

"You have to be me for five minutes. Ten minutes, tops. You can keep your name, but you have to be me."

"I have to *what*?"

"Be me. I mean, be the CEO of CompuPax. Harry Rutherford, CEO. You'll finally see what it's like to be self-employed."

"So far, it's confusing and unpleasant," Harry said. "And where are the reeking piles of filthy lucre?"

"Look, I'll explain later," Pax promised. "The courier's finally here with that delivery I was expecting this morning, but you have to accept it and sign for it, and pretend you're the CEO of CompuPax. And you have to do it as Harry Rutherford, not T. Paxton Brown."

Harry eyed him narrowly. "That's not illegal, is it?"

"Of course not," Pax told him. See? You did have to lie about stuff when you were the big boss.

"Then being you, even for ten minutes, wouldn't be illegal, only repugnant, is that what you're saying?"

"Harry," Pax cautioned him again.

"All *right*," Harry said. "I'll pretend to be you. And who are you supposed to be? Mary Poppins?"

"I'm Thomas. Just Thomas. I'm some guy who's come to fix your computer because it hasn't been working today."

"Oh, that's rich. You're the computer repairman? For a company that designs software? Why don't I have my own people on the problem?"

Good question, Pax thought. He hoped it didn't occur to Selby. Aloud, though, he said, "You want that bonus, Harry? You'd damned well better believe I'm the computer repairman. And so should the woman at the front door."

Harry arched one eyebrow peevishly. "Ah. It all comes clear. A woman is involved. Fine. I'll be you and you'll be the computer repairman. Won't this be fun."

Pax had to take him at his word and trust that Harry wouldn't screw this up. He started to lead his assistant back to the front door, then decided he'd let Harry take the lead, since, all modesty aside, he knew for a fact that the CEO of CompuPax wasn't much of a follower.

"Selby, this is my, um, employer. For today," Pax said when they came back into the living room, trying to keep her attention fixed on his face, because he feared Harry's expression might reveal too much of the ruse. Belatedly, Pax remembered that as good as Harry was at being rude and sarcastic, he was a terrible liar. "This is Mr. Rutherford," he introduced Harry further. "He owns CompuPax. I'm here working on his computer. Today. It's been causing him problems. Today."

Okay, so maybe, at the moment, Harry wasn't the only one who was a terrible liar, Pax thought. Why would his normally easygoing deceitfulness desert him now, when he really needed it?

"And Mr. Rutherford," he continued, turning to Harry and praying to every god he could remember from that humanities elective he took about world religions that Harry would please, for once, be cooperative, "this is a friend of mine. Selby Hudson. She works for the courier company who brought you this package."

Thankfully, Harry, being greedy and covetous of his Christmas bonus, played along. Oh, Pax could tell by his expression that he had no idea what game they were playing, and that he would demand an explanation as soon as was humanly possible, but for now, at least, he'd go along with it.

"Miss Hudson," he said. "So nice to meet you."

And Pax squeezed his eyes shut tight, because Harry was trying to do an American accent—maybe even a Texas accent—and didn't even come close. Maybe, if Pax was very lucky, Selby would assume Harry was from Scandinavia. Because, hey, all your most famous Swedes were named Rutherford.

For one brief, terrible moment, Pax was scared to death that Selby wasn't going to buy it. If she read even the tiniest part of the business section of the newspaper, or if she was the type to buy any sort of popular news magazine, she would know CompuPax was owned by T. Paxton Brown. She would know he was lying. And she'd demand to know why. And in that one brief, terrible moment, Pax's hands began to sweat, his heart began to pound, his vision grew blurry, and he feared he would throw up.

Then, "Nice to meet you, Mr. Rutherford," Selby said, smiling.

And then Pax knew an intense, transcendent sort of relief unlike anything he had ever experienced before. He remembered that Selby had only lived in Indianapolis for a few months, so she probably hadn't had a chance to familiarize herself with the local celebrities and such. For whatever reason, she didn't know anything about the genesis of the city's most important employer and biggest industry. And for the first time in his life, Pax was happy to be unknown and meaningless, a rather puzzling development, to say the least.

And then two more things happened that puzzled him. First, Harry smiled back at Selby, with what appeared to be a genuinely delighted smile, even though all the time that Pax had known him, he'd never seen Harry genuinely delighted by anything. And second, Pax realized he wanted to punch Harry in the nose for smiling that way at Selby. It made no sense. But Harry's showing even some small interest in Selby made Pax want to hit him. Worse, for one crazy minute, he actually felt uncertain about himself, worried that maybe Selby would find Harry more interesting and more attractive than she found Pax. For one insane minute, Pax was Tommy Brown again, pining for the kind of girl—no, for one girl in particular—he knew he could never have.

And Pax hadn't felt that way in a long, long time. In fact, he'd sworn to himself decades ago that he would never feel

that way again. He actually sensed the fingers of his right
hand curling into a fist, and he had to force himself to relax
them, and to relax the rest of himself, too.

This was nuts. This was Harry. This was Selby. And it
was all a big, fat lie, anyway. What the hell was the matter
with him?

Harry arched his eyebrows at Pax, silently requesting a
cue, but for the life of him, Pax had no idea what to say. His
thoughts were so scrambled by now, he wasn't sure what
he'd intended to do in the first place. All he knew was that
Selby was here, in his home, and for some reason, he wanted
her to come in and stay for a while. But he couldn't do that,
because this wasn't his place—at least, not to her. But he
didn't want to go out, either, because he wanted Selby *here*.
He wanted to share his place with her. Which, of all the
bizarre developments of the last few minutes, was the weirdest yet.

Thankfully, Selby knew what to do. She extended both
the package and the clipboard to Harry and said, "I'll need
you to sign, please, Mr. Rutherford. Right there by number
seventeen." And as she pointed to the line on the form, she
looked over at Pax and smiled. And suddenly, every fear,
every anxiety, every concern he'd been entertaining completely melted away.

Everything was fine, he thought. There was no reason for
him to be alarmed. Selby didn't think there was anything
odd about the situation at all. Because she trusted him
implicitly.

Dammit.

"There you go," Harry said as he returned the clipboard to
Selby. Then he turned to Pax. "So . . . Thomas. How's it
coming back there with the computer?"

"Ought to be done in an hour or so. Sir," he added, trying
not to choke on the word.

Harry smiled at Pax's discomfort. "Excellent." He thrust

the package toward Pax and said, "Take this back to the office when you go, will you? Thomas? I have to go out. Do let yourself out when you're finished. Have some dinner before you go if you'd like. That's what I'm going to do." And then Harry was gone, leaving Pax and Selby both standing in openmouthed amazement.

Well, hell, Pax thought. He'd wanted to get rid of Harry, sure. But he'd wanted there to be some small element of credibility in the situation.

"Wow. He's really trusting," Selby said when the door had closed behind Harry.

Pax did his best to shrug off the remark. "I, um, I've done work for him before. He knows me. And he's kind of eccentric." Well, that last, at least, was true.

"Funny accent," she observed. "Where's he from?"

"Um, Scandinavia, I think."

She nodded, but didn't look anywhere near convinced.

"So . . . you wanna stay for a while?" Pax asked experimentally.

"And watch you while you work?" she asked, sounding as if she would really enjoy such a thing.

Oops. Gee, that could be a problem, since Pax didn't know the first thing about repairing computers. He was a whiz at programming them, but if he had to take the back off of one . . .

"Ah . . ."

"I'm just kidding," she said, smiling again. "I can't stay. Even though this is my last delivery of the day, I should get home to grade some papers. Thanks, though."

"Well, have you had dinner?" Pax asked, still not wanting her to leave, in spite of the weirdness of the situation. Now that the shock of her sudden appearance had worn off—and now that he had her believing every fraudulent word he said—he wanted to spend some quality time with her.

"I haven't, actually," she told him, spreading her hand

open over her stomach. She turned her wrist over to look at her watch. "I could probably take an hour. No more than that, though." She glanced back up at Pax. "If you're sure Mr. Rutherford wouldn't mind."

"Who, him?" Pax asked. "He's such a people person, he wouldn't mind a bit."

He smiled at Selby. Selby smiled at him. And Pax knew then that not only was she buying everything he said to her, but that in no time at all, he'd be in like Flynn. Which, of course, went along completely with his plans for her.

So why did he feel like such a heel?

FOURTEEN

"SO THIS IS HOW RICH PEOPLE LIVE," SELBY said as she sat back in her chair and took in her surroundings again.

She still found it odd that the CEO of a major corporation had invited his computer repairman to stay for dinner while he was out. Even if Thomas had done a lot of work for the man in the past, it was still . . . odd. Maybe, like Thomas said, he was one of those eccentric millionaires, the kind who lavished gifts and services on those less fortunate. And anyway, who was she to criticize the whims of the wealthy when she had no idea what it meant to be a part of that economic stratum herself? The closest she'd ever come to this kind of money in the past had been watching them draw the Lotto numbers at night. Maybe rich people did this sort of thing all the time—that altruism and philanthropy stuff she'd heard about. Or maybe today was Take a Computer Repairman to Dinner Day and she'd just missed the memo.

In any event, if this was how the wealthy lived, she could be happy continuing on with her own life. Frankly, she wasn't all that impressed by the digs of Harry Rutherford, CEO. His place was pretty stark and spartan, with little color and less warmth. The furniture had probably set the guy back more than she'd make in her entire life, no matter how many jobs she worked, but there was nothing remarkable about it. On the contrary, with all those straight lines and the monochromatic feel, it was pretty boring. Her old, tweedy camelback sofa with the worn arms and squeaky springs that she'd bought for forty bucks at the thrift store had a helluva lot more character than Harry Rutherford's leather-bound conversation pit did. And his lamps made of twisted metal rods had nothing on the hand-painted ceramic pineapple lamp she'd picked out of a Dumpster a couple of years ago. Clearly money could not buy style.

"I don't like this place," she said as she stood up from the glass-and-copper dining room table and began to gather up her dishes.

Her complaint seemed to both surprise and disappoint Thomas. He still sat at his place, his arms folded over his expansive chest, leaning back in his chair as he observed her. But his expression was stunned and he sounded defensive when he asked, "You don't like it? Why not? What's wrong with it?"

"It's cold," she said. "There's no personality to it. I mean, this guy's got millions of dollars—"

"Billions," Thomas interrupted her.

"What?" she said, glancing back at him. He had his chair tipped back on two legs now, and all Selby could think was that the metal-backed seat looked so spindly, it would snap into pieces beneath him if he wasn't careful.

"Billions," he repeated. "The guy who owns this place has billions of dollars."

Her eyes went wide. *"Billions?"* she echoed. "Are you *serious*?"

Thomas nodded. "Nineteen-point-six billion, to be exact. Not all of it liquid, though, natch."

She decided not to wonder how he would know that. Instead, she just continued, "Oh. Okay. So. So then this guy has *billions* of dollars, but he can't afford a couple of picture frames for family photos?" She gestured toward the living room beyond the dining room, indicating the stringent decor. "He can't get a couple of houseplants? Some candlesticks? He can't buy some paint? A little color would go a long way here. This place is just . . . harsh. I mean, what kind of person would enjoy living in a place like this?"

Thomas's eyes went flinty as he said, "Probably a really rich one."

"Yeah, well, there's more to life than money," Selby said as she gathered up her dishes and turned to take them into the kitchen.

He expelled a sound of utter hooey. "Oh, really?"

She spun around at his tone of voice. "Yeah, really," she said. "What? You disagree?"

He stared at her skeptically. "Of course I disagree. Do you mean to tell me if someone handed you a check for a million bucks right now, you'd turn it down?"

"What are you, nuts?" she said. "Of course I wouldn't. But I wouldn't use it to buy ugly furniture and artwork a blindfolded monkey could have executed better."

"Hey, that artwork is worth a small fortune," Thomas said.

He only assumed that because it was purchased by a billionaire, Selby thought. He really shouldn't be so trusting. "Doesn't mean it's any good," she said aloud.

He gaped at her.

She laughed as she turned again and headed for the kitchen. "Well, it doesn't," she threw over her shoulder as she went. "Don't tell me you're one of those people who buys into the myth that just because something costs a lot of money, it must be valuable."

She heard Thomas's chair scrape away from the table and knew he was following her. "You think that's a myth?" he said as he entered the stark white kitchen behind her.

Like the rest of the house, there was little decoration here.

Only white cabinets and chrome appliances. And precious few of those. Clearly the owner didn't eat at home very often. Thomas set his own dishes on the counter across the room from Selby, then turned to lean back against it facing her, his arms folded over his chest again, waiting for her reply.

"Of course it's a myth," she said. "Do you really think money's all that important?"

"Don't you?"

"Not for what you evidently think it's important for."

"Oh, and what would *you* do with that check for a million bucks?" he asked point-blank.

Selby smiled as she mimicked his actions, leaning back against the counter on her side of the room, crossing her arms over her chest. "I'd use it to travel," she told him.

He seemed surprised, and not a little bewildered, by her response. "Travel?" he said. "Where?"

"Everywhere," she said. "All around the world. As many places as I could go."

He studied her intently for a moment, as if he were giving great thought to some matter. "You work four jobs," he said.

"Five, actually," she told him. "But how did you know? You only know about three."

He colored at that, his cheeks turning pink, and Selby was charmed by the fact that a man like him could actually get embarrassed about something. "I saw you," he said softly. "At Trino's one night. I would have said hello, but you were pretty busy."

"What were you doing at Trino's?" she asked. "That's a pretty expensive place."

"Yeah, I know. I know someone who works there," he said.

"Who?" Selby asked.

"One of the bartenders."

"Which one?"

"So why do you have five jobs?" he asked without answering. "And with all that money coming in, how come you live in the neighborhood you do?"

"First of all, it's not that much money," she told him. She made a quick survey of her surroundings again. "It's certainly not like this. And second of all, I don't like to spend money on material things. I'm saving as much of it as I can for something special."

"What?"

She smiled again. "Travel. All around the world. As many places as I can go. I'm planning to work for six more years, until I'm thirty, and stow away as much of my income as I can. Then I'm going to take a few years off to go around the world. East to west. North to south. I want to see it all. But I want to do it right. I want to take my time. That, to me, is where money can really be valuable. It can buy me time. And it can get me to places I want to go. And purchase a way of life for me. Not . . ." She shook her head dismally at the huge canvas that hung along the dining room wall, still visible through the kitchen entryway. "Not paintings that look like someone came in from the rain and wiped their feet on them."

Thomas studied her in silence for a moment, then, "What about jewelry?" he asked.

She didn't follow him. "What about it?"

"You don't like jewelry?" he said. "I thought all women went for that. Diamonds. Sapphires. Emeralds."

She laughed at that. "Oh, yeah, right. Do I seem like a diamond and emerald person to you?"

He seemed to give that some thought, too. But not for long. "No," he said. "You don't." And he sounded surprised when he said it.

"I don't care about stuff like that," she told him.

"Clothes?" he asked.

"Oh, I like clothes a lot," she agreed enthusiastically. "But

I like old stuff. Vintage stuff. The kind of stuff most people's moms put out on the curb."

"Cars?" he asked.

"Thomas, you know yourself that I don't own a car."

"But if you did own one, what would it be?"

She lifted a shoulder and let it drop. "Volkswagen, probably. They're kind of cute. But I like the old bugs better than the new ones."

He nodded at that, but he still seemed to be thinking hard about something. "So then, if you met some guy who had a ton of cash on hand, you probably wouldn't be too impressed, would you?"

"On the contrary," she said. "I doubt I'd want to have anything much to do with him."

"Why not?"

"People who have lots of money have it because they've worked hard to have lots of money, and they stayed focused so they can have lots of money," she said. "I won't say money becomes the most important thing to them, because that's not true in all cases. But people who have a lot of money have a lot of responsibilities. And they have to spend a good part of their life making money, and a good part keeping it. Money is definitely their focus. I would never be a priority with a man like that. His priority would be his job or his investments or his portfolio. He'd be more concerned with his wealth than he would be with me. And me, when it happens for real, I want to be the center of man's universe."

"Why?" Thomas asked.

She met his gaze levelly when she told him, "Because when it happens for real, he'll be the center of mine."

Selby wasn't sure just when it had happened, or why, but as she and Thomas had talked about money and such, they'd started moving closer to each other, narrowing the space of the room between them. So by the time she told him that any man she'd get involved with—for real—would become the center of her universe, she was standing nearly toe to toe with him, a mere breath of air separating their bodies. So it was no trouble at all for Thomas to reach out to her. And it was no trouble at all for Selby to lean into him when he did.

And the next thing she knew, he was kissing her, only not the way he had that night outside her front door, all desperate and demanding and fierce. This time when Thomas kissed her, he was gentle and solicitous and tender, as if this time he was confident of the outcome and was content to take his time.

"Thomas, we can't do this here," Selby whispered when he dipped his head to brush soft butterfly kisses along her throat.

"Of course we can," he whispered back. Kiss. Kiss. Flick of the tongue. Kiss. "We can do this anywhere. That's the beauty of it."

"But this is someone's home," she objected halfheartedly. "Someone *else's* home. Neither of us lives here. We don't have any right."

"The owner won't mind," he said as he brushed his lips over her cheek and along her jaw. "I promise you."

"Of course he'll mind. Two people having sex in his home when he's not here?"

Thomas halted at that and pulled away from her enough to gaze down into her face. "Is that what we're going to do?"

Only then did Selby realize just how explicitly she'd spoken. Just how explicitly she felt. "Aren't we?" she asked.

He smiled then, a wicked, wanton, downright devilish smile. "We can use one of the guest rooms," he said as he lowered his head to hers and covered her mouth again.

"But—"

"Shhh," he murmured as he kissed her. Again and again and again.

Selby, though, was adamant. Well, sort of. "H-how do you know which ones are the guest rooms?" she asked, her body melting into his, her hands, even as she protested, curling around his nape to pull him closer still.

"I'll take a wild guest. . . ."

And then he kissed Selby again, harder this time, deeper this time, and all her reservations fled. She didn't care about anything then except Thomas. Thomas and the way he made her feel. Thomas and the fact that she had wanted him this way almost since the night she'd met him. And maybe even before she'd met him. Because she'd dreamed about finding a man like him since she was a girl, one who was decent and kind and honest and good. Maybe Thomas Brown wasn't the most polished guy in the world, and maybe he didn't have the greatest prospects when it came to a career. But he was a good guy. Selby knew that much. And that was exactly the kind of man she'd always hoped to find. One who would appreciate her because of who she was—and, even more important, because of who she wasn't. One who would value her. One who would treat her with respect.

One who would love her. The same way she loved him.

Because she knew then that she had fallen in love with Thomas at some point. She must have. Otherwise she wouldn't be standing here with him now, in the home of a total stranger, caring about nothing except being with him in the most intimate way two people can be together. She wanted to share herself with him. All of herself. And that could only be because she was in love. Because she'd never shared all of herself with anyone before.

And then she stopped analyzing, because he slanted his mouth over hers and ran the tip of his tongue along her lower lip before skating it into her mouth. She welcomed him willingly, stroking her tongue against his as if it were the most natural thing in the world to do. And in that moment, it was. Because in that moment, nothing had ever felt more right than having Thomas hold her this way, in this place, at this time, the rest of the world be damned.

He dropped his hand to her hip, moving his fingers inward until he found the place where her T-shirt joined her jeans and jerked it free. He bunched the fabric in his hand, then dragged it and his fingers back up along her heated flesh, skimming his fingertips along her ribs until he encountered the lower band of her bra. But he wasn't put off by so delicate an obstacle, because he pushed the fabric higher and let his hand wander over her in a more intimate exploration. And as he covered her completely with his hand, he buried his face in the curve of her neck and shoulder, nipping the tender flesh lightly with his teeth, then laving the wound with his tongue as she softly cried out.

Selby dropped her hands to the hem of his sweater, pushing the garment higher until his chest was virtually bared. His skin was warm and alive beneath her fingertips, the finely sculpted musculature feeling like steel-fortified silk. As she tangled her fingers in the dark hair on his chest, Thomas pulled away from her long enough to shed the sweater completely, then went to work on the fly of Selby's jeans. He fumbled with the zipper twice, cursing quietly when his fingers failed him. Then he slowly . . . slowly . . . *oh,* so slowly . . . dragged the fastening open, dipping his hand unapologetically between the denim and her cotton panties, making Selby gasp.

"Thomas, no," she said softly, reluctantly.

"Selby, yes," he replied quietly, confidently.

And then he pushed his hand lower, extending one long finger to caress her in a place no man had touched before, and she had no desire to protest again. No, after that, her desire was for something else entirely. Thomas must have detected that, because he petted her again, channeling his fingers deeper into the damp creases of her flesh, sending a shudder coursing through her body she wasn't sure she'd survive.

"Oh, God, Thomas," she gasped. "That feels so . . . oh. *Oh. OH!*"

Her eyes fluttered closed as he continued to stroke her, and the sensations that shot through Selby, one after another, dizzied her, weakened her, but made her want so much more.

"Thomas," she finally said on a hoarse whisper, "make love to me. Please. I want you so bad."

"Bad, huh?" he said as he rubbed his fingers against her, inside her, again. When she opened her eyes, she saw that he was smiling. "Well, then, Selby, I'll do my best to be bad for you."

And without awaiting a reply, he scooped her into his arms and carried her out of the kitchen. Selby had the sensation of movement, but Thomas was kissing her again, so she looped her arms around his neck and held on tight. Not that she was afraid he would drop her, but for some reason she was worried about falling . . .

And then she was falling, onto a bed, and Thomas was falling down beside her. He helped her shed her T-shirt and bra, then Selby lifted a hand to his belt, touching it first only with the tip of her index finger, tracing the buckle. Then, slowly, methodically, she moved her hand to the leather, tugging on the length to free it from the metal ring.

"Selby," he whispered as she dragged it slowly through the loops of his jeans. But her name got lost when he covered her mouth with his once again.

Carefully, she lowered his zipper, then, without hesitation, tucked her hand inside. She located him at once, marveling at how rock-hard and ready he was for her, then moved her hand away, bashful about the discovery. She'd never touched a man like that before, and only then did she realize just how terribly inexperienced she was. She honestly wasn't sure what to do, hoped Thomas wouldn't be disappointed by her lack of knowledge. But he circled her wrist with firm fingers and urged her hand back into his jeans where it had been before. So with tentative, featherlike touches, Selby ran her fingers over him. Thomas pulled his mouth from hers and grew still at her caresses, bending his head to watch the motion of her hand between their bodies as it moved against him, and shuddering when she dared to make her movements bolder.

She loved the way he responded under her touch, was fascinated by that part of him and wanted to explore more. She brought her hand up over the top of him, palming the full head of his member, the slickness of his response aiding the rotating motion of her hand. Then she moved her fingers lower again, curving them around his thick, heavy shaft, and began to rub him harder.

"That's it," he ground out hoarsely, grabbing her wrist again. Together they stroked him, Selby's hand curling around his flesh, Thomas setting the pace with his fingers wrapped around her wrist, slow at first, then faster, rougher, until he felt beneath her fingertips as if he were ready to burst. Then, abruptly, he stopped and withdrew both their hands, lifting Selby's to his mouth to press a hard kiss into her palm.

"But—" she began. She didn't understand why he had stopped when he'd seemed to be enjoying himself so much.

But Thomas halted her objection by kissing her again, teasing the corners of her mouth with his tongue. Then he covered both of her naked breasts with sure fingers, squeezing gently, flicking the pads of his thumbs over the stiff peaks. After that, Selby didn't want to think anymore. She only wanted to feel what was happening to her. A hot, heavy river had begun to flow through her veins, and a hungry fire had flickered to life in her belly. Every nerve she possessed seemed to burst into flame as Thomas opened his mouth over her breast and sucked her inside. She wove her fingers through his silky hair and held his head in place, murmuring alternately that he should halt his eager onslaught and urging him to never, ever let it end.

Then she felt Thomas's lips move lower, to the underside of her breasts and then to her belly. She sighed when he dipped his tongue into her navel for a taste, then wriggled her hips as he tugged at her blue jeans. He dragged them down over thighs and knees, but she was still wearing her sneakers, so, with a growl of impatience, he took a moment to remove those and cast them aside, too. Then he parted her legs for a more intimate exploration, dipping his head between her thighs. When she realized his intention, when she understood that he meant to . . . to . . . to *taste* her, Selby opened her mouth to tell him to stop, because she'd never—

Oh. Oh, my. Oh, Thomas.

Any objection she might have uttered got caught in her throat when she felt the tip of his tongue flicker against her as softly as a butterfly's kiss. Never had she felt such exquisite pleasure, such a rush of staggering joy. Relentlessly, he savored her, and Selby could only lie motionless, her fingers knotting in the coverlet, her head turned into the pillow. But as the push of his mouth and tongue grew more insistent, ripples of delight began to unravel inside her, swelling one by one into eruptions of heat. Finally, an explosive orgasm rocked her, and she cried out at the intoxicating newness of the experience.

"Oh," she groaned as he dragged his mouth up the length of her torso again. "Oh, Thomas . . ."

Her eyes had fluttered closed, and in her pleasure-weakened state, she didn't have the fortitude to open them. But she felt the bed shift as Thomas moved upon it, heard the scrape of a drawer and then the unmistakable whisper of plastic. Later, she thought, she'd have to ask him how he knew he would find one of those in there. But when he returned to her and buried his head against her breast, sucking her again and launching an eager assault on her senses, she got lost in all the wonderful sensations he aroused in her. He seemed to surround and invade her, filled all the empty places inside her that had been cold and lonely for too long.

Selby helped Thomas shed the remainder of his clothing, then lay back down, allowing him to part her legs to kneel between them. She knew what was coming next, even if she had no experience with the act itself. She was about to find out, she thought. After having read about it, and fantasized about it, and wondered about it, now she was going to find out what it was really like. She readied herself for the pain— because she'd heard there was always pain the first time— but knew Thomas was a gentle enough man that he would do his best to make this easy for her. She started to tell him it was her first time, wanted to ready him, too, but he touched her again, running the pad of his thumb over the bead of her clitoris, and she gasped before any words could get out.

And then he was pushing himself inside her, deep, *deep* inside her, and her gasp became a small choke of panic.

"My God, you're so tight," he said, sounding delighted by the discovery.

And when she started to tell him again the reason for that, he pushed harder, and Selby gasped again, only this time it was because of the pain. And then he surged forward, and the pain became so great that instead of gasping, she could only cry out, and what she cried out was, *"Thomas!"*

Immediately, he withdrew from her, and she saw by his expression that she didn't need to tell him why she had yelled the way she had.

"This is your first time?" he asked. And now he was the one who sounded panicked. "You've never done this before?"

She shook her head slowly, weakly.

"Selby, why didn't you tell me?"

"I was going to," she said. "But it felt so good, I didn't want to . . ."

"To what?"

"To ruin it."

His expression crumpled then, and he closed his eyes. "Oh, God, Selby, this doesn't ruin it. It just makes it that much better. For me, at least," he added, and she figured that must have something to do with the tightness he mentioned. "But it's got to hurt like hell for you."

"It's okay," she said. And she was surprised to realize she meant it. It really was okay. Or, at least, it would be. "Just . . . go slow, okay?" she said.

He nodded. "And you tell me if I'm hurting you."

She smiled. As if he could ever do that. "Okay."

He moved between her legs again, holding his body over hers by bracing his forearms on either side of her. "Bend your legs," he said. "It will help."

She did as he asked, digging her heels into the mattress up near her bottom, spreading her legs open wider. He entered her again, more slowly this time, giving her a moment with each new foray to let her body grow more accustomed to the invasion. Little by little, he entered her more deeply, until finally their bodies were completely joined.

"You okay?" he panted then.

She nodded. There was still pain, but it wasn't like it had been before. And there was something else mixed with it now, something urgent and fierce and intense, something she wanted to learn more about. "I'm okay," she whispered. And she knew that, as long as she was doing this with Thomas, she was.

He pushed himself up on his knees then, circling his hands around her ankles and wrapping her legs around his waist. That position, too, eased some of the stress on her body, opened her wider, made it a little easier for her to accommodate him. Buried inside her as he was, Thomas reached and touched and heated parts of Selby she hadn't even known could feel. She reveled in the depth of his possession, clasping her hands tightly around the forearms he anchored on either side of her. And then, with a trust and a passion unlike anything she'd felt before, she let him sweep her away.

And sweep her away he did. Slowly, he began to withdraw from inside her, then slowly, he pushed himself back in again. Little by little, he increased his movements, each time stoking the fire inside Selby a little higher, until it eventually built into a white-hot conflagration. And just when she thought she would go up in flames with it, Thomas turned their bodies so that he was on his back with Selby sitting astride him. He gripped her hips and bucked against her, eliciting another cry from deep within her. Then he, too, cried out as he vaulted wildly against her one last time. Their climax came as one, both of them going still for one brief, scintillating moment, and then their bodies relaxed with their release.

Not sure what to do after that, Selby moved off of Thomas to lie beside him, facing him. She trailed her index finger along the length of his slick torso, his chest rising and falling in a deep, irregular rhythm. He caught her hand in his, holding it over his heart, his pulse leaping like a feral animal.

"Feel that?" he said. "That's what you've done to me. My heart will never be the same after this."

Selby smiled. "That's only fair. You've messed with mine, too, you know."

"Have I?"

She nodded, but couldn't quite bring herself to speak.

"I can't believe that was your first time," he said softly.

She touched her index finger lightly to his lip. "I'm glad it was you. I'm glad you're my first."

He said nothing for a moment after that, then, quietly, "Will you stay for a little longer?" he asked. "I mean, I know you have to go home—"

"And Mr. Rutherford will be back soon."

"Yeah, that, too," he said. But something in his voice when he said it felt wrong somehow. Before Selby could think about it, though, he hurried on, "Will you stay for a little while?" he asked again. "I just don't want you to leave yet."

She smiled. "For a little while," she said. "But then I have to go."

He smiled back and kissed her hand. Then, "I'll be right back," he told her, and rolled away.

The condom, Selby thought, grateful that he'd been coherent enough to think about that. She heard the bathroom door off the guest room click closed, then the sound of rushing water. She sat up in bed, wrapping the sheet around herself, unable to remember when they'd even turned it down. For the first time, she took in her surroundings. This room, like all the others, was sparsely furnished, but there was still something about the clean lines and muted colors of the decor that reeked of wealth. The clock on the nightstand told her she was going to be working late tonight, since she'd taken a lot more than an hour for dinner. But it was the assortment of other things on the nightstand that caught her attention even more. Because they were things that looked personal, things that suggested maybe Thomas's wild guess had landed them not in a guest room, but right smack dab in the master's chambers.

Uh-oh . . .

Beside the clock was a book with a bookmark tucked midway through it, Herman Hesse's *Steppenwolf*. Atop that lay a pair of reading glasses, and beside them was a single stray cufflink that—just a shot in the dark here—looked to be solid gold.

Oh, this was not *good.* They had just made love in Mr. Rutherford's room.

"Thomas?" she called out weakly, swinging her legs over

the side of the bed and reaching for her discarded clothing. What there was of it anyway. Where had she left the rest of it? "We have to get out of here," she added. But the water was still running in the bathroom, so she wasn't sure if he heard her. "I think you picked the wrong room."

The nightstand was constructed in such a way that it had a small shelf beneath the top surface, and as Selby bent to retrieve a sock, she saw lying on that shelf what looked like a leather-bound date book of some kind. She was about to look away when she noticed three letters embossed on the leather, and even though she hadn't been trying to snoop, she couldn't help seeing what they were. TPB. For a minute, the significance of that didn't deter her from her task, and she slipped on her blue jeans and bra without thinking. But then—

TPB? Thomas had introduced the owner of CompuPax as Harry Rutherford. *T* and *B* did not stand for Harry or Rutherford. But they did stand for—

The bathroom door opened then, just as Selby was pulling the date book out from its shelf. And if she hadn't already been worried about the discovery, Thomas's panicked cry of "Selby, don't!" would have finished the job for her.

Before she could open it, Thomas was in front of her, jerking it out of her hands. "That's private property," he said. "We should leave it alone."

She looked up at him then, still feeling a little woozy, though whether that was a result of their lovemaking or this new discovery—whatever it was—she wasn't sure. He'd slipped on a bathrobe and loosely belted it, a beautifully tailored garment that shimmered softly in the afternoon sunlight like silk. No, not *like* silk, Selby thought. It was silk. Because the owner of CompuPax could afford it and would demand the best.

"TPB," she said softly.

"What?" Thomas asked. But she could tell by his expression that not only did he know what she had just said, he understood what she was talking about.

"What does the *P* stand for?" she asked. "You never told me your middle name."

"My name?" he echoed.

She nodded. "Yeah. Your name. Your initials. Your date book. Your room. Your place. I'm right, aren't I? Harry Rutherford isn't the owner of the company. You are."

He said nothing in response to her charge, but a muscle in his jaw twitched once, and his cheeks grew ruddy.

"When were you going to tell me?" she asked. But before she even finished the question, she knew the answer. "You weren't going to tell me at all, were you? Because you weren't planning on this taking very long."

"Selby, it's not what you think."

She nodded. "Actually, I think it probably is."

"No, you don't understand."

"Yeah, actually, Thomas, I think I do."

But she didn't want to think about anything more than that. Not right now. Not with him looking at her. When she fell apart, she wanted to be alone.

"I have to go," she said.

"No, don't, Selby. You said you'd stay."

She did chuckle at that, a solitary, melancholy sound. "Yeah, well, you said a lot more than that that wasn't true."

"Selby . . ."

This time Thomas punctuated the plea by extending a hand toward her, but she took a step in retreat before he could reach her.

"I have to go," she said again.

As quickly as she could, she gathered up the rest of her clothing and put it on as gracefully as she could manage. Then she made her way back out to the dining room where she had left her other things. Thomas followed her through the house, saying her name again and again, trying to explain that which defied explanation. But Selby wasn't listening to him. She'd listened before, and that had only brought her to this point, and she really didn't want to be here. So she tuned him out, gathered her things, and left. He followed her to the elevator, but didn't get inside, his manner of dress—or lack thereof—evidently enough to keep him from going any farther. So Selby's last view of Thomas Brown was of the elevator doors closing over him, and him telling her a big, fat lie.

Because a man like him couldn't possibly love anyone.

FIFTEEN

HANNAH HAD BEEN INSIDE THE COMPUPAX Pavilion only once before, her visit confined to the main offices, when she'd come in the hopes of recruiting an executive of the company to sit on the board of directors of the Emerson Academy. That had been just six months ago, she recalled now, as she entered the main lobby at the side of the very executive she had ended up recruiting. But she felt as if she'd lived a lifetime since then, so much had her life changed. Adrian, whom she'd so innocently invited into her world, had turned it upside down and inside out. Because thanks to Adrian, Michael had stumbled into her world, too. And it was he, even more than Adrian, who had shattered everything she'd worked so hard for so long to build.

Even if, she'd been forced to admit, what she'd built had been constructed on a pretty flimsy foundation all along.

But that wasn't why she was thinking about Michael as she entered the cavernous glass-and-marble reception hall of the CompuPax Pavilion. She was thinking about him because she knew he was around here somewhere, listening in via the microphone in the pearls that encircled her throat. Although she had ended things with him—had it really only been a few days ago?—she hadn't been able to end things yet with OPUS. She had agreed to see this operation through to its conclusion, in spite of Michael's insistence to the contrary. And see it through to its conclusion, she would. She still thought that if there was even a small chance Adrian believed she was nothing more than Hannah Frost, overworked, overextended, overdressed, but egregiously underpaid—not that she was bitter or anything—director of a tony private school in Indianapolis, then she was obligated to do whatever she could to aid in his capture. In spite of Michael's insistence to the contrary.

Not that she'd heard about Michael's insistence to the contrary from Michael in person, mind you, since she'd done her best to avoid him after that fateful evening at her house when she'd realized just how deeply his clandestine intrusion into her life had gone. Oh, he'd tried to call her, and once he'd stopped by the house, but she'd pretended not to be home on every occasion. After all, pretending was what she did best. Pretending had enabled her to survive in the world this long, by God, and it would damned well keep her surviving long after Michael was gone. And she'd avoided him quite well, thanks, in not answering her door that day.

Unfortunately, not answering the phone hadn't been nearly as effective. Because Michael had left a message every time he called, messages that started off with something along the lines of "Hannah, you can't do this, it's too dangerous," and ending, always, with the quietly uttered words, "I love you." In between were attempts to explain and apologies for his behavior, but Hannah did her best to tune them out. She didn't want to listen to explanations or apologies. Probably because his behavior had defied both. Those last words he always spoke, though . . . Well. Try as she might, she just hadn't been able to ignore those.

She closed her eyes reluctantly now when she remembered the soft, uncertain way he had spoken them, but the action did nothing to diminish their impact. So she opened her eyes again, and tried not to think about it. Instead, she remembered how Michael had been earlier today, when she'd had no choice but to open her door to him, because he'd come to the house to wire her for sound and prepare her for the evening ahead. And if his hands had lingered on her bare shoulders a bit longer than was necessary as he'd fastened the clasp on the pearls . . . if his warm breath on her neck had felt like a turbulent sirocco over parched sand . . . if she'd thought she'd heard him whisper, as he dropped his hands back to his sides, the same three words he'd used to end his messages . . .

Well, it was his job to say and do things that lulled her into a false sense of security, wasn't it?

And he'd said a lot of things earlier today. But instead of making her feel secure, they'd put her on alert. Because everything he'd said today had been crisp, businesslike declarations of what Hannah should expect tonight at the reception. What she should expect, he had told her, was the worst, because Adrian Padgett was a time bomb waiting to go off. No one knew how far-reaching the damage would be until after the detonation. So they had to make sure they caught him before the explosion came.

Which was why Hannah would continue sticking to Adrian's side until OPUS threw a net over him. She could only hope now that tonight would be the night they snared him. A thrill of something vigilant and precarious skittered through her as she considered the enormity of what she was doing. Because Adrian, her escort, the man whose elbow she held with such feigned affection, might very well be planning to kill someone tonight.

Hannah could scarcely wrap her thoughts around the concept. He didn't seem like the kind of man who could commit a cold, premeditated murder. But then, she wasn't the best judge of character, was she? She tried to comfort herself by reminding herself that the CompuPax Pavilion was packed with people tonight. And as Michael had said, Adrian wasn't stupid. She was confident he wouldn't try to hurt her here. Probably.

She turned to look at him, noting how handsome and elegant he looked in his tuxedo, marveling that someone who claimed the looks of an angel could have such a cold, implacable heart. Of course, she thought further as she surveyed their surroundings, that did sort of fit in with the feel of the CompuPax Pavilion as a whole. She wasn't sure who had designed the place, and she supposed, for a high-end technological wonder like CompuPax, this was the perfect environment. But the towering glass room made Hannah feel as if she were trapped inside a giant ice cube. There was no warmth here, no affection for anything, as if the owner of the company had no familiarity with either emotion. Even the four wet bars that had been set up in each corner of the room were constructed of blocks of glass that looked like more ice. The floor was gleaming black marble, and at the far end of the room, another imposing slab of black marble acted as the backdrop for a waterfall of sorts. Someone had tried to ease the austerity of the room by placing lit topiaries throughout, but all in all, the effect was one of coldness and arrogance and imperviousness.

But then she'd heard that T. Paxton Brown, the reclusive monarch of the company, was much like that himself. Just like her escort for the evening, come to think of it.

"Have I told you yet how beautiful you look tonight?" Adrian asked, stirring Hannah from her wayward thoughts.

She ran an anxious hand down the front of the skimpier-than-she-usually-wore, redder-than-she-usually-wore formal, which she had donned in the hope that it might keep Adrian distracted. She inhaled a deep breath to steady her too-rapid heart rate and replied, "Yes, you did. Thank you."

He smiled and lifted a finger to the pearls around her

throat. "And the pearls are lovely," he added. "Just the thing to go with the dress. Though you've been wearing a different strand lately—tonight and at the restaurant the other night? They're not the same as the ones I recall you wearing before."

Hannah knew a moment of panic as he voiced the question. She was amazed that he'd even noticed the difference in the two strands of pearls, as OPUS had made this one the same length and size as her other one, and to her view they seemed identical. For a moment she thought about telling Adrian that he was mistaken, of course they were the same pair. Somehow, though, she sensed he would know she was lying if she did. And lying had caused her rather a lot of trouble lately.

"They're not, actually," she agreed, smiling. "I'm surprised you noticed. The others were a gift from my great-aunt, and these belonged to my mother. Auntie had mine made to look like Mom's."

Okay, so she'd told the truth *and* lied. It had been a damned convincing lie, she congratulated herself. Maybe she wasn't such a bad spy after all.

"I notice more than most people realize," Adrian said, and she wasn't sure how to interpret that. "But you look quite fetching, no matter what you wear," he added. Then he dipped his head to hers, moving his mouth to within millimeters of her ear. "And I can't wait to see you wearing even less later," he said softly.

His breath was warm as it stirred a few tendrils of hair Hannah had pulled free of her chignon and curled to delicately frame her face, but his words sent a chill spiraling through her. Before she even realized what she was doing, she sent a silent petition to Michael, to please, please, please be close by, and to hear what Adrian had just said and to make sure she stayed safe for the rest of the evening. Maybe he wasn't her hero, she thought, but right now he was the next best thing.

In spite of the way things had ended between them, she hadn't been able to stop thinking about him in the days since she'd told him they were finished. About the way his mouth always hooked up higher on one side than the other when he smiled. About how unabashedly earnest he was in his affection for his son. About how skillfully and tenderly he had touched her that day at her house when they had made love.

About how he wasn't the only one who'd told lies.

But her reasons for doing so, Hannah reminded herself quickly, had been generated by the fact that she had cared so much for Michael. She'd lied because she hadn't wanted him to know the truth about her, because he might have misconstrued the truth and thought her a different sort of person than she really was. She'd lied because she'd wanted him to see her for who she was now, not who she used to be. She'd lied because she'd wanted him to think the best of her, not the worst. She'd lied because she'd wanted him to like her, the way she liked him. She'd lied because she'd found herself falling in love with him, and had wanted him to fall in love with her, too.

So then how come, she asked herself, Michael's reasons for lying to her couldn't have been the same?

Because it wasn't the same, she immediately answered herself. That was why.

But herself wouldn't be put off so easily, because she demanded further, How? How was it different?

It just was, that was all. Dammit.

But *how*?

Hannah silently shushed the annoying voices in her head and tried to focus on her surroundings instead. Okay, so maybe she and Michael needed to talk, she finally relented. Maybe. If they survived the evening ahead. Because if anything went wrong this evening . . . if something happened to one of the candidates . . . or to Hannah . . . or worse, to Michael . . .

Well, she wouldn't think that way, she told herself. Everything would be fine tonight. It had to be. She just wished she could say everything would be fine *after* tonight, too. Unfortunately, she wasn't nearly as confident of that.

As if her thoughts had conjured him from thin air, Michael appeared on the other side of the room then, dressed, as he had been that night at the fund-raiser, in his faultless tuxedo. Before she could stop it, Hannah felt her heart soar at the sight of him. But just as it was arcing into a perfect rainbow of pure ecstasy, it went hurtling back to earth again, crashing and burning against craggy, windswept rocks. Because she saw then that he had accessorized his tuxedo tonight the same way he had the night of the fund-raiser—with the dreaded and dainty Tiffannee hanging from his sleeve. This time her dress was fashioned from some clingy, translucent fabric of sapphire blue. All the better to match her enormous, if rather vapid—well, they *were* vapid—eyes. The dress was every bit as revealing as the other had been, however. And Tiffannee was as perky and as dewy and as tiny—and, God, as *blond*—as ever.

Hannah tried to tell herself Michael had only brought his majorette along tonight to make her jealous. It wasn't because he and Tiffannee were and had been an item. Or perhaps they were an ittemm.

Stop it, she instructed herself. *You're being sillee.*

Evidently he wasn't going to be listening to her conversations with Adrian via the pearls, she realized. No, he was going to be listening in person. And when she realized that, strangely, something inside Hannah grew much lighter and easier to carry.

"Oh, what a surprise," Adrian said blandly when he, too, noticed Michael and Tiffannee approaching. "Who would have thought Michael would be here, too?" He pulled Hannah close, roping an arm around her waist with the fierceness of a boa constrictor. "My, my, my," he added when they drew within earshot, "what a feeling of déjà vu I'm having."

Michael smiled as he came to a halt, while Tiffannee, Hannah noted, looked as vapid as always. Well, she *did*. The adorable little thing.

"Déjà vu, is that what it is?" Michael asked. "Funny, but when I saw you, a totally different word went through my head. But it wasn't *déjà vu*. It was *scumbag*."

Wow. He wasn't even going to pretend to be polite, Hannah thought. That was odd. Before, he'd at least *acted* like he was tolerant of Adrian. What happened to playing cat-and-mouse? This was like one of those shows on the nature channel during "Shark Week!" where a big ol' great white comes popping up out of the surf to suck down a half dozen baby seals in one bite.

Adrian seemed surprised by the pointedness of Michael's comment, too, Hannah noted. For all of three seconds. Then his expression suddenly cleared and he began to laugh. But it was a strange, nervous sound that started off as a few doubtful chuckles and gradually built into laughter that seemed very confident indeed.

"Oh, Michael," he finally said. "You're always such a kidder. How could I have forgotten that about you? How could I have forgotten so many things about you?" Before anyone had a chance to comment on that, though, Adrian hurried on, "And you brought the lovely Tiffannee with you again this evening, I see. How nice."

"Hel-loo, Adrian," Tiffannee sang out with a smile, wiggling the fingers of her free hand in what Hannah supposed was meant to be a wave. Kind of. "It is *so* nice to see you again," she added in the same singsongy voice.

And then she winked at Adrian. But not very well. It was as if she were trying to keep the gesture a secret between just the two of them. All in all, it had the effect of making her look as if someone had just poked her in the eye. And when

Adrian only smiled blandly in response to her greeting, Tiffannee's expression fell, and she frowned like a Wink 'n' Pout Barbie.

"Aren't you glad to see me, too?" she asked him.

"Delighted," he assured her in a voice that sounded anything but. "Especially with Michael this way," he added. "The two of you look just . . . darling together. Don't they, Hannah?" he asked her, turning to look at Hannah now. "Don't Michael and Tiffannee look *darling* together? Don't they look as if they were just *meant* for each other?"

"Mm," Hannah said, wondering at his exuberance over the discovery. Wondering even more why it hurt her so much to hear him say such a thing about Michael and Tiffannee belonging together.

"Yep, two of kind, that's what you are," Adrian said with a quick, certain nod, his voice still tinged with a shade too much ebullience. "I don't know why I didn't see that from the start." And before Hannah could remark on his odd commentary and behavior, he asked, "Would you like a glass of wine?" Then he turned to Tiffannee. "I'll be happy to bring something for you, too," he said. "And I remember your preference for double letters. How about a beer? Guinness, perhaps?"

Tiffannee giggled prettily. "I'll go with you," she offered sweetly . . . if a little vapidly. Well, she *was*. "I want to see if they have any amaretto."

"Of course you do," Adrian said, crooking his arm in invitation. But there was still something about his expression that didn't sit quite right with Hannah, and for some reason, she was glad it was Tiffannee going with Adrian to the bar instead of she herself.

Tiffannee accepted the proffered appendage willingly, and then she and Adrian strolled off, leaving Hannah and Michael alone for the first time since they'd parted ways.

"I thought they'd never leave," he said as he watched them go.

Hannah battled the smile she felt creeping up, telling herself not to be charmed by him. "But they'll be back," she said with certainty.

When she turned away from the retreating forms of Adrian and Tiffannee, she found Michael gazing now at her with unabashed affection, undisguised longing. He took a step forward, closer to her, and just that simple gesture made Hannah's heart pound hard in her chest.

"You look incredible," he said, his voice quiet, rough, and earnest.

At the sound of it, something deep in her belly went hot and rampant. There was just something about the way his gaze was fixed on her face, as if he weren't going to let anything in the world deter him from . . . something. From doing some thing he was thinking about doing. Probably to her. As soon as possible. He took another step forward, closer to her, and her heart hammered even harder when she saw desolation warring with hopefulness in his eyes.

Oh, Michael . . .

"You look wonderful, too," she said, telling herself she needed to start being honest with him, but deciding not to think for now about why that was so.

"I wanted to tell you that this afternoon," he added, taking a third step forward, closer to her. "I wanted to tell you lots of things this afternoon. Hannah, we need to—"

She held up a hand, palm out, both to stop the flow of words and to stop his approach. "Michael, don't," she interrupted him. "Not here. Not now. We can't do this tonight."

"The hell we can't," he said. "I might never have another chance after tonight."

She said nothing in response to that, neither denying nor confirming his charge, because she just couldn't think any further ahead than this evening.

"Then when?" he asked, the hopefulness flitting from his eyes now, the desolation taking over.

Oh, Michael . . .

But then he took another step forward. Closer to her. Close enough that now Hannah could smell the fresh, potent, masculine scent of him, a scent she remembered too well and that carried her immediately back to that afternoon at her house, when they had come together first so explosively and then so tenderly. She remembered the skim of his fingertips along the ribbon of her spine, the brush of his mouth along the column of her throat. And she remembered the way his body had joined with hers, deeply, wantonly, completely, melting into her as if the two of them would remain coupled that way forever. She remembered way too much. And it wasn't nearly enough.

She shook her head slowly, doing her best to push all the jumbled thoughts away. "I don't know," she said, not even sure what question she was answering. "There's just too much going on right now for me to be able to think."

"And me, I've been thinking too much," he said, taking one final step forward, closer to her, eliminating what little distance was left between them. "Because, Hannah, I can't stop thinking about you."

Nervously, she lifted a hand to the pearls encircling her throat . . . and remembered that everything they were saying to each other right now could be heard by someone else who was listening in. It might even be being recorded by someone else who was listening in. Because Michael was a spy. And so was she, by default, however temporarily. And they were both in danger. Thanks to him, nothing in her life was stable, secure, or normal anymore. And thanks to him, her life would never be the same again.

Without thinking, Hannah moved both hands to the back of her throat and unhooked the clasp fastening the pearls together, then thrust the strand forward and shoved it into Michael's pocket.

"You're going to have to stop thinking about me, Michael," she told him firmly. "Just like I have to stop thinking about you."

"Hannah—" he began.

And this time he held out one hand, as if he were begging her to throw him some small scrap of hope that, somehow, things would work out between them. But all she could do was shake her head at him slowly.

"We have other things we have to think about right now," she said softly.

His response to that was a barely suppressed snarl. "I'm tired of thinking about other things," he hissed, any lingering sense of obligation to duty clearly having dissolved. "I want to think about us. Right now," he added emphatically.

"Michael, there is no us," she said.

"The hell there isn't."

"There isn't," she insisted. "There is no—"

"I love you, Hannah," he said, again interrupting her. But this time the words were spoken not as they had been in his messages, with petition and solicitation, but with defiance and challenge. As if he were daring her to object to his declaration, because he couldn't wait to prove how much it was true.

"Michael . . ." she began. But honestly, she wasn't sure what to say.

Michael, however, seemed to know perfectly well what he wanted to tell her. "This place is crawling with OPUS agents," he said. "You and I don't need to be here. We need to be together," he assured her. "But we don't need to be here."

"Michael, we can't just leave," she said. "Not now. You, at least, are on assignment," she reminded him harshly. "You can't just turn your back on that." And then, because she just couldn't stop herself, she added bitterly, "And the assignment means more to you than anything, doesn't it?"

He glared at her for a moment, her barb having obviously hit home. Finally, though, quietly, his voice as steady and even as steel, he said, "You're right. I can't turn my back on my assignment. Because it really does mean more to me than anything."

Hannah's heart fell to hear him say it. To hear him declare what she'd known all along. That he'd choose OPUS over everything else. That his first allegiance was to a faceless, merciless, relentless organization, and not to her. Or to his family. Or to the life he'd built here in Indianapolis. He really was the sort of man she'd thought him all along, as ruthless as OPUS itself. And now she knew without question that there wasn't any hope for them.

"You've noticed I'm not the one doing surveillance on you tonight," he said.

She nodded, but she didn't really see how that mattered.

"That's because I declined *that* assignment," he told her.

She narrowed her eyes in suspicion. "Declined?" she asked.

He shrugged a little awkwardly. "Okay, I didn't actually decline it. OPUS agents aren't allowed to decline an assignment. We're told to do something, we do it, no questions asked, no objections offered. So when my boss ordered me to do surveillance on you from a distance tonight, the way I had to do before, I pretty much told him to shove it."

Now Hannah arched her eyebrows in surprise. "You told him to shove it?" she echoed. "Pretty much?"

He made a sour face and clarified, "Well, I'd rather not repeat verbatim what I said to him. It was pretty crass."

Now Hannah gaped in astonishment. "Can you do that?"

He shook his head. "Not without getting tossed in the brig or put on trial for subordination or treason or something."

"*What?*"

"I really didn't care about that part," he told her.

By now Hannah's head was spinning with confusion. "Michael, what are you talking about? You just said your current assignment was more important to you than anything."

"My current assignment is," he agreed.

Not that his agreement in any way cleared things up for Hannah, but at any rate, they were moving on. At least, she *thought* they were moving on. Kind of. Maybe.

"The reason I'm not the guy doing surveillance on you tonight," he continued, "is because I told my boss I wasn't letting you out of my sight with that bastard Adrian on the prowl. I told him the only assignment I'd accept, from here on out, *forever,* Hannah," he added meaningfully, "is staying close to you. And it's an assignment, finally, that I want to carry out. An assignment I *intend* to carry out. For the rest of my life. Whether you'll have me or not. Because that assignment means more to me than anything. Staying close to you, Hannah, means more to me than anything. Because you, Hannah, you mean more to me than anything. I love you," he said again. And the pleading was back in his voice now.

Oh, Michael . . .

"Leave with me now," he said suddenly, impulsively. "You and I can go back to your place and talk. Or we can go to my place and talk. Just, please, let's go somewhere. Let me explain myself. Let me tell you how much you mean to me. Let me *show* you how much you mean to me. These other agents, Hannah, they can take care of Adrian. That's their job, not ours. Adrian has nothing to do with us anymore. He has nothing to do with *my* life anymore. You do, though. *You* are my life, Hannah. You and Alex. And I'll do anything I have to do to make you understand that. Because I want to be your life, too. Let's think about ourselves for a change. Just us. You and me. Forget about all the rest of it. It doesn't matter. You and me, that's what matters. Just you and me."

She wanted to say yes. Wanted so badly to do as he asked and think about nothing but herself and Michael. Because thinking about herself *was* thinking about Michael, she realized. He was a part of her now. He'd become a part of her the moment she met him, the moment she became so intrigued by him. She loved him. In spite of everything. And she knew that would never change. She didn't want to face a life without him. Not if there was some chance the two of them could be together. Whatever she had to do to fix what was wrong between them, she wanted to at least try. She wanted to be with Michael. To talk with Michael. To live with Michael. If there was any way she could.

She realized then that he was dipping his head toward hers, and without thinking—which maybe was a good idea, now that she thought about it—she felt herself leaning in toward him, too. His mouth hovered over hers, and he reached up to cup her jaw in his hand. Hannah turned her face toward his palm and closed her eyes, because being touched by him again, even in so small a way, just felt so good. So right. Yes, she wanted to tell him, they should leave and go back to her place. His place. Some place. Yes, they should forget about Adrian. Yes, they should think about themselves. Yes, they should talk. Yes, they should try to work things out. Yes, they should . . . Yes . . .

But just as she began to part her lips to receive his kiss, Tiffannee came hurrying up, calling out something that made no sense, something that sounded like "Raptor!" even though that word didn't have any double letters at all. And hearing the panic in the other woman's voice, Hannah jerked guiltily backward.

Raptor, she thought hazily. Why did she feel like she was supposed to know what that word meant . . . ?

"Raptor, I lost him," Tiffannee said in a voice that was in no way perky or dewy or blond. And where moments ago her eyes had been so vapid—well, they *were*—now her gaze was fixed entirely on Michael with clear, keen intelligence. "One minute he was there, and the next minute he was gone," she added, her tone clipped and cold and calculated. "He just melted into the crowd, and I have no idea which way he went. I'm sorry. I failed. Dammit, Raptor, I can't believe I let this happen."

Michael's response to the announcement sounded like the growl of a vicious, angry tiger.

Hannah's response to the announcement sounded more like, "Whoa, whoa, whoa. What's going on? Why does Tiffannee suddenly sound shaken, not stirred?"

Tiffannee's response was a roll of her eyes that indicated she couldn't be bothered with people like Hannah because they were just too vapid for words. That was made even more obvious when she disregarded Hannah completely, turned back to Michael, and said, "What do you want me to do?"

Michael thought for a minute, a minute Hannah used to inspect Tiffannee. Gone was the bewildered expression. Gone was the starry-eyed innocence. Gone was the look of a trusting little ingenue. In its place was an edgy tension and a clear intelligence and something else Hannah was afraid to get too close to. Involuntarily, she took a step in retreat. Tiffannee glanced over when she did and smiled, as if she were pleased with the reaction she'd generated. But it wasn't the smile of a Barbie doll, plastic and painted on. No, this was the smile of a desperado. Of a desperada. Of somebody really, really dangerous.

Holy moly, Hannah thought. Tiffannee wasn't a majorette. She was a spook!

When Hannah turned to look at Michael again, he was staring up at the soaring glass walls that surrounded them. "You know, it occurs to me that there's no place in here for cover," he said, as if he were just now realizing the fact. "If Adrian's plan is to assassinate someone tonight or tomorrow, there's nowhere for him to do it in here. Nowhere for him to hide. The debates are going to take place in this room tomorrow night, too," he added as he looked at Tiffannee. "So if he were planning to assassinate someone, where could he stash himself to get a decent shot?"

"Maybe he's not planning to assassinate someone," Tiffannee said, her tone of voice, like Michael's, indicating she was thinking as she spoke. "Maybe the whole assassination thing has just been a ruse. Or maybe it's been something we erroneously assumed. Maybe Sorcerer's surfacing here around the time a presidential debate was announced was just a coincidence."

Sorcerer? Hannah thought. *Who or what the hell is sorcerer?*

Michael evidently understood, though, because he nodded thoughtfully at what Tiffannee had just said. "Or maybe it was something he used on purpose, knowing he could jerk us all around. Maybe he's laughing at us right now up in his—"

"Office," Tiffannee and Michael said as one. And, lightning flash, they were both off.

Instinctively, Hannah followed them. She didn't know why. She was in no way trained for something like this, and it would have been safer for her to stay where she was. Nor could she have helped in any way by following them. But where Michael went, she wanted to go. Wherever he was, that was where she wanted to be, too. Obviously he wasn't the only one on assignment tonight. Because somewhere along the way, Hannah had accepted an assignment from herself that was similar to his. She wanted to stay close to Michael. That was all that mattered right now. She'd figure out the rest of it later.

As she followed their swiftly moving forms from the reception hall, Hannah saw Tiffannee speaking into the gaudy rhinestone bracelet she had been thinking was much too tacky for an affair like this. Her words were fast, clear, and to the point, brooking no argument from anyone. Hannah had to hand it to her—the woman issued orders and voiced directions with all the aplomb of a Bond Girl. No, not a Bond Girl. Like Bond himself. Michael, on the other hand, just acted. Acted with enough efficiency and ease and enthusiasm that Hannah began to worry that maybe this was the life he was more suited to after all. Worse, she began to worry that, in spite of his earlier words to the contrary, he might think that, too.

She didn't ask how they knew where Adrian's office was. That would be a given for OPUS operatives. Nor did she ask how they found an elevator waiting for them in the lobby. That, too, she was certain, had been prearranged. What was surprising—to all of them, she suspected—was that Adrian's office door was standing wide open when they got there. Even more surprising, Adrian wasn't standing anywhere at all.

But the screen saver that scrolled across his computer monitor on the other side of the room said, "Love ya, Raptor. But I gotta go. Sorcerer." Over and over and over again.

"What's 'sorcerer' mean?" Hannah asked when she read it.

Michael blew out a long, weary sigh, but Tiffannee pushed him aside and dove into the office, tearing through everything that wasn't nailed down. Somehow, Hannah got the impression she wasn't doing it so much because she expected to find anything as she was because she just wanted to beat the crap out of Adrian right now, and beating the crap out of his office was the next best thing.

"Sorcerer was Adrian's code name when he worked for OPUS," Michael said. "This is his way of signing off."

"Signing off?" she asked, more confused than ever. "But he hasn't killed anyone yet. He hasn't done anything at all yet."

"And maybe he's not planning to kill anyone," Michael told her. "He is planning to do something, though."

"But I thought that was what you guys figured he was planning," she said. "To assassinate one of the candidates. I thought that was what this whole operation was about."

"OPUS never knew for sure what he was planning," Michael said, sounding more tired than ever. "They just assumed, with the presidential debates being scheduled here, and him surfacing shortly after that announcement, that the two events were connected." He turned to look at her. "It wouldn't be the first time OPUS was wrong about something, Hannah. It doesn't happen often, but it does happen."

"Yeah, and it really pisses me off when it does," Tiffannee said as she ripped a shelf from the wall and sent its contents scattering violently to the floor.

"And it usually happens when Adrian is somehow involved," Michael added.

"*Bastard,*" Tiffannee muttered, summing things up nicely, in Hannah's opinion.

She turned again to Michael. "But what do you mean when you say he's signing off?"

Michael shrugged. "He's leaving."

"How do you know?" Hannah insisted. "He hasn't done anything wrong that you can prove. How do you know he's not going to hang around?"

Michael sighed wearily again. "Because when we were partners, 'Love ya, Raptor, but I gotta go, Sorcerer' is what he always said when he concluded an operation. Always."

"So you think he's concluding this one?"

"I know he is."

"So then . . . he's finished?" Hannah asked hopefully.

Before Michael had a chance to reply, Tiffannee replied for him, with almost maniacal laughter. Hannah took her response as a no. And she also took another step away from Tiffannee.

For the sake of clarification, though—not that clarification was really necessary—Michael only shook his head. "No. He's not finished. Whatever he's up to, he'll just come at it from a different approach next time. He never quits until he gets what he wants. There's just no way of knowing what he wants. Which will make it tough for the agents who go after him."

That was twice, Hannah noticed, that Michael had referred to OPUS in the third person, indicating he did not include himself in the mix. "But—" she began again.

She never finished what she was going to say, though, because Tiffannee's efforts to disembowel Adrian's office took on new life. She jerked out drawers and upended them, sending their contents flying, then began kicking Adrian's chair.

"She-Wolf," Michael called out to her. "I think you've done enough. Save something for your partner, will you? I think he'll want a piece of this, too."

She-Wolf? Hannah repeated to herself. Tiffannee was called She-Wolf? Who on earth came up with these code names? Then again, she thought, reconsidering Tiffannee, judging by the savagery of her anger and the way her perfectly coiffed hair was now flying wildly about her face, maybe She-Wolf was an appropriate name for her.

"Right," She-Wolf—*She-Wolf?*—said, calming down. A little. "Right." She relaxed her grip on the crystal paperweight she'd been about to hurl through the computer monitor and began tossing it into the air as if it were a Baccarat baseball. "Don't want to be greedy," she muttered. "And like you said, he'll want a piece of the action, too."

"He?" Hannah asked Michael. "Who's 'he'?"

"I'm 'he,'" a third voice spoke up then.

Hannah turned to the office door to find a half dozen people standing on the other side, led by a very large, very scary-looking man with jet-black hair and piercing green eyes. Hannah wanted to talk to him about as much as she wanted to talk to Tiffannee.

"And 'he' is . . . ?" she asked Michael, leaning toward him and keeping her voice low so as not to alarm anyone.

"He's the guy who works with She-Wolf," he said. "They're partners."

Partners in what, Hannah didn't want to know. There were just some things that didn't bear thinking about.

The weight of her situation came crashing down on her then, and she realized the only thing she wanted was to go home. And then something significant slammed into her. She wanted to go home with Michael. Her home, his home, it didn't matter. Because wherever she went with him, she realized then, she would be home. And once they were home, she wanted to pour them both a glass of wine—a really big, really full glass of wine. And then she wanted to talk. And she wanted him to talk, too. All night if that was what it took. And then, maybe, if all went well with the wine and the talking, she wanted to make love. And in the morning, she wanted to wake up and realize this had all been nothing but a bad dream. Except for Michael. She wanted to roll over in her bed and find him to be real. And she wanted the air cleared between them.

"Do you have to stay here?" she said.

"Only if you do," he told her. "Like I said, my only assignment from now on is being with you."

"Whether I like it or not," she clarified, smiling tentatively.

He smiled back, too. Tentatively. "Yeah, well, I hope you'll like it," he said. "Otherwise it could get awkward."

"So then," Hannah said, "you don't have to hang around and be debriefed or anything?"

He smiled. "Not by these guys, no."

Good thing, Hannah thought. Because she remembered what it was like to be debriefed by an OPUS operative. And anyone who was debriefed by Tiffannee/She-Wolf might not survive. Not to mention Hannah would have to bitch-slap the other woman silly for laying a hand on the man she loved.

The man I love, she repeated to herself, a strange mixture of hopefulness and dread splashing through her belly. Could they really make this work?

"So then you can come to the house?" she asked. "You can take me home tonight?"

His expression sobered when she asked what she did, and he didn't answer her right away. Instead, he circled her wrist gently and tugged her out of the office and through the wall of OPUS operatives, ignoring Tiffannee/She-Wolf's and *his*—funny, how no one had mentioned Tiffannee/She-Wolf's partner's name—questions about where Michael thought he was going. Then he guided Hannah down to the end of the hall, where they were alone and could speak without being overheard.

"Yeah, I can take you home, Hannah," he said softly, seriously. He met her gaze levelly, as if he were searching her face for the answer to a very important question. "I just want to make sure you want me to take you home for the right reasons, that's all."

She swallowed with some difficulty, worried about his concern. "What do you mean?" she asked.

He inhaled a deep breath and released it slowly. "I mean if you're just feeling stoked right now because of a dangerous situation and you need to get your ya-yas out by steaming up the sheets with me, then I don't want any part of whatever you have planned."

"Well, aren't we sure of ourselves?" Hannah said, biting back a grin. She couldn't help it. He was just so cute when his manhood was threatened.

His face fell at her remark. "No, I didn't mean . . . I mean, I'm not . . . not *at all* . . . I'd never assume . . . Hannah, that wasn't what I . . ."

She started shaking her head before he even finished speaking—mostly because she feared he would never finish speaking. "No, that isn't it," she assured him. And it hadn't been that the first time, either, she realized now. "Right now," she told him, "the last thing I want to do is have sex with you."

His brows arrowed downward with even more concern. "I'm not sure I like the sound of that, either."

"I want you to take me home so we can talk, Michael," she said. "About everything that's happened. About us. About what might happen in the future. And then . . ."

"And then . . . ?" he prodded.

"And then," she said, smiling tentatively, feeling tentative, too, "if you say all the right things, and if you and I both want it, I thought maybe we could . . ."

"What?"

She lifted a hand to his face, cupping his jaw in her palm. And very softly, she said, "Maybe we could make love."

He, too, lifted a hand toward her face, but he hesitated for just a moment before moving it to her hair and smoothing it over the crown of her head. "Is that what it would be?" he asked her. "Making love?"

She nodded. "If everything goes right, and we can both understand, then yes. It would be making love."

"I know that's what it would be for me, Hannah," he continued. "Because I love you. But is that what it would be for you?"

She smiled, feeling encouraged, but she wasn't ready to reveal herself just yet. "Take me home," she said. "We'll talk and see what happens."

They reached for each other at the same time, each leaning into the kiss. They joined briefly, uncertainly, affectionately, because there were others standing so close. But they were left looking at each other with the knowledge that they were by no means finished.

Then, "Come on, Hannah," Michael said softly. "Let's go home."

SIXTEEN

SELBY BEGGED A FRIEND OF HERS, ANOTHER
teacher, to substitute for her in her returning
ed class the week following her discovery of
who Thomas Brown really was. She knew there was no way
she could face him just yet. Truth be told, she didn't know if
she would ever be able to face him again. She had no idea
how she could finish teaching the seminar with him sitting
out there staring back at her every time she looked up, knowing how he'd deliberately misrepresented himself to her, and
knowing how easily she'd fallen for it. Knowing how much
she'd come to love him, and how she'd given him something
she'd never offered any other man. Knowing how he would
haunt her forever because of that.

And where before, his steamy gazes had bothered her
because she could only imagine what it would be like to be
with him, now she knew. And the knowing was so much
more than the imagining had ever been. She'd had no idea
how it could be between a man and a woman. Not just physically, but emotionally, too. Because as much of her body as
she'd given to Thomas that day, she'd given a thousand
times more of herself.

She was at home on a Sunday afternoon, mulling over her
dilemma, wondering if she could afford it, financially, to

give up her night class entirely, when someone knocked at her front door. And she realized immediately that her problem was a lot more pressing than she thought. She'd figured she had another thirty-six hours to prepare herself before she had to face Thomas again. But who else could it be knocking on her front door? Her friends weren't the kind to drop in for an impromptu visit.

Belting the sash of her short, flowered kimono over the baggy boxer shorts and T-shirt she'd slept in—she didn't care if it was two o'clock in the afternoon, she didn't have to get dressed if she didn't want to—Selby shuffled to the front door and peered through the peephole to verify her suspicion. Then, after only a small hesitation, she unlocked the deadbolt and opened the door. But it wasn't Thomas, after all, she saw when she got a fuller view of him. No, it must have been that other guy instead. The one with the initials TPB—the one who had nineteen-point-six billion, to be exact, not all of it liquid, though, natch. Because Thomas had always looked arrogant and full of himself, and this guy looked anything but. And where Thomas's uniform was ripped jeans and oily T-shirts and leather jackets, this guy was dressed in khaki Dockers and a brown tweedy sweater.

T. Paxton Brown, she knew now. She'd done some checking on him over the past week. She probably should have realized right off who he was, since the guy was a local, even international, celebrity of sorts. And she had recognized his name, once she knew what it was. More than that, she remembered having filled and shipped orders for him during her weekend shifts at Mathilda's. The local billionaire, one of the other salesclerks had told her, went through women like most men went through six-packs. And he always sent them something sexy and expensive from Mathilda's at some point during his wooing—or whatever it was men like him did with the women they set their sights on.

Of course, he'd never sent Selby anything from Mathilda's, she'd reminded herself at the recollection. And she'd hated it when she realized how much that bothered her.

"Can we talk?" he said now by way of a greeting.

She lifted one shoulder and let it drop, but the action was jerky and nervous. "Sure. I can talk. I've been able to talk since before I was a year old. Sounds like you can talk, too, if you can articulate a question like that. So I'd have to go with, yeah. We can both talk. In fact, I'll say one more word to prove it. Good-bye."

She began to close the front door, but he shot out a hand to flatten it against the door, and shoved it back open instead, with enough force to send it slamming against the inside wall. Selby gasped and took a step backward in response, her heart leaping into her throat, her stomach plummeting to her toes.

"I didn't get my turn yet," he said coolly as he took a step forward, over the threshold. And just like that, he was Thomas again. The Thomas she'd met that first night of class, confident, swift, assured. The Thomas who had both frightened and intrigued her. The Thomas she had ultimately found so irresistible.

"You're not being fair," he added, his voice dripping now with sarcasm.

That last, she could tell, had been said to get a rise out of her. But she wasn't going to rise. Not for him. She'd fallen too far for that.

She swallowed with some difficulty and screwed up her nerve. He'd surprised her with his vehemence, but she was confident he wouldn't hurt her. Not any more than he already had anyway. "I don't want to talk to you," she told him certainly. "Not ever again."

"Well, that's going to be a little tough, since we've still got more than four months' worth of classes to get through," he pointed out.

Oh, like she needed that reminder. "Then I'll talk in class, and you can take notes," she told him. "That was how it was supposed to work anyway. Had we stuck to the plan, this never would have happened."

He shook his head. "No, that wasn't how it was supposed to work, Selby. And believe me, I did stick to the plan." His expression and voice both softened as he added, "For as long as I could, anyway. Until it blew up in my face."

Oh, no, she thought. She did *not* want him softening. Because soft Thomas had been *really* irresistible. Soft Thomas had been wonderful. And he wasn't soft Thomas, she reminded herself. He was T. Paxton Brown, billionaire playboy, ruthless and careless and loveless.

"I don't know what you're talking about," she told him honestly.

He expelled a long, weary sigh, and suddenly looked exhausted, as if he hadn't slept for a week. He looked empty, too, she noted. Hopeless. Helpless. She knew the look well, after all, since she'd seen it every day in her own mirror.

"How it was supposed to work, Selby," he said, "was that, after meeting you, I was supposed to charm you and mislead you and seduce you and overwhelm you. Then I was supposed to use you sexually until I got tired of you. Then I was supposed to dump you and break your heart and hope you never got over me. That was how it was supposed to work. That was the plan. At least, that was the way I intended for the plan to work that first night I walked into class and saw you sitting there."

A dark hole had opened up in her belly as he'd spoken, and it had filled with something cold and unpleasant with every new word he spoke. "Well, then," she said quietly, "sounds like you got exactly what you wanted. Sounds like your plan worked just fine."

He shook his head, his eyes flinty now and never leaving hers. "Not quite," he said, the two words coming out clipped and cold.

She nodded, then made a production of smacking her open palm against her forehead. "Oh, that's right. I guess I messed it up by finding out who you are before you finished using me sexually. Because screwing a virgin one time couldn't possibly be satisfying. You'd have to screw me a lot more, get me all broken in, before you got any enjoyment out of it. Sorry about that."

He eyed her in silence for a moment, his teeth clamped tight, a single muscle twitching in his jaw. "I didn't screw you," he said softly.

"The hell you didn't," she said.

"And I'm the one who messed it up," he added, ignoring her remark.

"Yeah, you got that right."

"But it wasn't because I didn't get a chance to get tired of you, Selby," he told her. "It was because I fell in love with you."

Oh, no, she thought. Not that again. She wasn't about to listen to that.

"Don't you dare say that word to me," she told him, her voice edged with her fury. Her grip on the doorknob tightened, and it was through no small effort that she didn't slam the door in his face as hard as she could, regardless of where he stood. "You don't even know what it means to love someone."

He dipped his head forward, closing his eyes briefly, as if he were agreeing with her. When he opened them again, though, he fixed his gaze relentlessly on hers. "There was a time when I would have said you're right about that," he told her. "Because there was a time when I didn't—couldn't— love anyone. But that changed, Selby."

"The day you met me, right?" she asked bitterly.

"No," he said, surprising her. "It happened the night I met your friend Deedee."

Okay, now Selby was really confused. "Deedee?" she

repeated, recalling that night at Trino's. "For one thing, Deedee's not my friend. And for another thing, what the hell does she have to do with anything? How do you even know her? And how did you know I know her?"

Not that Selby wanted to even acknowledge her relationship to Deedee, however dubious. She'd been so sure that by moving away from Dorsey, Indiana, she'd be able to start anew and leave her unhappy past where it belonged—half a state away. But Indianapolis was a big city, and it drew people from all over the state and beyond, so she guessed she should have realized she'd run into someone she knew from high school sooner or later. She just wished it had been later. Decades from now, when the wounds of her youth weren't quite so raw.

"I was there that night at Trino's," Thomas said in reply to her question. "I was sitting on Deedee's other side when you came up to the bar. You were standing right next to me when you got change for that twenty."

He'd been there that night? Selby thought, recalling the details too well. Had he overheard what she and Deedee had said? she wondered. Well, he must have, if he knew Deedee's name and knew she was there. So then he must have heard about the blimp reference, too, Selby realized. He must know now what a complete loser she'd been in high school. And gosh, here she'd been thinking this situation couldn't possibly have gotten any worse . . .

"That's how you knew I worked at Trino's," she said, recalling how he'd mentioned her additional jobs at his home that day.

He nodded. "And that's how I know Deedee is a mean, nasty bitch who used to do mean things to you in high school. I overheard her telling her friend about you after you left," he said.

Oh, and Selby could just imagine what Deedee had said . . .

"About how they used to treat you," Thomas continued.

Oh, yeah. She was in Loserville now, Selby thought. Hell, she'd just been elected Mayor of Loserville. She hated it that Thomas had been privy to that part of her past. Then she wondered why she cared, since he wasn't going to be a part of her future anyway.

"And when I heard her talk about the mean, nasty way she'd treated you back then," he continued, Selby barely listening at this point, "I did something mean and nasty to her. It wasn't nearly enough to pay her back for what she did, but . . ." He finished the story with a careless shrug that was in no way apologetic.

And that was when Selby realized what he'd done. "You're the one who spilled the drink on her that night," she said.

She'd been able to hear Deedee's scream all the way back at the service bar. Jeez, the guys in the kitchen had heard that scream. Everyone in Trino's—and probably in restaurants a few blocks away—had heard that scream. Selby had gone running back out into the dining room to find every eye in the place directed at the bar. And when she'd looked that way herself, when she'd seen Deedee standing there in what had once been a beautiful white sweater outfit, all covered with something mucky and disgusting and foul . . .

Well, Selby had laughed. A lot. And then she'd gone back to work.

"You did it on purpose, didn't you?" she said now.

"Hell, yes, I did it on purpose."

"But why?"

"Because I wanted her to know how it feels to be the object of ridicule," he said.

"It doesn't change anything that happened to me in high school," Selby told him.

"Maybe not," he told her. "But it sure took the sting out of some of the things that happened to me."

She narrowed her eyes at him, starting to understand. "You were fat in high school, too?" she asked cautiously.

He shook his head. "No, I was a geek. A complete loser that nobody liked. Except when it came to having someone to belittle. Then they liked me a lot."

Selby nodded, thinking about that for a minute. It explained a lot about Thomas, she supposed. About the chip on his shoulder and his attitude toward women. But it didn't excuse anything. "So you've made it your life's work to get even with all the popular kids," she guessed, "on behalf of outcasts everywhere, is that it? Living well isn't the best revenge, after all?"

"Oh, living well is *excellent* revenge," he told her. "But it's not enough. There's still . . ."

"There's still what?" she asked when his voice trailed off without him finishing the statement.

"There's still something missing," he told her.

She softened a little at his comment. Mostly because she understood that, too. "Well, whatever it is that's missing, Thomas, I hope you find it someday." And she hoped she found it, too.

His expression went almost bleak at that. "I did find it, Selby," he said, his voice tinged with desperation. "With you."

Oh, no, she thought. *No, no, no.* She wasn't going to fall for that.

"But then I lost it again, when I lost you."

"Thomas," she began, lifting her hand in front of her, palm out, in a physical display of her objection.

But he interrupted her, taking her hand in his, weaving his fingers through hers. "You're everything I ever wanted, Selby," he told her, "without even realizing I wanted it. My life is completely different since you came into it. Nothing has changed, but it's totally different. Do you understand? I thought I had everything, but I was still unhappy. And then I met you, and I realized I had nothing, and that was why I was unhappy. And then, that afternoon when we . . ." He swallowed hard, his expression growing desperate. "After that I finally understood what it meant to have *everything.* Because I had you. Suddenly I realized how much better my life had been over the past month. Because of you."

"Thomas . . ." Selby tried again. But she halted, not sure what she wanted to say. His hand on hers was so warm, so tender, and it felt so good to be touched by him again, even in so innocent a way.

"That night at Trino's," he began again when she didn't finish what she had started to say, "maybe I was already beginning to realize how much better you'd made my life, and because of that, I wanted everything to be better for you, too. Maybe that was why I dumped the drink in Deedee's lap. Because somehow, maybe it would undo a lot of what was done to you back then."

"Did it undo anything for you?" she asked.

He hesitated, then shook his head. "No."

She sighed heavily, her gaze alternating between his dark, anxious eyes and the two hands linked so earnestly together. "Thomas," she finally said, "I don't want to change anything that's ever happened to me. As bad as it was, even if I could go back and make it all different, I wouldn't. Because everything that happened to me in the past, it contributed to what I am in the present. Even if I could change it, I wouldn't."

"I would," he said without hesitation. "I'd change my past in a heartbeat."

"But if you did that, then you wouldn't be the Thomas I—" She thought she stopped herself in time, before he realized what she had almost said. But Thomas, she should have known, would be too smart to miss what she had intended to say.

"The Thomas you what?" he asked, his expression turning hopeful because he obviously already knew the answer.

"Thomas doesn't exist," Selby replied instead. "He was just someone you made up."

He shook his head. "No, Thomas is real, Selby. He's real, because you made him real. By falling in love with him."

"I don't—"

"The hell you don't," he objected, some of his certainty returning. "I felt it when we made love. You allowed me to be your first. And you're not the kind of woman who would do that unless you were in love."

"It doesn't change anything, Thomas," she said softly.

"Yeah, it does," he disagreed. "Because when you and I made love . . ." He shook his head slowly, as if he were still baffled by what had happened that day. "It was never like that for me before, Selby. Never."

"Yeah, because you've probably never had to bother with virgins," she said sadly.

"No, because I was never in love with any of the women I had sex with," he countered. "And none of the women I had sex with was ever in love with me. I know that now. With you, though . . ." He expelled a sound that was a mixture of longing and frustration and something else, something she only recognized because she felt it, too. "It wasn't sex," he said simply. "It was love. I love you. And I don't want to live without you."

Selby said nothing in response to that. Mostly because she had no idea what to say.

So Thomas spoke again. "You told me that day that you thought it would be the worst possible fate to be alive and have there be nothing left on earth that you want to do. Well, that's the way I feel without you in my life, Selby. I feel like there's nothing left for me."

"That's because you've already done everything," she told him. But the fight was going out of her. She wasn't sure she believed herself any more than he did.

"No, I haven't done anything," he told her. "Not with you.

And without you, nothing matters. With you, I can see everything, do everything, and it will all be new and different and unlike anything I've ever done before. But only with you. Without you . . ." He shrugged again, sadly this time. "Without you, Selby, there is nothing."

She understood that, too. Because she'd spent a good bit of her time since parting with Thomas thinking about her plans to see the world, and how little those plans meant to her now. What she had once considered the most marvelous dream she could dream now seemed bleak and weary indeed. Seeing the world alone wouldn't be any fun at all, she'd come to realize. Unless she could share it with someone else, someone she loved, someone who loved her, too, it just wouldn't be the same. It wouldn't be special. Not the way it would be with . . .

"Thomas," she said aloud. "Does anyone call you that?"

He smiled. "You do."

"Anyone else?"

He shook his head. "No. No one else. And I don't want anyone else to call me that. Only you."

Only you. She repeated the words to herself and liked the sound of them very much. Maybe even enough to say them back to Thomas. Maybe . . .

She took a step backward, into her apartment, moving enough so that he could enter, and she could close the door behind him. She wasn't sure what she was planning, but she did want to move forward. And that one step backward, for some reason, seemed to be the right start. Silently, she invited Thomas inside. And in doing so, she supposed she was inviting him into more than her home. But it felt good to her. It felt right. They had a lot of catching up to do. With each other, and with their pasts. But there was a future for them, too, she thought. And that was really all that was important.

Thomas smiled at her silent gesture, but immediately took

advantage. As he moved past her, his arm brushed hers, and a thrill of hope mixed with affection purled through her. No, not affection, she realized when she looked at him again. It was love that did that.

She pushed the front door closed and leaned against it, smiling for the first time since she'd seen Thomas standing on the other side. Because she was happy, she realized. Truly, genuinely happy. For the first time in her life. Because Thomas Brown had come into it.

"You'll have to be patient," she told him. "It's going to take some time for me to get used to this."

He arched his dark brows curiously at that. "Get used to what?"

"To all of it," she said. "To how wonderful you are, and how you feel about me, and how I feel about you, and . . ."

"And . . . ?" he prodded.

She smiled. "And how much friggin' money you have."

He laughed at that. "Don't sweat it," he told her. "It doesn't take any time at all to get used to that, trust me."

"The other things, though . . ." she said, and this time her voice was the one to trail off.

But he kept smiling. "Don't worry," he said as he closed the distance between them and pulled her into his arms. "We have all the time in the world for those."

EPILOGUE

HANNAH SAT IN THE BLEACHERS OF THE Iceland Hockey Dome and watched Alex Sawyer skate across the ice like a miniature Wayne Gretzky. Well, maybe not so miniature, she thought. The kid was tall for his age, easily the tallest fourth-grader at Emerson.

She gazed down at the diamond ring on the third finger of her left hand that Michael had presented to her two weeks ago—on Valentine's Day—and smiled. Soon Alex would be something else, too. He would be her stepson. And soon, the three of them would be a family. The kind of family Hannah had always dreamed about. Only better. Because this family wouldn't be a dream at all.

And to think she had an outlaw like Adrian Windsor/Padgett to thank for that. How strangely the world worked sometimes.

"What are you thinking about?" Michael said from his seat beside her, obviously noting her preoccupation.

But when she looked over at him, she found him following Alex's moves with his eyes. She loved that about him, how he could be equally in tune to both her and his son at the same time. It was just one of the many things she loved about him.

"I was thinking about Adrian," she said. "I wonder where he is right now, what he's doing, if some poor woman is about to fall for his suave, debonair act."

"If she is, she'll figure him out soon enough," Michael said with all certainty. "Women always figure Adrian out. Eventually."

Hannah hoped he was right. And she hoped it wasn't too late for whatever unsuspecting woman Adrian had on his radar right now. "I still can't believe I ever got involved in any of this," she said, leaning back in her seat. Alex was only practicing this evening, so the hockey rink was virtually empty, save the parents of the team members. So she kept her voice low as she added, "It seems like a dream in a lot of ways. Like something that happened to someone else, not me. When I think back on everything we went through, and how Adrian still managed to get away . . ."

"OPUS will get him, Hannah," Michael promised. "They've got some of the best men and women on it, so Adrian won't get far. Guys like him always turn up again. And OPUS will be waiting for him this time."

"Yeah, but where?" she asked. "The next time Adrian tries something, will it be thousands of miles away? In another country, even? Or will he just come back here?"

"He won't come back here," Michael said decisively. "This area is too hot for him now. OPUS has alerted all the local law enforcement people to be on the lookout for him. Even the feds are keeping an eye out. Maybe they didn't catch Adrian doing anything illegal here," he conceded grudgingly, "but he's up to something, and he knows OPUS knows that. So he won't try anything here again."

Hannah nodded. She supposed that was true. It was kind of ironic—Adrian had always basked in the limelight and loved being the center of attention. Now the center of attention was the last thing he could afford to be.

"If you're still worried," Michael said, "I can tell you this.

She-Wolf is still on the case, and she's tenacious as hell. And she has a one hundred percent capture rate. Adrian might get away for a while, but as long as She-Wolf is after him, he's going to feel the heat. She's got a baaaaad reputation, that one."

Well, that Hannah could definitely believe. Even if she still couldn't quite believe that the innocuous, diminutive Tiffannee had turned out to be a fire-breathing operative for OPUS. "And here, until the end of everything," she said, "I was thinking a much better code name for her would be Majorette."

Michael chuckled. "She's good at the dumb blonde act, no question. She-Wolf's smart enough to take advantage of people who are dumb enough to succumb to common prejudices. In fact, she loves taking advantage of people who are dumb enough to succumb to common prejudices."

"Gee, you sound like you know She-Wolf pretty well," Hannah said suspiciously.

He turned to smile at her. "And you sound like you're jealous."

She gaped at him. "I'm not jealous. I'm just . . ."

"What?"

"Surprised, that's all."

"Her partner is after Adrian, too," Michael said. "And with that guy, it's definitely personal."

"Oh, and it wasn't personal with you?" she said. "Your partner and best friend, who had an affair with your wife."

"It's different with She-Wolf's partner," Michael said, turning to observe Alex's moves across the ice again, clearly unconcerned with all the water under the bridge that was Adrian Padgett. "That guy hates Adrian more than anyone I know."

Hannah remembered her brief encounter with the agent at the reception the night Adrian had gotten away. She recalled a dark-haired man with almost opaque green eyes who hadn't said very much, but who had seemed very menacing, very angry, and very dangerous.

"Why does he hate Adrian so much?" she asked.

Michael shook his head. "Don't know. He's never said. But having seen the look that comes over him whenever Adrian's name gets mentioned, I don't want to be around when he catches the guy."

Hannah remembered that, too. Just the mention of Adrian's name had made Tiffannee's partner look like he wanted to tear something—or someone—apart.

"And what's his code name?" she asked.

"If I told you . . ." Michael began.

"You'd have to kill me," Hannah finished for him wearily.

"No, if I told you, I'd be lying," he said. "I don't know what his code name is."

"It's that top secret?"

"Evidently. All I know is that nobody says that guy's name out loud. It's been rumored that all who have spoken his name have been found shortly thereafter in little pieces. Oftentimes mailed to loved ones."

Yikes, Hannah thought. "Then what does everyone call him?"

" 'The guy who works with She-Wolf,' " Michael said. "Anyway, between the two of them, it won't be long before Adrian's pulled in."

"This is assuming he surfaces before long," Hannah pointed out.

"Oh, he'll surface before long," Michael said. "When a person has an ego the size of Adrian's, he can't stay underground for very long. He needs the attention and adulation of others in order to survive."

Hannah supposed that was true, too. Adrian had always taken control of a room the moment he'd entered it, and he'd commanded attention from everyone in it. The worst punishment he could receive would be the denial of praise and worship. But she hoped the reason he was ultimately denied it wasn't because he was forced to remain in hiding. She hoped it was because he ended up rotting in prison somewhere.

"They'll get him, Hannah," Michael promised her again. "Whether it's She-Wolf or her partner or some other OPUS agent, they'll get him."

"As long as it's one of *them*," she told him. "As long as you're not going after him yourself."

He smiled again. "Why don't you want me going?"

"Because I want you here, Michael. With me. And Alex. With your family. At home. Where you belong. I don't want to lose you. Not to Adrian. Not to anyone. I can't imagine my life without you."

He pulled her close, roping his arm around her shoulders, then pressed a fierce kiss to the crown of her head. "You won't lose me," he assured her. "Not to anyone. Because I can't imagine my life without you, either."

"You'll love me forever?" she asked.

"I'll love you forever," he told her.

"I'll love you forever, too."

For a long time they watched Alex—his son, her stepson-to-be—as he glided over the ice, dancing through his teammates like the naturally gifted athlete he was. They cheered when he scored, booed when he was fouled, and Hannah felt warmth spreading through her in spite of the cold arena.

"So, Raptor," she said as hockey practice drew to a close and the team skated off the floor to shed their gear and collect their things, "looks like you're going to have some time off from the spying game for a while."

"From the spying game, yes. But tax season is here, and that can get pret-ty dangerous, let me tell you."

"That kind of danger, I can handle," she told him.

"That makes one of us," he said. "I hope you can handle being an accountant's wife," he added. "It's not an easy job.

Sometimes it's unstable. Sometimes it's not so secure. Sometimes, it's anything but uneventful."

"I'm up for it," she told him. "As long as you come home to your family every night, I can handle anything."

"I will come home to you every night," he vowed as they threaded their way between the bleachers and made their way down the stairs. He circled her waist with one arm and waved to Alex with the other. "Wild horses couldn't keep me away."

"How about OPUS?" she asked.

"Nah. They won't keep me away, either. My family comes first."

"Mine, too," she said with a smile.

"Forever?" he asked.

"Forever."

"You promise?"

"I promise."

"Well, then, what do you say, Hannah?" he asked as he pulled her closer still. "You want to collect our kid and go home so we can cook our dinner and feed our dog and then pop some popcorn and watch some TV by the firelight?"

She nodded, her entire body wanting to join in the gesture, so eagerly did she agree. It sounded exactly like the kind of evening she enjoyed most. "Yes," she told him. "I'm ready to go home. I've been ready for a long, long time."

And knowing she was going home to something that was even better than a storybook ending, Hannah took Michael's hand. And together, they took the next steps toward their happily ever after.

Do you think you know everything
about your favorite Avon authors?

Well, think again!

Because in the following pages
you are going to learn
Ten things
You never suspected about
Four of your favorite Avon writers . . .

And, of course, you'll also
be getting a sneak peek
at their upcoming
Avon Romance Superleaders!

10 Things You Don't Know About
Elizabeth Bevarly

1. I will do just about anything for a slice of chess pie.
2. When I was twelve years old, I took home the blue ribbon from the Kentucky State Fair for "Best Chocolate Chip Cookies." (I will only reveal the recipe for a million dollars. Or, you know, a slice of chess pie.)
3. I secretly devour true crime books. (So I know how to kill a man a dozen different ways. Of course, I never would. Unless he tried to get between me and my chess pie.)
4. I was once almost crushed in a mosh pit at a Clash concert. (Some idiot skinhead slammed into me and made me drop my chess pie.)
5. I once kissed the singer Harry Chapin. (And he wasn't even holding a chess pie at the time.)
6. My first job was at the age of twelve, drying silverware in my aunt's restaurant. (They had fabulous chess pie.)
7. I was on the dance team at my high school the year they took first place in state competition. (There wasn't any chess pie involved, but I thought I'd mention it anyway. The pie, I mean. Not the dance team stuff.)
8. I was born on the cusp of Scorpio and Libra, which means I think a balance of emotion is extremely important, but I'm much too emotional to achieve such a thing. (But it doesn't affect my affinity for chess pie, so it's okay.)
9. My favorite color is green. (Unless it appears on a slice of chess pie, in which case I don't care for it at all.)
10. I have a fetish for china, crystal and silver serveware, especially if it's antique. (Krautheim's Millefleurs pattern, for instance, looks especially nice under a slice of chess pie.)

**And now a sneak peek at Elizabeth's
January 2005 Avon Romance Superleader**

Just Like a Man

*B*ut even all buttoned up and battened down the way Hannah Frost had been, he'd been able to sense a barely restrained . . . something . . . simmering just beneath her surface. He hesitated to ponder exactly what that *something* might be, though, mostly because it made something equally *something* simmer inside himself. Instead of a gray crew cut, her hair had shone like pure honey in sunlight, the elegantly twisted style making him think it must be long and silky when allowed to flow free. And instead of evil eyes, she had the eyes of an angel, as blue and as big as the heavens above. And as for persimmon lips . . .

Oh, baby. Nothing could have been further from the truth. Hannah Frost's mouth had been as soft as the rest of her promised to be, full and lush and ripe. It had been way too long since Michael had kissed a mouth like that. And there were other things he could imagine that mouth doing, too. Things to him, in fact. Things *on* him, in fact. Things he *really* shouldn't be thinking about when his son was anywhere in the same ZIP code.

So instead of mentally undressing Hannah Frost, he made himself think about the way she *had* been dressed, an austere study in gray. The suit hadn't suited her at all, yet she'd seemed perfectly at ease wearing it.

Because ruminating about Hannah Frost was as far as Michael would let things go with her. And that was more than he should be doing. She was one cool customer, to be sure. Too bad she didn't have the same cooling effect on him. She made his blood run hot and wild, even after one brief, passionless exchange.

Damn. This was an unexpected development he hadn't anticipated and certainly couldn't afford.

And what the hell did she think she was doing going anywhere near Adrian Windsor? Okay, so the guy sat on the board of directors of the Emerson Academy. After all, that was the reason he'd been instructed to enroll Alex at Emerson. And to the casual observer, Adrian Windsor was a forthright, upright, do-right, citizen. But Michael knew things about the guy no one else at Emerson knew. For example, that his name wasn't really Adrian Windsor. It was Adrian Padgett. And what he knew all added up to the fact that Adrian was trouble with a capital T.

If Hannah Frost was involved with the guy, that was really going to cause some problems. And not just for Michael, either.

10 Things You Don't Know About
Rachel Gibson

1. I got my first motorcycle in the fourth grade. It was a Honda 50—not quite a Harley.
2. My little toes are on sideways. I know that sounds freaky but is very cute.
3. I love to sing loud but can't carry a tune.
4. My name is Rachel, and I am a shoe-oholic.
5. I speak fluent pig Latin.
6. I am not crafty. I tried it once and burned my fingers with the hot glue.
7. I jumped in a pool of Jell-O and won a T-shirt.
8. I love to jetski and I'm learning to water-ski.
9. I have a terrible fear of grasshoppers.
10. I work in pajamas until noon. It's a good job.

**And now a sneak peek at Rachel's
February 2005 Avon Romance Superleader**

The Trouble With Valentine's Day

"*W*arn me if you're going to write your name in the snow," she said to break the silence.

"Actually, I'm standing here wondering if I'm going to have to wrestle that snow shovel out of your hands." His warm breath hung in the air between them as he added, "I'm, hoping you'll be nice and hand it over."

Her grasp on the handle tightened a bit more. "Why would I hand it over?"

"Because your grandfather is in there getting all worked up over you doing what he thinks is a man's job."

"Well, that's just stupid. I'm certainly capable of shoveling snow."

He shrugged and slid his hands into the hip pockets of his cargo pants. "I guess that's not the point. He thinks it's a man's job, and you've embarrassed him in front of his friends."

"What?"

"He's in there right now trying to convince everyone that you're . . ." Rob paused a moment and tilted his head to one side. "I believe his exact words were that you're 'usually a nice, sweet tempered girl.' And then he said something about you being cranky because you don't ever get out with people your own age."

Great. Kate suspected her grandfather's nonsense was directed at Rob and not the other men. Worse, she was sure he suspected it also. The last thing she needed was for her grandfather to interfere in her nonexistent love life. Especially with Rob Sutter. "I'm not cranky."

He didn't comment, but the lift of his brow said it all.

"I'm not," she insisted. "My grandfather is just old-fashioned."

"He's a good guy."

"He's stubborn."

"If I had to guess, I'd say you're a lot alike in the stubborn department."

"Fine." She thrust the shovel toward him.

A smile touched the corners of his mouth as he withdrew his hand from the front pocket of his pants and took the shovel from her. He clamped his bare hand over hers. She tugged but his grasp tightened.

She wasn't about to get into a tug-of-war with a man built like the Terminator. "Can I have my hand back?" He relaxed his grip finger by finger, and she pulled free.

"Damn," he said, "I was kind of hoping I'd have to wrestle you for it."

10 Things You Don't Know About
Suzanne Enoch

1. She used to attend science fiction conventions, but only dressed up once—as a Colonial Marine from the movie *Aliens*. Okay, she once wore a Han Solo costume, too, when her friends joined her as Luke Skywalker and Princess Leia.

2. She once appeared on national television as a romance expert on *E!* as part of the "Star Wars Is Back" special. She had more air time than George Lucas.

3. Her first part-time job was at Cinedome, a movie theater complex. She stayed for two weeks, until the runs of *Raiders of the Lost Ark* and *Star Trek II* ended—the ticket booth didn't have air-conditioning, and without Indy or Spock, it just wasn't worth it.

4. She won't eat anything which could potentially eat her. This includes shark, snake, and members of the squid family—and so far the karma thing has worked out, because she hasn't been devoured.

5. She mows her own lawn with a manual lawn mower. The idea was that it would be good exercise. What she didn't realize was that lawns grow so quickly.

6. She once went on a date with a guy who made props for "Pee Wee's Playhouse." He showed up wearing red-and-white nylon parachute pants and brought her a green popsicle model with a smile embossed on it. If the popsicle had been real, the relationship might have had a chance.

7. She was editor-in-chief of her high school newspaper, which together with her braces and glasses and good grades, put a crimp in her high school social life. She's since recovered, but agrees that she could still probably be considered a nerd.

8. While in college she submitted a script for "The A-Team." The script was under consideration at the time the show was cancelled.

9. Her great-grandfather, Vivian Whitlock, was also a published author. His book was titled *Cowboy Life on the Llano Estacado*, and it's been rumored that he once rustled cattle and rode with Butch Cassidy and the Hole in the Wall Gang.

10. She consulted her Talking Yoda 8-Ball about whether she would be able to sell her first contemporary manuscript. The answer was "Likely, this is." Yoda's always right.

And now a sneak peek at Suzanne's March 2005 Avon Romance Superleader

Flirting With Danger

*H*e started to take another swallow of brandy, then stopped as the skylight in the middle of the ceiling rattled and opened. With a graceful flip that looked much easier than it had to be, a woman dropped into his office. *The* woman, he noted, reflexively taking a step back.

"Thank you for getting rid of your company," she said in a low voice. "I was getting a cramp up there."

"Miss Smith."

She nodded, keeping green eyes on him as she walked to the door and locked it. "Are you sure you're Richard Addison? I thought he slept in a suit, but night before last you had on nothing but jogging sweats, and tonight"—she looked him slowly up and down—"a T-shirt and jeans, and no shoes."

The muscles across his abdomen tightened, and not—he noted with some interest—in fear. "The suit's at the cleaners." Her gloved hands were empty, as they had been the other night, and this time she didn't even carry a paint gun or a pack. Again she was in black—black shoes and black tight-fitting pants and a black T-shirt that hugged her slim curves.

She pursed her lips. "Satisfied I'm not carrying a concealed weapon?"

"I have no idea where you'd keep one, if you were," he returned, sliding his gaze along the length of her.

"Thanks for noticing."

"In fact," he continued, "you seem a bit underdressed compared to the other night. I do like the baseball cap, though. Very fashionable."

She flashed him a grin. "It keeps my long blond hair out of my face."

"Duly noted for my report to the police," he said, his mind still pondering the intriguing thought of where she might carry a concealed weapon. "Unless you're here to kill me, in which case I suppose I don't really care what color your hair might be."

"If I were here to kill you," she returned in a calm, soft voice, sending a glance beyond him at his desk, "you'd be dead."

"That confident, are you?" She wasn't armed; he could rush her, grab her, and hold her for the police. Instead, Richard took a sip of brandy.

"All right, let's say I accept that you're not here to kill me," he said. "Why *are* you here then, Miss Smith?"

For the first time she hesitated, a furrow appearing between her delicate, curved brows. "To ask for your help."

And he'd thought nothing else could surprise him this evening. "Beg pardon?"

"I think you know that I didn't try to kill you the other night. I did try to take your Trojan stone tablet, and I won't apologize for that. But thievery has a statute of limitations. Murder doesn't." She cleared her throat. "I wouldn't kill anyone."

"Then turn yourself in and tell the police."

She snorted. "No fucking way. I may have missed the tablet, but not all the statutes have run out on me."

Richard folded his arms across his chest. She hadn't taken the tablet. Curiouser and curiouser—and it didn't suit him to let her know that someone else had made off with it. "So you've stolen other things. From people other than me, I presume?"

As she glanced toward the skylight, her smooth, devil-may-care countenance shifted a little. It was an act, he realized. Fearless as she seemed to be, she would have to be desperate to drop in on him here tonight. If he hadn't been so accustomed to reading people, looking for weaknesses, he never would have seen it. She was good at what she did, obviously, but that moment of vulnerability caught his attention—and his interest.

"I saved your life," she finally said, her unaffected mask dropping into place again, "so you owe me a favor. Tell them—the police, the FBI, the news—that I didn't kill that guard, and that I didn't try to kill you. I'll deal with the rest on my own."

"I see." Richard wasn't certain whether he was more intrigued by her or annoyed that she expected him to make her error go away. "You want me to fix things so you can walk away from this, without repercussions, owing to the fact that while you've been bad elsewhere, you were unsuccessful here."

"I'm bad everywhere," she returned, with a slight smile that momentarily made him wonder how far she would go in her quest to see herself cleared of any wrongdoing. "Accuse me of attempted theft. But clear me of murder."

"No." He wanted answers, but his way. And not through some sort of compromise, intriguing though she made it sound.

She met his gaze straight on for a moment, then nodded. "I had to try. You might consider, though, that if I didn't set that bomb, someone else did. Someone who's better at getting into places than I am. And I'm good. Very good."

"I'd wager you are." He watched her for another moment, wondering what she'd be like with all of that coiled energy released. She definitely knew how to push his buttons, and he wanted to push a few of hers. "I'll admit you may have something I'm interested in acquiring," he said slowly, "but it's not your theories or your request for aid."

Returning to her position beneath the skylight, she yanked her arm down. The end of a length of rope tumbled into the room. "Oh, Mr. Addison. I never give something for nothing."

He found that he wasn't quite ready for her to leave. "Perhaps we could negotiate."

She released the rope, approaching him with a walk that looked half Catwoman and all sexy. "I already suggested that, and you turned me down. But be careful. Somebody wants you dead. And you have no idea how close somebody like me can get, without you ever knowing," she murmured, lifting her face to his.

Jesus. She practically gave off sparks. He could feel the hairs on his arms lifting. "I would know," he returned in the same low tone, taking a slow step closer, daring her to make the next move. If she did, he was going to touch her. He wanted to touch her, badly. The heat coming off her body was almost palpable.

She held where she was, her lips a breath away from his, then with another fleeting grin slid away to grab the rope again. "So you weren't surprised tonight, were you?" With a fluid coordination of arms and legs, she swarmed up through the skylight. "Watch your back, Addison. If you're not going to help me, I'm not going to help you."

"Help me?"

She vanished, then ducked her head back into the room. "I know things the cops would never have a clue how to find out. Good night, Addison." Miss Smith blew him a kiss. "Sleep tight."

Richard stepped forward to look up, but she had already disappeared. "I was surprised," he conceded, taking another swallow of brandy. "And now I need a cold shower."

10 Things You Don't Know About Karen Hawkins

1. Karen once caught her house on fire while trying to kill a large, hairy spider. Every plastic glass in her kitchen sink and the handles to two pans melted completely before the fire was extinguished. The spider was, of course, unharmed.

2. Due to an Unfortunate Meatloaf Incident in '04 that resulted in a trip to the emergency room and stitches, Karen now avoids all forms of cooking and has perfected the art of "the dial-in order." Due to the amount of tips she'd paid thus far, seven pizza delivery drivers have graduated from junior college and two have named their oldest children in her honor.

3. Karen's favorite motto: If you can't afford a housekeeper, have children. There's a reason the word "CHoREs" and "CHildREn" have not one, but FOUR of the same letters. Coincidence? She thinks not.

4. Karen's biggest writing challenge is ignoring her dog, Duke, a large, fluffy golden retriever who possesses the World's Saddest Stare. His Sad Stare has earned him countless table scraps, numerous pity-induced doggie treats, and thousands of consolation ear scratches. When Karen is writing, Duke will pin his penetrating Sad Stare on her until she stops what she is doing and takes him outside to play in the park.

5. When Karen sold her first book in 1998, she was working on her PhD in political science. On receiving "the call" that an editor at Avon wanted to buy her work, Karen did what all dedicated students would do—she burned her stats book on the front lawn while dancing about in crazed abandon. She has never once looked back.

6. Karen is a confirmed Anglophile and revels in All Things English, especially the hunky British Prime Min-

ister Tony Blair. She has a T-shirt, two posters, one life-sized cutout, and a set of coasters with his picture on them. If you'd like a set of coasters for your own viewing pleasure, contact Karen Hawkins, President of the Tony Blair Fan Club, at their website *www.WeDroolforTonyB. com.*

7. To increase her writing output, Karen has developed a Reward System. One month, every time she wrote ten pages, she gave herself $10 toward the purchase of a new pair of shoes. Another month, she got to buy a dozen chocolate covered, creme-filled Krispy Kremes. This time, she rewarded herself every ten pages with a shot of tequila. Needless to say, though she met her quota every day for two weeks, she was unable to keep any work after page thirty and now attends WAA (Writers Against Alcohol) meetings twice a week.

8. Last year, Karen's daughter reached the amazing age of sixteen and now has her driver's license. After two tickets, three fender-benders, a hefty new insurance payment, and many harrowing hours waiting by phone, Karen has hired a new hairdresser good at "covering up the white." She will report back on the results.

9. Unknown to many of her family and friends, Karen is a master-level bass fisherwoman. She's never caught anything, but she looks good in her Lucky Fishing Hat and has a lovely tan. She also has a heck of a cast and can untangle her own lines from trees, shrubs, and even an occasional goose's neck.

10. Unknown to many of her fans, Karen is a shoe addict. She is especially addicted to shoes on sale. She owns more than eighty pairs, many of which she has never worn, including a pair of thigh-high glossy black leather boots and some strappy sandals in an unlikely color combination of deep purple and orange sherbet. Like most addicts, even while standing in line at Payless, Karen refers to her addiction as "a little problem" and says, "I can quit any time I want. No. Really. I can. Do you take Visa?"

* * *

For more tidbits about this author, a chance to win an auto-
graphed book, excerpts from her books, and pictures of her
doing sit-ups, visit Karen on-line at *www.karenhawkins.com*!

And now a sneak peek at Karen's
April 2005 Avon Romance Superleader

Lady in Red

To many people, the Marquis of Treymount seemed a cold, impersonal man, but to be perfectly honest, Honoria knew differently. Irritating and smugly sure of his own supremacy, he was far from cold. He was, in fact, a man of fierce desires and unremitting determination. Few members of the ton had faced the man when he was pursuing something he really wanted, be it an ancient tapestry or a priceless Chinese vase. When in genuine pursuit, his coldly controlled mask fell away and one was treated to the blaze of determination and cold acuity that was rather intriguing to behold.

Honoria searched his face for some glimmer of his purpose, but none came. Irritated, she dipped a slight curtsy. "My lord, welcome to my home. I daresay you've come on a matter of business . . ." She raised her brows and waited.

His deep blue eyes raked across her, lingering on her hair. Honoria had to swallow the urge to make a face at him. It was a peculiar tendency of his, to pause and measure one before engaging in conversation. She'd seen him depress the attentions of any number of toad-eating position worshippers. Under that hard stare, most people found themselves stuttering, anxious to please. Thank God she had her pride to hold her head upright, even before such an imperious gesture.

Still, she couldn't help but wish she'd worn her good morning dress, though she doubted it would make any difference other than to make her feel somewhat more confident; the man was used to the finest of the fine, and even her good morning dress could not be counted as such. She glanced at him and waited . . . but still he did not speak.

A flicker of uncertainty brushed across her. Was he

silently taunting her? Or was it something else? Honoria's back stiffened. She did not like being put at such a disadvantage. Treymount's continued silence began to weight the air.

"Oh pother! Enough of this!" She crossed her arms over her chest, fighting the desire to merely order the cad out of her house. At least his rudeness freed her to speak her mind. "Treymount, what do you want?"

He bowed, an ironic smile touching his lips, his gaze still crossing over her face, to her hair and back. "I am sorry if I appeared rude but . . . did I interrupt you in something . . ." Again that flickering glance to her hair. ". . . important?"

Her face heated instantly. She was used to people staring at her hair whenever they first met—the streak of white at her right temple made a lot of people pause. Some stared. Some pointedly looked away. Some gawked as if she had two heads. But Honoria had faced Treymount more than once now. Surely he wasn't merely looking at her because of that silly streak.

She unconsciously touched her hair . . . Her fingers found something and her eyes widening. "Cobwebs!" She crossed to the mirror over the fireplace so she could see the damage, laughing when she caught sight of herself. Two frothy strands of cobwebs hung across her hair and draped dramatically to one shoulder. Worse, a faint smudge of dust lined one of her cheekbones. "Ye gods, I look as if I've been in a crypt! No wonder you were staring. I'm a complete fright."

His gaze met hers in the mirror, a surprising hint of amusement lightening the usual cool blue to something far warmer. "I was going to suggest you'd been counting linens from a dark, deep closet, but a crypt is a much more romantic location to gather cobwebs."

"Cobwebs are not romantic." Honoria whisked her hand over her head and cleaned away the sweep of misty white strands. "I am sorry to receive you while so mussed. I was assisting my little brother in locating something he's lost." That was what she got for even worrying about her appearance to begin with, she decided, shrugging at her own silliness.

The door opened and Mrs. Kemble entered, bearing a

heavy tray. "Here we are, miss!" She set the tray on the small table by the sofa and then stood back, beaming. "There weren't no more apple tarts left, being as how Miss Portia visited the kitchen not ten minutes before I did and ate every last one. But Cook had some pasties a-cookin' and so I waited fer them to be ready."

"Thank you, Mrs. Kemble."

The housekeeper curtsied, though she managed to look the marquis up and down as she went. "Will ye be needing anything else?"

"No, thank you," Honoria said. "I believe this will suffice."

"Very well, miss." With one more curtsy and yet another lingering glance at the marquis, the housekeeper was gone, no doubt to regale the kitchen staff with her impressions of their lofty visitor.

Honoria went to the chair by the table and gestured to the nearby sofa. "Will you be seated, my lord?"

He hesitated, and she smoothly added, "I hope you are famished, for I am." She busied herself with the tray, adjusting the cups and putting a pastry on a plate, and all the while her mind whirled.

Perhaps he'd come about an object he wished to purchase. It was unusual, but not unheard of. Certainly other members of the ton called occasionally when looking for something specific. Not often, of course. But still . . . Mentally, she reviewed the more recent acquisitions. None of them were of the quality that he normally pursued.

If there was something good to be said for the Marquis of Treymount—and she knew of only one thing—it was that he appreciated the finest of antiquities and bought only the best. She had to admire his taste, if nothing else.

He stirred, as if making a sudden decision. "I suppose tea would not be amiss. I don't have long, but . . . why not?" He came to stand before the table, moving a loose pillow from the sofa and setting it out of the way.

To her chagrin, Honoria found herself at eye level with Treymount's thighs. It was strange, but in all of her dealings with the marquis, she had never noticed this particular part of his physique. Now that he was directly across from her, she couldn't help but admire the ripple of his muscles beneath his fitted breeches.

The man must ride often to keep such a fine figure—

He sat, his gaze catching hers. His brows rose as he caught her expression. "Yes?"

Her thoughts froze in place. Ye gods, did he know what she was thinking? Her neck prickled with heat, then her face. Hurriedly, she began pouring tea into a cup. "I—I—" She what? Admired his well-turned legs? What a horrid predicament! She could hardly admit—

His gaze dropped to the tray and he frowned. "Miss Baker-Sneed, I believe there is enough tea in that cup."

Honoria jerked back the teapot. She'd filled the cup over the brim and tea now sloshed into the saucer and tray below. "Oh dear! What was I thinking?" She reached for one of the linen napkins not soaked with tea. Just as her hand closed over it, Treymount reached over and clasped his hand about hers.

Honoria sat shock-still. His hand enveloped her, large and masculine and surprisingly warm. His fingers were long and tapered, his nails perfectly pared and trimmed, and yet that did nothing to disguise the pure strength of the man.

Her heart hammered against her chest, the unexpected touch sending the strangest heat through her body. She was going mad. She'd faced the marquis time and again at numerous auctions and never had she felt this tug of attraction. But it was more than a tug. It was a powerful wave, pure and primal. It washed over her, crashing through her thoughts and leaving her confused and disoriented.

In her bemused state, she could only stare wide-eyed as the marquis pulled her hand to him, causing her to lean forward, over the small table. His hand slid to her arm, his warm fingers encircling her wrist.

"My lord," she gasped. "What are you—"

"That's my ring." His eyes blazed into hers, accusation and anger flickering brightly in their depths. "And I came to get it back."

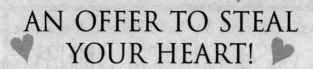

AN OFFER TO STEAL YOUR HEART!

RITA Award-winner and *USA Today*
bestselling author of *Daisy's Back in Town*

RACHEL GIBSON

"Funny, touching, steamy."—Elizabeth Lowell

❤ The Trouble with Valentine's Day ❤

Kate Hamilton knows why Valentine's Day stinks.
Dumped by her boyfriend, burnt-out by her job, she's back in
Gospel, Idaho, to regain some self-esteem. But her first pass at
a hunky stranger is completely rejected and she soon discovers
Gospel's Friday nights are about as hot as, well, fuzzy slippers.
And that's before she meets up again with Rob Sutter, former
ice hockey madman—and the hottie who told her to get lost.

Buy and enjoy THE TROUBLE WITH VALENTINE'S DAY
(available January 25, 2005), then send the coupon below along
with your proof of purchase for THE TROUBLE WITH VALENTINE'S
DAY to Avon Books, and we'll send you a check for $2.00.